www.wesmhenshaw.com

Wes M. Henshaw : Facebook

@wesmhenshaw : Tiktok

@weshenshaw : Instagram

I would really appreciate your feedback on whatever platform you're able.

First paperback edition February 2023

Book cover by Cherie Fox

Edited by Jon Oliver

(*Written & edited in Australian English*)


ISBN 978-0-6456561-0-7 (ebook)

ISBN 978-0-6456561-1-4 (paperback)

ISBN 978-0-6456561-2-1 (hardcover)


www.wesmhenshaw.com

*Aubyn & Hattie*

*Let wild dreams thrill you,*
*Let your heart guide you,*
*And let those amazing souls shine . . .*


*All my love to you both.*
*Love always.*

*Who am I? You may ask ...*
*Though, if you could, would*
    *I even know.*
*However, you cannot; you*
    *are no longer here.*
*You will return though ...*
*... one day.*
*Whoever, or whatever you may*
    *be ...*

*It hailed from everywhere, though nowhere could it be seen. A cloud of silence – or what could only be perceived as such. An unimaginable presence of nothing.*

*Though, he! He came through that silence, through that vastness of nothing, like a horror! The horror of knowing the fate of which was about to befall upon us all.*

*But, she! She was the noise, a noise that our souls could not scream. She sang a terrifying song: not that of resignation, nor despair, but a scream that our bodies could not vocalise.*

*It was a melodic roar of defiance, a roaring, rhythmic chant of challenge to he who would seek destruction and dominance of us all.*

Extract from 'A Dark Place to Live'.
Written during the third cycle of Drart.
Notated at the College of Rargarof by Alfeniti Larenta.
Acknowledged, thus sealed, by Jeremi Conteglio.

*It came from everywhere, alas! Though nowhere could it be sought. A majestic cloud of silence. An unimaginable presence of an absolute nothing.*

*She! She came through that silence, and that nothingness, like horror. As if Fear herself! The knowing of a fate which was about to befall upon us all.*

*But he! He was the noise that our bodies wouldn't scream – a terrific, terrifying noise: not that of resignation, nor despair – a scream of indignation that our bodies had failed to procure.*

*It was a deafening roar of defiance, a roar of a challenge to that which would seek desolation for all. A roar of rebellion for even the most primitive of creature. A roar for all!*

Extract from 'A Vellum Marked', dated during the sixteenth cycle of Inarellia.
Origin: unknown.
Author: ineligible.
Archived at the High Library's special archive: level six, square four, row three, column one, row seven.

# THE SCROLLS OF VILENZIA

# VELLUM I

## Festival of the Night

# Contents

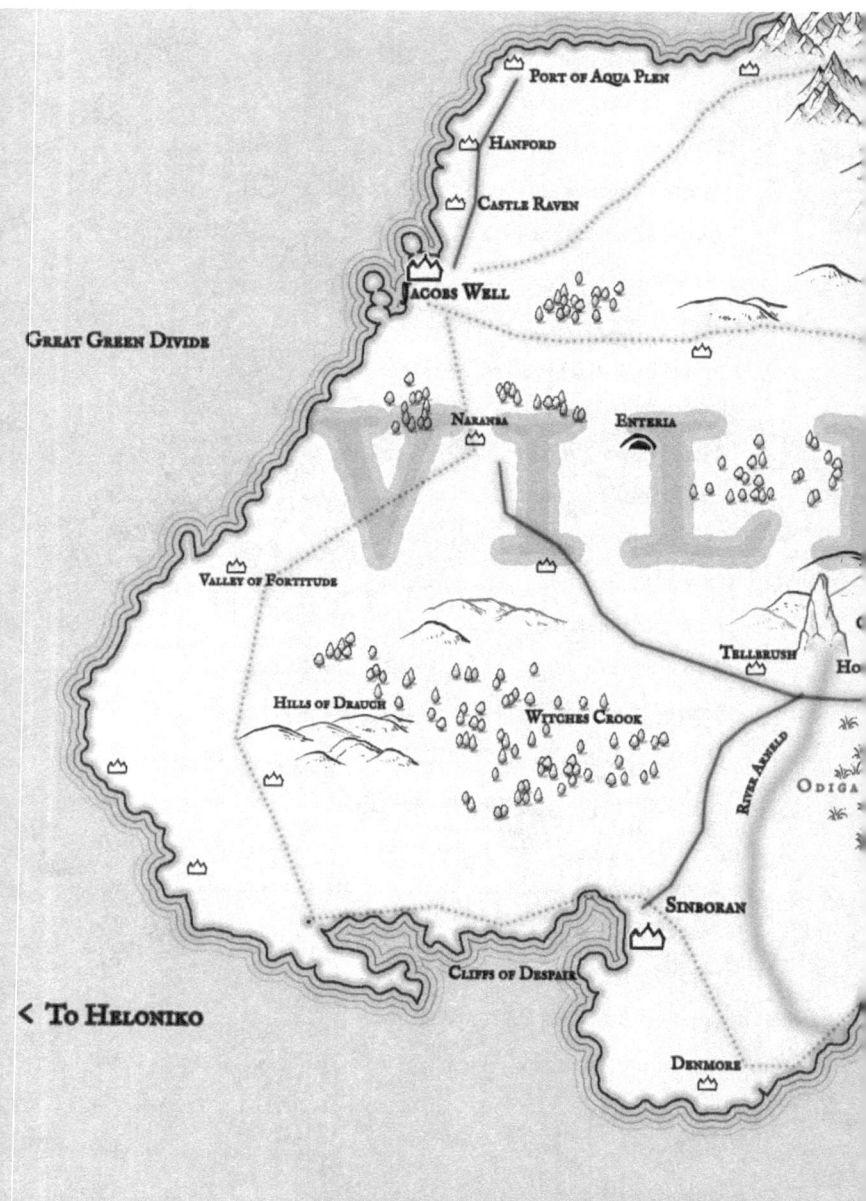

# CHARACTERS

**Altor** – the very first Onber

**Amaria** – Velosko's wife, accomplished violinist

**Anatoma** – castle mage at Jacobs Well

**Anna-Mary** – young, talented musician from Sinboran

**Arigal** – Mesfa's sister and acolyte of Sylteneria

**Bareleno** – boy persuaded by the darkness in Menton Green

**Belrough** – barkeep and landlord of the Ox and Cart in Jacobs Well

**Bendim** – muscle for hire by the dark mage Somendel

**Bertino** – one of Gurengal's crew, brother of Lento

**Count Atinna** – Amaria's father, count of Sinboran

**Countess Maria** – Amaria's mother

**Dagda** – one of the mysterious higher of the light

**Dresdor** – an eberactu and exuberant storyteller from the Famnagira forest

**Ebby Jink** – barkeep at Ebbys Rooms, a tavern in the City of Columns Third District

**Ebeno Jink** – Ebby's father

**Everos** – self titled God of Humour, resides on Seltero

**Getty** – a crippled boy, not of Inarrel

**Grehn** – princess in Jacobs Well, daughter of King Ben and Queen Jahnna

**Gretta** – Getty's mother, not of Inarrel

**Gurengal** – hunter with some magical abilities, has a large crew

**Holtonos** – known a God of All, Master of Matter, Binder of Worlds by those on Inarrel

**Jasquiera** – one of the Ancients of Inarrel

**Jentis** – once of the Third, bodyguard of Velosko

**Jhehbl** – known as Mover of Seas, Soul of the Oceans, Curator of the Land by those on Inarrel

**Kimo** – King Benjamin's twin brother

**King Benjamin Jacob Aurelia** – King of Jacobs Well and

its surrounds

**Kost** – one of the masters of the Third

**Lenjora** - known as Goddess of the Night, Giver of Love and Light by those on Inarrel

**Lento** – one of Gurengal's crew, brother of Lento

**Mala** – Molo's younger brother

**Malek** – middleman who spends most of his time at the Ox and Cart

**Marcos** – an apolit, Velosko's long-time friend. Also an accomplished cellist

**Master Johltor** – Onberseeler of the Third at the City of Columns

**Mesfa** – Arigal's sister and acolyte of Sylteneria

**Miss Nomellia** – aka Missy, a student of the Third

**Molo** – Grehn's friend, works in the castle at Jacobs Well

**Mother** Ursen – Onberseeler of the First at the City of Columns

**Morla** – ethereal form of one of the founders of the City of Columns

**Netiba** – one of Gurnegal's crew, excellent with a bow and arrow

**Peron** – member of the Third, enjoys travelling

**Queen Jahnna Aurelia** – Grehn's mother and King Ben's wife

**Semoni** –of the Third, a rarity for a pecbor to be studying at the City

**Sentok** – castle keeper and handyman at Jacobs Well

**The Slayer** – a mysterious woman who follows the Syltenerian way

**The Jester** – aka Jesse, a curious man not of Inarrel

**Velosko** – world renowned singer, blind, though very aware of his surroundings

# Prelude to an Eternity

The howl of the wind outside wasn't enough to drown out the crackling of the fire that sparked manically beneath a generously large timber hearth. A nightly constant that lit this musky room – if just enough – with a golden glow. It flickered shadows, throwing them to dance about the walls, to glisten tome titles; the majority, etched with silver, or gold, or both, reflected the sporadic spray of flamelight to make it seem as if they themselves, held fire. A minority … maybe once did.

There were two who occupied the room. Three, though, occupied the timber-cladded residence, sat halfway up a long sloped hill. The third remained behind the closed door, ear up close, listening to the generally one-way conversation; a low, rumbling mumble that carried its way from the older of the two occupants inside. She held a hand over her mouth to aid the suppression of any sound, anything more than a rush of breath escaping. She listened, intently, as the man dictated from the scratched scribble upon an ancient parchment. Some cursing too … which was not god speak – not any she had known of anyway. She heard the occasional rustle of paper unfurl and then the distinct sound of grinding, the scroll to be furled and tied once again, to be shelved once more, collecting dust until the next time it would be its turn again.

She sat there and listened after setting the child down for the night, and after she swapped with the man who read to the boy … a ritual constant. She did this *almost* every evening.

Stood on the upper rungs of a wooden ladder an older man reached up and grabbed a bundle of dusty, rolled-up papers from the top shelf, high above the rest of the diligently arranged layers of books that nestled in some kind of order of size on the shelves below.

'Well … what do we have here?' The man sparked a wink to the boy. 'Ahh, yes! I remember this one, hmmm — was it so long ago? It has been an age since I—'

'Which one is it, Papa?' asked the young boy excitedly.

'An old one, poppet! Tonight, would you be game to hear words written of ghosts, by ghosts, one could only assume, of a long ago past?'

'Yes, Papa … but how could ghosts possibly write? Are they real? They look very flimsy. Who would write on such a thing, instead of in a book?'

'Well, older generations would and … hmmm, others.' He absently looked up at the timber-slatted ceiling. 'They just did, I guess. Suppose they used what was available to them at the time. Let me get settled and grab my reading glass out of my pocket. This one is a tough one to read without. Even then, it is ineligible in parts. My apologies, child. I dare not touch this with anything sharper than my stumpy fingers to fill in the gaps … I will, however, fill said gaps anyway where I can, and with how I see fit.' The older man threw another wink at the child lying prone upon the overly large bed. 'Huh, there seems to be more than a few gaps since I last glanced over this text. Never mind, I will go on—'

'Yay!' the child exclaimed, expecting the usual flourish to the man's inventive improvisation.

'Now then. Are you settled, young one?'

'Hey! I'm not that young anymore! And of course I'm settled, how else could I be …' The boy's face flicked back a smallish, wry grin as he looked at his legs forever rested still, now atop the plush blanket.

'Ok … my little sprite. However, I will limit the cursing in this text for fear that your mama overhears and gives me that dark stare of hers, you know the one. And believe me, little one, these scrolls contain scripts from deep within—'

'It sure does look bigger than the ones you usua—'

'It is child. And this one here is only the first part of many alike! The continuation of this series takes up the whole space up there, the whole upper archives.'

'Who is it written by Papa? Is it Rehm? Or maybe Sarepo? Wait … Regala? It must be Regala, he has the biggest collection, it must be—'

'No child. These scrolls come from a different age. So long ago they are now considered make-believe.'

'Hmm … what do you believe, Papa? And why did they write on those curled up papers?'

'I just told you. It was the best of what they had, maybe their way of the time. I never thought about it too much. It does not matter anyway. It was so long ago—'

'I will believe then!'

'I know. I had hoped that you would …'

The man once again looked up, toward the ceiling, but this time he saw beyond the plain of old timber and imagined on to the unseen skies above.

Then even further beyond.

This exchange would continue on, and on, and on. Eventually, over time, the boy would begin to question further with more sophisticated questions.

But for now, the small boy's eyes rolled back before they closed peacefully as the man's soft rumble dictated the words upon the scroll.

# Jacobs Well – A Beginning

Grehn eventually woke. It was late in the day, just before noon. She had been dreaming peacefully, dreaming again of a beautiful and blissful world unbeknown to her. She had always wondered if it was somewhere of her own *world* or some other as written about by the most respected writers – *dreamers*, just like her, she thought of them.

She liked to dream; it took her away from the everyday life she lived. *Living* ... she thought often. Was it *living*? Or was it just that she was alive to experience the drab days and nights offered since she entered the world of *Inarrel* – sister planet to the much larger world of Seltero and the much smaller dwarf planet of Kinora.

She loved her parents deeply, offered no ill towards them, no matter how conservative for her safety they were and always would be. She also loved the people who were closest to her, those who resided – more often than not – inside the castle walls. And knew they all felt a deep dread, brought from deep within them, no doubt, whenever she asked to cross the *Masked Arches*, over the broken divide and into the main town. The mark she bore on her lower back, a mark of such importance, she knew that the seclusion was much warranted. She thought she understood, for she would ensure the same for her future children if it kept them from harm.

*I'm a princess, don't they all get hidden away? Till they are viable for marriage?*

Being who she was also meant there was always a hidden danger that required additional resources to combat: for detection, and then for elimination of such threat; cue the permanent guest, the mage granted, maybe gifted, by the upper echelon of the *City of Columns*.

She made her way to the window, following the source

of a small breeze that brushed by, one that brought in a little of the mist: of moisture dissipating onto the iron bars that crisscrossed the large opening. Then looked out beyond. Listened to the constant striking crash of large waves upon the craggy wall of stone below, the source of that fine mist of moisture.

Eyes closed, she inhaled deeply, drawing in enough air to savour where she thought it had travelled from, or through. She imagined the taste of the rivers and streams of a distant land, carried from afar. She longed to be there, anywhere really, anywhere to escape the lonely space she dwelled. Away from the massive monolith of a rock. A rock which sat abreast a great, deep channel. A channel that divided the palace upon a rock and a great ancient city. The city of Jacobs Well.

Grehn would often stand in front of the high, open window to gaze wistfully over the vast ocean: wondering, enchanted by the thought of sailing over the waters of the Great Green Divice of Vilenzia – the largest of four blankets of water that touched the shores of the Great States – and out onto the plains of *Dalmetonia* and to those forever beyond.

She caught a scent upon a wisp of smoke that drifted across the room from her nightstand. A final result of her brewed mixture of herbs and exotic spices before she added a sticky paste – one produced from crushing the bud of the flower Blueblood. She had been brewing this concoction since the midday meal the day before and then late into the night. Many seasons had passed before she was able to pick the bud of this special genus, the whole winter it had taken to germinate, guided with constant care and meticulous maintenance. A bud of the Blueblood was believed to contain a portion of a collection of souls, those lost to deep waters during the coldest months of the year – all lost during the year of its germination.

During the same meal the previous day, one of the many squires – and one of her best friends – that resided in the castle had bounded in, through the ancient large, flame-seared, oak-laden, double doors and arrowed straight at her, excitement flashed all about his aura.

'Grehn! Grehn … come look!' he cried.

A booming voice quieted the room. 'Molo! Molo, child! Calm yourself, young lad! This is not—' King Benjamin Jacob Aurelia looked at the bouncing child and held a glowering gaze. He was halfway through his gravy-laden rye, loaf, a spittle of gravy flipping off his bushy moustache and also dripping heavily off the red mane that grew south of his chin before he was cut off.

'Ahh, Ben,' A slow, low, gentle whisper could barely be heard escaping the sweet, luscious peach lips. Queen Jahnna leaned in close, and rested a hand on his chest. 'Go easy you big oaf, we both know why he is here.'

Ben chuckled. 'Oh … yes … yes. I heard from Anatoma this morning; I suppose it was only a matter of time before … Hmmm—'

'Apol-apologies, sire, I … I …' Molo stumbled, interrupting their subtle conversation.

Before he could continue, the king spoke, full of warmth and affection. 'No need, Molo. We know why you're here.' Ben looked at Grehn with a smile and a wink before he looked distantly away, toward the largest window on the courtyard side of the wall.

Jahnna noticed the cue, and gracefully glided over to the shuttered window, swinging both leaves wide open with a dramatic swoosh. Then she stepped back, leaving more than enough room.

Grehn rushed forward, followed by Molo, whose grin now touched both ears, bumbling past the statuesque servants and the long winding tables and their hungry punters.

As Grehn reached the window, she heard before she saw. A slight squeal, a melodic, haunting, almost intoxicating wail of the bud cresting from its cocoon. The ambient glow the shedding created was reminiscent of a lantern swaying on a gloomy night at sea – hovering above a wooden, wave-soaked deck of a tall ship.

Her mother drifted over to her. But, quickly, she held herself back to leave Grehn, tranced in a moment of expected pure bliss. She knew what this meant to her daughter: a delicate, complex brew, the final assessment of her long arduous schooling in Medicana and elemental studies. It was her last opportunity; failure meant another four long seasons.

She quietly backed away, hooking a long arm in front of Molo so he wouldn't bowl her only child out of the window. 'Wait Molo, just watch … and listen,' she uttered, barely a whisper.


Coming out of the reverie, and back to her room, the trail of smoke continued to hover, drifting slowly by her. Grehn edged closer to the cultivation of the precious bud, the last of a dozen that had made it through the past winter suddenly dawned on her and she quickly stepped not to lose her precious concoction to the ever-destructive element of fire.

She inhaled the intoxicating air that billowed up slowly from the pewter, the same that had now filled the candlelit room – the candles' wax were now short stubs from burning through each end during the night and the whole morning. Some had not made it that far and were now just stumpy blobs of wax.

The concoction brewing just a small distance from her was a recipe, of sorts: from the pages of *Delight of the Alchemist*, a compilation of writings and teachings by many scholars, alchemists, Medicana, and arcanists that lived, or had lived, in the City of Columns collated into one simple manual. It was deftly deposited into her chamber many years ago by he who was granted leave from the City to reside in the palace upon a request from the king.

Working the coals out from underneath the heavy iron pot with a set of long tongues she let it set on the iron grill to calm, she then grabbed a short, blue-glowing rod, infused with a small charge from the castle's *Collector*. She plunged the rod into the burning mixture, quickly cooling all including the burning hot pot.

With no hesitation, and thought of burning, the pot was lifted and taken to where a candle with an effervescent flame shone with a glowering flicker in the far corner of the large stone-laden room. This burned as bright and tall as she had left it the night before.

Her footsteps were muffled from any echo, aided mostly by the many tapestries hung on walls that once were used as rugs, woven by the *Women of Kallandur*. The very same whose name was attributed to this concoction's creation.

Once settled, the precious produce was ground to a fine powder that glistened like starlight beneath the candlelight, creating an almost sunset-twilight sky appearance. The next step was to add a serum of black leaf dew, taken from the forest a short ride from the city, harvested by a trader who delved in such rare provisions. She mixed until it became too stiff to stir and bound the resulted content into a short stump, just a little larger but the same shape as her thumb.

The chalk, crafted: the attainment, complete. Only one thing left to do now. Kneeling to the floor, she drew a glyph of a crude shape that almost resembled that of a flame, and whispered, 'Echa, echa, echa.' The markings of the chalk flared bright orange and a sharp heat instantly blew outward.

Eyes wide, she squealed with delight. Then she reached up to grab a handful of ground pink rock salt from a large translucent bowl and threw it to scatter across the stone slabs to snuff the glyph to show only a chalk marking.

She enclosed the chalk into a script engraved locket, the outer case ruby-encrusted, its innards lined in a purple velvet.

With a nod – one of approval – and a sigh of relief that she had *actually* been successful, she tied the chain around her neck. Thoughts now focused on the upcoming Festival of the Night – when night becomes the way through three full days.

'Then …' she said, clutching the locket, a small daydream flitted through her mind.

'Now …' She brought herself back. 'I must speak with Molo. I must also find some food …' *I missed lunch and supper yesterday through all of my excitement!*

\*

The day was beginning to darken already, almost the start of the yearly Festival in this town. The eclipse would last only an hour or so as the planets were beginning to warm up their annual extended alignment. The following day, roughly mid-morning, would be day no more. Nor would the day after. Only ending on the third afternoon. A morning of darkness followed by the Festival's crescendo of turning the darkness into a beautiful bright multi-coloured extended early evening. The lightshow would last until much later than the usual dusk. It had been known to hang around way beyond midnight – though not for many a year.

A celebration, yes … but also a reminder that light always overcomes the seemingly eternal darkness in the end. As it always had … as it always would.

Peron looked up slowly as he sat on a long, wide step: it was dusty, it was dirty, though it was one of the few that led up to the entrance for the world-renowned drinking hole. *The*

*Grousing Potter.*

He peered through fingers wrapped around his face, to once again look at a signboard that was posted at the bottom of the steps, hoping with all his might his mind was playing tricks.

It read, much to his dismay:

**Closed for circumstances out of our control. Graciously receive our deepest regrets. We hope to welcome you back soon though!**

*Nope … No!* thought Peron, still mortified.

He was close to weeping. Finally the chance had arisen to visit Jacobs Well, to sample the offerings of this wonderful place from afar – beyond afar, he would argue. Instead, a keening murmur crept out, which was more appropriate for the devastation and how low his soul currently felt.

Looking about, he saw the streets were still empty. They had been all morning – ever since he arrived through the unmanned front gate just after the break of dawn – save for a large hulk of a balding man that had been lugging a huge cartload of something in front of him he had unintentionally shadowed, for a fair distance. He had tried to catch up to the man, but it seemed he was obviously in no mood for a friendly chat. *Probably too tired …*

'Fan … fu—' he moved his lips silently to fill the gap of his curse '—tastic!' he finished, with much distaste for the scene he had found himself a part of.

Those words brought him back to where he sat: the large steps of the greatest tavern this side of Inarrel – if it could even be called a tavern anymore. It was rumoured to be like no other. The stories he had heard. The endless flowing taps spread across three majestical levels.

*The bards, the raconteur, the minstrels, oh … oh, the dancers,* he dreamt a little dream.

Of all his time being a member of the *Third*, he had never been posted anywhere near Jacobs Well. Well, not long enough to venture away from any given assignment.

'Damn … damn …' another sharp curse fumbled far underneath his breath.

Eventually, he stood, and faced the town square, leaving his backpack on the top step, his staff to lean against the large mural painted door and his dark blue robe to rest atop the same staff. He stretched an arm high towards the sky, he was about to close a clenched a fist to curse Everos – the self-revered God of Humour – when a soft thud emanated from behind him, which paused his flow. Peron turned. Excitement that the establishment was opening its doors was met with further demise of an already dampened spirit.

His robe now lay on the dusty step, staff poking out from underneath. Turning again to gaze into the sky, both fists now pointed to the bluish hue of Seltero hanging high above the horizon, another slight curse almost touched his lips. Instead, he laughed. Laughed deeply, and his whole body shook, eyes began to moisten with a foolish humour or anguish – or maybe both.

'Okay … okay,' he sighed, 'you got me! Got me good Everos, you bastard!'

Picking up his dusty belongings, he looked at the clock high above the large door at the entrance to the Grouse. Just past noon, the hands told. If all had gone well, he would have been seated just a small way inside, browsing through the more than thirty pages of a delectable menu – Jacobs Well's finest cuisine – coveting a mug from a selection of over two hundred ales from all over Vilenzia and, more exciting, beyond.

Redirecting his line of sight back to Seltero, he smiled. 'So long as I am here and not up there, I can at least find my way to another establishment nearby. The ladies will have to dance somewhere, and I will be able to listen to a few stories, tall tales told through beautiful or morbidly sad song … or by some raving, stark mad-drunk *raconteur.' Seems most likely*, he surmised.

He descended to the lowest step and looked about the place, then ambled into the depths of the long-cobbled street. Arching his neck back, he looked up to see a finely appointed brass lantern stooping off a high post – one of many scattered about on either side. He looked from the randomly arranged and stacked almond brick veneers dotted about the façade of houses and shops, to the reflective glass windows that added an extra brightness to the grey cobbles which the ample, soon to be snuffed, daylight provided.

The square he beheld was huge.

'A most beautiful city be here. But … where is everybody, and why is the damn Grouse closed for the Festival. Of all the places! Shit!' he murmured, disbelievingly.

He then looked higher and  across the tops of the dark slate roofs clustered to trail far beyond the square, all inclined to what lay even further. Then past the chimney stacks and high bridges to a final portrait of a scenery which seemed implausible. A large grey mass, rising high, jutted with cracks, the sea crashing and creating a misty, foggy appearance high in the air to make the large rock seem as if it was floating upon a cloud. Central to the rocky cliffs, a large structure connected this land with the island. Atop the island an expanse of a wall – not natural, but surely not made by man – seemed to wrap in both directions to the castle. The tallest tower of the castle itself almost touched the sky above.

A sharp shock of blue light, high up from within one of the towers that rose up from monolithic castle, caught his attention. But before he trained an eye on whatever it was, it had expired. Paying it no more mind, he returned his thoughts to the steps to where he once stood.

'Truly … a beautiful city. I wonder if the upcoming Festival has something to do with the town being so quiet?' he muttered as he looked at a map crafted for him by the strangest of cartographers during his brief stop at a town on his way to Jacobs Well. A small town named Naranba: barely fifty folk could have resided there, he assumed. An unusual thing for a map, it was made entirely of a soft fabric, not leather, nor parchment. The guide to Jacobs Well he held bore a big red cross stitched into the fabric, marking exactly where he currently stood., the first thing he had asked the map maker to include upon its completion.

Using the castle as a bearing in relation to the Grouse, he traced a finger to the east, then the first street south, away from the castle to a marker – one tagged as a tankard. The descriptive legend corresponded the symbol, "Tavern".

*As if I needed such additional aid.*

He licked his lips. 'Oh well, let's not waste the day moping, Peron,' he cheerily offered himself a little morale, trying to motivate himself. But the words were swiftly followed with a sigh as he trudged in the direction his finger traced when he felt a little lighter than he should have. He went back for his gear once he remembered and grumbled a little more, as did his stomach … he had always followed despair with a trip to the nearest dropping pot – be it sanitary or bush.

Halfway toward his destined turn down the wide street, he stopped as a loud ringing sounded. He quickly turned back hopefully to the Grousing Potter to see a big bell ringing from atop a tall spire of the building adjacent. A hand past noon, the clock now read. Immediately after the bell had stopped ringing, doors and shutters banged open and a bustle was now starting to establish itself with a cascading ambience.

A small boy ran by singing, 'Ten bell past highest sun, now all are free to run, may once again we be protected by they who—' The song trailed off as the boy moved further away.

Peron turned away from the scraggy looking thing and spotted a merchant quickly setting up a decent sized table at the corner of the entrance to the required junction, and the first person available in the day to interact with, save the strange fellow from that morning.

Peron started, 'Hello, good sir.' The merchant measured Peron up and down – there was no doubt he knew Peron was from out of town – and looked at his robe and belt. No doubt he also knew there was a coin or two to be had. 'May you be of help to a wayward traveller?'

'Aye, sure I can be of use, young fellow. What can I do for you? You have—'

Peron interrupted the man's reply. 'Sorry, but why were the streets empty all morning? And what is this ten bells past twelve business?'

Every city and every town, even the smallest of hamlets, had their own custom for the time during the Festival. So many so that there was now a side unit of study, though within an optional curriculum, one that could be taken as one of the specialist subjects at the City of Columns.

'Ah, just as I thought. You are from far elsewhere, good fellow. There be a few more of you round here of late. More than there usually be.' The merchant waved a dismissive hand. 'Nay mind, to satisfy that curiosity, it's the season of our Protector. He who be there to protect us from the darkest of souls.' He made a quick sign about his chest. 'We are forbidden to pray, eat, drink, laugh, love or cry, safe in our homes from sunrise till them bells' ringing be ended. Thus earning us our penance,' the merchant finished with a proud look on his face.

Before Peron could speak, the man shone him an untoothed smile, broadening it as he rubbed his speculative palms together. 'All ends on t' last day of the Festival, not more than three nights from now.'

*Obviously never left this town, he believes it's all about this town for the Festival ... All good,* Peron concluded.

Again, before Peron could get a word out, the merchant pressed on. 'Hmmm, may I ask what you carry in your hand there?'

Peron eyed the man cautiously, waiting for the attack of commerce to commence. *What is he selling and what is his tact?* 'This crumpled thing? Oh, just a map of the city.'

'M-may I see?'

'Sure ... here.' Peron handed it over. 'So, what wares will you be selling when you have finished erecting your stall and hanger, sir?' Peron asked politely.

The merchant reviewed the map. 'It be made of cloth ... why? We have paper, ye know!' Peron raised an eyebrow, acknowledging the fact. The man then began to pull at the stitching that marked the big red cross, located where Peron had been stood at noon. 'Won't be needing that anymore, boy,' the man chuckled. 'And ... looks like I be selling information so long as you part with some hob for some of *my* merchandise?'

'Here we go,' Peron whispered, air slowly filling his lungs, and smiled inwardly. 'What's for offer from your plentiful looking stock of wares? and why'd you remove that thread?'

'I sell charms and the like, boy. The very best of. Not just wares you should know!' The man's scowl hinted at a withheld anger and resentment. But he continued on. 'Bracelets: some magical, some not, some could be, though they'd need to be charged with a spell or some other enchantment by someone ... someone *other than me*.' He overemphasised the last, just to make the point clear. Not that Peron needed such guidance away from the man's ability.

*All the same in my world.* 'I will take that one there, that little trinket *righhht* there.' He pointed to the smallest charm in what he assumed the non-magical pile – not that any pile could be attributed as such – sticking up high out of its assigned basket. 'For two hobs, as per that there, small "must go" sign.'

Peron offered out the hobs, holding his hand open quickly, knowing this was probably more than double what he should be offering, though he still expected the merchant to make out as though he had been pilfered by the gods themselves.

'The Grousing Potter?' A stern gaze prompted the man as he held out the hobs, ready for an exchange.

The merchant's reply was swift. 'Laddy, what is it you require to know. If I *can* assist, I will. But if I do not, I can only direct you to where you need to go to seek what you may require. But such a small offering won't bring you much. You have only earned what you have asked thus far.'

The merchant turned away from Peron to continue setting up his stall. Eventually he handed Peron a small open box which contained the purchased charm – a bracelet. Though upon closer inspection, it certainly was not worth a third of what was offered.

'The Grouse?' he asked again with a slight nod. 'Kind sir … two hobs?'

Peron finally handed over the two worn – lightweight for their size – metallic coins.

The merchant looked down the street toward the Grouse, took the two coins and dropped them to the cobbles below. Hearing a satisfying clink, he scooped them up and deposited one into his wooden safe box. The other he slid into a hidden side pocket as he looked sheepishly about the place. He winked as if Peron would have known why he would do such a thing – an unspoken joke that maybe he was not party to. Holding the small box in front of his newly found customer, he spoke. 'For the first hob, I can tell you that the tavern will not be opening any time soon …' he paused for effect: none was taken. 'As for the second … I can advise as to a short why.'

He leaned in closer, as if not to be overheard. 'They say …' he looked about before going on, 'the cellar there has been overcome with some sort of darkness; a presence of something foul. Of this world they claim. Even maybe of this city. However … if you wish to know more, I wish to offer no more,' he smiled nervously. 'Good day to you, sir!' he finished after a brief pause then quickly snapped the box shut and thrust it into Peron's midriff.

'Well, at least can you tell me where I can find a refreshing ale?' he asked – now the one looking pained from the shittiness of the deal that had taken place.

The merchant picked up Peron's map and handed it back to him. 'I see you were already on your way, boy. Head past the bright artisan's house half-way up this street here, to the left, and you will smell it before you see it! And you may even find one willing to offer answers in there!' He smiled again, gave him a wink, and finished. 'Good day once more, young one.'

Peron walked down the narrow and winding street – it seemed, and felt, more of an alleyway because of how tightly the buildings seemed to be arched overhead, high above the cobbled divide.

'So, it sounds like it could be a while before I get into the Grouse. Lucky I'm here a few weeks, eh?' he muttered to himself.

Coming up on his right was a colourful, patchworked house – that of the Artisans Guild, identified by a sign that hung over an arched, mural-painted wooden door. He watched as their artwork was brought outside onto a slither of a balcony, to add to the already advertised pieces hanging in the front windows. *Impressive. I wouldn't doubt there to be a few collections and pieces from a high talent back home, from up high in the City.*

Looking forward, he saw a small way in front of where his feet were taking him, and where his finger was tracing the map – the one made of no ink, *no chance for a smudge, I kind of like it* – and raised his eyes higher, now directed a bit further down the street, to see a more than a few people milling at the front of an old looking building. One that split the small alleyway in two – the offshoots looped around the old looking tavern to converge behind. It was obvious the tavern had stood since long before the street was eventually paved, and even before any of the real estate that now sprouted up high on either side of the cobbles.

Coming closer, he saw the slow milling of people quite clearly. After a quick tally, he guessed at approximately thirty-five. As he gazed a little longer he counted the true number. *Exactly thirty-six, losing it Peron.* They were forming a non-descript queue. The majority: older looking. And that majority: men.

An unpleasant scent wafted through the semi-enclosed passage, twinging his nostrils slightly. Looking at his map, he was almost there. There, where the people milled about, was the *Ox and Cart.*

The parting wink, full of sarcasm, from the merchant had given him a clue as to what kind of establishment he was to be heading to having been unsuccessful with gaining entrance to his favoured the Grousing Potter.

He smiled. Broadly. The grubby old merchant obviously did not garner any indication of Peron's taste during their brief exchange.

Peron joined the queueing punters. His stomach grumbled with unease, a regular occurrence these days. *I'm now fully regretting that decision to eat at the hovel of a place last night, but damn it was tasty*, he thought as his tongue dragged across his lips to sample any still lingering spices, while at the same time rubbing his stomach to mentally ease any discontent happening deep down within, managing only just to hold it all inside.

He gauged a few outsiders in the queue from the way they held themselves, trying to look as though they belonged to the city. They stood out like asses on a canoe to Peron. He wondered as to why these people would feel obliged to fit in, every town and city he had ventured to before welcomed outsiders, not necessarily for their personal company, or larger than life bravado, but for the generosity of the coin they brought with them, and the many stories – no matter how embellished they may be.

When he eventually ventured inside, he felt a small breeze blowing through the inn from the back to make its way out of the main entrance, to naturally ventilate the place, moving the rancid, hoppy air about, forcing it down through the big opening and then down the street from where he had ambled.

Surprisingly, the inn was quite well kept, the tapware and the lines that sprouted off were well polished, showing no hint of rust or smear. And the low ceiling seemed to amplify the low ambient noise and the subtle stench of the newly admitted inhabitants – the latter he sensed since laying eyes upon them from back up the street.

The floor was cold but immaculate, swept, scrubbed even. And the large stone slabs felt good on the soles since the uneven cobbles outside bent the foot in all kinds of angles, especially with the soft soled shoes Peron had worn to grace the Grouse.

Peron made his way to the bar. He was the first one to

touch the large wooden plain – a long and seemingly ancient earthy bar top – before he settled his elbows and then exhaled.

'Your recommendation, barkeep? I see a large selection on offer,' a punter asked from just over his shoulder, obviously not from town. Peron knew to never ask an unknown barkeep what he would recommend. More often than not, he would smile and offer up the house special.

Peron shook his head, and before the barkeep could offer a response, he spoke sarcastically. 'I will have anything else …'

The barkeep smiled, ignoring Peron. 'Look 'ere, then, laddy.' He walked to one of the taps which had a small amount of frost congealing around its spout. 'Now, try this! See if this sample 'ere soothes that thirsty, flapping, tongue of yours. The house special! A nip on the house!'

He passed it over Peron's shoulder to the lanky man behind as Peron rolled his eyes. 'Much obliged, kind sir,' said the punter.

Peron was dumbstruck by the grace of the barkeep. *How very gentlemanlike of the man. A free swig of his finest house! Usually they make you pay first!*

The scruffy middle-aged man took a long sip of not much, savouring the drop. He sighed with pure satisfaction: no doubt the tap, or line, or both, had some magical element installed to keep the drink coming through the nozzle cool; it looked icy throughout. *Probably to disguise the flavour, a common swindle.*

Peron was not alone in his observation: the sigh of pleasure was also keenly observed by all that were waiting, some impatiently, at the bar.

The barkeep poured ten mugs of the more than satisfactory ale and sat them on the bar ready for an immediate sell off all to the first ten lucky punters eyeing them, and the exchange that had taken place.

Peron brought himself back to his normal calm, away from his gullible view of the picture unfolding. He whispered to the barkeep, 'Not fooling me. I see the game here,' and then he winked at the barkeep.

Settling to the back of the pack, Peron watched with a smug look on his face as the unwitting clambered over each other to offer their coin for the house special, noticing a few others stepping back also, aware of the potential ruse being played out.

There was a large groan of disappointment when all the pre-poured ale had disappeared off the bar, and the barkeep had announced, 'We're now out of the special. However, good folk, an alternative keg will be tapped from a well-known brewer from the state of Helfern, where the large plains produce the silkiest of wheat grown with the purest, crystal clear water that spouts up from the deepest of the *Springs of Serenity* below!' He finished with a flourish and a sweeping bow.

Those graced with the house special made their way to the area with ample seats. Peron eyed them while waiting for the other keg to be brought up and tapped, expecting them to hurry over and begin their complaints to the effect of robbery.

Peron was amazed when he heard a chorus of satisfied sighs, if ever so slightly exaggerated, joined by all in the seating alcove, followed by a clink and a raucous rumble.

'Damn, you!' Again, he looked to the sky but saw only the rafters holding what seemed to be the floor above – dark beams and freshly painted boards that did not care for his curse.

The barkeep did not miss this little exchange with his ceiling and chuckled quietly. He looked at Peron and shouted over the wriggling mass, 'Stranger,' he pointed a thick forefinger at Peron, 'come 'ere.'

Peron made his way to the end of the bar to where the

big man was chuckling: his squinty eyes glaring at Peron underneath a large and wrinkled, sweaty forehead, the little fur above his top lip and his long-braided beard flopping around while he had his fun. Peron grumbled another curse, this time to himself.

'You see all those men, them over there? They are the locals around here. We know what goes on in other parts of Vilenzia, the ruse is so my regulars … Well, they stay my regulars, if you know what I mean?' He winked. Peron understood all too well.

'But the fellow from out of town then … he who asked for your recommendation? He surely isn't part of your little ruse … is he?' Peron protested.

'Well, he is from out of town, I suppose. But, he do live with a niece of mine,' he chuckled again.

'Why such a big show if there is no profit in it for you?'

'Because, my laddy, you see those who followed you to the back of the throng that began pushing toward the bar?'

'Yes,' agreed Peron.

'Well. When I announce to the tavern in a short while we will be bringing keg upon keg of the stuff in tomorrow, they will have at least four … maybe five or more with 'em, thus increasing my profit tenfold on *my* lovely house special.' He rubbed his hands greedily together.

Peron looked incredulously at the man, he himself … fooled. He could easily make a show of the whole scheme to the unsuspecting but thought better of it.

'What if I go and tell that poor folk you would swindle them for some cheap ale, probably from that nice clean grate over there collecting the swaths of spilt ale?'

'Aye, ye can, laddy, but it would be fifteen to your one word, would be fruitless.' He paused to size up the smaller man. 'I do, however, have one left. It be from the cellar at the House of Jurengor. Three hobs though …'

Peron sighed inwardly. *Robbing bastards, town seems full of them*. Though he was thirsty, he knew the brewery and the cellar well. He'd been there many times. And he was mildly impressed by the man's guile. He shook the barkeep's hand uneasily. And again he released more of his hobs; at least one more than he thought necessary.

'Agreed. But … a name from my early afternoon tormentor?'

'Belrough be my only name, and this 'ere be the most fabulous inn on this side of Jacobs. Well, for the most recent of weeks now, since a few changes have aired 'emselves within the district.'

Belrough leaned back a little and breathed in a deep one. 'We have serene, magical music, as such from that bunch there lugging themselves in just now.' A couple of unkept and youngish looking boys and a much taller, more refined girl came bundling through the large doorway dragging each a large case that housed their mammoth instruments. Belrough continued on after another deep breath. 'Many stories and tales of the deep and of wonderous treasures hidden around Vilenzia from our resident raconteur sat over there.' He pointed to the regulars all leaning in, as if listening to something.

'The most exot—' he tried to carry on but was interrupted by Peron who could hear something but saw nothing.

'Where is he?'

'There!' Belrough pointed to the middle of the troupe now well settled in the alcove. He was a bit put out by Peron's interruption as he composed his own sonnet, exaggerating his tavern's greatness.

'Oh, the fellow looking at us with one eye, the other eye looking at the stairs?'

'No, no, laddy. The short one, looks wider than tall … that be him!' Another chuckle.

'Ahh … yes I see him now. So you were saying?'

Belrough continued. 'The most exotic—'

Peron continued for him. 'Dancers? The best ale in all of Vilenzia? The most luxurious rooms? All decorated by the Goddess of Love herself? Per chance?'

'May I be introduced to such-a-smart fella before he be ejected back onto the street he came from?' Belrough said bluntly, glaring at him now with all seriousness.

'Good man, I … I jest! Peron. Peron I am known as. I have travelled far from the other side of the Great State of Vilenzia. I am but a weary traveller.' Peron lowered his head to resemble, he hoped, an offering of apology.

'Well. Peron. Before I again start to think about ejecting you from the Ox – *my Ox* – you may apologise with one of those shiny grets your lot seem to carry with you.' Belrough pointed towards Peron's small satchel, tied around his waist belt.

'Here. Take one, so long as I get to stay long enough to enjoy this supposed remarkable Jurengorian ale. Which I have already purchased, may I also add! As matter of fact, I was here to—' Peron held a strangled look about his face, trying to wrangle a question: one that he had been trying to figure out in the back of his mind while the whole exchange was taking place. 'Hold on for a moment barkeep.' He composed his mind enough to finally ask the question that had stumbled into his mind. 'What … what if one of *my* good folk happened to be in that muddle for the Jurengorian ale?'

'Well …' looking at Peron as if the answer was obvious. 'Well. I suppose then they'd soon enough become another one of my regulars.' He boomed a large laugh, all the way from the stomach, and slapped Peron's shoulder, knocking him back more than a touch. Peron took it well enough, a little too well, but Belrough was too away with his laughter to not notice.

'Come to think of it, that bunch over there do look a little odds and evens. Might I join them? Wouldn't mind resting my weary legs and hearing some long tales.'

'Huh …' Belrough seemed slightly miffed at Peron's quick reaction but responded just as quick. 'Aye, laddy, but were you in the middle of asking me something else?'

'Ah! Yes! The Grouse?'

Before he offered an answer, he rubbed a finger and thumb around his platted beard. 'Some bad business be that …' Belrough lowered his eyes to the polished timber bar, then across it, ultimately fixing then on a man Peron had failed to notice earlier – something he never did. Belrough gave a quick nod, and the man began to slowly amble over to join the pair.

'Good business for me though, hehe. Bringing the likes of your lot in 'ere.' Belrough waved his big thick arm to coax the sly looking figure over quicker. 'Malek. This 'ere be Peron. Thinks he's clever and asks questions like he be the district constable. I'm assuming he has quested many a mountain, sailed the five oceans, and plunged into the deepest caverns of Longerwhere.' Peron looked to the man, ready to confirm that he had indeed done *most* of that. But he held his tongue. 'Just to satisfy a curiosity garnered for the much talked of, and enamoured, Grousing Potter and its otherworldly charm and offerings. Correct? Friend …'

'An accurate surmise.' Peron nodded to Belrough then to the newcomer, Malek. 'Good day, Malek. I'm Peron.' He stuttered, before realising he had already been introduced as such. The air suddenly felt thick about the dodgy looking chap who stared dark, sunken eyes intently at him.

Belrough interjected, cutting off Peron's stammer. 'Laddy, Malek is one of those men who offer bounties. There be only a few of them be permitted to in this town. I let him hang around here as there are always some dealings to be done that … well, that I don't want any part of, other than my cut! Ain't that right, Mal?' Belrough winked at

Malek and accompanied it with a quirk of a smile.

No such smile was returned, or anything to acknowledge he had even been spoken too. Belrough dabbed at his forehead with a tatty, well used rag, before excusing himself. But not before handing Peron the ale he had bought. He then began to use the sodden rag to wipe the bar between them, and moved on to serve the remainder of the now grumbling punters.

Malek spoke softly, though Peron was sure not to mistake any danger this man possessed. 'My friend, the Grouse is closed. For now ... at least,'

'I know! I just happened to be there.' Peron's response was cheerful. A little too so.

'What would you *wish* to know?' Malek's response was as blank as his demeanour. No humour, no malice, just ... blank.

'When will it be open again? For starters at least.'

'Ask the landlord's door keep. I'm sure he will be around here later, if not sooner.' Again, blank. Devoid of any hint of the slightest change in emotion.

*Okay*, thought Peron. The conversation was heading nowhere. 'A mighty fine pleasure to meet you, Malek. Good afternoon.' Peron turned toward the seating area where most of the earlier clientele had mingled. It had only been a few minutes but already a few were heading back to the bar for their second helping.

'Wait!' Malek spoke this time with an urgent sharpness as he turned away, having gazed swiftly across the golden embroidery emblazoned on the hilt of a dagger Peron held strapped on the inside of his jacket, revealed after he had exaggeratedly raised his arm to leave.

'Hmmm ... you may yet be of some use yet, young man.'

*Did he form a smile, just then as he spoke*? Peron was unsure – once again. He would entertain this cryptical, nonsensical episode only a fraction longer. 'I'm still here. Not where I want to be. Can we at the very least take a seat then?'

'Of course, this way sir!'

They headed away from where they had stood taking up precious real estate at the bar.

Malek dragged another tall chair close to where he had sat moments earlier, to sit at the end of the bar – the common area where finished drinks were to be deposited for a *thorough clean*. Malek offered the seat to Peron.

Peron shook his head slightly, thinking of what this little interchange would entail.

'Do you wish to grace what magnificence the Grouse offers while you are still here? The town's folk would be relieved, very relieved to have the jewel of their city back, hopefully before the festivities of the Festival begin … or at least by their close.' Malek looked intently again at Peron, as if trying to gauge something in him, or about him.

Peron slung his cloak on the chair. The staff he then wedged into an angled join in the wall. The backpack rested upon his knee as one elbow propped his head up against the timber slab.

Malek turned his natural, cold gaze toward the group mingling in the seated area. 'The one you will need to aid you is over there.' He pointed to the regulars now slapping knees and rubbing shoulders. 'You have to persuade him, otherwise the folly began will be as useless as that old staff you carry with you. Not to mention that overbearing cloak.'

The strange man was correct; the staff was indeed *all for show*, to help him fit into his respected column in the City – they all seemed to carry one with them. And the robe did *only* hold a small amount of charge, though it did enhance the appearance – *quite considerably*, he thought. But what Malek would not have known was that the medallion around his neck held as much power as if the robe and staff were charged by a master arcanist from the most ancient column of the highest Pillar.

'Boy, you have a power about you. I espied it while you were outside, milling around – the only one trying not to fit in, I might add. You carry the embroidery of *The Shadow of the Path.*' The last words were barely a whisper.

Peron now eyed Malek with his own blank look, trying to not escalate any further the evolving situation. It was now Malek who was smiling – it looked odd, far out of place for such a dark fellow.

He knew. He had seen Peron ghost to near the front of the pack. While all others were fixated on the entrance, there was one who was fixing a stare the other way.

'Fictional tales and fae stories, Malek,' Peron bluntly advised. 'You'd do well to remember that and not press any further.' Without taking eyes off the man, Peron now had his staff held in his free hand.

Malek tried to make sense of the fact of the observation that presented itself suddenly in front of him: Peron sat with staff in hand, bag still resting on his thighs. It had been a long way out of reach but a moment earlier, and Peron himself seated. Now he sat grasping it. 'My apologies, just an old man rambling,' he stood quickly and helped Peron fold his cloak. 'Go and speak with Dresdor, the shortish wide looking fellow over there, the one rambling on with all gusto. He has a good story to tell about your precious Grouse. When you have finished speaking with Dresdor, come back and see me for I have an item you will need. If you can manage to persuade him that is …'

'Why not just give it to m—'

'Go. Speak with your man Dresdor first.'

Malek, gave Belrough a quick nod to get his attention and gingerly shook his head. A quick warning, a silent piece of advice for Belrough to assist with any of Peron's needs – and not to throw him out on his arse.

Belrough looked back at Malek. Malek's face was now pale and held a mild twist of angst. Seeing this, Belrough, having moments ago been ashened by Malek, now shook with a shiver, and dropped a metallic mug to clang on the stone floor behind the bar. He crouched down to fetch it and clutched the talisman wrapped around his neck, then stuttered a little prayer as though he had been cursed by one of the greater gods.

Startled, he jumped and banged his head on the underside of the thick timber as he noticed Peron leaning over the bar.

'My good fellow, could you bring that ale over? I'll be seating myself at the table with the man they all call Dresdor, your resident storyteller. Bring him one too, eh! That gret should cover the expense, I assume …?'

Stumbling about behind the bar, Belrough mumbled something that resembled a stutter as affirmation.

Peron grunted a sharp acknowledgement. 'Finally! Now we're getting somewhere,' he muttered impatiently.

Peron made his way across the space between.

*How had he seen it? Not once do I remember exposing the hidden pocket of my jacket, for even only a fraction of a second, and he saw it.* Peron thought of the small dagger attached to the inner cloth of his lightweight jacket. He looked back over his shoulder at Malek, still searching for a shift, some haze about the bloke, anything that could reveal the suspicious man's true nature or intention. There was nothing, just a blank image. He had heard of people like Malek, people who could search for something that was not gauged from the outer self but deep within. Nothing magical, just an innate ability to read a person, a skill Peron would do well to develop further it would seem. Turning back his attention to the tables he was heading to, he smiled at the mixed looking group, most of them already well into their second draught.

*Surely just a guess, expecting me to confirm or deny. And I gave him enough to conclude. Stupid.* He continued to roll through on reflection.

'Good day to you all. I'm here to have a friendly, if brief, chat with *he* who'd be your afternoon entertainment.'

Peron had interrupted a small ballad being composed, not very graciously, by the short, stumpy fellow. But the man offered enough charisma to hide the off keys – no doubt later on when the man was full of drink, he would be much better.

Dresdor looked up at him. Then stood.

Peron looked down. And tried to stifle a chuckle.

Dresdor chuckled back, knowing full well the cause of humour and what Peron was so amused by.

The chuckling stopped.

'Ayeah! Stranger, what be happening here, eh …?' Dresdor grumbled, abashed at being interrupted and no doubt flummoxed at the brashness of such regard to his height – or thereof lacking.

'Yeah! We were getting to the part where the lady gets burned to ashes for hiding an evolen stone,' grumbled a patron, followed by a chorus of ayes from all those gathered around the tables.

'Don't worry, gentle folk! I just need a moment of your man's time. I will reimburse you all with another house special. Isn't that right? Barkeep!'

Predicting a potential physical conflict, Belrough had already rushed over with the two requested mugs, as promised. He was but a shoulder length away from Peron when he heard Peron finish speaking. Dropping the mugs down briskly on the table beside where the exchange was taking place, he wheeled back toward the steps to the cellar. But not before shouting, 'Absolutely, my good fellow! Right away! Coming right up! I will just check if any deliveries have been ! Should be here by now.' He wiped his forehead again before disappearing behind a wall at the end of the bar.

Belrough could then be heard scurrying away, down the stone steps to the acrid cellar.

'How'd you get into that stubborn bastard?' Dresdor asked incredulously. He only then noticed the dark figure at the end of the bar give a slight nod toward Peron.

'Right lads! That's your lot … for now at least. The man has recompensed more than plenty. Surely more than my lame compositions ever could.' The short man laughed – if a little nervously.

They grumbled but necked their tankards in anticipation of their refill.

'Name's Dresdor.' He held out a big thick hand. Peron took it.

'What's got that there resident bounty organiser so twitchy? Hehe …' Dresdor showed a big smile, but still nervously offered. 'Suppose you're here to coax me to go down into that cellar of the Grouse with you hey?'

'What … the Grouse? Waaaaiit! Why would I find myself in the basement with what is supposed to be down there? I know I'm keen as a goose to get in there, but …'

'Because, matey, that fella over there looks like he's seen a ghost himself, looks scared more than half silly.' Peron looked back at Malek who still held the same blank gaze, so he shrugged off Dresdor's observation 'What did he offer ya? Gold, jewels, an enchanted tome? He has 'em all, let me tell you. Let me guess …' The short man rubbed a finger and thumb about his chin. 'Aha! The bloody membership to the Potter?'

'What! He has a-a what? A membership. Why would a man like that have a membership for the finest tavern in Vilenzia? He looks quite … well, not the type.'

'Not quite, lad. It was promised to whoever clears that cellar of whatever be causing them taps to ooze out nought but bile. Something down there be causing all the best ale in the world to congeal and sludge out. Tap the barrel and it be fresh as new – between the barrel and the tap, only the gods know what was making all the folk sick; the smell drove them all out after a short while.

'Then they saw something, a misting in the cellar. It formed to a shape. Do you know why that man asked you to come here, to me?' Peron shook his head slowly. 'Didn't get that that far, eh?' Dresdor looked down. After a moment the slightest hint of a glisten formed around his eyelids, shining from his averted gaze. 'That shape. The rumour be it materialised into a well-formed and distinguishable shape of a man, a man with an anguished face about him, a man I knew well …' Looking back at Peron, his face returned to its initial pose – hard as stone. 'Hmmm, it would surprise me if it were old Steff … to be truth.

'You see, they had him chucked out a month or so back, said he was driving folk away with his batty outburst about a coming storm that would flatten the known world, a storm from that big blue thing up there.' He made a quick sign and kissed his wrist.

'Why would he be there now? In spectral form?' asked Peron, now finally intrigued by the whole episode. This was the Shadow's business to seek out information of anything that would aid the Path and their deployment of resources from the Third Pillar. The madman, or so the folk of the *Grouse* believed, a man named Steff who was possibly a seer, though terrorising the cellar of the Grousing Potter seemed unlikely. But there was a means to an end here.

Dresdor continued on. 'Could just be the cellar boy's wits gone awry. When them goosebumps appear, folk see things ain't there.' He tapped a thick finger against his temple to emphasise the point. 'Steff ain't been seen since he was booted down them steps. Was a rumour he stopped off by the house on Eldwin Street a few weeks back. Said to be a few in there that ain't the good sort, if you know what I mean.' He shook his head. Took a swig of ale. 'Anyway.

Me and Steff go back. Way, way back! There's no chance he would have anything to do with it, not a chance!' He continued to shake his head. 'If I were a betting man, my money would be on that witch that lives down the road from the Grouse, always berating the folk who come out of the tavern. "Unholy! Heathen! Scum!" she shouts. Always there.

'And she ain't been seen for weeks either. Suppose with no patrons to berate that would make some sense.' He looked again to Malek, who was still watching the conversation from afar. 'He thinks that if it is Steff, I may be able to talk him around. He is dead set that's the case.' He brushed a wide hand through the majorly greyed mane. 'That's why *he* sent *you* over here. Hmmph!'

'How much are they paying him, or anyone, to get rid of the problem?' Peron asked, also eyeing the shady character.

'As I said, a lifetime membership. Not just an ordinary one, this one would give all area access. Full use of the master suites, including all the accompanying amenities.' Dresdor winked as though Peron would know what was meant. 'Reserved for only royalty, the highest nobles, and the most influential entertainers of Vilenzia, and those from far beyond.'

'What's in it for him then?' Peron asked.

'The gold that be offered too. Maybe. Probably … it's all very private, you don't see. All only rumours. But something be 'appenin there, and they're trying not to scare the good folk off for good.' Dresdor shot Malek a fleeting glance. 'He has a key, one given to all the bounty organisers and even a few competent mages in the city, which ain't many.' He clasped his hands together. 'Apparently, they the ones that make the deals to get things done. They negotiate the return on the bounty.

'Look, matey. I am keen to clear my good man's name. Wherever that old sod is, he ain't in there!'

The mug Dresdor had been supping from during the exchange was now halfway dry. Peron lifted his mug, measuring Dresdor again, looking him in the eye, looking for some sort of elaborate swindle. When he was sure there was none, he offered the slightest nod.

Dresdor lifted his half-empty mug and banged Peron's. Ale sloshed up and out of Peron's mug and onto the clean hard surface below. They then both downed the cool, crisp content that remained.

Wiping the froth from his upper lip – the now empty tankard sitting on the table – Peron looked toward the shady character of Malek again. 'Okay, Dresdor. Friend! Let us go see what we can purloin from your mysterious little friend, and this utmost urgent little errand.'

They walked back across the stone-slabbed floor, past the only clerestory window of the inn, the one high up at the wide porch; the sky seemed darker than it should be, only slightly, but Peron did not miss such an adjustment. The Festival of the Night was beginning to warm up, and with it, the annual festivities. Those which would begin on the following day, when the subtle eclipse would become much more prominent. Much more permanent.

# Depths of Enteria

The cavern was dark and very much unwelcoming. Not a full darkness, but plenty enough to lose yourself if you had no aid for means of guidance.

The split-rock laden surface – moist from the seepage that made its way through to the void from the terrain above, then down into the massive chasm below – seemed to soak away the little light that was emitted from the two burning torches being carried down the makeshift trail.

A slight cutting of a pathway led a long winding slither, then disappeared as it met another couple of torches hung either side of a jagged cut archway. The archway's opening itself rippled ever so slightly with seemingly unnatural liquidity – much akin to that a feather may cast across a lake upon contact.

To step across this spacious, ancient cavern was a privilege bestowed upon only the most devoted. They were those who had been tested and had been judged worthy to grace what lay beyond the rippling archway.

To step across this cavern unknowingly, oblivious to what lay beyond the opening, would be to enter nothing more than another opening, a mirrored opening sending you walking in the opposite direction to that by which you entered.

To those who dared to set foot onto the rocks of the cavern floor with ill intent, they would be incinerated by a surge of power that would emanate through the splitting veins that ran through the rock – the flitting natural seeming cracks jutted all over its surface.

As the pair approached their final destination, a constant ripple lurched outward and across the large opening forming almost a quartered bubble out from the rock face.

They chanted aloud. Quickly, and in absolute tandem:

*"She! Oh, she who will save all,*
*I come here, blessed for all we have shamed.*
*You have shown me how to stand tall.*
*As your faithful servant,*
*Grant me entrance, to your place of rage.*
*Through the doorway, ascending from this plain,*
*So, I may add to your many pages."*

The archway bubbled much more fervently. Then a hulk of a being stepped forward, bobbing its head as it crossed the high threshold, mindful of the hard frame. It was adorned with leather straps acting as bracers, many old small bones threaded through the leather that crossed over both shoulders of its musked, muscular body. It held a large double-headed cleaver in one of its hands – the size any normal being would struggle to hold with two hands. It stopped a short way before the two well-revered acolytes and spoke, a grinding monotone gargle. 'I am the Gatekeeper!' Then it pointed with its free hand, and swayed a finger to hover over both in turn. 'Choose … you! Which of you will step forth to carry themselves through this boundary? To beyond. To that of perpetuity?'

A soft voice spoke from under one of the two dark green hoods. 'We are as one, our lady came to us both, proclaiming greatness to come.'

'Yes?' It laughed before cutting off abruptly. 'But to both? I think not!' An excruciating drawn-out gurgle and matter of fact demeanour escaped its purple, bulbous lips.

It clutched four blade-like fingers around the hilt and pointed the sharp two-sided weapon towards the other unspoken figure, before it asked, 'And so, what say you? Who will step forth?'

The figure who had yet to speak stepped forward, dropping the dark emerald hood, letting it slump around slightly built shoulders. She met its scornful gaze full on with burning eyes of her own.

Suddenly staggered, the large being stepped back two short steps. Swooping the weapon behind its back, it knelt, head low, so low its lumpy bloated face could feel the moisture as it hovered close to the cold damp stone.

Looking down on the large being stood a woman – beautiful beyond measure. A wayward breeze let an isolated strand of glowing auburn hair fall loose over her left eye, hovering past her petite, pointy nose. She brushed the loose strand back behind her ear – re-joining the mass of long raven hair – and stood tall. Confident. She used the same hand to prompt the first speaker forward with a low swinging motion.

The other figure came forward, slowly, to stand beside the woman, shoulders a finger's breadth apart.

Sensing the approach, the creature peered up from its deep obeisance, trying hard to not meet the eyes of the woman standing above, nor her face – the very replica of the many statues that adorned the place beyond the opening from where it had appeared.

It almost grovelled.

As the other dropped its hooded cloak, the creature raised its head slightly higher to see what else could be beheld, then fell flat on its stomach, seeing the other woman, the mirror image of *she* already standing over him. The only difference, the gentle glowing streak of hair that was a different shade of colour – fuchsia.

Tears began streaming to the ground, dripping profusely off its bloated face. Tears that glowed a subtle pink as they dissipated on the dark, rocky surface: plenty enough for the cracks to glow slightly, and reveal themselves fully as they drained the immortal's moisture away.

Now the grovelling did begin, in earnest. It spoke quickly and with little pause as it spat the words out. 'Almighty! My hands have been tied for generations into this, and many other interrogation alike! It is as it always was! Until now … none have passed as a pair …ever! You should know that before relieving me from my endless duty. End me now … here! Do it so you may both be granted permittance.

'My part is done. For only two entities may be permitted to step forth through the portal. I gift my soul fire to you both, to see you both through. See and remember this as my final sacrifice for our cause …'

The being held itself flat to the stone and pushed the cleaver forward to the pair. Then tensed, waiting. 'You'll need this to pass.'

Stepping forward quickly, the last to approach the creature was first to react. She reached down low and grabbed the large cleaver, picking it up as though it was a scalpel. And began to spin the weapon above her head – as though spinning a weighted string – before arcing it downwards, the spin cascading higher in pace and tempo the lower it raced to the ground.

A whispered whimper could be heard from the now obedient being. 'Thank you. I will be your most faithful! When I meet you both in the afterl—'

The smooth, efficient stroke across the middle of its back sliced the thick, muscular being into two. The resulting emanation of dark green liquid oozed across the floor, cutting the demon's slurring words to nothing more than a short gurgle – its pitiful worship for the two cut off before it was able to finish.

Then the floor became alive, glowing vibrantly in the same colour as the ooze that discharged from the cleanly exposed faces of the split open Gatekeeper's body. More ooze was discharged as the two parts of the being twitched violently before they came to a slow halt. She threw the weapon back to the floor. It sparked brightly as it clattered toward the upper half of the torso of the beast, before eventually falling to rest not far from where the blood flowed into the fissures.

Both women looked at the carnage – if a little perversely.

They slowly outstretched an arm, raising it up toward the black of the cavern's grimy soffit, and chanted an unknown ancient or foreign language. Globes of sparkling light appeared in the palm of each, lighting up the vast cavern. Strings of darkness rose from the ground and flowed into the two women through the orbs, draining the life source from the flaccid being.

Suddenly the light dissipated: a rush of wind shot outward from each woman, blowing out all torch light, creating an immensely dark space inside the cavern.

The first woman began to tumble then fall slowly forward, her streaking auburn hair now glowing a violent violet hue.

'Mesfa!' the second woman shouted, dropping her now extinguished torch. She moved quickly to catch the brunt of her companion's fall before she could clatter into the hard surface face first. 'You take too much. Here. Let me relieve some of the soul fire you have absorbed from that—' she looked at the shrunken remains of the being '—thing.'

Mesfa spoke with a wavering but strong voice, one that punched through her innocent appearance. 'No, Arigal, the moment, this … place, it all just … overwhelmed me. We're so close! The entrance beyond, we are about to fulfil our long-held dream: one we both have held true for more than a lifetime.' She touched Arigal's hand. Grabbing it as an aid, she helped herself to her feet. 'The Gatekeeper's soul! It was so dark, so powerful, even more so than the whole soul fire we have consumed over the last few years – decades even!'

Mesfa brushed the grime off skin-tight black threads and her loose-fitted cloak with both hands. Mesfa looked to Arigal, *almost* a mirror image: the beauty, the determination, the inner darkness seemingly identical to her own. 'Now we must advance. Let us pass … Sister.'

Arigal nodded, turning her attention to the large portal now humming and rippling turbulently then snuck a side glance at her best friend. Both knew the prophecy.

*She of fair complexion who melts and melds the hearts of men.*
*She who bears the streak of power in her hair.*
*She who seeks darkness becomes the darkness.*
*She, a reflection of Our Lady.*
*She will lead us to a new dawn. She will be the end!*

Mesfa didn't miss the attention of Arigal– she never did. 'Sister, we are destined to become far more than the children we once were.' She turned to face her as she continued. 'Know that my love for you has no bounds, as yours to mine.' She tapped her chest with two fingers. 'This! This is what we must become to fulfil our role as the New Dawn of Sylteneria eventuates. Our love for each other will overcome. If we are destined to face each other, it will be what it will be. That love between us will be carried by the victor with the blessing of the fallen.' She snickered as a wicked smile appeared. 'And we both know who that is to be!' She laughed as she avoided a swift jab from Arigal.

An unexpected screech, that of an echoing voice filled the cavern, emanating from the arched portal and blurring out all other sound.

*"Pleassse do not disssappoint, forrr you have been chosssen, you mussst relibquishhhh your petty feelingssss. For thossse not worthy to fulfil shhhall not passss!"*

The echo eventually trailed away to allow the void of silence to fill the cavern once more, save the occasional drip from above that disturbed from its tiny vibrations.

Arigal grabbed Mesfa's hand, and brought it up to her lips. 'I would make you proud, as you would me. Whoever it may be! Let us begin the journey, *our journey* … together!'

Stepping up to the portal, Mesfa noted the torch handles were moulded from a disfigured creature's appendage: a long, sinewy limb with a fingered fin of more than ten long branched fingers, a once webbing, no more. Both held a black orb, the low flame now nothing like it blazed but moments earlier.

Still holding hands, they moved at a steady pace toward the rippling bubble.

Upon the slightest touch of Mesfa's fingertip, the ripples stopped. A bubble expanded and encased the two inside. It expanded even further, to swallow the halved still form that lay on the ground behind them. Then a flash consumed all darkness, so much so that only a bright light could be seen.

They looked forward. And braced themselves.

'I would have expected nothing less … from either one of you, Blessed. You may now pass!' The voice from behind should have startled the two women, but they were no more perturbed should a breeze have touched their hair.

In sync once more, both women spoke without the slightest hint of hesitation. 'Lead on … *Gatekeeper.*'

The large creature moved in front of them both. Though less than half the size it was when it first appeared, it still towered over the two. It waved the now glowing cleaver in the air they had left on the ground, spinning it faster and faster. The runes on the blade glowed brighter and brighter, creating a vortex that looked to travel for an infinity beyond.

It spoke again. 'We go now. We must be away from here! The first temporal alignment is imminent …'

# What Happens in the Dale

Peering through a small growth of heckle bush, he could now *finally* make out its body shape – it was a sight to behold, almost magical, almost the terror seen only in a nightmare. Was the creature none the wiser of where he currently crouched? Was it still unaware of his nearby presence? Highly unlikely. This was a creature deserving of the lofty respect in which it was held, renowned for its cunning and relentless hunting – it had been known to stalk for many a day, even weeks – if there was potentially a greater prize to be garnered from its long, drawn out, silent and, in the end, brutal pursuit.

But. This time, *it* was being hunted. The culmination of a full seven day round trip, venturing out into the epicentre of the dale, then back to near where they had started out, through an alternate winding track to where they would lay their own ambush – the winding a tact to throw their scent to a path of their choosing so as not to confuse their prey.

The expansive dale was nestled between the large town of Horgshead and the small city of Tellbrush – the distance between their respective closest neighbour as a direct route was an arduous travel by foot to the lowest point of the dale. A slow descent through marshes, middle brush, and the unavoidable bands of dense forest which wrapped the valley – these bands a myriad of trees and clumps of massive unnatural-seeming oaks that stretched upwards beyond the more opulent palms and expansive creepers that were native and prevalent to that part of the state.

Three of those seven days were spent venturing out, locating and awakening the beast. The remaining four days luring it back to the camp where the trap would be sprung.

The beast's natural instinct would, no doubt, conclude it was tracking the *hunters*, its prey, oblivious to the hunter's lure. The lure, concocted seven days earlier when attending a parish get together at the church before their expedition began. Old folk, young folk and parishioners who could easily be overcome – a reek of innocence from the congregation that would attach itself and linger upon the aura of anyone for days. For they would not be battle-hardened, easy, and ripe for the picking. To feast upon, satisfying the creature's hunger for a little while longer.

The lingering scent of the parish about the air would attract the beast from its slumber. The feast consumed, the two weeks prior would enable it to rest for a mere few weeks, maybe a month at best. The hunter knew these creatures were not the most sociable and were rarely seen out in the dale, or anywhere. It would also grow faster, stronger, harder the more extended their hibernation – so long as a decent amount of the essence of innocence was absorbed. This boosted their strength quite significantly – or so it was spoken around whatever social circle was frequented …

The impossible to reach hollow, high up the precipice, where the creature resided, sat high up the sharp rock of a mountain in the middle of the dale. An unnatural monolith that rocketed high up from the lowest point of the River Arneld. During the driest month in an age, the usually raging river slept as soundly as the creature resting above, which made the journey all the easier.

The high rocky face that elevated sharply above them was legendary, it was said to have been carved by the hands of Drecordian himself – a massive rod of a rock, dropped from the heavens accidentally long ago to forever remain part of this landscape.

The creature would hopefully, eventually, inhale the scent that drifted up from below. Wafting into its lair, the reek of weakness, carried by the clothes of the hunters below.

Just as the same scent of weakness had made its way through the nostrils of the creature three weeks earlier in the small hamlet of Gurado – just a short ride and the nearest settlement to Horgshead. A reek that would be detectable by the beast's heightened senses, detectable for more than four nights, clinging to the hunter's clothes. Hopefully. Depending on the weather – the driest wet season for years would help their cause.

A faint whistle was heard. The sound was not too close, but close enough, a signal that all was ready back at the makeshift camp.

The creature heard also. More than likely it also heard the two runners set off on their loop back to the camp. The runners knew they were safe, they knew the beast coveted the bigger reward from its shadow hunting. The promise of a sweet banquet of the weak.

He watched patiently through the brush as it stood up, high, on its two hind legs as it searched, looked around erratically and sniffed the air constantly for a scent, elevating itself to a height of almost three times his own paw to maw. After a short while, it extended concealed wings, spanning at least five his own outstretched arms – claw to claw.

This is what Gurengal had been waiting for. He was no match for the *orcindall* while it was mobile, with its wings encased under its large, muscular arms. He had to be quick: if the beast unfurled its wings fully and took flight, all back at the camp would be in dire peril, no matter the number of arms hidden in the tents and quick slumber sacks. All would perish.

If it sensed the trap, closed its wings, and was able to get past him: again, all at the camp would perish – they were prepared, but only prepared to fight this thing if he was around to help.

Just as half the entire school in Gurado had not been

*prepared*, the grounds left littered with small bodies and those of their educators were evidence of that – the ones that were lucky to be left behind, those bereft of the torturous weeklong feast, that no doubt would have been endured back within its lair.

Those taken, those not fully paralysed by the creature's nibble, those were found by the hunters in the mud of the Arneld at the base of the mountainous rock. They chose to succumb themselves to the stratum far-far below, rather than the horrible slow digestion they would have witnessed during the creature's feasting of those whose bodies had been numbed to the point of immobilisation by its incapacitating venom.

The whistling hunters, who set off moments earlier, were the camp's early warning. The whistle was to alert the camp of their impending frantic approach.

The orcindall preened its expansive grey, translucent wings as it began to stretch them to their maximum breadth – undoubtedly stiff from being cramped during its time in the narrow hovel of its lair, plus the four long days of crouching in such an unnatural carriage as it followed the hunted hunters. Now it knew its destination, there was no need for stealth, it was confident enough to take flight and was looking forward to consuming the non-existent habitants of the non-existent village – the hunter's camp.

*Would they be ready in time? They'd have no chance against this thing.*

The sight brought a moment of terror to his senses. The massive bulk combined with the speed of the creature almost betrayed its keen intelligence. Another small thought, though, crept in; that of five-hundred silver hobs – a third of the town council's total yearly reserve that had been offered for this mad bounty. It was almost outweighed by the sharpest shock of terror. *Almost* …

He had been in much worse situations than this, but not many. He knew what was expected of him. His constant reconnaissance and research enabled him to know the enemy. He knew how it moved, how it hid, even how it relieved its bowels – and it was not the least bit pretty. He also knew that within mere seconds, one beat of its massive, oversized wings, and it would be done. It had to be so. He was just overawed by the sight of the mighty beast stood before him.

Waiting for that *one* precise moment that was needed, he remained crouched behind the bush. The scented essence of the bright berried and favourably bloomed bush was hopefully masking his precarious position, including thought and instinct. All of which was required to shadow himself from the bounty's innate ability to sense even the slightest mood change within such a vicinity, to where he crouched low, and bent his entire being.

The creature set itself to make its skyward leap, its scaled head pointed upward from atop a long, angular and slimy column of a neck. Suddenly, it snapped a sharp, fleeting look behind toward the thicket it had trudged from, then toward the hiding place of the hunter.

*It knows I'm skulking here! Shit! And … was that a nod of acknowledgement of some sort? To whom, or what?* the hunter thought to himself? Without chancing a moment to consider even another thought of what had occurred, the beast quickly crouched to set itself once again, readying to plunge skyward.

An instant later, the hunter burst through the heckle bush – ignoring all the spikes, punctures, and incisions as the brush clawed away at him, trying to pull him down back into its clumping mass. He lunged through, sword swinging swiftly in an arcing motion. His braced left hand was followed by his right hand holding a small arcane-engraved shield – the etching began to glow slightly as he neared the creature.

He charged – toward *one* of the offspring of ancestors misplaced upon this world – covering the more than twenty strides in a one-two large stepping motion. He completed the sword's arc and struck the upper tendon that held taut underneath one of its wings, that adjoined adjacent the armpit. The shield came low, completing its own arc to block the slash from the creature's other wing, just as he had anticipated. *Lucky*, he snuck a thought in.

Completing the string of the premeditated and fluid spiral of parrying motions, he leapt up and over the sweep of a tail that whipped around from underneath its now slumped wing. All happened within a fraction of a breath. All had been as he had hoped. Thus far.

Gurengal turned to face the wounded and forever grounded animal – if it could be attributed as such. He had a miniscule moment to compose himself before his next move. An age though appeared to play itself out ...

Post Gurengal's age of reflection upon the scene that had played out, the orcindall screeched a terrible cry. Not only did it rumble the surrounding trees, knocking loose branches to fall to the growth below, it also rumbled Gurengal's composure as he caught a glimpse of something beyond. Even through the commotion of erratic despair, the creature looked again to where it had glanced a few moments earlier.

Nothing more to do about it now, he had to take down the creature before it could speedily slink away. Either toward the camp, which was now most unlikely, or from where it had been tracked, back into the forest. It was not flying anywhere though, not anymore, now not free to come and go as it pleased to terrorise the innocent for consumption that would build its own strength beyond that which was naturally necessary.

Grabbing hold of the creature's now limp appendage, he

hoisted himself up to slash a strike, true and hard, across the front of its twisting neck. The shield batted away the force of an enraged, piercing shrill and potentially lethal poisonous bite as it tried to snap at his legs.

Striking a solid, deep blow, the creature's immobilising cry was muffled by the force that cut considerable depth through the thick muscle, and through to the windpipe. A snapping writhe was followed by a large crash as it flopped down onto the grasses beneath, the resulting draft of the dropping wings shook the trees once more throughout the whole clearing.

Gurengal, cast a cautionary glance as he dropped to his knees – toward the direction the orcindall had silently called for aid. The trees again shook as the air gushed outward from beneath the falling creature's flanged wings. Then he finally saw. The briefest of a flicker of something not of the forest, but that which what was not supposed to be seen was now exposed, clear as mud, in that flickered opening between branch and leaf.

Quickly he turned away, muttering a quick prayer, playing dumb, acting none the wiser as to what was out there. Trying to not show any alarm at what he might have seen, he walked toward the stricken creature, which had now began to dissipate away to nothing. Clouds of a purple, dusty powder had begun to puff and swirl away from the still form. *Hmmm, another creature of darkness! They always seem to fade away like that, to nothing. Pieces of shit they are!*

Before it fully evaporated, to whatever afterlife took such vile things, he swung his blade from high above his head and hacked off the closest claw before it too had the chance to dissipate to nothing, and quickly deposited it into a black velvet sack. He tied it closed quickly, then uttered a single word, –'Myloth' – one spoken to bind the sack with an unseen seal to prevent the talon evaporating away. He needed such to collect the sizable coin offered. Proof to show the town council of the bounty completed.

Casually, he walked back toward the gauntlet of a gap in the heckle bush, back through where he had burst out into the small clearing. As he did all the hair stood on the back of his neck. Anticipating an attack from behind, he walked ever so stiffly. He would be no match on his own for one of the High Clerics of Sylteneria. *Or would I?*

He had to move. Had to retain that measure of calm, to elude any speculation that the cleric had been exposed.

He listened for any change, be it the reverberation of the trees, any subtle pressure differential about his immediate surroundings. And readied …

The expected ambush didn't eventuate, and he did not wonder why.

The shadows slowly faded all about him, and he looked up through the canopy of dense greenery to gauge the sky beyond. It had begun to darken.

'So, now it begins.' Whispered words, barely audible for sake of detection.

Once deep beyond the thicket, once upon a slightly worn trail and hopefully out of eyesight and whatever other sight was being used, he finally made haste. And ran as fast as he could, back to his men. Back to some sort of sanctuary.

*And hopefully a long soak in a warm bath.*

Away from the small open clearing, roughly three thick tree growths back, the dark-grey-skinned *pecbor* had cloaked himself with an enchantment: one of concealment as the orcindall moved forward in its slow, silent pursuit. A simple one for cover, much more than the shadow of the bush ever could offer – just in case.

Curiosity had led him to follow the trail of the shadowy creature – one he had sensed to be as such, almost immediately as it entered the wider proximity of his then locale. The non-descript hunters had passed dangerously close to where the High Cleric of Sylteneria and a small number of his acolytes had gathered to temporarily reside in an abandoned sawmill.

A buzzing, one that vibrated the two nodes atop his head had alerted him of a presence of something akin to that found within the peaks of Ellemenda. The mix of an essence of Ellemenda and aura of darkness had him intrigued. The Ellemenda Peaks were known to be home to many mystical, mythical creatures, many more than those that roamed the balance of lands around Inarrel. The cleric, known as Somendel – the Revered Somendel, he would argue – knew this to be true. He was a well-seasoned sorcerer, one who had delved deep into the dark magical arts of trapping such creature. He was, however, not limited to just such a creature to furnish his lust for fulfilling The Lady's blessings. The Lady, in return, by some intervention or benevolent impression, would bestow enhanced abilities depending on how rare and powerful the specimen, even more so if they were endowed with a magical ability.

At first, Somendel had believed the humming throb pulsating through his elongated nodules – a detection of a … sought after presence – had emanated from the orcindall. It was not until he caught up to the creature that he detected a much larger vibration, almost too much for his sensitive nodes to bare. A euphoric sensation, one that almost caused him fall to his knees, dropped with such sadistic delight.

Somendel had now made it an issue: an issue full of intrigue. One he must now see through, no matter what had been requested of him or his minor acolytes.

Facing the creature, he held up both hands to show no cause for fight or alarm as it snapped a silent warning. It did not turn its head to Somendel face on but kept an eye trained directly at him.

He ushered the two acolytes who trailed his path to move back and take cover behind the low, cobbled stone wall at the edge of the overgrown garden that lead away from the redundant mill. Turning back to the orcindall, he kept his hands raised and began a slow and steady pace in its direction.

The creature eventually turned to point its prominent snout toward him. Then it sniffed at the air toward the direction in which Somendel approached. Nostrils flared, it stood on its back legs and let out a booming echoing roar of challenge. It started to advance, closing the space between.

Not slowing, nor changing his composed gait, Somendel began to utter an enchantment. The distance between the two diminished as the words were spoken, the words became louder and echoed all about the place. Suddenly, the chant stopped, and within an instant, a crackling sound filled the air. The immediate atmosphere surrounding the two became statically charged and he stopped his advance toward the creature, just before it looked around. Instantaneously, a bolt of shock-trail appeared from Somendel's raised hands engulfing the orcindall in a clinging web of entrapment – the zapping, snapping cloud encapsulated the creature.

Somendel began another chant: one of binding. A binding not to imprison, nor to subdue. But a spell of coercing the mind with his own.

It fought back though. Fighting against the disturbing mental intrusion. But it yielded in the end as the chant went on. Subsequently it knelt down to the ground, both its short scaly legs brushing the under scrub of the undergrowth away from its hulked form. A show of subservience, the /creature understood its master's commands. All such transmitted within an instant during their flawless psychological connection. The two-way communication gave the High Cleric enough intel on the troupe he needed.

Somendel looked on through the few trees, to follow the sequence of events that were taking place, a series of motions he knew would eventually unfold.

The creature was to follow the small group for a couple more days while he used the time to conjure enough power and strength to be, at the very least, a match to the apparent leader. Then, once he was ready, he had instructed the creature to fly into the air and take out the runners to prevent any flanked counterattack – or so the creature had assumed. He knew the creature would not get the chance to lift itself off the ground, no matter its agility.

He had need to gauge the troops leader and how he would deal with such a threat from one of the *lost* creatures. Thus, how he himself would be able to eventually subdue the mind of this seemingly mad but powerful foe.

*Another trophy to offer up for The Lady's cause*, he pondered. She would undoubtedly imbue a small portion of the man's powers into him, adding to his already impressive repertoire of proportioned soul fire.

The eventual outcome came. Two days after the connection, and in the smallest of clearings, the creature took the bait, the runners and their whistle: the implanted cue.

The creature snapped its head around. Somendel flicked both his wrists upwards, as if to imply *Leap! Quickly! Leap, you damned thing*.

All from that point was but a blur. A brief exchange, the two rumbling out in the middle of the clearing, only one outcome. A disconnect between he, and the beast.

He smiled through the ensuing carnage: his flopped front lip now curled upwards to show his short blunt teeth, while the creature looked behind in bemusement and with no small amount of stark terror, felt deeply within his own being due to the connection as it faded. S*uch a terrible, evil creature, yet not so devoid of innocence, so it would seem,* he mused.

Thinking to himself he would one day, in the near future, trap one of the other few *orcindall* known to roam Vilenzia, to inhabit his own personal playground of sin – though a creature of the shadows, it had taken a liking to hiding out and acting of its own volition.

A quick glance in his direction from the hunter froze him back to sense. He was confident he would not be seen. A cloaking spell would have been enough, even this far back, to not alert anyone in the vicinity of his presence. But then again, he was unsure, but now majestically aware of this hunter's capabilities: those that he dare not bring to the table for a fight *just yet*.

Seeing the hunter turn back toward the bush, the same way he appeared without any second glance gave him the slightest amount of comfort. He now knew where their camp was situated, just outside of the town of Horgshead. They would no doubt settle in the town for a few nights to rest before they headed off in search of another bounty, and enjoy the festivities the town may offer for their petty little Festival. *Opportunity*. But he also knew that would not be enough. He needed to act now, before nightfall, install a capable crew to entice him out, away from his people.

He speedily made his way back to the mill within an instant, via the mini, swirling, temporary portal he had hung near the mill before he followed in pursuit. The power he had generated was no use for physical interaction – not yet! Instead he created the other end of the portal where he now stood. Some of that energy would be absorbed back to the earth. The man was much more than he had estimated, and a round-about guess was not something that Somendel did lightly.

Somendel reappeared just a short walk from the glowing oval opening, back through the overgrown garden that lead back to the mill. He passed two twisted bodies of the two acolytes that had taken cover, who were now strung upside down from a thick branch, the ground charred and blackened beneath where they swung in the small breeze. There were indents of a round, deep darkness about their chests, the black holes still smoking from carrying charge to the mini portal. There had been just enough life source within them both, enough to have given him the power needed to be able to flee in an instant if needed, or battle through and make the return on foot. An energy he planned to use if he was uncovered during his pursuit. Now it was much welcomed as he walked past them both. He would use what they had left in them, and maybe a few more of his little lambs, though he would not diminish his flock completely – he had enough from which to choose – for him to send forth a troupe of his own to flush out the man who would haunt him while he rested tonight.

He walked inside the mill and closed the rickety doors as the shadows in the woods started to fade. None of the other acolytes moved from their bow of obedience towards the statue of their Lady, not showing any alarm as though he wasn't even there.

Somendel walked to the fore, beyond where the remaining acolytes were bowing, and joined them to start another prayer. One which was echoed by all through the mill. Almost all.

A small group stood at the back of the mill, snickering as they sharpened their knives and tied up gear. The nod from Somendel as he watched them on his way through was taken as an order to prepare for a fight. The group grumbled. Of the loudest, a big man paced about, muttering disapproval of something or nothing.

# The Third Pillar

Up high, overlooking the Sea of Faith. Behind, looking up towards the peak of the highest mountain in Vilenzia, and probably of all Inarrel, *Hollowloft* , the City of Columns sprawled from the shore of the large emerald blanket of silk and crawled up the slopes of the massive monolith.

The cascading mountainside formed the backdrop to most of the city, from an aeons past eruption, the half-mooned caldera was now home to students, teachers, masters and more. The brightest of all from the Great State of Vilenzia, and more than a few from all other known regions that formed the world of Inarrel. A city built upon foundations of metaphorical Pillars – five in total.

Columns represented these Pillars in physical form and were built to support each faction's house of practice. For each Pillar, ten structural Columns structurally supported the building at the central plaza of each faction.

The city itself consisted of seven neighbourhoods, two more than the number of the original five factioned settlements. The factions themselves had a maximum intake quota for each, something which had not changed for centuries as the limited space could not accommodate any change in residence due to unavailable real estate. The city since, though, had spread to the sea and outward, creating a swath of expanse in every available direction.

One swath pushed to the west, unable to expand any further beyond *Morla's Pass* – a break through a large cliff, two hundred feet into the sky, an artificial entrance to the city, the beginning of a huge trafficable canyon that lead to the budding market town of Growfell, a fair distance away on the other side of the never-ending plateau.

The opposite outcrop of the city, almost a full league from Morla's Pass and crossing four of the seven rivers feeding the Sea of Faith, expanded beyond to the red tinged forest of *Famnagira,* home to the *eberactu.* The eberactu were a race known for their formidable strength and knowledge of mechanics, not to mention their well-known love and craftsmanship of brewing. The eberactu were short and stocky in size, not many stood eye-level to the average man's chest, and very few ventured out into the world beyond the forest settlement's main gathering place of *Famcor.* But when they did all were welcome in any establishment where they could spend their abundant supply of silver, gold, and the many other crafted materials they seemed to mine deep within the massive red-leafed, violet barked, enchantingly hazed forest.

The very few eberactu that delved into the world beyond the Famnagira had a knack for storytelling, and an almost hypnotic ability to draw in a crowd of any sorts, leaving them with a belief that all that was told was nothing but truth. Many of these tales were pure fantasy, tall stories. But a few that would have been thought of as make-believe, the tales most farfetched, those were more than likely from the millennia old recordings written upon hearing the words being spoken from the Union's most upper echelon: the Onberseelers themselves. They, the Onberseelers, would frequently visit the ancient groves of the Famnagira: for many, a place of solace. For some, a private place to discuss the Union's dealings.

It was recorded in the texts that the pass was created by Morla – one of the early founders of the Union of the Jenine and the City of Columns – who was eventually elevated to rank of Onberseeler, the highest rank of each of the pillars. Only the One Onber had a higher station to command, as overseer for each and all of the Pillars.

The Onberseelers were supported by their Tembor, one for each Column, a rank of ascendance up from the regimented factions' most elite, most trusted, though not necessarily their brightest, students. These stations of command included the induction into the mysterious and much speculated about, though such speculations were heavily rebutted by those within, the Union of the Jenine.

Each Pillar was dedicated to its own unique discipline. And sometimes its students, dependant on their pedigree or ability, would be given a chance to study under another Pillar. A student who could master all knowledge of their designated Pillar would become *Seeler*; a higher, more influential rank above the other students. Students who had mastered three of the Pillars gained the possibility to ascend to the rank of Onberseeler – only seven students had gained such a title in the past century. Students who had mastered all the Pillars would be given a secure path to the One Onber – a course only two had completed fully as required for the study of each faction's elemental Columns in the last three hundred years.

Assessment was offered on mastering the Pillars periodically; a flawless routine during rigorous examination of the many compositions that made up *the* stipulated Pillar: the Columns. Each Column was, in itself, a complex component of knowledge that directly linked to the upper discipline of the Pillar's call.

The *First Pillar* was situated just below the old town, high up the mountain slope, and was dedicated to aid, relief, and healing. A faction devoted to the development and issuance of items, techniques, medicines, and advanced healers. All to benefit the elimination of, or at the very least to soothe, the pain and suffering that was commonplace and prevalent throughout Inarrel.

The *Second Pillar*, although the next numerically, was situated highest up the old town. Its cohort were tasked with garnering knowledge of Vilenzia and beyond. Books, tomes, scripts, scrolls, any type of text, recordings of people's personal events, stories – no matter how farfetched. If it was new, it was coded and archived in the vast, vaulted library sculpted into the mountain face, a maze of never-ending pockets carved into the huge caldera, worming their way up and into the rock. The vaults now spiralled upward as the original level and three further additional levels had been plenished with history's greatest, and it's not so significant, events: be it a whisper, text or some other potential of the unknown. Even potentially relevant dreams were recorded – whether good or bad. All had to be preserved.

The *Fourth Pillar* overlooked the First Pillar and represented the mystic arts of the world, and beyond. The pupils initiated to this faction would mostly outlast all other pupils from the other factions. Thus, spaces in this Pillar were limited. This was not usually an issue with the other students who were less likely to manage the strenuous education without first, the natural ability, and secondly, the mental capacity for the strains that would be applied upon their mind. Nor the ability to control the workings of the inner spirit to influence the material world.

The *Fifth Pillar*, the central hub of the old city, was mostly populated by royalty and high-ranked noble offspring. It offered the ultimate study of politics, accounting, brokering, and bargaining, amongst other controversial studies such as seduction and persuasion.

Every student in the city, no matter how wealthy their family or respected their lineage, had all been selected on ability, potential, and any benefits that they may bring to the cause. One of the first lectures all members – not only students – sat through, was a mandatory obedience for all others residing in the city, no matter their status. There would be no lesser, nor any higher stationed or controlled until the ascendance to Onberseeler, the respect for each and all was what enabled the city to stand as it had from the dawn of its inception and construction by the six inceptual

Onberseelers.

Altor, first One Onber – elected by the other five original Onberseelers: Morla, Dawan, Maapoi, Yurengar and Psilinto – was a master of almost everything, the most experienced by far in all the factions of study offered today at the city. They were all vastly influential in the creation of the City of Columns. There was no hesitation from those assembled as to who would lead the Union into a new era, a construction of a new city to increase the resources to fight those that would see an end of order, those who would preside over and welcome the destruction to all that was good.

*The Third Pillar* was accessed through the Fifth via a large crevasse in the mountainside. The large crevasse into the mountain sat directly below the Second's library, a library supported by ten massive columns, rising at least fifty spans to the carved-out rock soffit. The Third had no house of practice to support; the Third Pillar's house of practice was all about actively operating throughout the outside world. There was, however, an average, non-descript looking building not far from the precinct delineation line – on its border with the Fifth – one frequented by elder eberactu, those not already selected to study the Columns among the students of both the Third and Fifth.

Its members were trained in all the arts of judiciary, deception, hand-to-hand combat, swordplay, disguise, and deception. All the traits to be fully useful in extracting information, the extraction of certain goods, or for extracting a person, or persons. They were schooled, not necessarily educated, on how to lead a small army, or to sit quietly for a while in an unknown village, town or city to listen and not act, and report. This Pillar's selective crop was known by all at the city who studied the Columns as The Shadow of the Path.

The second lecture to the newly amassed was on the way

of the *Jenine*, that the city itself was part of a much larger establishment and that those who studied there must be bound to the Union's secrets and its many dealings. The bond if broken, was known as *The Forfeit*, the memories of all those with whom they had divulged such taken, including their own, leaving them to wander about the world with no recollection of who, or what, they once were.

The small plateau on which the Fifth and Third stood was adorned with an almost constant hue of gold that emanated from multiple globular lamplights arched on iron poles, perched high above over the pretty landscaped and manicured footpath. The footpath itself was paved with a dark marble and wound a slithering snake-like circuit from the non-descript building to a much livelier place. A place where men, women, and creatures alike would congregate to share tales of their stimulating quests out into the known world. This wonderful place was the real centre of the Third.

All the eberactu were welcome there, as they were welcome anywhere in the city. Not a few would remain here for days, more often than not after lugging the sweetest amber ale up the mountain to *Jink's Rooms*, the name of this wondrous place, from deep within the magical forest of the Famnagira.

A deep rumbling sound not unlike that of a voice could be heard, emanating from within.

'Word … my young fellow,' a large frame of a man hovered a humorous gaze at his underling from beneath two twitching, bushy eyebrows, 'has been intercepted of some trouble in Jacobs Well.' Kost continued to look at the young pecbor, struggling to keep a straight face, waiting for the offered bait to be taken.

He continued on, when he knew no bite was forthcoming. 'Seems some trouble has arisen at the Grouse,' a small pause ensued, waiting for a twitch of something, 'closed ...' again, he looked at the pecbor, the two small nodes on the top of a scaly little head showing no sign of movement, nor his mouth. 'Semoni ... you know, you can be so damn irritating sometimes, if not for most of the it!'

Suddenly Semoni twigged the man's attempt at jest. Semoni looked up with a small crinkle now appearing around his eyes, his little teeth now showing something that could resemble a smile. 'Ahh ... aha!' Kost nodded invitingly at him. 'Master Peron! What has he done now I wonder?' Semoni lisped with the barest hint of humour that belied his widening smile.

Obviously not enough for Kost.

'Merciful Holtonos! He has done nothing. Nothing yet ... I hope. He should be just arriving there. That's why it's so damn funny to me. And should damn well be for you too!' He banged the table, sloshing liquid up and out and then back into their metal tankards; the smallest amount made its way down the sides of the container. 'All he had barked on about for weeks, last I were here, months ago, was spending a few nights, there at the Grouse. Hehe. Now it's closed, has been for a few weeks!' Kost sputtered out another chuckle, then settled the cough with a large sip of the amber ale.

Semoni finally rose to the bait, finding himself bent over, releasing a low shriek and a wheeze of laughter, them both ending up rubbing their knees on the floor as their hands patted the same comically.

'Oh Peron!' Semoni slapped the floor again, emphatically. 'I wish I could have seen your face when you got there.' Pulling himself together he went on. 'I had word arrive from him only two days gone. He was to arrive before noon on one of the most joyous days of the year, for the Jacobs Well's festivities before venturing over the stone bridge to the palace to meet Anat—'

'Ahem!' Kost reminded Semoni. 'Ears everywhere,

young man.' They both rose to their feet and sat back on the sturdy timber benches.

'Sorry, sire. *Our* palace cleric.' Propped upright, he cocked a leg over the bench to sit facing Kost.

He looked across the room, to the only other inhabited table. Then he looked at Kost who gave a wink and a slight nod in their direction: an invitation for the other sole occupants of Jink's to come on over.

'Fellas!' A young woman of slight build nodded to both as she approached behind.

'Kost! Semoni.' The latter she showed a wider smile than the first. 'Greetings to you both.' Another older looking gentleman peered at Kost suspiciously. 'So what's got you two bludgers all in a heap?' Without pause, he followed the question up with a chuckle of his own. 'Surely, I do know. I read the missive too.' The man chuckled after he finished. 'Peron ... the brunt, no doubt? I presume. Correct?'

Before Kost or Semoni could confirm, the young lady accompanying spoke again. 'Leave the good man Peron alone, Shanlar! You know how excited he was to be back out there. Been cooped up in 'ere way too long. Especially when he heard his latest assignment was travelling across over to Jacobs Well, and ... especially during the Festival.'

Silence ensued for a moment, before all three men burst into another fit of laughter, wiping tears away and rubbing hands under running noses. Those not seated already took a pew at the table to calm themselves, the lady amongst them looked on at the moronic display with little pity for them.

'Where is that blasted Ebby? We have been here for at least ... well ... long enough!' grunted the girl. 'Probably hiding and supping away the slosh himself. The hairy little—'

The fresh faced – young looking for his race – stocky barkeep had jovially sauntered out from behind the bar area once he heard the atmosphere brighten dramatically. The eberactu then ambled up quietly to stand beside them. 'Beg ye pardon, Miss Nomellia!'

Startled, Miss Nomellia turned, quickly inhaled a sharp breath of air, and banged a knee with Semoni's in the process.

Blushing, Semoni stuttered, embarrassed. 'Oh my … so sorry, Missy. Here, let me …' He began to rub Miss Nomellia's knee before he realised all were looking at him. He let out a startled yelp, his smooth grey cheeks now awash with a crimson tide.

With the comedic atmosphere already hanging as dry tinder, the now abashed youngsters set them off again.

The barkeep, none the wiser, joined in with a wonderful boom of hearty laughter and settled four metallic tankards down, one in front of each seated patron. Then he rested his arse on a finely curated log for a stool, its plane crested just a bit higher than the benches that accommodated the others – one of many scattered about the rooms – a seat for his own kind, enabling him to rest his arms on the tables.

After taking a long sup of Semoni's draught, letting out a gracious sigh at the flavour of the drop, he said, 'Will, perchance, any of you be stopping over here tonight? Not had a quarter full house for too many a moon!'

Semoni resigned himself to another night sober as Ebby Jink dropped the rest of the tankard's contents.

All looked at Ebby Jink, especially Semoni who watched on as Ebby wiped away the froth from his low dropping moustache. It was Kost, though, who answered for them. 'Not tonight, my good friend. We've been summoned to attend her Onber tonight. Seemed quite urgent her request, and … we have been advised we may be there late, even past the next sunrise.'

'So urgent the Grace does not request you immediately?' Ebby tipped the tankard steeply to take in any dregs that remained. 'Ah,' he then replied, 'I heard a few *youngers* say there have been a few of you *seniors* appear in town this morning.' Jink looked at Semoni and Miss Nomellia directly. 'Hmm and a few … hmm. Well, you know who.'

They both looked at each other, then back at Jink. Now it was Miss Nomellia's turn to speak. 'Yes, apprentices. We get it Jink. Just don't forget we will be seniors, even Tembor like these two here one day. Even you, Jink! You started out same as us, drafted in on a whim once, you know, your papa was taken. Took you a few months to fit in.'

'Suppose you're right there, Missy. Apologies, forget myself sometimes, I too felt the same, thought I knew more than most. Probably knew more than them seniors, even more than those blasted Tembor.' He laughed again and slapped a palm to the table. 'No offence, gents. That was the world back then. World's changed since, though, Missy, a lot more than you couldn't know.' The last remark brought a look of rebuke from her.

He scooped up Semoni's empty tankard, turned on his seat, and prepped himself to hop off. Missy touched his shoulder to stop him. He looked back at her, then settled back in. He gave her a quick smile, one returned with genuine warmth – matching that of the crackling fire that burned underneath a thick hearth adjacent the main bar.

'Soooo, Jink!' she began. 'We still on for that trip down to Famnagira this coming eighth day?' She looked at him pleadingly, sparkles twinkling in her eyes, reflecting the flickering flames just out of her direct line of sight.

A nod. 'Already gotten word to the Master Brewer in Burrinda Glade to expect us to be arriving once the coloured lights have settled themselves at close of the Festival. Asked him no expense be spared. A welcome to the glade with one of its finest ales, and two luxurious guest rooms in the glade: one for you and one for Master Shanlar.'

'Sounds lovely! Can't wait. You care to join us, Sem?'

Semoni glanced shyly at Jink, who immediately nodded his approval – if only a slight one – expecting the unspoken request before Semoni then sheepishly turned his eyes to his master.

Kost had a stern, straight look about his face. With all seriousness he muttered, just loud enough for all at the table to hear, 'We will be busy here till tomorrow night.' Semoni's cheeks sank, disheartened. 'But tell you what … we get done by midday, then aye. Aye, ye can go!'

Semoni burst inside, he was about to burst out but saw that Kost still held a serious pose which quelled his flicker of delight. He shushed him before he spoke and carried on with a low mutter, still serious, 'But … remember, laddy … Jink only made a request for *two* rooms!'

This set all but one member of the small group off in a raucous uproar of backslapping and over the top laughter.

The silent one flushed once again, glowing brighter red, redder than Jink's long bushy hair – the pale grey skin of Semoni's cheeks unable to hide the hue from deep beneath.

After the commotion calmed a little, Kost asked Ebby Jink to send forward word to Burrinda Glade to expect two more guests who would lodge in any available stable or grain house if no accommodation was forthcoming – he knew they would not be staying in such, the request offered borne from generosity.

Shanlar spoke. 'Well if ye be accompanying Jink and Missy, then I think I will hold back that half a day to catch up with an old acquaintance. You keen to follow on with me Kost? Let your lad leave in the morn?' Shanlar winked a little too obviously at Kost. Who winked back just as flamboyantly as he dropped his head to emphasise he knew full well why.

Semoni rolled his eyes dramatically. Miss Nomellia squeaked with as much gusto to outshine his impossibly contained delight.

# Heavens Above

Holtonos made his way the through large arched doors of his chapel toward the outside, out from his forever home, the doors out of proportion for his tiny abode. The air this far above one of the swirling oceans of Seltero was light but abundant with the required ingredients to sustain their – and their helpers – needs to survive.

He was flanked by Lenjora, who wore a flowing dress that dropped just below her knees, tied with a criss-crossed lace that zigzagged across her back to conceal virtually nothing beneath.

And Jhehbl, wearing his usual brown robe still as new after so many years, accompanied with a yellow sash. They walked through the inner courtyard and then out of another pair of doors, out fully into the open.

They walked on, eventually standing before a warped, crystalline bridge that traversed the massive expanse below. The *Bridge of Hope* they had named it.

Holtonos looked beyond the vast expanse, to a large mass of rock that floated at the bridge's terminus. He waved his hands with a twisting motion and the bridge rearranged itself to form a wide walkway. The path sparkled and glistened from the rays of the bright orb glowing low in the sky – hovering directly above the rocky structure they were heading to.

Before stepping onto the walkway, he turned to both following, then in turn looked deep into their eyes, and looked behind, beyond them, to where *their* world of Inarrel was cresting above the chapel.

Finally he spoke, softly. 'Now, as you well know, the first pass is upon *our* world of Inarrel. Are you ready to observe?'

Both nodded slowly.

They proceeded to cross the walkway, suspended high in

the air. The only sound to be heard was that of the wind, gushing to whistle beneath the bridge. That, and Lenjora's boots clinking on the hard, semi-opaque surface. The vast ocean below, the *Weil of Purity*, could not be heard this high up. There was also no base for the waves to crash against as the rock they now almost graced was elevated above – suspended by the essence of grace that evaporated from the purest of waters below.

They reached the other side, reaching a platform on the huge non-descript rock that stood in the middle; the single monolithic structure held a haziness about it. The shrouding mirage was extinguished with another wave of Holtonos's hands.

A large oval contraption appeared, balanced on its side, held with some metallic mechanism which looked as though it was used to rotate to view from all angles. A mystical viewer it was known as, trained intently on *their* world, no matter the orbital co-ordinates.

A smile appeared on Lenjora's face. She loved this time of year. The Festival of the Night was a time when those below would rejoice and show they were no longer afraid of the dark, or those that lurked in the shadows, creeping around unseen. Also, it was a time to repent – this brought the most kudos to the oceans below, before they were sent on their way to the light and the *unknown* – prior to their long metaphorical expedition through the night. A journey mingled with a heightened sense of love, laughter, merriness, and quick and slow dancing to music played at high and low tempo. Not to mention the accustomed, throughout time, fermented brews, crafted especially for this time of year. The latter more than occasionally followed by a false promise, brought about from the consumption of such lofty a brew. All the same, throughout the majority of the world, until the close of the long, long night, every populous grouping – be it a tiny hamlet, or big city – had their own unique custom as token of offering to the higher, their gods. Even if they were not such … not quite that level.

Lenjora, Goddess of the Night – a parody as for the darkness, a name gifted by herself from the enjoyment of the festivities she would spout when visiting, known as the Giver of Love and Light to those who called Inarrel home, even those who followed the path away from the light. The curator of all that was good in the world. Not a goddess, not as such. A higher being most definitely. But she *was* viewed as a goddess by the majority of all below.

Just as Holtonos, God of All, Master of Matter. The Binder of Worlds, or so the folk below believed.

And then Jhehbl. Mover of the Seas, Soul of the Oceans. The Curator of the Land.

Their true being: *The Greater*, as they were known beyond this little system of planets.

The denizens of Inarrel worshipped them as holy beings. As gods, those who wove the thread all of their lives would be comprised. Though they were at the basic level of understanding, only a conduit to what lay beyond, to a light above. Prayers and offerings were funnelled through their planet and then on to the holy unknown. The holy unknown were beings that were not quite of this universe but of something more. An unknown but sure form felt by all, no matter their station.

Their peers, The Greater, were spread about everywhere in the cosmos, and undoubtedly beyond even that, through time even … populating and curating projects of their own. Generating the goodwill and prayer to fill the bucket of the holy unknown.

The reason? Unclear. Just as is the way of things throughout nature.

Lenjora was now becoming excited and had a skip to her

step as she strode to the viewing mechanism. 'I have not celebrated with my beloved for many years. This year I may revel, a little ... at the very least, on the last day of the Festival, for it is always such a glorious day!'

Holtonos glanced at her. Gave her the slightest of nods, accompanied by the merest sparkle of a glint in his eye – showing acknowledgment with a hidden smile.

Jhehbl also looked at her, though he carried a grimace. He remembered the last time they both ventured to the Isle of the Dream Keepers, then on to Inarrel. The Isle was situated not too far from where they stood on Seltero. A connecting portal was operated by a select few, enabling travel between the two worlds as opposed to their traditional methods, ones not used for generations, and only then when utmost peril was becoming.

Though, to Jhehbl, that was not the issue. The issue with Jhehbl and his reluctance was what happened in Vilenzia four cycles prior. 'I think I may leave that travelling and revelling with you, you *young ones*.' Sarcasm was not his usual forte and when it was it was terrible. For they would be roughly the same age. Aeons had passed; they had always retained their mature features. None of them knew youth but none of them would ever age. 'At least there would be no shadow wolves up here for me to banish back to their dark realm or wherever they hale from. On the fourth attempt of trying, might I add?' he finished and looked away and over the ledge to the waters below.

Oh, they were mortal. They too could be *extinguished*, just as easily as a burning candle dropped into an ocean – and just as quickly. Higher powers do not bestow an eternal flame. A jab in the right spot with a dagger is just as deadly as a poisoned chalice. However, having the ability to create such a beautiful world from only a floating bare rock had its advantages.

Though, where their – and no doubt their peers –

creativity touched or touches, so too did the darkness in almost equal proportion. Their beautiful creation like a flaming beacon of life to be snuffed or devoured, attracting The Greaters' opposite, those who would gladly fill their Lady's bucket with slosh from doing evil, and all their dirty little deeds. These things were known as *The Higher Souls of Garoth*, Sylteneria's finest and most trusted.

The problem with venturing through the large spatial divide to Inarrel, the reason Jhehbl was so perturbed with the notion, was their abilities seemed to be nullified to a point where they were incapable of producing even a fraction of their usual energy to defend themselves. And then, it was only ever useful on those not of their own design – those that the darkness had imbued upon the world. It was still probably more than any being on Inarrel could muster, but  wolves do not usually hunt alone. And … these were not the average canine kind.

It had required them all – Holtonos, Lenjora and the elusive Everos – to infuse Jhehbl with enough energy to send the wolves … to who knew where, back to wherever they had come from.

The darker creatures had grown in strength over the past few decades. They all knew, more than felt, a climax during this age was coming. They all also knew that none knew when.


All three stepped around the device to stand at their allotted station. Each used a small spyglass on the device and adjusted their lenses to focus where they set their sights on the lands of Inarrel. Though not directly aligned to view Inarrel, they had floated a device linked to the mechanism to view as if so.

Lenjora spoke. 'Just a quick observation would indicate all is well at the Columns. Cloaked in a small scattering of … cloud cover.'

Jhehbl countered, 'Seems too the pass between the North and the South has … at least for now, has become … our shadow.'

Holtonos looked at where the sun still crested the horizon, then back to where the world of Inarrel had disappeared behind the chapel. He felt a squeeze, a sharp pang of unease. The angles were not quite set for the distant planet to adorn the shadows at that exact moment. Was this an omen coming to fruition? He quickly walked to stand beside Jhehbl. 'Jhehbl. Can you tell me what colour hue proceeds the supposed shadow of ours?'

Jhehbl turned to look at Holtonos as he moved in close, and choked on a sudden chuckle.

'You sound croaked, are you alright, Holto?' he offered as he bent backward from where Holtonos hovered. 'It's dark, it's grey, black in parts. Not a full shadow, but … dark, a shadow' was his eventual answer.

Lenjora was monitoring the exchange from the corner of her eye, still holding her looking glass below the other. 'Answer him, Jhehbl. The question is of importance as you well know. Burying your head in the sand will not be good for you. Nor I. Nor anyone else.'

'Yes, yes. I was hoping that well … you would mention it before me. The line of shadow extending to the north does have a kind of …'

'What …?' Holtonos lowered his brow, concerned.

It was Lenjora who answered. 'There seems to be a slight, indistinct, crimson corona preceding the shadow, Holto.' She turned away from the device, giving Holtonos a view of both worried eyes.

She was not quick enough. He was already away, pacing swiftly back across the bridge.

Making a move of her own, she hooked the looking glass over a metallic frame of the device and moved quickly to follow, pulling Jhehbl's hood to swing him in the same direction she was heading, before picking up the pace to follow Holtonos.

The sound of slapping from Jhehbl's sandals and the clinking of Lenjora's boots caused Holtonos to pause and hold both arms out wide. As he did, the two running behind him halted after a synchronised skid. All three looked above the chapel just as the small, devilish glowing planet of Kinora rose to block their view of Inarrel. Lenjora gasped loudly, blocking out the loud curse both men in her presence spoke as they took in a breath.

Everos smiled.

He was plumped sideways atop an extravagantly large daybed. He lounged at the pinnacle of his own tower high above the other smaller turreted towers that adorned the skyline of the Isle of The Dream Keepers – the only other parcel of habitable land to grace Seltero. He had his own looking device, one for viewing the majority of the denizens below. It was a combination of a sheet of thick parchment stretched over a large window combined with a spell, cast to magnify the world of Inarrel. The image was projected from a drooped crystal affixed to the soffit of his lounging chamber – he also had the same type of device scattered throughout his unhumble abode.

'Ahhh …' A long breath preceded the chuckle. 'Peron, my old friend. What are you getting yourself into now? Hey!' He let the rest of his breath escape to offer himself a slight chuckle.

He watched on as Peron took the key and clasped his stumpy, though nimble, fingers together. 'Here we go. I will see you soon, so it would seem, my good man.' He rubbed his palms together, this time a little more briskly.

Everos had followed the exchange from the moment Peron had muttered the initial curse, one meant for him. Knowing that he would be in for, what he thought, a few hours of drama, he perched himself comfortably, resting his back on a few plump pillows, and readied himself for the forthcoming entertainment …

He was not wrong. For he was in for a gluttony of such.

# Requiem, of Sorts

Grehn walked purposely through the vaulted corridor with an open facade that let a little light in from the outside courtyard through slim, though tall arched openings. She walked away from the bottom of the only staircase that spiralled for an age back up to her rooms. The covered walkway ran adjacent to the central courtyard, its landscape manicured proficiently and constantly. A spectacle that could have been observed through the constant flicker of openings as she strode along – she chose not to observe, her head was set firmly forward, she dare not let any distraction take her.

Her riding boots echoed throughout, amplified by the quietness and inactivity of the castle during the accustomed routine for the set daily lunch.

Not all was quiet, though. A scrubbing sound eventually caught her attention. One not so remiss of the usual scrape of a spade or hoe. She halted her stride and failed to miss Molo tending to the walls of the large well stuck in the middle of the courtyard. The legendary well. The birthing structure of the now populous city of Jacobs Well.

Molo had been tasked with cleaning the mildew off the stonework that covered the lower walls of the well; he had seemingly left it to the last moment, *Much fool him*, she thought quickly before flitting the harsh thought away from her mind.

The well was now far enhanced from its humble beginnings of just a hole in the ground, much larger than it needed to be – a statement of its significance? Perhaps. One that was storied, over and over, by the ruling monarch to mark such importance events as the yearly Festival. Her father had the honour, once again, this year. She enjoyed hearing his booming voice carry across the courtyard; the awe on the guests' faces invited from all over the city was striking – those lucky enough to be selected from the annual, city-wide ballot. The *King's-ballot*. One hundred folk from all walks of life selected as guests on the second day of the Festival, to celebrate, and be hosted as equal to the monarchy themselves.

The achromatically dull shade, a dull darkness that the first day of the Festival brought, would be extinguished on the second, punctured wholesomely with large colourful flamework, built and ignited by the castle keeper. Explosive produce procured by he named as the castle keeper – Sentok.

A joyous day for all those lucky enough to rub shoulders, clink a tankard or glass, and talk shop with the humble King Benjamin Jacob and his family. Also, to score a dance with the iridescent Queen Jahnna would be a welcome bonus to any, no matter their carnal sway.

Her father would retell a story, one that had been passed down from every generation. One that had not changed for hundreds of years. A telling to all of those that would be present on such a special day. A tale to spread and reinforce, no doubt with added embellishment beyond their own premise.

Hopping over the stone-clad wall and through a skinny, arched opening, she waved to Molo as he scrubbed hard and fast, muttering something inaudible, to himself.

He didn't hear her calling to him as he scrubbed fervently away, a small smile touching his lips after every word of a song he was whispering. It was only when he stood and stretched his arms high, to crack his back, did he notice that Grehn approached, walking through the pristine garden beds adjacent the arched walkway.

'Grehn!' Startled, he dropped his arms, then began to rub the dust and grime off his baggy green trousers. 'Didn't see you there.' He put his small brush down atop the thick wall of the well, then shyly snuck another look at Grehn, trying hard not to stare too long as she strode toward him, or glare at her riding boots. 'Grehn!'

She cut him off as she grabbed him with both arms to give him a tight squeeze that expelled all breath from his already hard worked lungs. 'It worked Molo! It actually worked!' She loosened her grip ever so slightly. This, though, brought little relief to Molo even if pure delight glowed about his face.

'Show me! show me!' Molo shuffled his body a little to let out the words, excited too.

She showed him just enough to bring intrigue. Enough for confirmation though. Then quickly hid the locket back beneath her shrift. 'Not here, Molo. I need to take this to Mother Ursen. So I want no mishaps!' She held a hand over her chest to cover the locket beneath the cloth of the shirt. Then she nodded an affirmation and smiled.

As did he.

'She is travelling here, with the Medica Column. They are heading this way and should be here this afternoon. Maybe they are setting up down the main square by now, hopefully before all the chaos begins tomorrow.' She smiled at the last.

Word had been sent to the Medica months before, Grehn's final examination was at hand. In surety, more than anticipation of a successful completion, word had been sent back in the affirmative to attend, during the Festival and that Mother Ursen – who held the rank of the second-highest station at the First Pillar – should be present to offer the distinguished accolade.

A bird chirped and they both looked at the greywing that sat atop the high-pitched roof of the well. Grehn held out a hand, then reached up, trying to get closer to the bird's temporary perch. The bird twitched its spiky feathered head then obliged, accepting the invitation offered. Settling on her hand, she leaned her head toward the fluffy little thing. 'Baston,' she whispered softly, 'where have you been these past few days?'

Still twitching its head, it looked at Molo.

'Whoa, Baston, easy … easy.' Molo knew what was coming next. Baston flapped his wings quickly and landed atop the scruffy hair of Molo.

Grehn let out a giggle. 'I saw him floating around the bluff far beneath the bridge,'

Molo, softly, with one finger, stroked the bird's fluffy mane after he had untangled its claws out of his knotty hair. 'I think he has been busy with his new lady friend … hehe.'

The bird made a squawk, embarrassed by Molo's implication of it possibly courting. It hopped back over to Grehn. She leant in again and it rubbed its soft furry head against her soft red cheek.

A crashing sound at the gate startled them all. Baston jumped high then swiftly opened up his wings to fly back to safety atop the well. Molo and Grehn looked over to see what the commotion was at the gate.

A large figure, bald as a well-worn pebble, emerged as the gate was pushed open. The gate was usually manned by two guards – their dual strength was required to open each of the large wooden doors to admit any that would not fit through the single door hung as a hinged panel as part of the large gate.

The hulking form of Sentok pulled a wagon through one side of the double gated opening. He was sweating profusely but looked none too disturbed by that fact, as shown by a big grin offered to both youngsters.

Grehn and Molo both rushed over to the gate to greet Sentok. Molo's buffy, curled hair would press only as high as the man's chest; Grehn's not past his shoulders! But both – so small in comparison – almost bowled him over.

'Yikes! Look at you two! You're both almost taller than I. Damn you little sprouts, I have only been gone for a few months.' The large man smiled still, widely, almost past the limit that his large, hulked frame would allow.

'Come! See! Come see what I have brought for this year's Festival!

Sentok had, once again, been tasked with supplying the necessary sky flame for the Festival. After three years of his seemingly heroic exhibitions, the mighty successful three years of explosive and brightly coloured fire in the sky, he was now entrusted with the annual errand, away from his usual role as castle keeper for the couple of months preceding the Festival to source such rare material.

Holding aside the thick braided cloth at the rear of the cart, he showed them his wares purchased for this year's fire and flame show. Atop the pile of small tubes, coils, and boxes sat four huge pipes wrapped in fogging foil.

'Those beauties there should be visible to even the gods! And then to even whoever or whatever they offer prayer! Hopefully!' He split another wide smile, shadow shaded cheeks crinkling with delight at the thought of this year's exhibition of the manufactured concoction of colour, his creation.

Grehn hopped onto the wide timber step dropped low at the back of the wagon. She then scrambled into the back of the cart to rummage, as she usually did, to poke around to see what else he had brought along.

She knew he always brought some very rare trinkets, or even harder to find items back from where his travels throughout Vilenzia, and sometimes beyond, had taken him.

Understanding her impatience, Sentok grunted. 'Grehn, I wouldn't go moving stuff around in there. Just the slightest spark would remove this castle from the rock on which it is meant to rest!

'Here! What you're searching for be in my satchel.' He

pulled out a sack, bound tight, and dropped it into Grehn's eager palm after she had bounded triumphantly out of the cart.

Unlacing the string, she shook the bag upside down into her other palm. When nothing fell out, she looked dubiously at Sentok. 'Ha … ha! Very funny, Sentok!'

'No, Grehn, *the sack!* That is what I brought back for you.' He grabbed it back from her and looked around, nervously looking for something large. Not finding anything of use, he jumped into the back of the wagon. After he fumbled round for a short while, he came out with one of the large sky flames that had sat atop the rest. 'See here, watch this!' He opened the sack's collar as he let it slump on the ground. Then, once happy with its position, he slowly guided the pipe cautiously through the hole it offered on the pavement.

To the amazement of all others present, the pipe – the same that stood at the same height of Molo – disappeared into the sack, into nothing as Sentok tied the sack closed.

She gazed at Sentok; her face full of awe as he passed the sack back to her.

The sack held the same flimsy weight as it had originally.

Curiously, she untied the sack and tipped it upside down. Then proceeded to shake it about.

'Grehn! No! Shit!' shouted Sentok. 'No! Don't—'

The pipe dropped out and made a loud clanging sound as it hit the stone cobbles beneath their feet.

As close to instant as could be, Sentok grabbed both Grehn and Molo under each of his thick arms and ran toward the well causing a few feathers to fall from Baston as he flew like an arrow, making his escape from such commotion, before drifting effortlessly high up, then over the castle's high wall.

They arrived briskly at their presumed shelter behind the well's half height wall.

A fizzing sound preceded the large boom that filled then echoed around the courtyard. Their vision was filled with sparkles that held a multitude of colours.

When all had settled, Molo peered around the side of the well, only to be dragged back again by Sentok just as a blaze of blue sparks fizzed all around them.

The two youngest giggled with glee, and a hint of relief. 'Wow, Sentok! That was close. I can't wait for tomorrow night's show.' Molo looked again behind the well to see if all had come to a close. Seeing the pipe was now only smoking with no flame, he stood, followed by Grehn and Sentok. They walked toward the wagon. All three brushed themselves down of the dirt that had been caught in that sliding by Sentok.

Sentok looked at Grehn. 'Damn, Grehn! If that had gone off in the direction of the wagon and not us, we would have all been blown past Kinora!'

Molo looked back at the well and sighed. The stonework of the well was now scorched with something more than grime, though it held not much of the earlier mildew. But now it bore scars of the premature flamework. It would be a long, long evening …

\*

Grehn saddled her ride at the royal stable yard and was helped up, to straddle the ornate saddle, by her father. Once she was settled onto her mount, Ben slung himself over a tall, dark stallion, the most prized steed in all of Vilenzia. He had asked Grehn if she minded if he accompanied her over the divide, and then deep into the city: to where the Medica would, no doubt, set their shelters up in the main square. He wanted to be the first to congratulate her on completing her arduous studies.

'Your mother is so, so proud of you, darling. She is setting up a little congratulations party on the seaward deck.'

Ben then turned his gaze to the two sturdy warriors sat stationary on their mounts just behind the royal pair. He asked sturdily, 'Is the bridge secure, Kimo?'

'Yes, Captain!' was the firm reply. Being the most senior in charge of the city's military, the king was referred to – as he always had been – as "Captain". He head even lead the region's army himself, out on the battlefield, on many occasions whenever was warranted – though not for a long time, as peace had reigned for years. There had only been a spattering of unrest, quickly quelled by his guards and their commanders.

'Has the city's guard been deployed?' Ben raised an eyebrow, expecting only his expected response.

'Yes, Captain. They wait … throughout the side streets and inside the allotted safe houses. If the need may arise, they will be at *your* call within but a moment.'

'Good. Good work, Kimo, once again.' Ben tilted his head toward Kimo, a show of affirmation toward his most trusted.

Grehn looked toward Kimo. He didn't look like a battle-hardened, ultra-trained warrior. He was a big man no doubt, but his gentle face betrayed the horror he could, or would, and should, inflict if provoked; no less forced to defend any of those residing in the castle. She had seen it firsthand … many times – too many times to forget.

The attention was noted, then returned with a small smile and accompanied with a wink to bring in some comedic value. Reassurance personified; something she felt within him, a knowing that he would defend her and her father against any foe that would mean to do them harm … to the death, be that his own.

She would have no one else wear his boots. He was a frightful adversary to anyone, but he was also one of the gentlest men inside the castle walls on any given day. Pushing just into his fifties, he was now showing a slight grey about his cropped hair and a few extra lines that wrinkled at the edge of his forever friendly green eyes.

His hands, though, were as fast as ever. And his strong arms had lost none of their cutting strength since the first time he had lifted her high above his head when she was just a little child; he was still able to swing her over his head, and just as easily. The doting uncle. Ben's twin held no disregard for his eventual station, nor any ill feeling toward *his* king or any of Ben's family. He was a stalwart defender for his own kin.

Ben swiftly raised both his arms to motion the two stable hands into flight and to fulfil their last task. They were quick to obey the king's command and opened the large doors out into the courtyard.

As the lunchtime feast had concluded, the four guards were now back at their post and opened the heavy gates that led out to the usual bustle upon the bridge known as the *Masked Arches*. The road had been cleared, though not fully, as it always was when royalty were to cross the deep divide – it was the same for any other known royalty or their dignitaries from any other city throughout Vilenzia and more beyond.

It was also not lost on Ben as to what had taken place in the central courtyard during the lunchtime feast. The large boom had shaken the dining room, dropping all to the floor, taking their food and drink platters with them. He shook his head at Sentok who had now stationed his wagon at a safe distance far away from the inhabited sections of the castle.

Sentok returned the offered scorn with a large grin and Ben chuckled to himself; he had experienced as much as Grehn had that afternoon – maybe more than he would ever disclose.

'Oh, to be young again hey, Kimo?'

Ben's sibling looked at Sentok. The big toothy grin

disappeared as Kimo's mask faded, leaving a gaze to stare fully upon him – akin to a solid sheet of green ice. The bald man may have been the biggest in the castle but even he knew Kimo would not hesitate to take his head should any harm befallen Grehn or any other close to her.

'Aye, Ben, I remember … I remember all too well!'

They made their way across the granite slabs atop the Masked Arches, cantering their way through the squabble of residents who were permitted to remain, brushed off to each side – the permanent residents who would come up from below to set up their shop, shops that were commissioned by the castle, thus all profits above the offered wage were put back into the city, whether to increase its defence or attack capability, or to construct something else for the community, such as the newly constructed hostel for the less privileged children. The vendors were vetted before employment and allowed to reside close to the castle walls, settling in makeshift cabins while away from their families – some even had set up permanent residence on the bridge with their small families, though they remained out of sight of the main route.

The cross breeze always blew the same way. So the stalls, when set out atop the bridge, would all face the same way, facing away from the ocean whipped winds.

Grehn, atop her mount, stretched her neck high and inhaled the salty fresh aroma. *Nature*. It was usually mixed in with the stalls' many different wares. *Life*. The many infusions set off some kind of sense within her; every section of the bridge offered a different mix from the other: from the scent of exotic spices to the apricot-infused puffs of perfume to the charcoal-smoked brisket.

She loved it all.

Their ultimate destination would take them through a few less desirable districts, those where disdain for the royals was spread by way of misinformation and the plight of a poorer existence. Grehn knew that, though she loved every experience outside of the castle walls, she would sympathise with the town folk; she sensed their pain, but also their strong will too, which offered itself in abundance and had her often close to weeping, from their resilience through such adversity. She wanted to give them all a big hug to convey *I feel you,* but she knew their reply would be along the lines *"Sod off you perky bitch"*, or one of a few cruder lines, of similar ilk, often thrown at her, transmitted through an ignorance she would forgive each time.

She was also fully aware of the occasional shutter left slightly ajar during their descent into the guts of the city, *never quite free.* Knowing eyes would be watching from the merest gap. Roughly one in twenty of the houses that adorned the narrow streets were occupied by the city guard. Positioned as such as the need would arise. Any hint of the slightest danger, then a signal from Ben or Kimo – or whoever was in command – would bring a horde of the highest calibre of soldier clattering into the streets.

What she was not aware of, though, was the two entertainers that unintentionally blocked their trail with their overly large float, that consisting of a flutterby's flowing wings. Two stunningly beautiful and exotic women were prancing around on high stilts, their bodies bouncing with a flair that was matched by their outstretched painted arms; a faint bounce of a drumbeat and subtle sway of guitar matched their stride and swing. Grehn laughed as the two put hands on hips and then blew a kiss to Kimo, who blushed enough, she thought, for his mount to feel the heat. Immediately recomposed, he proceeded to send the two performers on their way, barking orders at them as they kept their seductive, flaunting glances at him.

She slowed and clapped in tandem with the beat which accompanied three tumbling acrobats crossing the street, each dressed fully in puffed up clothing, each spinning a large hoop. She laughed even harder when her father had to duck underneath one of the flailing hoops as it was let loose, obviously from the hand of the least experienced, youngest of the spinners. The now sheepish troupe bowed and offered their apologies before making their way down another side street on the opposite side from which they had heralded.

Kimo grunted profusely and pointed forward to move.

The royal entourage did little to stifle the enthusiasm of the residents this time. They had come out in droves to greet their king and his beloved little girl, if all were not entirely gracious. Offerings of all kinds were presented with displays of utmost love, though intended, or for show was unclear, but all were heartfelt. Offerings to the divine seemed to be always the most heard, offered to keep the king and all the royal family safe from harm.

The cascading effect that rippled through the city was always the way. By the time they made it to the city square, there would be a welcoming party of hundreds to greet them. *Also a hundred potential threats*, she thought, reflecting the same thought Kimo's gaze showed.

The castle mage, Anatoma, had been sent to scope out their final destination a few hours earlier to detect any anomaly excreted from the aura surrounding the square – any other than that of the Medica putting down their wards. If the slightest hint of threat or malicious intent had been detected, he would meet them at the crossroad between Second Street and Third Avenue – after he set off the emergency flare. At that junction rested a safe house with an elite guard unit residing permanently, and a bunker compound which led to the start of a maze of escape tunnels stretching out beneath the city, down to a dock at the base of the jagged cliffs beneath the Masked Arches, or weaving in the other direction to open out beyond the city's main gate.

*

Anatoma skulked about around the main square. He had moved about uneasily from the very first moment he'd arrived there. Having heard the rumours surrounding the closure of the tavern, he was now beginning to feel the truth of those whispers. A few other citizens had made their way to the main square too to have a gander at the arrival of the band of wagons, cloaked generously with swathes of all shades of green. He was keen to be done with the charade of playing a local beggar. And he knew Mother Ursen well, she would no doubt sniff him out if he ventured anywhere near her. The two had shared many a conversation surrounding a variety of topics – mostly political – about the wider world. Also, too many an eclectic drop of a variety of red wines during his studies and training in the city. He had also received a few lessons on how to behave ordinarily to blend in as one of the local residents – within reason, depending on the size of the population.

He looked to where the swath of green was now encamped – the only other faction that would regularly leave the city, though they left in a tranche unlike the Third's operational requirement of, at most, master and apprentice. They made the square look as though it was made for them. *Such military precision for a group that is so far from that brutal ilk.* Anatoma admired them as they regimentally assembled.

A few of the wagons had opened up their canvases ready to reveal a selection of herbs, potions, tomes, and books below their much worn and haggard coverings. There would also be healers who would invite the residents to share their burdens with a hope of relinquishing any pain; whether of the mind or the body, or just to ease with understanding and an offer of a way forward to go about their lives. The one wagon that had not yet revealed its innards just yet was

Mother Ursen's. He knew it to be hers by the markings along the wraps and straps, sensing the hum and radiance emanating from them: strong shielding glyphs creating a magical shelter that encapsulated the wagon with an impenetrable web. The web would catch any intrusion and absorb any physical damage. It also acted as a barrier to keep any prying eyes or ears from any insight into what may be happening beneath the bereft tarp, though it was not as frail as it appeared from the outside.

He was about to make his way to his set position, one agreed prior with Kimo where the royals would pass close by and allow him to follow at an easy pace at the instructed distance behind to avoid any scrutiny. Suddenly panic erupted from those waiting nearest the steps of the Grousing Potter. A scattering of people then darted away from the big door of the Grouse, knocking over a signboard in their haste.

Two men had burst out through the large famous doors – now splintered and scattered across a wide area of cobblestone – hounded closely by something even larger, a wrathful apparition that resembled dark sin, all arms and legs with a frightfully bulbous head, mouth full of rotted, but still razor-sharp, teeth.

Anatoma gulped in a wad of air.

Both men fell down the steps and into the square, bringing up clouds of swirling dust with their body slides across the unswept cobbled road. Both turned gingerly at the thing before they began lifting themselves up. The much taller of the two had hold of a large medallion which had previously been wrapped around his neck. The chain had been snapped, more than likely in his haste, and his shirt, jutting from the front of a finely woven jacket, had been torn open to release the medallion from its resting place upon his chest. The much smaller of the two stood to begin a mad hobble away from the foot of the steps, shouting several curses as he struggled to get away. He was limping even before he hit the awkward surface of cobbles.

'Peron …?' Anatoma muttered to himself. 'What have you done now? You little shit!'

Peron turned to face the phantom menacing their heels, bringing the talisman high, the chain slumped to either side of his wrist, then he started to shout an enchantment. Before he could finish, one of the long flailing arms of the spectre extended slowly, becoming almost twice as long as it snapped at Peron's arms, knocking the medallion away. *Oh shit! It can strike with physical form,* he instantly thought with shock.

*Shit.*

Rushing from his place of calm, Anatoma was joined by Mother Ursen as he passed close to her enclosed carriage. They both raced toward where Peron and the eberactu were backing away toward where the carriages were stationed. Both had their arms raised, pointed at the spectral form closing in on its stuttering prey.

A translucent strand of emerald leapt from each of Mother Ursen's hands – a similar turquoise strand shot from Anatoma's. Their enchantment and the strands began to blend in a finely tuned chorus as they merged then enveloped the large form.

Peron looked to see where the energy had appeared from, immediately he recognised both faces. Turning back to where he'd scrambled from, he saw the glint of the medallion hovering precariously over a vent to one of the foul drains. He moved quickly forward to retrieve the medallion, having to duck backwards a step to avoid a swipe from the now partially immobile thing. He regained his balance and a small amount of composure and leapt into a roll to avoid another strike. He picked up the medallion as he finished the acrobatics.

He began his own trap by raising the medallion up to the spectral form and spoke clearly. 'Humra, banerar, beloria! Begone!'

The entrapment folded in on itself after Peron had reached into a small band around his waist and threw a miniature chest at the thing. The little box jumped around on the cobbles then calmed after a moment, before making one last vault, just high enough for Peron to casually catch it with his free hand – though smoking, Peron showed no discomfort from the supposed heat.

He then looked at the two newcomers to the party and smiled. Dresdor did likewise … only much wider.

The small royal entourage made their way into the square just as the commotion was subsiding, breaking out of their hurried canter to a small trot as they moved toward the steps of the Grousing Potter.

Kimo did not miss the small scattering of townsfolk, nor the distressed-looking frame and hinges of the entrance to the tavern.

'Halt!' he shouted, once they were almost over the top of the panting Anatoma. 'You were to come to us if you had any inkling of trouble. Why must I find you here now, looking like you have just seen a ghost.'

'Because my lor—'

Ben interjected. 'Kimo! Look! Who's that? There in the doorway!' he croaked, interrupting the exchange, and saving Anatoma from – at the very least – a verbal bashing.

Kimo looked to where Ben had pointed. There, a figure skulked not far inside the entrance. He strained his eyes to see, but once his eyes trained on the figure, he slumped to quickly dismount to the cobbles below. Eyes still focused just beyond the entrance, he whispered, 'No … it cannot be …'

Ben was now also off his mount and moved toward

Grehn. 'Grehn, listen to me. Turn your ride around right now and go!' he whispered up toward her as she leant down to him. The urgency in his tone, the worry in his eyes, set her to shaking.

'But, Father! What … what is it?' Perplexed at the sudden urgency, she almost held the proud smile she'd held on her way.

Mother Ursen stood among the wagons in the courtyard, a short stroll away. She looked at the older lady and saw the same as she had seen in the origin of her father's expression. Looking up toward the entrance where her father and Kimo had locked their steely gaze moments earlier, a figure turned and walked back toward the innards of the tavern.

'The White Lady of the Well!' came a cry from the townsfolk behind them. It started a drumroll of an echo, a concern that rippled panic throughout the square.

Kimo barked at Anatoma, 'Get her away from here! Now!'

Instantly, Anatoma took two large steps toward Grehn, flicked his head to the side to motion her to not leave her saddle, to move back, and swung atop the horse almost catching Grehn in the face with his worn leather boots. Plucking the reins from under himself when mounted, he slashed them with both hands. The steed moved with a fast jerk and headed toward the crossroads to the haven designated for such a passenger in peril. 'We will come back, I promise, but now we must go, and fast!'

No more than halfway down the street toward the safe house, their ride skidded to a halt and caught its hooves in the jutting cobbles, throwing Grehn forward. She grabbed hold of Anatoma's shoulders to try and remain seated, but the forward momentum was too great, and they both lurched forward.

Both hit the surface below, hard.

A few moments passed before she came to her senses.

She knew she was bleeding but was unsure how much damage she had taken. Anatoma had taken the brunt of the fall and hit his face and body on the hard surface under the crumpling form of Grehn. A groan gave Grehn insurmountable relief that he was at least able to breathe. That relief was undone when she noticed a figure standing in their path, no doubt the cause of Anatoma pulling up on the reins. The same figure that moments earlier had disappeared into the tavern now stood before them.

It made a quick, unnatural move toward Grehn, but stopped to hover just beyond an arm's length from her. Muffled shouts came from behind them. The voices were now very familiar.

*Father*, she whispered.

The figure looked at Grehn, dead eyes emanating fear. It spoke, a rasping squeal escaped its mostly toothless mouth. 'My child … it has begun. You must be ready before the final joining.' Looking past Grehn, the spectre resembling that of an old lady pointed toward the tavern. 'Find me. Find me before I pass this and every other realm. You must …'

Grehn looked toward the tavern, beyond the onrushing figures of her father and Kimo. She turned her head back to the old woman who had spoken to her only to see a wisp of smoke disappear to be one with the air.

Shaking her head to clear the nauseous space between her ears, and to also aid her hand to clear the blood dripping down into her eyes, she leaned down to help Anatoma to his feet, spattering him with a few spots too.

Now conscious, though less than lucid, he thanked her then looked to where he had seen the figure before the dramatic halt. 'Lady, forgive me. I am sure I saw her. No, I am absolutely certain she was in our way!'

'Easy. No need to apologise Anatoma,' she replied.

It was Kimo who reached the fallen duo first. It always was. Immediately he pulled the sash of his station loose and tied it around Grehn's head to stem the blood pumping out of a nasty split across her forehead – one that traversed from the extremity of her left then up and over to the beginning of her right eye. As soon as the makeshift bandage was applied, Grehn asked Kimo, 'Who is she?'

But before the answer was given, she slumped to fall into his arms. A crimson mist was the last she saw as she finally succumbed to the welcome darkness of peace.

Peering through timber boards nailed to the top window of a decrepit and abandoned building directly across the square from where the commotion was taking place, Ezekel watched on as the local resident he had planted weeks earlier – whom he had entranced and set upon a path of destruction – burst out of the main doors, now fully engrossed in its rageful, spectral form. Giggling to himself, he was just about to depart his hiding spot when he saw a glint of mirrored orichalcum held by one of the fleeing punters of the Grouse. Holding his breath, he watched as the whole scene played out – from the encapsulation of the drunkard he had snared so promiscuously to after the two who fell whilst trying to escape its manacled clutches.

*Who was that? The one who leapt from the cart? The only one I could not penetrate.* The thought ran through his mind. *And what were the princess and the beggar – Anatoma – running from? Why did that fool from the City rein in like a maniac? And who did that spoiled little princess talk to before she dropped into the arms of that … that brute?* He would not gain any answers by remaining in his temporary squaller.

He decided he would finally make a move, the first movement in days, away from the much unaccustomed, dank, and dark room.

Once the square had calmed enough, he made his way across to the back of the Grouse through a roundabout way to avoid any suspicion, to where the gargantuan amount of stock would be dropped through two large, grated shutters. He dropped down inside then froze. Staring at him was the old lady who he had tried, but failed, to trance into his mystical bargaining. She who had refused a lifetime of forever beyond the mortal realm. She who had evaded him as she threw a mixture of powdered silver and sulphur into the air between them.

But now she was here. Staring at him as though she had been waiting for this very moment. As if she had read him from his very first pitch. He looked back up toward the grated entrance to the cellar as it was slammed shut by an unseen force. He did not have time to turn back as the old lady in the cellar dove at him with another force, though this one was physical and far beyond the shrill of a silhouette she appeared to be – one that felt like a thousand piercing spikes all striking simultaneously.

The pawn of evil spattered all about the cellar floor in an unquantifiable amount of unidentifiable shreds of flesh, bone, and all the things in-between.

She wiped the stench of an unnatural ooze of darkness from her hands and spoke to herself, or to the thing she had just decimated, matter of fact.

'Filthy, dirty beast!'

She then let loose a shriek which shook the whole tavern to its core, dropping the main entrance's splintered door frame fully to the ground.

A shriek so vociferous it would most probably have been felt, or at the very least heard, far beyond the city walls.

She hoped.

For she had little more left.

The royal decree for the first day of the Festival was that no-one was to step foot beyond the bounds into the *Grousing Potter* until further notice, affirmed by the king himself. The effect on the populous' spirit that resided in Jacobs Well, was palpable. The jewel in the crown of the city, the tinder to the celebrations that would extend from the tavern, out into the city square then on to the many winding streets and then all the way to the castle gates themselves. Now snuffed out. The celebrations would go on though, but understandably, somewhat subdued.

Sat in a low but expansive candlelit room, one well adorned with intricately laid out seating, the one and only room that linked the two main towers of the royals castle, Ben asked Kimo, 'Why now? Why now does she arise from her holy god forsaken ashes to torment me or, more so, us? And what timing! Damn! Damn that witch …'

Kimo was the only member of the small council brave enough to offer advice at this time. He knew Ben's moods well, and a bad one was not often seen, but he understood him in this moment. 'My lord, during this eclipse, this conjunction … maybe this has something to do with the timing? It would make sense.' Kimo pondered something for a short moment and then spoke. 'The why? This one seemed different … I can't be certain, but the shadow seemed to proceed with a blooded tinge as it passed through. You know the prophecy, Ben, and what that means. You cannot bury your head now. Not with this one …'

'Aye, Kimo.' Ben nodded to his brother and seemed to settle a little, though the pain of his daughter, no less the sight of her flailing for solidity over the neck of her mount, still hung heavy. 'But it has been thousands of years since that prophecy was scribed, one of hundreds too, and the rest, may one add, all mostly written by madmen, or spoken by some proclaimed god or goddess. Who I would deem, just as mad …'

Kimo looked at Ben sceptically. He knew Ben was

holding back on what he was prepared to divulge to the wider group who they held in forum.

It was Peron who offered further reason. 'My lord. Lords,' he nodded to Kimo, ' may I suggest why.'

Ben hmphed, but accompanied it with a nod to Kimo, who only nodded with the same toward Peron, offering some approval.

'Well, my lords, back in the city, *our* city,' he looked to Anatoma, 'there has been some rumblings and ramblings, mostly surrounding the interjection of Kinora and the slightest change to its orbit. I was sent to Jacobs Well to speak with Anatoma, then I was to venture on to—'

Peron was interrupted as Anatoma coughed. 'Peron!' He wiggled his finger, advice to not divulge any secrets of the Shadow.

'Yes … Well, I was to venture on and visit another three of our *agents* in the area, up toward the north, to collate any information of any disturbances that were away from the norm. Out of the norm, like, as in any disturbing occurrences.'

'Oh come on! Cut to it, Peron!' Kimo barked.

Peron jumped back sharply from where he was leaning against the large table in the middle of the room. 'Ghosts!' he managed to squeak out before he regained his composure. 'Ghosts, and the like, my lord. Also, any occurrences of people becoming, well, not themselves. Never knew about the bloody Grouse, would never have come otherwise …' he wrung his hands together. 'They believe a reckoning is upon us, and Jacobs Well, along with this part of Inarrel, is going to be the sweet spot. The maximum shade cast from both those planets up there which just happened to slot right between us and the sun and—'

'Peron! You're doing it again! Just get to it!' Kimo reminded Peron, along with a slight neck tilt and its resultant crack.

'Sorry, my lord. They calculated the epicentre of maximum shade that would be created by the alignment was to be somewhere near here …'

Ben had been watching the exchange, taking all in. He then spoke calmly, and measured, to the only silent person in the room. 'Mother Ursen, is it a coincidence that you are in this city at this time?'

A long pause ensued. Eventually, she looked deep into the crackling fire and let out an extended sigh. 'No …'

Ben spoke again, well contained anger creeping into his eyes even as his voice stayed level as he asked, 'So, you let me bring my daughter down to that … that filthy square knowing what was—'

'No!' Mother Ursen shot back. 'We had no idea what would transpire from this planetary alignment. We are far removed from those others who preclude so much from their own findings, it is of no concern to our cause.' She then pointed to Ben, who shrunk ever so slightly, but just enough. 'Do not take out your anger on me, you old—' She held her tongue at the last and what she was about to let loose. 'Look, Ben. I'm sorry about what happened with your daughter, with Grehn. We had every intention of recognising her achievements and welcoming her to the fold and, one day, to eventually study at the city, just as we did Jahnna. We were hoping to take her back before the Festival began, though we were caught up with a few strange occurrences of random madness, thus halting the journey. And don't we know what happens around here during the Festival and with Grehn being that age where—'

'Not another word from you, woman! Hold that riddling tongue of yours,' Kimo barked, interrupting. Then, realising what he had said, he began to make an apology which was abruptly dismissed by Mother Ursen.

'Save it, Kimo. I know you are still hurting from the

afternoon's events. No need, you are a good and true man. I would never hold to a word spoken against you.' She turned her head to speak to Ben. 'I see … I see I was right.' Mother Ursen began to rise, ready to depart, when the doors swept open revealing an emotionally forlorn Jahnna.

'Mother …' she croaked as she stepped a little quicker, to seek the warm embrace that would coddle her addled heart.

'Sweet child. Look at you, such radiance, such beauty. How long has it been?' Mother Ursen swept Jahnna into her arms as she came close. Jahnna nestled her head under the taller older woman's chin.

'Too long … far, far too long,' she whispered.

'How is she?' Mother Ursen flicked her chin up and toward the door.

'Sleeping. She came somewhat awake, though let out a strained groan, so I administered the *broth of polentia*. Then, lights out, just as quick.' She smiled brightly, holding the older woman at arm's length, still tightly.

'Excellent choice, my dear,' Mother Ursen replied, showing her a warm smile. Her eyes also beamed with pride at Jahnna's proficiency. 'You go, rest now, it is getting late. I will fetch my large sleeping sack and lay up in her room and continue the administration of the broth until the morning. That should be enough time for her to not move about so much and let the wound heal somewhat. As best it may.'

'Yes, that's Grehn. Always about the place.' She let out a croaked laugh but then bundled her head back into Mother Ursen's chest, and sobbed uncontrollably.

All the men in the room grumbled, though not loud enough for any others to notice. There would be no more talk of what happened that afternoon, at least not tonight.

No more barbs to be shot at each other via spoken word.

Nor via any unspoken gestures or dagger-like glances. No man present would be brave enough to get on the wrong end of Mother Ursen in the presence of her adopted daughter, Queen Jahnna.

# Elegy of the Lady

It had been almost a full day since they had both seen the light of day upon Inarrel. Their current setting on Kinora bore no such radiance, no matter how much the glowing sun offered. A planet that spun on no axis, only on a random rotation swayed by the large bodies much closer than the communal sun. A large floating rock that continuously made its way around the two larger sister planets in a figure of eight pattern.

Stepping out onto the balcony, a large extended girth of extruded rock that jutted out implausibly from the face of the highest peak of Kinora – *Vane of Shadow* – they both looked to the sky above and the short horizon. The red hue – as also observed from Inarrel – was created by the many vents sprouting from the surface below spouting their molten vapour; a magnificent sight for them to behold, however how hard it was to breathe.

Mesfa, still looking upward, spoke. 'Such a beautiful visage, but also … so very much malicious. I have dreamt much of this sacred place, scoured many a page found in so many different texts we have read. Sister!' She grabbed Arigal by both shoulders. 'We are finally here!'

Arigal, looking not now at the sky above but to the terrain below replied, trying her best to hide any hesitation she felt, 'Yes, we made it. What next, I wonder, awaits us?'

Before Mesfa could respond, a small, crooked being appeared, hunched over in the broken archway behind them. It made a snorting sound to grab their attention.

'*Child* of the night! Come. Come here, now!'

The non-plural notion – children – offered by the decrepit little being wasn't lost on either woman: It was meant for one, not both. The one that would be elevated to the subsequent station, leaving the other to rot in the dirt of whatever surface onto which they would fall.

There was no need for such niceties in their current residence. It was as it had always been: to serve the Dark Lady. If you didn't like it then you wouldn't be there. If you didn't accept it, then you were not one for the cause – and the small being knew that, as would any other being that found itself permitted to grace the barren red rock.

They had travelled through the portal of *forever*, a conduit to the depths of the mountain they currently stood high upon. If they had not been pure of commitment to the cause they would have been extinguished during the small mesmerising journey through the unknown space between – no matter what trials preceded, the passing was one of the final tests. Now both women had passed through, the keepers on Kinora knew that their new occupants could be trusted with the final training before the next ascension could proceed – one that would involve many strenuous activities.

Making their way toward the opening where the creature stood glaring at them, Mesfa asked for its name.

'Esfell. Esfell is my na—'

Before it could finish, Arigal backhanded the creature across the face, the force of the blow knocking it back to the carved stone wall. 'Another test, Mesfa.' She then walked casually over to the now stung creature. 'Speak like that again, to either one of us, and you will be nothing but fuel for this planet's core! Understand, you little grub?!'

Showing no fear from the brutality offered, thus received – which was expected of all who resided on Kinora – it nodded, backed away, then scampered with a limp down the spiralling steps it must have appeared from, but not before it pointed to the large wide steps leading upward, through the guts of the mountain.

Esfell hissed a whistle as it departed, the composition a haunting tune, the melody fading away the deeper it stepped.

The stairway they now beheld seemed to extend forever as it made its way up through the mountain.

Mesfa looked slightly perplexed and commented on the newly offered observation. 'Surely the mountain is not that wide for these stairs to extend so far upward?'

Arigal nodded. 'Nothing is as it seems. Surely *you* should know that by now …' She smiled and pushed Mesfa toward the first step. 'Go on, *Child of the Night* … haha'

They both laughed as they started stepping up the elevation, through the innards of the mountain.

Making their way up the stairs, they eventually saw the mirage for what it was; they saw themselves becoming larger in a wall at the top of the stairs the higher they climbed. The wall the mirror was affixed to was tilted at such an angle to directly reflect the angle opposite the stairs to form such an illusion. Reaching the pinnacle of the stairs, a landing showed itself. So too, did two doors on each opposite side of the landing.

Stepping onto the landing, the mirror suddenly shimmered, then rearranged itself, a burning, golden script now visible on its surface which was dictated with speech that floated and echoed about the air.

'*Choose … Choose your path.*'

Arial and Mesfa looked to each other, moved closer, and held hands. Mesfa nodded to the door on the right. They started to make their way to the door when the mirror shattered, showering the two women with glass. Shards of glass pierced their skin. They knew not to wipe them away; they would pluck the shards out when they had a chance. The mirror then replenished and rearranged itself.

'*Choooossse!*'

As an act of defiance, they walked closer to the mirror.

With the mirror again whole, they staunchly began to pull the shards wedged into their faces using the assistance offered by the reflection.

The mirror rippled with another shimmer then recalibrated itself, only to return somewhat whole again, save the reveal of another opening in the centre.

The opening led through and onto another balcony – on the opposite side of the mountain from where they began their ascent. It stretched at least fifty paces out toward the red, menacing sky above, stretched beyond the shorter horizon they had both been used to.

The balustrade surrounding the floating balcony was made up of multiple small stone stubs acting as balusters, topped with what looked to be the long bones of some creature unknown. Upon closer inspection, they could see the massive spans appeared to be wing support bones of some sort, the spinal digits that would have no doubt housed the sinew and flange of a massive wing were now curled up to create a battened effect now moulded to the balcony's perimeter base with the multiple broken body parts of much lesser creatures.

A figure hovered beyond the balcony's edge with a slow bobbing motion, hood drawn over its head, was facing away out to the lands beyond. Still, it sensed their approach, and spoke. A similar voice to that from the cavern, though with not a hint of the screeched high pitch; softer, almost angelic. 'Well … I wondered when you would be joining me up here.'

Both women continued to move at a slow and steady pace toward the shadowy figure.

'You should know, I am not she—'

'Then who are—' Before Arigal could finish the figure turned with a dramatic twist, eyes black as coal trained on her. The rasping screech now returned with full force, an disproportionally sized mouth howled at them, blowing their hair back, requiring them to shield their eyes.

'Dare interrupt me again, child. I dare! You speak when I say and only when I say. Those minions here, do not let them shush you. But, for me … I will have the skin off your bones without hesitation, even from who you are destined to be! Hear me?'

When the tirade was finished, both bowed their heads in obsequiousness. It had been drilled in from a young age, do not speak to those of a higher station unless directed.

Arigal should have known better. Mesfa wore a wry grin. *Score to me?* she pondered.

Arigal also hid a wry grin. Her bowed head, she dared not make a sound though, that would set them both off in fits of laugher – *not the place.*

'Now then! Now that I have your undivided attention, I will explain what you need to know and only what you need to know … is that clear? Your ascendance here will be short lived unfortunately. I need you *both* back there!' The figure pointed to Inarrel. 'Understood?'

A slight drop of the head from both was appreciated by the figure, who nodded.

It was female, from that angelic voice. Arigal surmised a spell of some sort was carried to hide her true identity. However, she did not mistake that the figure was not hovering through her own devices. Peering through the bones of the balcony, she noticed two large globular, black eyes bobbing in tandem with the figure that was berating them, appearing then disappearing below the parapet of bone. *What is that!?* she thought. *Surely a creature able to hover, but so still?*

The female figure made an upward motion with both hands then flattened them when the creature raised her at a height high enough to step onto the balcony's railing and hop off on to the balcony's pavers. As she stepped down, she threw her hood back to reveal herself and offered a small smile to Arigal, even though the disciple's heads were still drawn to the stone below, she was amused. 'Arigal. Child, come closer. Come see!'

Arigal left the idle and prone Mesfa to smoulder where she remained. Raising her head to meet that of the figure who beckoned her, she fell half a step back. This drew another smile from her caller.

That half step was followed by a drop of her knees. The kneel, dissolving into a statuesque offering, head to the stone, compliance to her immediate tormentor.

Mesfa waited where Arigal had left her, as petrified stone. A twitch to her left eye – the side at which her sister had been summoned from. She knew her sister's quiet outburst and her general inquisitiveness had impressed the *thing* that now stood above them. She dared not raise her head, not in the slightest. The itch to look was eating away at her solidified composure. *Be bold, it is not her Lady!* She stood and was ready to move forward, only to mirror the same subservient pose as Arigal upon seeing the face of the lady stood in front of them.

Though, as Mesfa began her ascent off the floor, the creature that had been carrying their unbeleaguered host revealed itself in an instant to ward off a potential threat to its mistress: a mess of fully extended limbs, twelve in all, of perhaps maybe sixteen or more that it may have once had, judging by the few stumps moving in tandem with the other limbs. It stood high above them on two of its thick, solid legs, raising and stretching the remainder. Hair, chitin and sinew. A massive, twitching head and a multitude of fangs sticking out proud of its snapping maw.

*Be bold!*

When she completed her ascent, she looked at the figure, then began to descend back to the floor after the figure shook her head at the probability of unspoken disobedience, but not before the creature spewed a stringy webbing which encased her entire body – save her neck and head.

'You can stay in there for a while, Mesfa.' The woman raised an arm to halt the advancing creature, denying it a hearty meal. She spoke again, 'Disobey me once more and I will not let Bambam leave here without feasting on your flesh and bones ... understood?'

She lay prone under a sticky mass of webbing, knowing she had erred. Though this woman was not the Lady, she was one of her immediate disciples sent from afar. *Shit* was the simplest, but most compelling thought she could muster.

The woman turned to Arigal. 'Now we chant, together, you and I. One that you have been told not to utter aloud. Hold my hand, I will lend my strength as a new power surges through you.' Before the chant began, the woman spoke to both. 'Your time down there is not yet done, we return. Together! Before the end of this night! Apologies we must leave so soon after your arrival here but needs must. My needs *must* be met!'

# A Bash About the Town

Gurengal opened the crudely made curtain ever so slightly to let the thinnest of the early morning rays of light into the small room. The night before had been a heavy one for most of his men, those who remained now slumbered, scattered about the wooden floor of the small, rented room above some non-descript tavern. A few grunts met the incoming rays of a low hanging morning sun.

'Hush men!'

Peering out of the window and down the long wide street he saw nothing of note. 'While you louts have been feasting and drinking in the ale rooms beneath, and wherever or whatever else, I have been here, warding these rooms so you all could sleep sound as babes smothered by your mother's tits.'

'Never met me mam,' one of his men mumbled a grumble.

He pulled the makeshift curtain off the makeshift rail above the window and threw it back onto the bed from where he had drawn it – the sheet – from. 'We need to be ready, gentlemen. Ready for what that devilish being has in store for us. He will be no doubt scheming something. It won't be pretty, can guarantee that. It won't be obvious too, unless he has diverted from his seemingly usual tact. It will catch us off guard though, and when it does, I don't want to be rousing your arses off the floor or off whatever or whoever you be lying on!'

A big hulking form by the name of Jurengor lay sprawled on the floor, the light not waking him, nor the deep resonating voice of Gurengal stirring him. As Gurengal stepped over the man, he let his heel clip the big man's quivering lips and shaking nose. Gurengal twisted enough to squish them flat to his face …

Still nothing. 'For 'sakes men, what did you do to him?!' A swift boot to the clobber's ribs – toes digging deep – startled the lump, who finally drew in a big snort.

Now awake, he stared through bloodshot eyes at Gurengal. 'Huh! Whit thit fir?'

'That was to make sure you were at least able to be woken if I needed you! Last night I have very little issue with boys. But ... that will be the last until we are out of and far beyond this town. He is coming and we need to be ready for when he is here. The gods only know what he will bring to the party.' Walking over to the one who was the most with it, he asked, 'Where's Lento and Bertino? I told them no matter what happ—' He shook his head. 'That whoever's bed they ended up in, to be back at daybreak ... It's now passed that time!'

It was Jurengor – the lump on the ground – who spoke. 'Thim girls, sumit ab:t thim ... huh, Bilty?'

'Aye, boss, they were some cracking looking lasses who they left with, both of 'em in tow. Had 'em in all kinds of knots,' added Bilty, showing a knowing smile of what the boys may have been up to.

Gurengal eyed both Jurengor and Bilty. 'You say! Knots? Kinda knots you talking about man?'

'Well, aye, them lasses that came in late last night. Lento were hooking onto another pretty lil lass and Bertino were all over some other floosy, locals them be. Well, anyway, they came in and everybody were obviously interested t' see who were comin' in, ne'er heard such a quiet noise from this rowdy lot. They made a straight arrow for those two larrikins. Wasn't much competition be honest for what they were hanging onto at the bar. Both just dropped them girls and ... well, few minutes later they're gone! Outta front door.'

'Bil, answer me this and be quick about it. Do you remember what them girls looked like?' Gurengal's tongue was sharp and direct.

'Aye, how could me forget. Well, they were… hmmm. Well, they were girls, gorgeous I recall, but … heck! Canny remem—'

'Shit. I should not have let you boys out last night. My wards only extended to this room and out to the corridor from the stairs. Fuck!'

Jurengor added, 'Mintal Biss, I f'git too!'

'Shit!' Gurengal confirmed his thoughts.

Another voice aired; it came from one of the three that had yet to speak. He rubbed his eyes. 'I didn't get a good look, but I heard what they said, well, a little what they said. Said they would be taking a walk down to a lake south of town, just t'other side of the woods that encircle the town. Asked if they would be good for a … a swim under the darkest of nights?'

'Shit! Shit! They're already here, the bastard. Jurengor, get your fat head inside your battle helm and quickly come with me. Rest of you lot, stay here, in this fucking room! You hear? And arm yourselves up. But do not leave these four small walls 'til told. Understood!'

Grumbles, affirmative grumbles at least. It was just enough for Gurengal.

The big man, Jurengor, moved like a fleeing cat – unbefitting his huge, solid form. His head would no doubt be swimming around like a shoal of small fish contained within a small bowl from the night's consumption – it had been many times before. He was the most able, even with a foggy head; the others with theirs would be less than useless, and a surety of hindrance. He would give them all time to recover. He would stop on his way down the hall to the neighbouring room, housing his three most trusted compatriots.

He needn't have banged on the door as they were all ready to move, as they always were – sober as chalk.

Lentino and Bertino had barely slept a wink all night. What had promised to be a night of fun out in the most basic of settings quickly became a night that would haunt them for the rest of their days – though they may only see very few, if any more, at all. Being strung up high inside a cage that prodded at multiple points with small spikes to all parts of the body will do that to you. Add to that the inclusion of an occasional prod from an extended onyx-clad spear tip – then that would keep you wincing.

They had learned the hard way – the smooth-talking duo, whose words flowed like honey out of well-rounded mouths, were batted back with a force tenfold in the end.

In the end, to whimper was the way, the only way.

'You wretched shits will stay up there until we return. We will finish you off then. And take what little soul fire you possess! Which, from first impressions, may only amount to that held by a worm  For now though, you will remain as bait.' The big gruff of a thing swung around. Its makeshift cloak spun outward with a slightly delayed unison with his arm, catching the face of the small figure sat close by on the ground. Not looking behind, he spoke again, this time to the victim of the opulent spiral. 'And you, my little fettle, will remain *here* and make sure *they* remain up *there*. No communicating with them! Okay? Oh, they will try, believe me, they will. But you shut your trap till we get back!'

'Yes … if I must,' came the meek response from the small and wiry looking being. Its green eyes shone as it peered up toward the two hanging baskets above.

'Now, come on you little whores. Let's go have some real fun. Ripping the guts out of all them up in this town.' The burly man pointed up to the swinging pair of men trapped in their cages. 'Starting with their sorry crew!' This brought giggles from the two enchantresses who had led the jovial lads to their impending doom.

'But were we not to remain hidden until our master arrived, Bendim?' The small being, the one told to remain behind, spoke softly, momentarily halting the bulking form from leaving the makeshift grove.

A sharp swinging rasp across the face was followed by a hissed verbal barrage. 'Dare utter my name again, slug guts, and I will end this apprenticeship of yours. A role I had no part in arranging, only agreeing to it through long, mind-numbing submission. It will end with your face ripped off though, I presume. Now, quiet!'

*

Stepping through the undergrowth, Somendel had been eavesdropping on the conversation during his slow walk from where his mini transportal swirled. He was too late to stop them from their escapade into the city the previous night, and total disregard of his explicit orders to wait for him.

The bubbling anger was replaced with a smile on his petite, grey, and normally placid face as he entered into the clearing.

The large oaf of a man turned and looked at him, his jaw slightly ajar, knowing he had erred.

*You idiot! You egotistical, incredulous oaf. I will make a statement of obedience of you. Mostly from your innards.*

The man was obviously frightened of what he saw. A wide smile that complimented the small eyes and large nodules was not a good sign.

*Good, feel that weakness that you are now feeling, non-believer.*

'I … I … No … We? Yes, we! We waited, Master, we waited. We heard they was to leave town this midday. We had to move.' The big man stumbled through the impromptu excuse.

'Fuck off! Shit we did. You only had an inkling; one you seem to have made up!' one of the fair-haired enchantresses butted in.

'Silence! Both of you! You, Bendim, have been found out, your insolence is boundless, so to the only punishment. What say you to her Lady's executioner? *Your* executioner!'

He dropped to the ground pleading and grovelling.

Somendel looked down at the pathetic Bendim, the cocky, confident bruiser now retching around like a split worm. *I will take pleasure in finally ending your insolence.* 'Stand. Stand and accept your fate. You know that the Lady's lenience has worn far beyond thin, especially with this final act of your one-man barrage, through insincere and unworthy offerings.'

'Please, Som—'

He was cut off with a bang to the back of the head – a blow from one of the two enchantresses – which led to a snivelling from the big man.

Somendel raised his head, nodes bubbling with an internal frothing sensation. 'Shhh! Everyone, be quiet.'

The whimpering died down from the man now lying on the ground, but up above them, a new whimpering began.

The men in the cages had a better vantage to see beyond the undergrowth. They could see the approaching shadowy figures wading through the trees, four silhouettes proceeding a larger one that walked a few steps behind as they made headway toward their precariously hung location.

Their muffled cries were not loud enough to alert their potential approaching saviours or to warn the troupe as to what lay below. They advanced, coming closer.

*Gurengal!* Lento's hopes had risen considerably. He had hoped they would have been missed, from not being back at base! Back at the tavern, for when the sun crested the forest. That encouragement for rescue soon dissipated as the leader of the troupe was finally distinguished – swinging around a ribbon, strung upon a loose skinny branch.

The silhouettes escaped from that mirage of hope, and stretched out shadows now approached from the low hanging sun. They were but children. Children, heading toward the monsters that milled below.

\*

Somendel brushed past Bendim, who was now only just quieting, still crouched low to the trampled grass. He made his way to the low topped bush that divided themselves and the approaching band of innocence. He could sense their innocence as soon as they entered the surrounding woodland.

*A dilemma! Maybe I subdue you small things and come back for you once I have dealt with my main prey. What to do?* Somendel chuckled at the thought.

The sound of laughter brought on by jovial taunt came closer. Lento could see the monster below, one hidden inside pecborian skin, weaving some sort of spell. He felt a rage trying to burst from within him, one that he was unable to let out.

The sound of laughter broke off and turned into manic screams, broken by the whistle of a large arrow, which landed abruptly in front of them. Somendel heard the thud of the arrow as though it had hit him in the head. *They are here!* Turning back to face the small and disobedient squad, he raised his hand, now pointed in the direction of Bendim, and somehow lifted the big man to his feet with an unseen force. He spoke loudly and clearly. 'Go out there and follow the flight path of that arrow. If another one hits you, I will know from where it came. If you do not go out there … well, you'd better not find out, hadn't you?'

The big man looked up and winced at the dark mage; he

knew he was in a hard place to bargain but would, in the end, comply. *Time … time I may still have, you horrible looking cretin.* 'Aye, boss, give me a moment I must—'

'Get the fuck out there now, you imbecile!'

The pecbor pulled its arms over its body in an arc, toward the planted arrow; the hold still had a connection to move Bendim who in turn arced over the brush like a cantankerous child throwing its dolly out of a pram.

Landing inches from the still shaking arrow, Bendim raised himself up gingerly, hiding behind the small margin of girth the shaft of the arrow offered him – the slimmest of defences to whatever was out there.

\*

Gurengal put a hand on the archer's shoulder immediately after the bowstring had been let loose. 'Just one more should be enough to draw them from their advantage and out into the open. Put it a bit further in this time, see if that teases them out.' He looked to where the archer had aimed and judged the distance it had flown to be at least five hundred yards, but no more than six.

A sudden change about the air hit him, floating on that same stream – *Screams, children are in there.* 'Halt!' He quickly grabbed the shaft of the bowed timber and pulled to loosen the taut string. 'Children! Engo, Jemal, get in there now. Full haste! Go!'

Attributed with sustained speed over long distances, they raced toward the tree line and disappeared into the growth just as quick.

It didn't take long for them to reappear, others in tow. The children had obviously not been far from where the initial strike had landed, hence the urgency of their flight.

'Shit!' Relief hit Gurengal like a horse-cart full of manure. He had no idea the children were in there; they must had been cavorting about in the woods like children do just before they arrived in the street. He saw five small figures appear from the tree line followed by the two rangers.

'Shit! How many were in there?' Quickly he ran to the scattering of children and aimed for who he thought would be the eldest, and most able to communicate.

'Child, are you all out safe?' Nothing. *Shit.* 'Child, what is your name?' Still nothing. *Fuck! Did Netiba impale one of their friends. Does that animal have more of them? Fuck!* To Gurengal's relief the child eventually nodded.

Slowly they made their way back down the street toward the inn, looking to find a haven for the distraught young ones in one of the large houses to either side of the main street. Not long after, he caught that strange feeling of unease. Sure enough, as he turned to look back toward the woods, a hawking figure stood where he trained his eye.

It raised its arms and slowly started to walk towards them. When it was halfway between them and the opening, it lay flat on its stomach.

Gurengal motioned Netiba to aim the bow, then he turned to motion the two rangers to approach the now prone figure which had casually elected to lie face down in the dirt.

The man looked at him directly and smiled. Gurengal could see the toothy grin was meant for him and it most likely included parlay. 'Halt, you two. Keep that bow trained on that scumbag, Netiba. I am going to have a quick chat with him.' Netiba eyed him warily, but Gurengal patted a forearm – a forearm containing more than just a small shiv.

As he approached the smiling lump of a man, it spoke. 'He's in there, you know. Get me away from him and I can give you all the information you could ever need. Or coin, if that's your thing?'

'Who? Who's in there? And what could a shitbag like you give me? I am not a man for the coin … well I am, but not for bargaining the life of scum like yourself. Ahh, now I recognise that shitty face of yours, seen it plastered on all the towns notice boards wherever we have been recently.'

Ignoring the jibes, the man lying on the floor went on. 'My supposed master, he is the one in there, he is no ordinary kind, but he be one of 'em. He does things, has things, can do things … is evil is he.'

'You are selling a great bargain here aren't you, nothing for shit. What is it you want? Or more importantly, why should I care?'

'He has a … how should I put it gently? Yes, he has a *thing* for you. You really throbbed his nodes. Very romantic, hey?!' the big man chuckled grotesquely.

Gurengal crouched low, hands rested on his thighs, and steadied himself. He then grabbed the man's hair. 'Times up. Why give yourself up? What are you? Some sort of decoy?'

Bendim laughed. 'No. No, I have been exploiting their bullshit for many years, didn't know they were properly involved to begin with. Been offering false prayers to …' He looked about. '*Her Lady.*' Not bothered by the rough hand grabbing his hair, Bendim looked up as he uttered the word, expecting some sort of strike from the heavens, but realised where he was looking, then corrected his vision to the floor below, waiting for the ground to strike from beneath him. Nothing came.

Gurengal had heard enough. He slammed the man's head roughly into the dirt. 'Tell me what I need to know. Now, and quickly. If we make it back out of those woods from the help you are about to offer, you may live to see the sun after the longest of nights. Not before we have decided what to do with your sorry guts in the morning. It seems that is the best option. And for you, the longest option to remain alive at this point, or am I mistaken?'

Nose bloodied, Bendim nodded and smiled with a red, toothy grin. 'I do be in agreeance with the offered opinion.'

He spat blood to the street below, just missing Gurengal's well-worn brown leather boots. He began to rise, lifting himself up on to his knees, once the large span of a hard hand had released its grip of his greasy hair. Swaying slightly as he leant back, he began to laugh loudly. A burst of cascading laughter that became louder and louder with every breath. 'That nobble-headed bloke in there says he wants you as his pet.' Turning his head, he coughed to spatter blood over the pavement, and continued. 'Why's that?'

'Your guess is as good as mine,' Gurengal resumed his inquisitive crouch. 'What is your name, grub?'

Again, a burst of wheezing laughter escaped the big man's mouth. 'Name's Joe, yours?'
Gurengal steadied himself for a moment longer, then smacked the big man's flopping cheeks. 'Liar. Name … now!'

'Alright! Jeez, man! That was some swipe. Can't feel me darn face.' Rubbing his jaw, he eyed the man crouching in front of him. He could see he was losing patience. But he knew the longer he delayed, if these men could not fight off the grey man in the woods, he could use the excuse he was delaying them. *Delaying them for what?* he thought. He was the bait. What advantage in delay was there? *Suppose I never thought that through.* Just as he was to answer the man, someone else beat him to it.

'Bendim!'

A crackling echo reverberated through the wide street, emanating from the opening in the wood. Stood there, flanked by two larger feminine figures, stood a cloaked figure.

'Traitor! Your life has just ended. I will finally get to relish the chance to take your head!'

'Oh fuck,' mumbled Bendim.

Grabbing Gurengal with both hands, he pleaded, 'Take

me away from here, take me to your wards in the inn. I know things most folk don't know. I can be of service, believe me!'

Gurengal looked at the fool, almost with pity in his eyes, as he rose back above him. He shoved him aside, then walked purposely toward the three new figures that were making their approach onto the street. 'Take that oaf with you back to the tavern. Jurengor! With me.' Netiba was about to protest but was silenced by Gurengal's piercing blue eyes. 'Only Jurengor, rest of you back to the inn, get behind those wards quickly. This one will be a bit of a tough one. Been expecting him though, but not so soon!' Netiba hurried the rest of the crew and the children back toward the inn, but not before he glanced back toward the three standing at the end of the street.

*Only three of them?* thought Gurengal.

Bertino looked across the space between, over to Lento. Was it such a surprise they'd both been snagged? Together? The memories of the previous night had slowly dripped back into his head – *such arrogance.* The two girls who had attracted all the attention of the room made a beeline for the two; the easiest of prey, so distracted from their own nuances to that of the opposite sex which addled them every time. This time was different though, it was early in the evening. There was no beguilement or the perplexity of consumed, over the counter, intoxicating liquid, nor the sweet escape from reality by way of the *Narcodias'* inebriating, exorbitant substances. Or so it would seem.

A haze was starting to lift from their minds, and with it came a sense of guilt which outweighed the dread of what they were currently facing. A predicament which could have been so easily avoided had the crew not been so resolute in attending another meaningless night down in the tapping rooms of the inn, away from the upper room from which

Gurengal had strained himself, almost to breaking point, to protect from those who would now want to break them into pieces.

As the cloud of confuddle lifted, so too did the chained memories of the events leading to their eventual immuration. The two women who just departed the clearing with the cloaked figure, they were their captors. Even though it seemed they possessed immense beauty, it was now clear that they were not anything of the sort. Replaying the first moment they entered the inn in his mind, Bertino saw what was masked beneath their inebriating presence: *Scottles!* A race of she-demons, from south of The Divide, who preyed on the vulnerability of vain and often wealthy men. Though not demons as such, they may well have been, for they possessed the same lust for indulged carnage.

*Shit!* 'Lenny!' shouted Bertino. 'Lenny … you awake?'

'Yes … yes, Benny, have been the whole time!' grumbled Lento. 'We are in deep shit, huh …'

'Yes. Yes we are, Lenny. Do you remember them two girls?'

'Aye. Not girls though, hey?'

'Nope …'

'Scottles?'

'Uhuh …'

'What we gonna do?' asked Lento with little amount of hope in his voice.

A sigh of resignation preceded the response from Bertino. 'Not much we can do, just wait … see what Guren—'

He was cut off by a loud shout, one that penetrating through the woodland from the direction of the town.

'Looks like we will find out sooner rather than later, brother …'

'Maybe …' Lentino peered out the side of the makeshift cage, down to the one who remained below. 'Who is that?'

Bertino shot an eye below. 'Still down there?' He asked the question not expecting any sort of result.

The small figure spoke, loud and concise given the distance between them, an obvious amplification through some magical means. 'I am to be your saviour. I will guide you out of here. *But* … I ask one thing in return …'

The brothers eyed each other warily, obviously still stinging from their previous night's escapades and its culmination of ending up in a cage, high above the woodland floor below, seduced by otherworldly charms of horned she-devils. The adherence to beautiful women was one thing, the fellow below, offering to pull them down and lead them out to safety was surely on par therewith.

It was Bertino who responded, 'Who are you? And are you not with them there monsters who just casually ambled past you and told you to keep us up here to remain as bait?'

'Oh, you heard that, hey?' A hint of humour was left trailing.

'Yeah, and we know who you're with, you dirty little bastard!' Lento spat from the cage just missing the unaware fellow below.

'Why don't you go and follow your little horny, horned bitches out of here before we come down there and slap your face in! You little fucker!'

The target of their verbal barrage only glared up at them. 'You're both fools. Can't see what's right in front of your dicks,' he said, pointing a finger, one on each hand, at each of them.

A blast of crackling wires shook them both into semi paralysis.

Lento and Bertino were still quivering when the figure leapt up from the ground below and clung to Lento's cage. It looked inside and breathed a small enchantment, soothing Lento. Then it leapt to the other cage and did the same. Both were now dazed, and not shaking violently anymore.

Lento looked into its green eyes. They seemed to be glowing, and constantly shifting as though expecting a strike from wherever. 'Who? No … what are you?'

'As I have advised you already, I am your liberator …'

Bertino looked at Lento and shrugged. Seemingly over the whole ordeal, they would be better off on the ground and out of these makeshift bait cages though.

Gurengal had not been blind to the townsfolk re-shuttering their doors and windows – those already opened for the day. It was early still and not many folk about. But with the brightening day, they were all surely eager to get out into the street to prepare for the upcoming Festival. *I wonder how they will celebrate it here. If I sort this shite out, I may indulge this evening.* Shaking his head, he looked back to where his attention should be trained – toward the now advancing dark mage! *Shite, only one night. This one must be keen to settle something!*

He motioned Jurengor to begin the advance to meet those on their own approach. The man in the middle of the trio was circling his hands, creating some sort of magic projectile he guessed. Gurengal was also whispering something to counter whatever was thrown at him from the spinning arms of the pecbor. He was sure a confrontation would arise from the botched attempt with the orcindall. He also knew what, and from where, the force had originated from beyond where he was spied upon, being watched through the canopy of branches the previous day. He expected the dark mage to at least mass a considerable force before coming to attempt any secondary ambush.

But no, it seemed this one had other ideas. For he had walked back to the exact spot from where he had been watched – after taking the claw as bounty – and, once he had seen the small, cloaked figure skulk away back to its hidey hole, he had sensed the darkness within the air; the air had felt heavy and damp, full of a rank sensation of evilness which could only be emanating from one foul source, one he had sensed many times – that reek of a higher stationed Syltenerian.

Then it came, much more powerful than he'd anticipated. The blast put him on his arse quite a way back from where he had been struck, no chance to avoid and get his counter away it was that quick. Jurengor, however, had remained steady in his pacing toward the pecbor.

Rising back to his feet, he began a quick enchantment to block any salvo toward Jurengor who was now the most advanced of the two; his judgement was once again misplaced. As he threw the cloak of debuff around Jurengor, a second slap of energy hit him, a boomerang of energy from the first blast surging through him on its way back to its caster, striking the fallen Gurengal once again.

*Different.* He looked on as Jurengor halved the distance between the two parties. The rage on the big man's mind would hopefully not cloud his judgement. Jurengor was met halfway through the same space by the two enchantresses that confuddled the entire inn the night before, still cloaked with a mask of splendour. Jurengor did not care for such female conditioning, nor what was offered by such beauty They were not his type; he had no type or preference, hence Gurengal's instruction to include him for this street fight! For that reason they would not sway the big man's groin.

All became apparent to them as they failed to release the maniacal twist to his face with their seductive intention, and it brought not a small amount of shock to the two she-devils as he swung his half mace, half axe, toward the closest skull of the two as the pecbor remained static, holding still some charge about his wrist behind them.

The head of Esmirel was split in two from the force of the axe, the very same which was now swinging towards the horrified, wrought face of Damragella who had now shrieked away from the attack at the sight of the upper part of her sister's head spinning up through a spraying fountain of blue luminous liquid, high into the air. The shying away had saved her own life though, for Jurengor had assumed the flight path of both women would not falter. He missed the scalp but took a few drifting hairs along with his handle. As the handle pulled through Damragella's hair, it dragged her sideways with its swing.

She followed with the unintended arc and spun around the hulking man to climb onto his back, hair still stuck to his weapon. Jurengor swung the weapon around, bringing the scottle back over his head. She sprawled across the ground after a large clump of hair was ripped from her head. She crouched up and hissed violently back at Jurengor.

Before he was able to swing again at her, he was struck with a blast of air from where the cloaked man stood. The pressure barrelled into the scottle he had tried to take a swipe at and took her into his midriff; he could feel one of the hidden horns dig into his thigh, just above the knee. Jurengor screeched loudly and rolled away, blood flowing freely down his thick tree trunk of a limb.

The women had now lost their abilities – run out of magical capability, assuming the flair of their appearance would be enough to dazzle their enemies into submission. But now she sat on the floor in the middle of the street and in full view of the town. Those that had braved a peek of what was transpiring in their normally sullen town banged whatever shutters had not been shuttered at the sight of what was sat there – the very same beings written about in multiple texts archived in the town church.

"*A real scottle!*" they must have exclaimed prior to an ensuing prayer to whatever deity they held true.

Getting back to its feet, it made a mad dash toward Jurengor, screaming its sister's name as it lashed out with sharp dagger-length fingernails that glinted, akin to steel, as they reflected the barest cast of sunlight, catching him multiple times around a barrel like chest

Jurengor managed to grab back hold of his mace, and once again tried to swing at the manic being slashing away at him. The sharp claws felt like ice as they sliced through his leather tabard. He was foiled, once again, when another blast from the cloaked figure hit him.

He sat up quickly from where he landed, only to duck back down just as quickly as he remembered Gurengal's most recent plight. He glanced over at Gurengal, who was slowly muttering something, hopefully a counter spell of his own. *Okay, boss, I will gain you a few more moments to finish whatever you're doing.* He shook his senses clear, then made a straight, albeit hobbled, scuttle for the dark mage who had another charged spell ready to project, to fire it once again toward Gurengal. A sudden whistling sound shot past his left ear as an arrow struck close to the grey figure, but did no damage as it fell harmlessly to the floor from an unseen shield. That moment of consideration the pecbor had given the projectile gave Jurengor the slimmest opportunity to close the gap. And no sooner had another arrow whistled past, he decided to follow its path and leapt with his good leg the remaining distance to the cloaked figure, barrelling them both to the cobbles below, raising up a cloud of dust all about them.

Gurengal had been chanting a spell of static crackle to null the magical ability in the street – he himself would be included – to eventually settle this day with a good old fist fight. He would also like to have a chat with the bastard in the hooded cloak. So he had to restrain himself and not dissipate the thing to pulp with his fists.

A second arrow flew at the cloaked figure. Again nothing doing until Jurengor smashed into the cloaked figure hard, knocking them both down to slide a good way back down the street. The scottle was now heading in the same direction, a piercing wail carried with it.

Raising a hand high into the air, he twisted his wrist and released the energy that simmered around his immediate aura. A blaze of bright purple crackle left his raised hand and mushroomed out around the whole street forming a small dome that encompassed all within the radius of the beginning of the woods and back to the tavern.

Netiba raced over to him, bow drawn, then released the string, firing another long and heavy arrow at the scottle, hitting it dead centre in the middle of its back. It rolled forward and howled a noise as it fell flat on its taut skinned face, only steps away from where its sibling's head had come to rest – staring back at her with blank sockets that once each contained an eyeball, the very same that now gazed up at the sky from where they lay between the top and bottom of her skull.

Gurengal watched as Netiba raced on past as the struggle continued further down the street.

Even though the figure was small in stature, he assumed Jurengor could see the nodes now quite clearly – he knew this race was quite wiry, canny, and stronger than they looked. The mace at such close range was useless and trying to get the small dagger out of his sleeve was complicated by the fact he was stopping the grey man from doing the same.

*

Jurengor had seen the crackling light emanate around them as they were struggling. *Lucky. Would probably be a toad by now*, he assumed as the advantage seemed to be swinging to the small man as he gained the upper hand and crawled onto his back as he lay face down, the wiry thing holding an arm behind his back. He heard, before he felt, a cracking in his arm. *Little bastard is strong!* But as that thought left his mind, he felt the weight lift off him. Toward the tree line at the end of the street, he could make out two small glowing green orbs. He surmised correctly they belonged to another small creature. *Backup! More of em! Shit!* he thought incorrectly.

Lento and Bertino both hurried their pace, glad to stretch their legs, keeping up with the strange, small figure that seemed to float as it ran across the brush. When they reached the end of the narrow man-made thoroughfare that opened out of the woods to the town's main street, they skidded to a halt as the figure stopped a short way beyond the opening. Lento looked at Bertino and shrugged.

They both beheld the carnage all about the street. A crackling energy charged through the air as Gurengal pointed toward the sky. Jurengor lay on his stomach, grappling with the newcomer from the woods this morning, and – what they could only assume – the scottle that had befriended them the night before, tearing toward the scuffling pair. The very same monster from the woods was being chased by Netibo. Netibo loosed an arrow to despatch the first danger, then readied another as the pecbor wriggled free and raced toward them.

They both jumped for cover. Should the arrow miss its intended mark – which was unlikely – they were in the direct line of its trajectory.

The strange being settled itself back between them and began to hover, legs crossed. It spoke in some unknown tongue, but swore the local lingo when nothing happened as it raised a hand toward the pair scuffling around on the floor.

'Yeah, buddy. That sparkle in the sky there. Seen it before, a few times: magic blocker or summat like that! Don't know how you're still hovering though?'

The creature turned its head and spoke. 'Would seem I'm out of that barrier's reach, that horrible thing though . . . is not. You might want to make a move before he escapes that barrier. I think he saw me floating here and realised where the encasement's perimeter could be. Quick, go! Go and get him!'

Both ran toward the now escaping pecbor, its little legs moved as a blur followed now by the limping Jurengor. Netiba must have seen them both and had decided not to let loose one of those thunder bolts as it was still cocked and followed the pecbor. The little man turned away at an angle and decided to run behind the last dwelling of the street. But as soon as he was away from the line of sight of the two, Netiba let loose once more. The pecbor had enough sense to keep on running, albeit its little legs were moving not as fast with a large feather bobbing up and down protruding from one its arse cheeks and the point pivoting, in opposite tandem, through its thigh.

Gurengal waved at them both to keep up the chase as he followed behind, walking slowly in the direction they were all heading with his arm still in the air. Moving with him, the perimeter of his barrier's magical radius in line wherever moved.

The green-eyed fellow dropped to its feet and began to follow them, but, as it touched the unseen barrier it hissed and backed away. 'I must remain here, you two go on. When you are done with him, I must relinquish its life force to never again touch this or the next. It has done much harm to my kind and those who would call our habitat home, and no doubt much more damage beyond our borders.'

As they closed in on the now scampering pecbor, a sudden jolt shook the ground. It knocked Gurengal to his feet and he faltered. He tried but failed to reignite the sky full of crackle before a red hue enveloped the entire town.

On the horizon, the sun had begun to appear over the trees as a crescent due to the incursion of the red orb of

Kinora.

*Shit! The Festival was not due to be in fruition till this midday!* The shock of the horizon shook him more than the rumble of the stones below. He regained his composure, and stood. All he could see was Jurengor and the two he was sure were gone forever and a confused Netiba looking around as though lost in a dense misting fog. The small grey man had disappeared into thin air, using the moment of confusion to his advantage.

As they all stood around milling for any sign of the creature, they heard a commotion somewhere from the bottom of the street. All raced down the street then turned to follow from where the sounds of scuffle had emanated from.

They bowled each other over as Netiba stopped suddenly.

'What?!' exclaimed Netiba.

'Well, that was most unexpected. Seems we may have found a new friend.' Gurengal rubbed at his chin, suppressing his grin from widening.

He crouched down after they had made their way down the road that skirted the tree line, to see Lentino and Bertino sat atop the pecbor, keeping him compressed as a small figure stood next to them speaking in some unknown tongue as the pecbor hissed at all three of those around him.

Gurengal grabbed one of the nodes atop the pecbor's head. Feeling the vibrating hum, he mouthed a small enchantment, and it throbbed even harder. 'What's your name, you repugnant little shit?'

The pecbor spat at him through the slimmest of slits between its lips.

'*Its* name is Somendel,' the small fellow with the green eyes offered.

'Ah. One of the gracious *ectoritor*, I am honoured by your presence.' Gurengal bowed graciously then kissed a clenched fist and offered it for him to touch.

'You know of us?' The ectoritor did the same and touched a fist to Gurengal's.

'Yes, I know your kind very well. I believe you will be wanting to take this … this thing with you?'

'Yes indeed, we need to interrogate him to discover where and what he has done with more than a few of my own, and many of the mighty creatures that should, rightfully, inhabit The Divide.'

'Hmm, you are in real shit now. Somendel, was it? But before I leave, why? Why so soon?'

Again, the pecbor spat. 'You will soon feel the wrath of Our Lady, I am but a pawn for her to do with as she pleases—'

A whack to the pecbor's head with a meaty clenched fist cut the words short. 'Answer. The. Fucking. Question!'

Spitting what could have only be described as blood, Somendel continued. 'You would have been a perfect addition to my gratuitously decorated wonderland. We will meet again, you and I. But you answer me this, who are you and how did you know?'

'Know what?'

'I was there?' The pecbor shook his head.

'Just an inkling …'

'And that I would come here!'

'Hmm, very well. I sent those boys down in the bar last night.'

Jurengor, who was the only one present who was in that bar last night, bar Lentino and Bertino, looked incredulously at him. 'Now, now boys. I could have extended those wards beyond the inn if needed. I needed them to think they had the upper hand if they came sooner than I thought.

'Your imbecilic crew thought they would have some fun with my boys. But did they actually try to harm them, or did they just use them as bait? Instructed or no?'

'Damned fools. You spread the word you were leaving town on this morn? And they quit waiting for me. I told them to wait … idiots!' Somendel looked up the street. 'Speaking of idiots, wait … where is that bloke who submitted himself for succour?'

*Shit!* Gurengal slapped the pecbor with a big right palm once more.

He looked to the ancient one. 'He is yours now. Do with him as deemed necessary. You know the prophecy as well as I, ancient one. There is a war coming, look at the sky, this is no time for festivities. But tell me, what is your name?'

'Jasquirea …' he said in a melodic accent.

'Well, friend, may I ask why you are here. At this moment?'

'This traitor from the south of The Divide had been marked. One of our drifters had spotted him trapping a golden orik. I was issued a command to infiltrate. That is all you need to know. If you wish to know more one day you will be much welcomed.' Jasquirea bowed to Gurengal. 'You know how to find us … I presume?'

'Aye, your presumption is correct. Now, this oaf we picked up before, is he dangerous?'

'Yes, he is very dangerous in the wrong hands. But only to himself it would seem … look.' The green-eyed creature pointed back down the street. The two rangers dragging him back toward the inn, he was unconscious, head hanging to the side and feet dragging along the bumpy cobbles that lined street.

'He knows much, do not waste that life so soon, he has plenty to offer, much more than he realises …' The small Jasquirea pondered something for a while, twitching his head as if it involved an internal conversation before speaking again. 'I will take him, in this *thing's* stead. I will drain the memories of this foul creature to gain the knowledge I need. But, let me take him.' He pointed to the now unconscious Bendim. He may be more useful to me than you realise.

'Are you sure, ancient one? His demise would surely be a welcome relief to your kin. '

Jasquirea nodded understanding, but shook his head as he pointed up at Bendim.

Bowing deeply, Gurengal spoke softly. 'Very well ancient one: *Am i entumira su loma.*' – "May all in this world be as one" – 'He'll be yours, but later, I have my own questions to ask of him first.'

*'Um e sendaria su toma. Em undari, po lecoli,*' – "Our world is always, as one." 'We need to unite all that would call this world home.' Jasquirea pulled out a small dagger, the hilt more solid than the blade that shimmered slightly, and nodded at Gurengal. He nodded back, knowing what was to come.

The blade sliced smoothly across the throat of Somendel as foul soul energy leached out, much brighter than the eyes had portrayed. The pecbor did not succumb though to the afterlife, for the blade was not crafted with physical material but was a blade of something more of the ethereal. He threw Somendel back with a rough kick to Gurengal. 'Here, take him. See he serves a justice befitting. We have no more need of him. I know now exactly the location of his sordid playground.'

The Syltenerian high pawn slumped forward, to still take mortal breath, the only kind he would now ever know.

'I will wait here until you're done.'

∗

Later, away from the fray of battle, back behind the wards of the inn which now extended to include the tap rooms below from which they *all* supped, Gurengal took a long, sustained gulp and placed his tankard on the large table as he sighed. It was a sigh he offered through a smile. 'Told you bastards he would come soon. He wanted me for himself it seemed. He must have a zoo full of magical beings! Size of Vilenzia, it would seem … And I told you I would need you all to play ball for whatever was coming.

'And you unknowingly did. I just didn't know those she-demons from the South would be in tow …'

'So, you didn't know? We could have been killed or, worse, mauled at the groin by one of those … one of them *scottle* bitches!'

'Not a bad way to die, Bertino. Could think of worse ways to go … like having my head ripped into two, hey Jurengor?' Gurengal began to laugh as he replayed the earlier scene, as half a scottle skull flew through the air. A laughter followed by all who had gathered.

The big bloke in the corner, though chained, let out an audible chuckle, albeit a quiet one, obviously finding some humour in the crudest of circumstances – no matter his own.

Bendim knew his demise was now far from where he'd earlier assumed it would be as it *should* have occurred today from one of many hands! And it gave him a smirk of confidence. It had not happened though, and he was glad for it. He looked at the man dropping jugs now quicker than wenches' breaches on a victorious battle party homecoming. *He may well be just as evil as that prick Somendel. Maybe …*

No sooner had Bendim's thoughts ended had Gurengal thrust himself at the man in the corner. 'You maggot, you think you know what this is all about? Stop it, for fuck's sake! See the world for what it is and not for your own benefit of coin! You have no idea! A war is coming. And you do not matter to anyone save your failed parents!'

'Very harsh. Still … bullshit, my father left my mum the night he would've paid a few grets for her time!'

'And there! There it is! A hate for the world … The world owes you, doesn't it? Why? Because you feel some scorn for one piece of shit who was, as it seems, exactly like you? Did you know my father did the same? He left my mother to bleed out upon her death bed, the same bed I was deposited onto at birth, mages and Medicas did not prevail in preventing her death. Where was my father? He was there, hiding behind the cloak of invisibility, he could have saved her, but the bigger bastard picture got in the fucker's way—'

A big hand touched his shoulder. 'Izzy big min, izzy.' Jurengor had limped over, seeing that Gurengal was ready to rip the waste of spew's head off. 'Till im why, biss.'

'No, he doesn't deserve to know. Get this piece of shit upstairs and locked away, for the Festival be gaining traction soon. No one needs to see this piece of shit; they've seen enough for truth.'

Jurengor looked at Gurengal. 'Rid sky, Biss?'

'Yes, Jurengor. I noticed. Just get him out of here will you.' He looked at Jurengor, and nodded too his concern that the sky should resemble a crimson tide, nor should had it begin to darken for a few hours yet, the beginning of The Festival was a few hours away yet. 'Has anyone tended to your leg wound yet? Or those nasty looking slices I can see through your leathers?'

'Nit yit biss … I allrit.'

'Mate, do you know what those bitches drink? could be any number of toxins running through your body, no matter how small the wound, they are not a—'

'Biss, I fill fine.'

'Ok, well, just keep an eye on them wounds, the leg one looks deep too. Just do it for me, Jurengor. And will you drop that sack of shit on the outskirts of town before late? He's off on a journey of his lifetime, it would seem!' *Wonder what that is all about.*

Gurengal nodded to Bendim only to receive a snigger as affirmation.

# A Return Home

A large crowd milled underneath and spread out beyond a grand portal of intricately carved, arched stonework. The Great Music Hall was situated a short walk away from the gated archway, not far from the port of Sinboran. They were there to see, or rather listen to, and be entertained by, the well renowned singer, and his equally gifted companions from *Dalmetonia* – one of the other greater regions of Inarrel, from across The Great Green Divide.

They had drifted into the main jetty of Sinboran aboard a large vessel – the *Ethereal Dancer* – one commissioned by the *Overarch* of *Heloniko*, the capital of *Dalmetonia*. The vessel consisted of three large central masts supported by four smaller masts either side and two between – the massive ship could easily contain within its hull all those that had attended the Feast of the Night at the Great Hall – a side gig to the Festival, usually reserved for those who had enough coin to purchase such a rare ticket. The punters had come from all across Vilenzia and beyond to see this show, for rumours swirled it would be their last in Sinboran for many years.

As Velosko disembarked, he made his way along the jetty, flanked on either side with decorated vessels that bobbed following the wake of the other ships making their way to their designated pontoon. Most had personal guards still aboard or at the gangway that touched the jetty, to ward off any of the street urchins. Others were still being tied to the dock, their patrons not yet prettied up for the feast of music and the other delights the extra-long night would bring. He stopped for a moment to inhale the unique air of Vilenzia – it always had a familiar feel, though if never the same.

Either side of the tall and predominantly grey-haired

singer – noticeably slim for a profession addled with forever offerings of the finest of indulgences – walked his two most trusted friends, whom he had known for many years since the beginning of his attendance at the University at Heloniko, many a year ago.

Marcos, to his right, was a handsome and gentle faced figure with small, folded-in ears that accompanied an upturned but petite nose. His skin seemed to absorb the light due to his pasty, matte peach complexion. He stood taller than Velosko by a short margin. What was most remarkable was that only three nimble digits protruded from either hand. He had absconded from the sparsely populated eastern and middle region of Dalmetonia, and had been found playing with a heavily bandaged, and most likely stolen, cello on the streets surrounding the university where Velosko had studied. He had been brought in by one of the chancellors of the arts, who he had mesmerised plucking away at the strings of that makeshift cello with a most complex musical sonnet of "The Silent Dance". The chancellor had noticed his hands and thought it impossible to strum such a harmony – a harmony that required, at the very least, two accomplished cellists to strum concurrently in absolute harmony. Even though he lived on the street, he had retained all his charm and natural grace that belied the fact he had had to scrounge every coin to keep himself nourished, if lightly.

He was an *apolit*. Had he been born as humankind, he would have been the most beautiful being in all of Inarrel, just as any of his race. Even though he was an *apolit*, he would still attract the absolute attention of every patron he would ever meet. They would be in awe of his striking facial structure and flowing locks that swayed like his music when not tied up so. The ears, nose, and hands did not seem to deter folk; that he was the most accomplished cellist on Inarrel only aided that focus. When he played, his music seemed to magnify the resonance of his soul and would have crowds swooning, weeping, and silently praying to whatever god they so desired. Rumours, which most believed to be true, told that if he ever looked at you directly, during one of his pieces – which was a very, very rare occurrence – he would have you sitting as though looking through a window into the very paradise you so desired.

On Velosko's left, strutted the woman, his own paradise, who would often beg him to stop this madness and settle down somewhere far beyond the reaches of all monarchies, slimy benefactors, and those who preyed on her husband's generosity and good nature – she the very source of all such rumours of retirement ... folk talked and addled the speculation with emancipated gossip.

She had been there, beside him, since the very first day he had endured an unwarranted onslaught, caught in the *tunnel of initiation;* a harsh, and very much malevolent welcome to the university for the freshly enrolled younger residents.

She remembered the events prior and post ... all too often.

Those forming the tunnel were the most likely to fail the rigorous tutelage at the prestigious university.

She remembered immediately seeing a young man crawling on his hands and knees, dressed in what she would later discover were his best clothes: smart jacket, trousers, and, his most prized possession, the extensively polished brown shoes handed to him from his father before he had journeyed far across the ocean; the last gift he would ever receive from his father "What says that of a man, for but a view to the world they have tread, then even to where they wished to".

Above him, hands from either side formed a tunnel for him to navigate his way through, it snaked throughout the middle courtyard and seemed to consist of the full cohort of the upper years, for she had never seen it so long in the three years prior. All would have been well but for the fact that the older boys were kicking dust from the gravelly ground. He expected such, but as he ventured further through the cascading tunnel, the boys who had seen early on that their kicking of dust had not damaged the boy's spirit – the majority oblivious to the boy's plight – re-joined the end of the snaking column as they were permitted to inflict further punishment, thus to add some gratification to satisfy their own fulfilment of the evening's proceedings. She remembered giggling at first, the poor boy clambering between the brigade of legs of the  human tunnel. The other boys had made it through and were patted and padded down by their elder peers as they coughed, spluttered their discontent, and found that their disorientation seemed to give the elders the satisfaction they sought to end the trial after only one or two rotations.

Velosko's initiation, however, was only just beginning after the second rotation. With a keen sense the surrounding sound and movement, he raced through the first and second, then the third rotation without a bump of the knee or a hook to the ribs, nor strike to the chin from the pointed black leather shoes of the elders. It wasn't until the snake had circumnavigated the courtyard fully that things started to get messy … and not the slightest bit ugly.

With barely a scratch on his soft, pale face, nor the merest of a wheeze offered from the kicks aimed to the middle, the tunnel closed in, and made sure there was a connection for every blow they now swung his way. This was not enough for some for those that could manage and those with enough reach – luckily for Velosko not many of them could reach him – unbuttoned their trousers and began to urinate on the boy as he passed by them.

A heightened sense of smell was not needed as the warmth of the fluid could not be mistaken, bouncing off his back and the back of his head before the stale aroma eventually penetrated sensitive nostrils.

To be fair on the boys that began the initiation, a few of the elders had backed away and decided enough was enough and did not want any part of what was now being dealt out to the young man clambering about on his hands and knees, and then his stomach, all before the retching began.

Amaria, who had joined in moments earlier with the giggling and cheering, began to see the charade for what it truly was. She was shocked into nausea that she had cheered, even promoted such filth. Almost vomiting herself, she had had enough. She ran to the boy now weeping silently flat on the ground, pushing past the boys who had circled around the graduate. A few fell backward from the force of her barging like skittles, only to end up with soaked breeches themselves. This brought a cheer from almost all of those in attendance. A couple of them, tempers flaring, began to start at her but a fiery outburst and kick stayed them as they fell back down, bringing another cheer from the crowd. She knew the boy would never forgive her for the embarrassment he would face during the following years, but she did not care. Pushing the remainder of the boys away, she grabbed the now whimpering boy by the arm, up onto his knees, not bothered by the stench now rising from the grey jacket and now slick hair. She knelt in front of him and grabbed his hands. She held both in hers and held back a breath upon the touch of his palms. So soft ... soft as a silk purse.

It was then she realised what the other boys had not. Before she was able to speak, he smiled at her and spoke, ever so softly, casually, as if no bother had befallen upon him. 'Ah, joy ... is it over?'

The soft rumble of his voice crept deep down inside her and brought with it a euphoria that had her skin bubbling with gooseflesh. She inhaled, a little too sharply, and was unable to speak.

'Who? Who is holding my hands? Such warmth,' he spoke again, bringing a shudder through her body which he felt from the shaking of her small fingers. 'I do recall an angelic laughter from earlier, pray it be my saviour.' The boy smiled with no ill, nor malice, just an air of hope which shot around his blank eyes.

She blushed, and was able to compose herself enough to at least croak out a name. 'Amaria. And maybe I was laughing a little before, but my laugh was far from such a want.' She laughed a little but held it before Velosko smiled even harder at her. She blushed deeper; she was sure she escaped such resonance with his disability. 'Why put up with that stupid charade for so long?' She helped him to his feet and walked him away from the staring crowd, over to the shelter of a large elm. 'So, you're the one the prefect was talking about.'

'Whatever do you mean?' he said, blushing a little himself at the attention.

'The boy who cannot see but has the ability to see beyond that which cannot be seen.'

'Did he use those words? Well, he flatters me. I have never been able to see, Amaria. Though I feel almost all, I used to want to see, wished so hard for it, but what would I be if I could? Normal? I'm not sure I would want to be any different than what I am today.'

'What, stinking like that? In that dusty old suit?' she let out a shy giggle.

Velosko had let the slight of his attire slide. 'No ... no. The absolute joy of being able to feel a heart flutter, like the fastest flutterby's wing. Or hear the sweetest melody hidden inside such a voice, such you could never know of ... when you speak.'

Amaria fell back a full step, then pulled him fast out of the courtyard. Away from everyone and anyone who'd dare torment him again.

Now, Amaria absently clenched a hand around her flute, only to squeeze fingers into her own palm. She usually carried it with her, though had been persuaded to leave it, along with her other stringed instruments, with the muscle that followed along in the entourage behind. "You never know who is lurking around here. Better to leave it with the group of minders," Velosko had said to her. And no one would be foolhardy enough to approach that bunch. The flute had been a gift, offered immediately following her acceptance of her and Velosk'os forever vows. Velosko had, painstakingly, crafted the instrument himself, hellbent on making sure every note when played by her would be beyond the purest sound ever heard from any other instrument of the same kind. She treasured it above anything else – anything other than Velosko and Marcos.

They made their way to the edge of the wooden jetty and, as they stepped on to the large stone slabs laid in a herringbone fashion to form the beginning of the street, the one that would lead them to where they needed to be, Amaria noticed Velosko halt for a second. He turned with a big smile to face them both.

'You alright there, Vel ?' she asked.

'Ahh … yes. It was a long voyage. Smooth most of the way, but I still feel the motion of the waves moving me to and fro. It feels wonderful and sickening all at the same time.' Velosko spoke gently, calmly. Amaria would describe his voice – as many times he had hers – as angelic.

'Well make sure those waves stay down, my dear. We wouldn't want to have that lot behind us making a fuss over the mess you created, nor those queuing up ahead at the Great Hall.' She nodded ahead toward the milling crowd. 'I think, though, they have spotted us. Hopefully, they have the sense this time to not act like complete idiots and cause some havoc before we are ready!'

The last time they had attended the Great Hall was four years earlier. Their minders had bashed a few of the eager folk away, and more than a few ended up in the drink over the revetment wall that lapped at the edge of the docks.

'Let them come, Amaria. I am always enthralled by their energy, their passion it's—'

A bell rang. Those milling around the Great Hall began to form an orderly line which had now begun to wrap itself round the street, ending not far from where they were headed. Heads turned their way, and a few of the more excited gave the three welcoming and emphatic waves. The bell signalled that the Hall was ready for the sitting. It would take a few hours before all was settled and they were not due on until well into the afternoon – though they had once played first, which gave hope to all filing into the hall that their judgement to attend early would be well merited. Just in case the miracle was repeated.

It gave the trio and their entourage ample time to freshen themselves up at the count's residence. The count and his wife would welcome them and ask them to take up temporary residence in the large, cosy reading room where they would welcome their daughter and her husband with light refreshments. Not to mention the many hugs, tears, and the pressing to tell all about their travels. Handshakes, backslaps, the clanging of battered tankards and the chink of intricate crafted crystal flutes would also be prevalent.

The argument would come later after the feast over how much they would want their daughter to remain in Sinboran. Velosko would try to agree with them but would be struck down by the veracity of his beloved, Amaria.

Amaria knew how much her parents missed her, being away for years at a time she knew it was hard; she and Velosko understood. Why, on Inarrel, would they send her away to study in a foreign land if they didn't want her to experience all that life had to offer? They recognised early on that the amelioration of her art was best suited to Heloniko – as legend would say, the birthplace of magical arts of the acoustic variety. Though Sinboran was building a reputation of its own, it still paled in comparison.

Once the formalities and catching up was concluded, Count Atinna led Marcos and Velosko to the visitors' residence, reserved only for Amaria and her guests – including the hefty entourage. Amaria was left behind to attend Countess Maria, her mother, and all her further prodding for stories of years gone by.

Velosko knew Amaria would be a while away, an age almost would ensue before he would finally get the chance to wrap his arms around her without constant prying eyes. The second wing – one separate wing unattached to the visitors' residence – was where he would reside with Amaria for the next few weeks, long beyond the Festival – longer, he hoped. He enjoyed the company of her father; he was a person of great intellect which had bred itself into a constant wiry wit. Atinna was also passionate about the arts which he respected deeply.

Count Atinna was into the final chapters of his existence but was determined to leave behind a legacy. A legacy to emulate that which was being produced over in the Dalmetonian capital. It was a long-term project though, which would continue long after he had been cremated and sent off ceremoniously into the oblivion of the unknown. Atinna had mentioned to Velosko that he would like the two of them to seriously consider coming home to assist in a mentoring role, to educate the staff at the Sinboran College of Musical Arts. Even so, in the few decades since its inception, it had inaugurated some of the brightest musicians from Vilenzia; the majority of those not born into a wealthy or prestigious upbringing. The wealthy were sent over The Great Green Divide to Dalmetonia, unless they displayed other special attributes that would interest the guilds at the City of Columns. The City of Columns would also consider those who did not have the required coin for the voyage.

This utterly did pique the interest of Velosko. Now into his late forties, and Amaria edging over the mid-century mark, he so wanted to aid the development of the arts and had given himself and many thousands of the general populace of wherever he went, joy; a reason for existence maybe. Enough for some … maybe. Enough for him though? absolutely. The University at Heloniko was pushing for him to return to his original tutelage in an advisory role; he knew this was also a marketing ploy against Sinboran to persuade the elite musicians to attend the traditional home of the arts and spend their vast reserve of coin there, rather than the second, its perceived copycat by those in residence there. A perception he knew all too well.

It had only been an hour, which was much quicker than the few previous occasions, when Amaria came walking through the white-framed and glazed double doors. The quickness and the bounce of her steps resounded inside his mind; she held a bounce about her aura and seemed happier than she usually did upon her return as she graced the threshold of their temporary residence.

'You seem spritely this morning. Very much so … Good news or are you just glad to finally have me all alone?'

'Hey! Never mind, you always seem to know. And if you must know, Mama and Pop have arranged for Leonard to mind over the city, as caretaker for a few months,'

'Huh?' Velosko said sharply, confused.

'Yes … from when we depart,'

' No, I still don't follow you,' Velosko said, still mystified.

'We all depart for Jacobs Well … together!'

'Oh, well … your idea, or your mama's? Safe to

absolutely assume that it was not your father's notion. He hasn't left this city in more than a decade, and that was only to get the seal granted for the commission of the art college here.'

'Wrong!' She slapped a palm to his chest playfully. 'It was actually my father! Can you believe that?! He is determined to fill more spaces in the college by visiting the major cities and towns of Vilenzia. He wants to strike a chord with their rulers and overseers to offer scholarships to the most talented via contests, and he will be the judge … well him, you, me, Marcos, and a nominee from the representing ruler. Oh, I can see him now aboard the *Speardrift*.' She glanced over an imaginary galleon, a firm hand held flat to rest above her eyebrow as if gazing at a shoreline as they drew closer.

'I can also imagine such … him hanging, bent over the taffrail, feeding all the creatures of the sea his last meal.'

'Oh, don't be a wretch!' This time she aimed a soft jab toward his chest. But he instantly moved away and twisted her to fold her in a close embrace.

Speaking softly, and in close proximity, he said, 'My sincerest apologies, I just cannot keep my hands off you. And apologies, once again for …'

'For wha—'

Before she could reply, he smothered her words with a passionate embrace of the lips, which was not relinquished until they reached the border of their bedroom.

'Ahem …!' A few hours had passed before Marcos appeared in the antechamber that adjoined their bedroom with the outside.

No response.

Louder now, he spoke, his rough voice rumbling through the arched opening, 'Vel! Maybe we should be heading off soon? It's darkening no end out there.'

A rustling could be heard coming through the archway, and then something being knocked over, followed by a yelp then a giggle as two pair of footsteps could be heard patting on the stones to, or from, the small bathing room.

Marcos smiled and whispered to himself, 'Ahh, where is *my* Amaria hiding? I *will* find you one day, wherever and whoever you may be …'

A shout came through. 'One day, Marcos, the day you do will be the cause for the greatest celebration of all time!'

Not surprised at being overheard, he shouted, 'Vel! Hurry up man!'

'We are not showing until the concluding act tonight, my good friend!'

More giggles could be heard.

'Very well, I will wait for you to get ready. Come and grab me from Amaria's father's cosy room. I saw him lighting some lanterns in there a short while ago. Pre refreshments, I presume … I should hope!'

Amaria replied this time. 'Okay … yes, Marcos, he has some good news for y—' She squeaked, cutting off the rushed response.

Marcos knew he would have a while to wait, so he would make himself comfortable and share drinks and hopefully a few nibbles with Count Atinna – he enjoyed that man's company, enjoyed the man's constant jibes. His stomach grumbled too. *Those marinaded prawns would be good to settle you,* he thought as he rubbed away the grumble.

Humour appeared in his voice, and he spoke louder, so that any in the courtyard would be able to hear, 'In that case, take your time … Especially you, Vel!'

# Interlude

'Pappa, why have I never been able to move my body?'

'But you do, you just don't remember when you do.'

'Why can I not remember then, when I do?'

'Well, there are things that happen that we cannot control …'

'Do you and Mama still love me?'

'Always. Why such a silly question, poppet?'

'Then why does she not read to me anymore? It feels as though I haven't seen her for months.' The boy closed his eyelids slightly.

On the other side of the door, the woman clasped both hands over her face and stepped away silently and quickly as tears flowed freely; a release of absolute anguish contained within.

A croak unintentionally slipped out.

'Is that Mama?' The boy looked toward the big wooden door.

'Why yes, yes it is. Probably busy making some broth for us to devour; she makes the finest broth, hey?' The man ruffled the boy's thick head of hair. 'Give me a second, I will go see how long she will be. She still does come to kiss you goodnight, every night, even after all these years, hey.'

The man stepped through the door and walked the short landing to where the woman was crouched, resting on her haunches against the wall.

'Now, now … come inside, he misses you. He is barely awake these days when you come in to sit beside him—'

'He is not my son! He is not your son! You have to tell him. It's breaking my heart! The longer we lead this charade, we will break his heart even more than our own!'

'He *is* our son! We took him in when he was offered to us from the Higher Beings. We have to lead the way; the salvation of our world, the salvation of all worlds is supposedly in his, thus in our, hands.' The man gently rested a hand on each of her shoulders.

She shrugged them both away.

'Bah! Cow's shit! So, what? We just keep going on like this, reading old rolled up scribblings to satisfy his curiosity?'

'No, we have to give him the full etchings of Aladur that were given to us. We have to give him the knowledge of *all* the writings and what they possess.'

'But where are these stories coming from? They change so often. How could he, *Aladur,* know all?'

'He wrote all, literally, all from his memory at the end of the time. He wrote … as so they told us. The apparent goddess only gave us what we needed, that what we possess must be important, and most vitally hold a deeper meaning. A snapshot of a history that was relevant, and will be relevant again. We have but a fraction of the writings, copied, or so we have been told, from the Great Library of Onentillia.' He shrugged heavy shoulders as her face remained passive, resigned to what she was about offer.

'But why would a god hold the fate of this realm in the hands, or teachings, of a small boy who can only hold enough consciousness to listen to a scroll, tome or book being read to him?. Let alone able to move …'

The man bristled, and felt a surge of urgency to convince the woman he loved to carry on with this *charade.* 'I can feel him growing stronger. I saw him the other night running through the woods outside. He is getting faster. Whatever is coming, when it comes … *our* boy will make us proud.

'I'm so, so sorry … I do love him, so, so much! Sorry. It's just been bothering me for a while. I hate seeing him like this … he will understand … one day. And I hope that there will be another day that he may forgive us for our secrets.' She dropped her head and buried it into the man's chest.

The tweed jacket soaked away all the pain her tears held.

# Revelation Amongst Revelry

The sky had dulled, quite considerably from the beautiful sunny day it had promised. Grehn had woken with a throbbing headache that stretched across her forehead and down to her jaw as she tested it with a move of a hand to the chin. She didn't remember even climbing into her own bed.

*Who dressed me in my night gear?* She struggled to remember. She eventually looked around, away from her nightdress, and saw Mother Ursen inspecting one portion of the apparatus that was scattered around her room. *Ah … I wonder what broth they gave me!*

'Awake dear?' Mother Ursen didn't turn her head around, but Grehn sensed a smirk beginning to widen on Mother Ursen's face.

'Just …'

'You slept longer than we all expected,' she said, her gaze still upon the mortar of stone upon the stone benchtop.

'Well … that's what happens when you administer such a large dose of *polentina*.' Grehn began to rouse a little more, then rose up.

'Very good, child. How did you know?' she said as she wiped clean the contents of the mortar with a dramatic tut at the state it was left in.

'It's sat on that stool there. I can tell by the vile smell and the brown trail of residue that dripped down the side of the bowl.'

'Very observational, even in your state,' she said, still with her back toward Grehn as she lifted and inspected all other manner of apparatus around the room. 'Lucky …'

'Lucky?' Grehn asked, still sporting a foggy head.

'Yes, lucky you have a stone floor and not a wooden floor, otherwise your glyph would have burned right through. Probably to the kitchen or whatever found itself beneath the stone beams below, looking at these etched marks left by the salts!'

'What happened, Grandma?' she held a light blanket around her neck.

'You tell me?' Mother Ursen raised an eyebrow before continuing on with her assiduous inspection of Grehn's equipment – trying to decipher what else she had been concocting.

'Uh, well … umm … I saw a lad—'

'Go on,'

'An old lady, though very familiar. She told me to find her. She seemed angry, or so it fel—Oh, Anatoma is he—'

'He's fine. He should have been quicker on that horse, the useless fool!'

'Who is she, Grandma?'

'I can only assume she is the one who gave you that mark!' Mother Ursen pointed where it would be beneath the sheet.

'But why?' She threw the blanket down to her legs, to reveal the mark on her side, twisting her hips to get a better view.

'Rumours only, but believed by many, including those high up in the Columns. So, I pay attention and listen. The mark was placed on you to identify, to us, that you must be protected at all costs … and some.' Mother Ursen spoke as she investigated every crevice of Grehn's equipment.

'Again, why?'

'That we do not know. What else did she say to you, Grehn?'

'I cannot really remember … something about finding her is all I really remember.'

'Then you—*we* … must. She is the one who started this whole damn prophecy business.'

'Who is she?' Grehn asked again, more direct.

'She is what remains of a woman once named Morla, one of the original Onberseelers, founders of the City of Columns. I am supposedly … of her ancestry, generations upon generations ago. I don't know how she got her claws into you though. Your family tree descends from—' She cut herself off before offending Grehn about the origins of her mother's family's heritage, and all the drama associated with. 'No matter. Where did she say to find her?'

'She didn't. She assumed we would know. But she pointed back to the Grousing Potter, so maybe that would be a place to start?'

'Well we will go back there, to that bloody hovel. Though only when you're ready will we depart. That clear? And only we, is that also clear?'

'Did I pass?' Grehn looked at Mother Ursen expectantly for a long moment. She was answered by a shrug of the shoulders. One she remembered so fondly from when she was but a child.

Mother Ursen finally finished her inspections and stood, hand on hips, looking toward her, and pointed an emerald ringed finger at her neck. 'Bring that there locket with you … we shall find out … soon enough!'


Peron peered up and over and then away from the cards he was holding to look at the big man sat to his left. Once no notice of such attention was received, he moved to stare intently across the round table to the man sat opposite. Hard unblinking green eyes glowered back at him. Quickly he turned his nonchalant, sweeping leer to the man sat on his right.

'The gods have not been kind this hand!' he sighed with resignation.

Sentok, Kimo, and King Benjamin all grumbled before they resigned their cards to the felted table in disgust. All as Peron placed his limp wager.

'Hey! What?! What are you all doing?!' His voice was high pitched, mildly perturbed, as he scraped what little was left on the table to his amassing stacks.

It was Kimo who answered first. 'Don't try to fool me, little man.' He flipped the cards over and pushed them away. Peron smirked ever so slightly.

Sentok chuckled. 'You're such an easy read, you should learn to keep your mouth shut, Peron.' He too pushed his cards away after showing a middle hand.

Peron held his pose, elation almost bubbling to a froth.

It was King Ben's turn to chuckle. 'You should listen to your man there! Do you hear this man to my right speak a word when he has highest card and cube? No. So what did you have?' King Ben, one of the most powerful rulers in all of Vilenzia, picked up then threw his cards to the felt top. Peron did not dare move a facial muscle.

Peron eventually let out a humph and threw down the second worst hand on the scale of *Paper and Stone*.

'Fu—lip me!' boomed Sentok,

Kimo shook his head. 'You little bastard!'

King Ben could only chuckle at the deviousness. 'We should really wrap up soon. There is too much going on that needs my attention. No, my apologies, you gents carry on. I will leave you to your—'

'No!' Kimo stood and clasped a hand on Ben's shoulder. 'You go, we all go! Ain't that right men?'

Peron thought better than to grumble at the bullishness of Kimo. He stood. 'Aye!' he shouted a bit too emphatically which drew more stares from the others.

Sentok placed a hand on Kimo and Peron's shoulders, then squeezed. 'Let's go celebrate!'

Queen Jahnna sat comfortably in the attending room, a small, enclosed space between the main entrance and the expansive ballroom. It was custom for her and Ben to welcome each and every guest to the castle and share a few pleasantries before they ventured on to their allotted seat. They would be dined and wined before the festivities moved outside. where a few more spots of lighter entertainment would ensue.

Jahnna sighed inwardly, bracing herself as the first of the hundred moved toward her. Extra security had been placed at the entrance following the earlier events in the town, and only one party – a duo – at a time were permitted to enter. The small amount of despair she felt dissipated as a firm hand rested on her shoulder; she knew the touch instantly, and loved all of the forever warmth it brought.

'Ben … you took your time! Of all days to be late …' The warmth was welcomed. The tardiness was not.

'I'm not late, I'm right on time …'

'Welcome, sir, madam. With whom do I have the pleasure of sharing your presence?' The duo were mystified and could not offer anything. 'Welcome to our home, we would see you well fed, and we would very much love to speak further once we're introduced to all our guests. Go … enjoy the feast and all the other activities.'

The awestruck couple bowed and made their way through to the main hall, ushered away by one of the many servants.

This continued on until the selected hundred had been welcomed. The actual number through the doors ended up at ninety-seven; apologies were made for the unlucky absentees.

The tables were arranged to reflect the sign of The Snake – this year's prominent constellation. They rotated the setup through the six more well-known constellations: The Dragon, The Supple – a large, wide fish which was native to The Great Green Divide – The Butterfly, The Alaca – a large animal not dissimilar to a moose but twice as large – The Boar, then The Pertoni – a large purple-blue flower with large folding petals. Banners were also raised to reflect the sign of the year as the table arrangements would not always outline the required figure exactly.

When all had been seated, the main table took centre stage. The two head seats were occupied by the king and queen, and either side was occupied by the general public selected by ballot; the seating was arranged in sequential order from left to right based on the hundred seats balloted.

King Benjamin stood. Gradually the bustle began to quiet until the silence was absolute. 'All! We are joined here this afternoon by folk from all walks of life. We see no one here as higher or lesser, including myself and my family, and the purpose of the ballot is such. A tradition that we have upheld for generations. I won't hold you too long as I know you are eager for the food soon to be brought out. So … enjoy! We'll all be having the same dish, one of my father's favourite, before we head to the courtyard for further festivities.

'Now … be ready! For here the delights come. The resident head chef and his unrivalled team have been preparing the dishes throughout the night.'

When the king took his seat, a long train of servants bustled out of three double-leaved doors, flowing in tandem, all holding a dome covered silver platter. They took their designated spot and, with a flourish, dropped the plates onto the tables where a marker was placed for such deposit. As one, they removed the cloche, revealing a steaming pot of orange sauce with chunks of goose breast contained within. Immediately after, the aroma filled the room. Jahnna was sure she heard no little amount of saliva being sucked back into mouths as the platters were revealed. Herself included.

Jahnna rested a hand on Ben's forearm. 'Curried goose? Are you feeling alright Ben?'

He looked at her seriously, then let out a small chuckle.

'Aye, they're easier to catch than those hogs that tear up old Jack's farm. Well, he said he needed them to repopulate at least for the next couple of years anyway, so he offered the geese. They're taking over the place apparently, he said. We should have some left over to last us more than a few weeks, though I'm sure we will grow sick of goose over the next few days. I might commission them as royal gifts to a few of our guests here, and let them leave with one each. He had that many of them culled, would be a shame to waste.'

'That brute … We should look to another source.'

'He is the royal food source; his family have been running that acreage for generations. What would you have me do?'

She screwed up her face before looking out of the main window, to the south-east. 'Look, Ben. The sky, it's beginning to darken; the Festival is nigh. The Festival will have started on the other side of Vilenzia hours ago! Oh, can we pause this whole thing for one year so I can go home and enjoy the beginning of the Festival at the City? Next year may be a stretch but can you consider the following?'

Ben spoke quietly. 'My dear, this has been the way for generations. We can't just up and leave, it's unheard of.'

'You can't, but I can. How many times has the king himself or the queen been at this function by themselves?'

'Yes, but every living monarch has attended, it's what brings this city together!'

'Ben, we will talk more later. Your voice is beginning to rise, and the guests are also beginning to glare at us.' She looked around, an artificial smile cast to reassure the guests that all was well.

'Yes, of course, we'll talk some more later. I suppose Grehn will be feeling the same, couped up in this big block of a home!'

Jahnna read it as his way of conceding ground. *Yes, Grehn would love to finally break free from the chains shackled to her. I wonder if she, or Ben, is ready for that to happen?*

Peron was milling around the courtyard as Sentok began preparing the flame dancers, an addition to the sky flames. 'Hey, Sentok, how do you know how much to put in each tube?'

'I don't. I ask the supplier to do all that stuff. I just tell them the colours and how high and how wide I want the explosion to cover.'

'Oh, that must be hard.'

'It is, it's hard trying to find the correct mixture. The guys who sell this kind of stuff don't just reveal themselves willy nilly! You have to gain their trust.'

'So, what I'm getting from you is they're dodgy!'

'Yes, very much so.'

'So why deal with them?'

'Because the dodgier they are, the better their flamework!'

'Seriously? You deal with those kinds?'

'I know you know I do already, Peron. Why all the questions?'

'Just habit I guess.'

'Well, that habit will get you into a lot of trouble one day if it already hasn't!' Peron nodded at the truth to the man's words.

Sentok continued to walk around the courtyard placing tubes and boxes in places no one would think to look, unravelling a coil from a reel he was moving around with him.

Peron, biting on a long bay leaf's twig, watched Sentok do his thing. 'So, what you're saying is, you're aiding thugs?'

'No, just trying to entertain the majority, my good man.'

'But the guys you get this stuff from, they have caused havoc the past few years?'

'Yes, but have they killed anyone?'

'Well, yes … yes they have!'

'Who?'

'You know!'

'The uprising. Those mad bastard's who supported the uprising years ago. If so … then damn, what a damn shame!'

'How long are you going to be? Shouldn't you have done this already? Like, long before now? You're cutting it a bit close.'

'Just be quiet. I'm almost done! Those young ones stuffed my timing up!' He looked to the well. 'And shouldn't you be somewhere else?'

'No and, yeah, Kimo was very pissed at you! I don't think you will escape his wrath for a while, if ever!'

'You're telling me. The glare he gave me as they left for town yesterday … it was brutal!'

Peron was now leaning against the centre point of the courtyard, the well's wall. He was looking around as the sky began to darken. It didn't escape him that not only was it getting darker, but the temperature had also begun to drop significantly.

He spoke to Sentok who had now begun to drop the intensity of his flamework preparation as he rubbed a sodden towel over his bald head. 'Hey, Sentok … you feel that?'

'Feel what, Pe—'

'That chill?'

Sentok left it a few seconds before he replied, 'What is that?'

'I have an idea, but only from what has been suggested, which I cannot divulge any further …'

'So, its bad eh?'

'Yes, potentially!'

'Kinora?'

'How? No. How … You—'

'Just take it, Peron. Your masters at the City of Columns

may know a fair bit, but there are things happening that get talked about round the towns and villages. Which, may I add, have some talented—'

'Yes, yes that's why I'm here! There is something going on. It wasn't supposed to happen this year but … oh, looks and feels like it! Especially with all the strange happenings.'

'Huh, why are you here again?'

'Reconnaissance!'

'Ahh … you hear much on you travels across Vilenzia on your way here?'

'No, not really, I didn't want to listen to much gossip. I was supposed to head up to Castle Raven after the Festival, then on to Hanford, then on again to the port of Aqua Plen. Looks as though I will be here a bit longer!'

'Why's that?'

'Just a feeling. You should have seen that thing, Sentok. The thing that chased after me and that eberactu fella. Was not of this world or the next, that's for sure! Then that woman, if you could describe her as such, she was very familiar, and I knew I'd seen her before somewhere … Bah, I'm getting goosebumps again just thinking about her. How long are you going to be with all this stuff? I heard they all come out here after their lunch to play games and eat more food.' He looked to the doors, then added, 'I'm starving.'

'Thanks for reminding me, Peron. It's not why I'm out here at all.' He let the sarcasm wash over Peron. 'I'm in charge of setting up the boar spits. Can you come over here with me and help me start up the fire? Need to get the coals heated.'

'Suppose I could. Where are the boars anyway?'

'King Ben had his personal chef skin and baste them overnight. Should be a real treat to them folk who were lucky enough to win a space here today. The lucky boars won't be brought out until the annual traditional speech of welcoming has begun. The servants will then bring them out.'

'Damn. Was hoping for some tucker soon!'

'Help me here then we can both go find your eberactu friend.'

A servant came out of a slim wooden door adjacent to the outer wall. He was about to sit down when Sentok barked, 'You there … laddy! Come 'ere!'

The young man jumped as Sentok's booming voice echoed around the courtyard. He rubbed his hands on his black and grey chequered trousers. 'Yes, sir?' he asked, gingerly.

'Tell me, boy, have you seen a short, stocky fellow, no taller than your chest skulking around the halls? Most likely with a large tankard in hand. Sporting a big fuzz of orange hair and a beard to match?'

'No. Sorry, sir.'

'Hmm … You sure?'

'No, sorry. Should I have seen him?'

'No, it's all good.' Sentok dismissed the boy with a nod back to the door from which he came.

Peron watched the exchange and was about to carry on with helping Sentok, then thought better of it. 'Wait! Come back here for a moment, young fellow.' He reached into his pockets, pulling out a small amount of coin. 'Here, go find he whom my good man here just described to you.'

'Aye sir. Will I find him wandering the halls?'

'If you haven't seen him there, then no. Maybe go see if he is in the castle common room.'

'But it should be empty, everyone but the barkeep are, or should be, in the main hall.'

Sentok replied, 'You'd be surprised where to find people at the best of times young man.' Rubbing his stubbled chin, he looked at the boy. 'Run along …?'

'Mala. My name is Mala.'

Sentok chuckled and ruffled the young lad's hair, a little

rougher than he meant to. 'Of course. Molo's younger brother. I should have recognised the resemblance soon as you came through that door. Do you at least know where your brother is? Could do with his help down here.'

'Heard him say something about waiting for Grehn somewhere. Said he hadn't seen her all morning.'

'Ah, that's bec—'

'Shush, Sentok,' Peron jumped in, holding a strangled expression.

'Because … she is busy studying …' Mala side-eyed Peron who only sighed and began to walk away.

'Don't worry, Sentok, everyone knows about her fall; word spreads fast in this city.' Mala, too, turned to walk away, but not before he gave the big man a wink. 'Secret's safe with me.'

\*

Dresdor was sat in the middle of one of the finely appointed seating nodes. He rubbed a hand on the well-worn leather. *Hmm smooth, polished from those wide arses of the royalty.* The other hand held one of the scrolls he had grabbed from the many stuck in a number of timber slots attached to the wall at the far end of the polished brass bar. He'd had trouble reading the inscription carved into the old brass tab above the square void he had removed the scroll from, the text ground to almost nothing from the constant polishing they seemed to do around this place. 'Probably because there ain't nowt else to do,' he muttered to himself. He took a guess at what it may once have read – *Cremornean Bootleg?*

A good guess it would seem, one garnered from a brush of a thumb across the tab. A guess confirmed as he read from the top.

As he worked through the text – which was in much better shape and infinitely more legible than its identification – he took mental notes as to what apparatus would be needed to make such a seductive broth. He had not yet made it to the ingredients listed, nor the concoction required which would render the mental notes useless due to the apparatus not being found for thousands of years. Pausing a moment, he peered over the top of the scroll to the man fidgeting around behind the bar. 'Do you ever stand still?!' The placid fellow only glanced at Dresdor for a mere second before carrying on with his nonsensical chores.

'No, sir, what if one of the masters appears and I'm leaning an elbow on the bar, or sitting doodling my finger around on this magnificent piece of metal?'

'Hmph … well stop that and bring me another amber ale, none of that shit from anywhere but the sweet forest harvest of my home. You have any cured meat to nibble on too?'

'Coming right up, sir. Do I add that to your tab, or will you be kind enough to pay in coin for this one?' The barkeeper, Mamitelander, offered a pleading smile, hopeful for some sort of extra commission for the constant service.

'Nah! stick it on the tab and—'

He was interrupted when the door was barged open, a familiar face coming through.

'Ahhh, Dresdor, there you are! Are you going to spend all day in here? Does the king's pleasantries in allowing you to stay the night extend through the day? Not what he agreed! Come on we have things to sort and settle …'

The bar keep eyed Dresdor curiously, then after a few moments began to realise that the order would not be added to the short fellow's fictitious tab. 'Just wait there one minute. Pay up or you won't make it out of here!'

Dresdor barked a deep belly laugh, until he saw a glint of reflection flash from one end to the other of a large, curved battle sword, rising from behind the bar.

'Easy … easy!' Dresdor said as he backed away.

Peron interjected, throwing a small coin purse onto the

brass bar top. 'Should be ample there. I'm sure it will far cover this lazy bastard's tab also, allowing some credit for yourself.'

'Thank you, Master,' Mamitelander gave a slight nod in Peron's direction, then turned back to Dresdor with a look of disdain. 'That shite you have been drinking was actually from the fields of Arengor, not your precious Famnagira!'

'You little shit ...' Dresdor made a march to front the barkeep. 'Come here you ... don't you dare—'

The barkeep again raised the shining metal; Dresdor held his tongue for no more than a moment, though the sight of the sword didn't deter Dresdor from continuing on – the eberactu pride taking to the fore. 'I'm gonna rip those fidgety arms off your torso and stick them both up your ar—'

'Hey! Hey! Both of you ease up!' Peron swung his hand quickly into the air, signing an imaginary glyph with his fingers at the same time as he muttered a short sentence in an ancient language.

Before Dresdor made it close to the bar, and before Mamitelander was able to swing the large sword in such a confined space – the sword was most likely used to deter any aggressive clientele – both became confuddled and dropped whatever they were holding. Dresdor's metal mug and the sword held by the barkeep made a clanging sound as they hit the floor, echoing about the bar. Instead, they began to scratch their heads in unison.

'Barman, why are you scratching your head like a madman?'

'Hello, good sir. I have no idea. Why are you also scratching your head? An outbreak of flealice maybe? Ouch!' Mamitelander placed both palms on the bar with a strained effort then asked, 'What can I get you?'

'Oh, nothing, we were just passing through,'

Dresdor looked at Peron conspicuously, with contrition.

Peron just shrugged and made a motion to head for the door he came from.

'Aye, let's go …'

Sentok had just finished the coal settling when he saw two shadowy figures skulking toward the main gate, keeping close to the outermost wall of the courtyard, trying to avoid detection which piqued his interest. *Why would people be sneaking out and not in?* Curious, he left what he was doing and followed. As he made his way closer, the larger of the two, without looking, raised her hand toward him and shot a green puff that mushroomed out toward him, meant for a full body encompassment. However, Sentok knew magic, and how to avoid it. Falling into a forward slide, feet first, he slid beneath the cloud of puffing aroma that was meant for his inhalation.

Mother Ursen hadn't felt the resistance back off the spell which always came from a casting of that sort – she began to kneel and had to halt her advance to the main gate. This time both hands were raised. Palms outstretched, she began another spell. The large man was now only a fraction of the distance he was when they had begun to sneak around the most direct route to the outer gate thinking everybody would be inside the main hall. The spell did not emanate, there was no need to complete the enchantment; Sentok was sat on the ground with both legs outstretched and a big goofy grin on his face. He had recognised the cloak Grehn was wearing.

'So, where are you two off to?'

Mother Ursen answered for her. 'None of you damn business!'

'Sentok, you must promise me not to tell anyone we have left the castle grounds. Please!' pleaded Grehn.

'But look at your head, Grehn. You sure you want to head out like that? Hey? You're not going back there are you? Grehn … come on!'

'If you knew what was good for you, big fellow, you would keep your mouth shut.' Mother Ursen was now pointing at Sentok who thought it would be wiser to just agree.

'But what about those two guarding the front gate, how will you convince them?'

'Don't worry about that, big man.' Mother Ursen winked as she patted her apothecary bag. Grehn grimaced.

The door where Mala had appeared earlier now swung open with two figures venturing out: Peron and Dresdor would match the silhouettes that appeared in the gloom. Mother Ursen grimaced. Grehn allowed herself a small smile – she now knew they would not be going over the Masked Arches as a duo but, at the very least, as quartet.

*

Four now made their way over the Arches as the sunlight was slowly being consumed by the red planet Kinora and much larger Seltero.

They walked silently, so much so they could hear gasps and concerned chatter amongst the prayers being offered to multiple gods. They made it halfway across the Arches when Grehn let out a sharp yelp whilst clutching at her side as she dropped to the floor.

Dresdor was the first to crouch down beside her. 'Deary, you alright?'

'Does she sound alright, you idiot!' Mother Ursen knelt down beside him and fiddled around in her cloth sack. She pulled out a long belt – a hand width thick and adorned with many symbols and text that wrapped both faces of the belt. 'Arms up, child. Here, this should ease the pain.' She wrapped it around Grehn's midriff, covering the side she held as she fell.

'That hurt so much! My birthmark, it began to burn and

got hotter the more I touched. I have never felt that sensation before now.'

A nod from Mother Ursen. 'The belt should mask whatever is calling you, for now. However, I imagine that it will only get worse as the next few days evolve.'

'What do you mean? Calling me …'

Mother Ursen looked to Peron who had been standing close by, not knowing what to do other than to wring his hands together, looking concerned at what was transpiring. 'A word, Peron?'

'Ah, maybe not here, maybe someplace on the way to the Grouse, maybe …'

'It wasn't a question, Peron … a word, now!'

She left Grehn with Dresdor who acted with grace, comforting the lady in need as he wrapped a thick arm across her shoulders and cradled her gently.

As Mother Ursen led Peron to the edge of the bridge, close enough to peer over the waist high parapet, and the only thing separating the road from the long fall to the crashing waves below, Grehn pulled away from the embrace and spoke to Dresdor: though it was not Grehn's usual soft voice that he heard. Nor the sweet wide eyes he saw that were now glazed completely white; they gazed right through him. The croaking rasp of a whisper escaped her lips. 'You waste time. Find me. And be quick about it, or all that we know, and all that has been before, will be gone forever, surrendered to darkness.'

Peron's wide eyes at to what he was witnessing gave Mother Ursen but a moment of indication. She turned and charged at pace back to where Grehn was now kneeling.

As she approached, the face of Grehn remained passive and calm as it turned in the direction Mother Ursen was approaching. Four words Grehn shouted, *'Aldacantra Detribunim, Daldolenta Fresa!'* Then the world stopped all around Mother Ursen.

'Leave my grandchild's mind alone, Morla. Now! We're on our way!' She showed no nerves as to what had just happened, standing her ground with hands on hips as all around her had been frozen, save the merest flicker as Peron blinked once at the extremity of her peripheral vision. *Hmmm that one is more than he lets on, the sly pup.*

Grehn stood gracefully, breaking Mother Ursen's summation of Peron, then looked with wide eyes at the belt around her stomach, the glyphs and text burning brighter than when she had strapped it on tightly to cover over the birth mark during her burning fit.

'That was once mine, as you know. That is why you couldn't shut me out. I know how it functions, know how to alter the waves of impulse around the age-old wards that *I* scribed. I mean her no harm: quite the opposite … Magala—'

'She speaks the truth.' A beautiful melodical sound came from one of the two spectres closing in through the now reddish gloom. The only other things that moved in the frozen space.

'I second that!' the other figure spoke. A voice of authority and unlimited wisdom. 'Magala, ease your mind and see for what the child is. She is the saviour, so it would seem, if you believe the prophecies. But … I'm sure you already knew?'

'Holtonos! How long has it been?' She dropped the stony façade, and raced to him, embracing the tall being tight. Then around the other, squeezing the two of them as an arm slung around each. 'Lenjora!' She kissed her cheek. Lenjora reciprocated the gesture.

*

Peron remained solid as stone, viewing the interaction between the three and smirked. *Mother Ursen, the Rock of the First, acting like a younger just out of her first uniform.*

The smirk slowly appearing on his face wasn't missed by

Holtonos. 'Peron?' *Shit, whatever have I gotten myself into now …?*

'Yes, Hol—'

'Come on over, we have much to discuss …'

He only shrugged both of his shoulders as he made his way over. 'So … how long has it been?'

It was Lenjora who came over to Peron, she held both of his hands. 'It has been six years! Since we were last supping in Jink's.'

Peron nodded, squeezed her hands a bit tighter. 'Everos?'

'Hopefully he will be here soon. We sent a message yesterday when we first saw the trigger sign. He said he is readying something to do with a *reflection* of some sort …'

'What's that other grumpy old bastard up to?'

'Oh. Jhehbl? He is mustering something back up there too, but I think he is stalling, scared of the last time he was down here.'

The conversation was cut short by the croaking drawl from Grehn as Morla's words. 'Let us draw this little reunion to a close. You must be here … *there*, before full alignment. Time is short and so is my patience. Be warned, one of the ill was here, he was the one who cast the demonic soldier, as a lure it seems. I took care of *him*, though I'm very sure there are more. His apparition was merely a puppet, the puppeteer also another puppet. Be warned …'

With the conclusion of the words, Grehn dropped to the ground, and all started to move with a buzz about the bridge again. Peron reached her in time before she hit the stones for a second time in as many days.

Walking swiftly over, Mother Ursen spoke. 'Dear, are you okay? What do you remember? Did she say anything to you? Anything we couldn't hear?'

'No … no, I don't think so. The burning? It was so hot! I also felt as though trapped inside honey, just like the ancient esqueros in the museum's collection. Everything went hazy, then I could sense a presence … That was it, me just stumbling and our new friend catching me. I feel sick, let me go a for a moment, I think I'm abo—'

Mother Ursen managed to turn her body away as the projectile release left Grehn's stomach. She also found it in her to shield Grehn's dignity from the assembled party. Peron was not so lucky, as a few spots bounced off the pavement and onto his plush shoes. A few of the Arches' residents dared to look at Grehn, but Mother Ursen shot them a look of contempt that would have frightened them enough for them to leap to the safety of the waves below.

Her mouth still frothed with the remains of the last convulsion. Even so, Grehn looked at her grandmother with concern. 'I thought I saw something, before I fell I … I think I saw—'

Mother Ursen pulled her in close. 'We must go on, you understand right? We need to. My being here was no coincidence, Grehn. More so I hoped that it would only be an initiation, but this probability has been tracked for many years. Your father, bless his blessed soul, knows more than any and why we have to go on.'

'So he knows we are out here?'

'Oh heavens! No child! He would have me—no both of us dropped down the well till the sun came back to sunder the darkness. But he will know soon enough, believe me …'

'I understand. But why the Grousing Potter? Why is it connected?'

'It isn't. Well … not directly. You see, the evil of this world, which I am sure your father, or at least Kimo, have talked to you about, view what we hold dear: fun, laughter, spirit, beauty, music … love! As something to sway in their own sadistic ways. It's all relatively pertinent to what they wish to dissolve. I suppose the Grouse holds many of those, and at least generates a lucidity to the values we would hold dearest. There is more happening in this world, far more than the everyday mortal's view could ponder. I'm sure you are aware of that *other* world, Grehn.

'When you were born, the Mother at the time, Mother Folia, bless her beautiful spirit,' she made a quick sign in the air close to her chest, 'held you up for those few gathered in attendance. Not long after, she was unable to hold her tongue any longer. It wouldn't have mattered anyway; they would have discovered as soon as she took the swaddle off your little bottom. She pronounced – rather dramatically, and with all kinds of exaltations – that the fourth prophecy had now shown itself. Or so, had rather been delivered to the world.

'The joy wrapped across your father's face was suddenly replaced with sinking dread. Even so, he was over to you in a heartbeat, swearing to the gods that no harm would befall you, for he knew then, that on top of your inherently gifted station, you would be the prime target for those who would destroy all those values we all strive to live for. Second to that flow of cursing, he asked everyone in the room to swear an oath, one that all of what had been said in the preceding moments would remain inside those walls; a pact. One which all swore to hold your life above their own. Your mother had lost consciousness the moment you had almost arrived, thus had no idea of the proclamation, nor your father's words to those assembled. It was for me to tell her when she eventually woke.'

Grehn continued to nod at the revelation – one she was not surprised at – as Mother Ursen continued.

'Your father lost some faith in me on that technicality. He wanted your mother to think all was rosy, as if nothing had transpired. I know she would have done the same if the shoe was on the other foot, but it wasn't. She had the right to know, Grehn, and she would have found out as soon as she saw your mark anyway. So I don't hold any guilt in that regard.

'Do you ever wonder why your father wears that bracer on his left arm and never takes it off …?'

They continued to walk, Grehn had been listening to the story intently, she had been wondering who else could have been in that room when she was thrown headfirst into this world; she knew her father, mother and her grandmother were there. A question struck Grehn. 'But is it not the king's duty to wear the gold bracer?'

'Yes, it is, child, though only when presenting court. You see, the first time he held you, your birth mark glowed hot, so hot, though it did not seem to bother you back then. While your father was cradling you in his arms, your birthmark scorched the skin on his wrist – but not the cloth of the swaddle – searing the shape of the three planets in almost conjunction just as they align at this very moment. And did you know that the pain he felt that day still lingers? For he asked Mother Folia to take pain you felt just earlier away from you, and to scorch him. She did it, reluctantly. Now your father feels that pain on his scorched skin whenever you are near to him, probably even from where we are now. But I assume from what he has told your mother, once we are across the bridge, the pain will fade … then he will know.'

'We best be quick then, Grandmother! It won't be he I'll be worried about!' she said with a smirk as she foresaw the icy, green eyes of her uncle pinched to dots, pointed at her.

Lenjora had been listening from a short way back. Though she was not in *that* room – not in person at least – she remembered the whole episode well. She had also uttered the second oath: the first she could not hold from those around her on Seltero.

The chill in the air suddenly cut deeper at the skin.

And all shuddered.

# Famnagira

Semoni, the young pecbor, strolled along as the two who ambled ahead constantly horsed and joked around. *More than likely at my expense*, he assumed as they continually glanced behind.

They had left a day earlier than planned, seemingly all the stars had aligned to enable such to occur. More so, the forest during the alignment was too much of a splendour to pass up.

It soon became clear they were not the only ones who had heard such tales of wonders that occurred during the eclipse of the worlds. All manner of creatures, the smaller more so, would become confused and act in a quasi-mindless display of a disorientated dance: ranging from ground dwellers such as the possomo – a six-legged marsupial with four bright glowing eyes that flashed a multitude of colours depending on its mood – to the smallest of insect that would leap from branch to branch in search of food … or a mate, or both. It was rumoured – predominantly throughout Inarrel – the ancient forest would display its lustrous side and provide its own show through copulation of nature.

They had passed no fewer than fifteen couples, four large families and thirty roaming individual souls: the former, to copulate amongst the magic. The latter, marching hopefully to follow suit with the animals' mindless revelry. Not to mention those who had already made, and those who had yet to make, the journey.

As they approached the middle of the wide-open clearing, stuck in the middle between the dregs of the City of Columns and Famnagira, the border of the forest became more prominent. The outer ring was now adorned with a luminous, auburn glow; the eclipse now in transit made it easier to see the hue created by the millions of flying insects throwing themselves around the large macadamia trees that densely populating the perimeter of the largest forest upon Inarrel.

Semoni looked up again after a short way of looking where his footing found the scrub, toward the two walking ahead as they came closer to the forest. Miss Nomellia hadn't turned back since they had come to the edge of the clearing. She was no doubt mesmerised by the sight that beheld them all; the sporadic zipping around of the insects created a resemblance akin to a blaze raging all through the forest.

Semoni looked at the haze now bearing down upon them. *I hate bugs,* he shrugged a thousand imaginary bugs away. Then again he looked past her at the burning haze that was all across the façade of the forest.

*And fire,* he concluded.

Miss Nomellia was eager to drop the niceties; Jink was a true gentleman and knew how to cause a ruckus and throw a joke around, but that's all he had done since they left. She had persuaded Kost to let Semoni be relieved of his duties. And though Kost had eyed her curiously, he had reluctantly agreed, but on one condition, *'He sleeps in Shanlar's reserved room. On the floor, at least until I get there.'* She had agreed, knowing, without doubt, Semoni too would be glad to agree to that … He had, which she was hurt by initially, though ever so slightly. She thought, and hoped, he was only venturing along to be in her company, which assuaged the sense of slight despair. She sensed there was chemistry between them, and she was aware that Kost knew there was a possibility of that chemistry. *But why let him leave without you?* she thought as she listened to Ebby Jink crack another jibe, again at Semoni's expense. He then cracked another, this time about one of the single folk gone crazy and who was running at speed away from the forest – obviously, the pull of the forest had sent the man's little mind way off kilter. She had also felt a little dissimilar of mind. The closer they approached the more she felt … *phantastic.*

Jink didn't miss the slight sway about her as she moved with a melodic, rhythmic, motion. 'That be the forest, Missy … isn't it a wonderous delight!'

'Huh?' she replied, a dumb expression held to hide the fact she was indeed feeling movement to some unheard, and unseen, euphoria obviously affecting her.

'The forest, my dear: my home. I feel it, even up high in the city, it's with me. I feel it ever so much more whenever I'm drawn back. It feels as though the ocean washes through my body, over and over as would its coastal waves, offering nothing but grace to fill my soul. Even in my dreams, I feel her pull, her motion, her breath of tide … in … out, a presence I don't know what I would do without. It's as if she is us, and we belong to her! But during the annual eclipse, it seems to spread to all souls across these lands. Our kind believe we are the forest. We all believe our ancestors help generate that energy needed for her to survive: their life energy transcends through the roots of the trees when we bury our passed-on relatives, thus reciprocated a hundred-fold through the earth to help us survive through her offerings of bountiful grain, fruit and … well, just the general aura of the place is brimming full of her magic!'

'Yes, that's how I feel, all of that! As though I'm on a ship breasting large waves.' She turned back to Semoni – he was looking at her again. Whenever she turned he was looking at her. 'Hey, Semoni!' she shouted, jovially. 'Hurry up will you!'

Semoni smiled – for a pecbor, he had a charming grin – and nodded, and shouted back, 'This is surely a wonderous place. Thank you, Jink!'

'For what, laddy?' Ebby Jink walked back a way to meet with Semoni as he began to hurry his short, slinky legs.

'For letting me tag along with you both.'

'No worries, Semoni. And don't worry about Master Shanlar, and also Kost, if he does indeed decide to travel, they will catch us up after they have had their meetings and what not. Say, did Miss Nomellia mention to you why they would be venturing out here in the first place?'

'No, I assumed it was for some sort of reconnaissance or maybe study of some of the plants or grains that are grown here. That's the usual trip …'

Jink bowed his head and smiled, knowingly. 'Strange you didn't ask, Semoni. You're close, though. Reconnaissance, yes … with one of the Onberseelers. Study, yes, but not of any vegetation, Semoni: but of a new creature I was told arrived from out of nowhere, and which is currently being watched closely by the *Flame Guard*. It wanders the forest, glowing, even during daylight it glows with luminescence akin to a purple orchid. It arrived a few weeks ago, word came to me not long after. It seems content to wander, the Guard tried to communicate but it acts as though they are not there …'

Silence ensued for a short while before Semoni spoke. 'Is that it, Ebby?'

'For now …' Ebby Jink grinned as he motioned his hand forward, motioning for Semoni to lead on.

They began to close the gap to Miss Nomellia, who was still standing starry eyed at the forever changing canvas before her.

\*

Missy waited for Semoni to catch up before she put an arm around his waist and turned him toward the forest. Still holding an arm around his lower back, she inhaled deeply, her face glowing in the firelight, a big, wide smile accompanied the inhalation of magic from the air, then she spoke, more a whisper. 'It is ... as wonderous as they say! And we are not yet even amongst the thickets! I cannot believe I have never had the chance to head down here ever in my life.'

Semoni thought the motion he was feeling in his body was from the nervousness a schoolkid held, out on his first real outing with a girl he admired. It wasn't until Missy asked him if he could feel the lapping energy of the forest. He was, however, not so fluent when he spoke. 'M ... Mm ... erm, Mis—'

'Spit it out then, Sem!'

'Erm, I was just about to agree with you, it truly is a sight to behold,' He was caught by the light that flickered off what little her half closed eyes offered. She suddenly opened them fully and looked at him, and he immediately blushed, though the light flickering through the darkness covered the rosy blemish – a shine he was so accustomed to – on his pasty, grey cheeks. He was not the typical pecbor, he had angular features in all the right places. His nodes were not as pronounced for any other his age, and the pigment in his skin had not been scorched away from the searing heat and constant blustery wind – extended time spent away from the arid region of Pecboria seemed to lessen the onset of the typical pecborian features.

Her smile widened, then she squeezed him, just a little tighter.

Jink was the one who began the march to the periphery; he gestured back to them both with wide arms and shouted, 'Come on! Best not dawdle for too long,' before he disappeared into the glowing glade.

Semoni composed himself enough to speak with some coherence. 'Let's follow Jink, we don't want to get lost.' But his composure was shattered with an atypical squeak when Missy grabbed his little, bony, pecborian arse and pushed him forward to follow on.

Meandering along one of the few worn and frequented tracks through the forest, sounds could be heard all around, and not from the resident inhabitants – obviously some had not ventured far before the magical euphoria about the place had taken hold of their senses.

Nervously, Semoni looked at Missy. She was covering her mouth, muffling laughter, the crinkle about her eyes only added to her mischievous demeanour, brought on by amusement of the unseen passion echoing throughout the forest. The crescendo of such seemed to be in tune, and sequence, with the sway of firelight that bounced and rippled all around them.

They both walked and talked. Giggled and swayed, all in rhythm to the melodies floating silently about the groves. Ebby Jink watched on with glee in his heart, happy to show his close friends the delights of this, *his,* and the *eberactu's* sacred land.

After roughly an hour of trudging gently through the forest, discussing all manner of things, not only of what the forest offered, a large clearing began to open itself up further ahead. The haze was making it difficult to see what lay beyond the glade, but there were colourful blurred images that would present themselves – if fleetingly.

Semoni quickened the pace to join Ebby Jink who had now trudged a little farther ahead. 'Is that Caliopa?' he asked, the rising hope in his voice not undetected by Jink.

Jink stopped, waiting for Miss Nomellia to catch up, and then stepped ahead, before he turned and opened his arms wide. 'I *wonder* why it took so long for you to come to speak to me …' His grin widened, which it always seemed to do when he asked things to make people blush; the two of them did just that. 'You see … No one uninvited, and not born from within the Famnagira, can enter beyond a hundred paces of its sacred entrance. Many a person has tried; many a person has failed. Only the residents and their guests may venture deeper. Turn around and see!'

Both Semoni and Missy turned in unison.

They both inhaled sharply. Being so caught up in each other's company, they had not even had the chance to look too far from their immediate surroundings. Now they were dumbstruck, they should have seen nothing other than trees skirting the long narrow pathway behind them, for they had ventured for over an hour. They saw only the pathway that lead back to the entrance of the forest, and could quite clearly see in the distance, through the small narrow opening, the glowing city climbing the slopes of Hollowloft.

They turned back in disbelief. Jink was still smiling. 'Now, are you ready to enter the forest for real?'

'We … We thought it was a myth, kids talk and that … well, that—'

'All true, my dear. Well mostly … they mostly do hold truth. Say even I peddled a few of these myths at Jink's Rooms. Heck … my father, Ebeno Jink, had been filling you youngers full of dread and wonder for decades. Felt only right for me to carry on the tradition from him, and many a Jink prior.'

Missy asked, 'Whatever happened to Ebeno, Ebby? I have heard stories, all different mind you. Which one is truth? You never talk about him. I was there, as you know, but never heard the end of it or him …'

'Not here, Missy … not here. Maybe one day, one day soon, but not here. Just … enjoy yourself.' Jink shuffled the belted sack hanging to the front of his waist, and turned it to hang around the bottom of his back, clearly agitated, but he didn't lose his warm friendly smile. He knew she meant no harm, she was just curious as to the sudden disappearance of his father many years ago.

She had never before conjured the courage to ask such a

question, her master had forbidden her to speak of the event, but here, in the forest, it seemed all inhibitions had been cut loose somewhat. She had been a new initiate, only a few months in when she was first allowed in the taproom of Jink's Rooms, rather than just the sitting room while her masters muttered away. She remembered the first time she had graced the much talked of stone tiles after only just ticking over the age of sixteen summers. Ebeno had always been very courteous and most of the time jovial toward the novices waiting around playing board games and card games and the like contained in the sitting room, waiting for their masters to reappear from their discussions, as they sat around the common tables of the tap room – sometimes after several hours.

Though, the first time beyond those stained-glass and wooden doors where they all talked, had also been the last she would see of Ebeno Jink. Four cloaked men had suddenly appeared from the antechambers where the high-level meetings took place, wearing the same shade of green the third pillar adorned. A heated discussion took place before the tallest, and who seemed the most senior, cast something quickly, something that could only resemble a spell, to render the old eberactu to silence. From that point all in the room were ushered out by the other cloaked members of the *supposed* Third pillar. She was the last to leave, and the only one to look back before the doors were slammed shut. She remembered the last image like it was only yesterday – Ebeno, stood behind the bar, she was sure she saw the man smile, not a smile of malice, but a warm, friendly smile and she was even more sure he moved his lips as if speaking to someone unseen before the doors were locked off and guarded by the three.

She left the wondering alone for the moment.

Ebby Jink led them to the opening to what Semoni had hoped was Caliopa.

It didn't take long before they crested the opening and were now standing in the midst of the first town on the trail. It was unlike any other they had travelled to before. It was, though, just as depicted by the paintings at the City. Surprisingly, none of the small houses were made from timber: instead, they were constructed of large blocks which had a consistent earthy shade all throughout the town. All the roofs had many rusted patches and even more patches of paint where repairs had taken place. *There must be a metal deposit of some sort and smelter in these woods as the only smelter anywhere near this place is within the Fourth Pillar, and nothing has been commissioned for Famnagira. Especially not crinkly metal!*

One other stark image that bestowed itself upon them was the massive well in the centre, it could be clearly seen from where they stood at the outskirts of the town, the same blocks as those that made up the houses structure were arranged around its perimeter. It was a massive structure, one that should be replicated in every town they visited in the Famnagira.

The wells, along with providing crystal clear water from the springs beneath the basalt terrain below, gave access to multiple other villages and towns of the eberactu within the Famnagira. The tunnels had been a project started by one of the earlier Onber who had travelled to give advice to the eberactu on all manner of subjects, including networking and defence; thus the beginning of a project that had been under construction for hundreds, if not thousands, of years – only nine of the major locations had been connected so far. Based on the progress to date, it was expected to be another sixty years before all the locations required to be connected would be so.

Semoni asked, 'Hey, Jink, why not make use of the abundance of timber in these woods?' He gesticulated widely with his arms to add focus of the point. 'Why only the doors?'

Ebby's reply was delayed as he too looked to the magic of the woods. 'Sem, we only take what She grants us,'

'But the doors, Ebb?'

'Given by the winds: aged limbs of timber, chopped to planks. We only take what falls from the trees and nothing more!'

Missy joined the conversation. 'How old is this place?'

'No one knows … we keep no records of our long ago past, only the significant events, and nothing before we were approached by the earliest Onber. For we have always dwelled in these glades, well before your forebears' initial contact. We have all we need, all we have ever needed, right here. The wonderous creatures to the south are the only inhabitants of Inarrel who can pass freely through the glades, for it is believed – through generational speak – they provided the forest for us to live as to not disturb their habitat. It is also believed that we were once mountain dwellers who lived high in the mountains. Another thing to note is that—'

Ebby was cut off by a loud shout from not too far away.

A plump woman trundled toward them – tall for her kind. 'Ebby! Jink!' She waved her arms in the air before pointing profusely at him. Now it was Ebby Jink's turn to blush, his red hair and red beard now matching the colour of his cheeks. 'Ebby! Don't you dare move, young man!'

Ebby made a sound. 'Shush! You two, keep quiet. No, actually, both of you disappear … but not too far, hey. Go, get gone!'

'But Jink, our masters instructed explicitly, and under no circumstance, were we to relieve ourselves of your company.'

Ebby grumbled. 'Well … just go over there, and quick!' He pointed toward the well.

They were not quick enough to escape the cyclone of

arms and cursing that headed toward them. 'And just where do you think you're going, child?'

Semoni was abashed, though he tried to reply before she cut him off.

'And you, you little tart! What do you think you are doing with my Corella's to be? Her promised, Ebby?'

Missy also tried to reply, but was again cut off. The flustered woman turned to Ebby Jink who was cowering and holding his hands high around his throat as if expecting another pair to soon be wrapped around tighter than his.

The older eberactu woman was waiting, hands on hips, looking at Missy, waiting for an explanation to be offered for her pointed query. Jink began to speak but again the woman cut off the interruption, 'Was I asking you? You little cockslinger!'

They were saved from further rendition of scorn by another one of the stumpy folk who appeared behind the lady. 'Now, now, Comola, be easy on young Ebby. You know the reasons surrounding his sudden comeuppance, to tend to Jink's Rooms.'

'Aye, Ped. But leaving Corella like that?' She said, suddenly looking pained – now that the burst of pent-up anger had been released. She turned that hard gaze once more upon Ebby. 'If she were 'ere, Ebby, you know she would have thrown you down that well before you ever got a word in. Heck, I might still throw your arse down there myself!'

'You know I can't discuss why, but I do offer you an explanation. The demise of … sorry … the unfortunate passing of my dear father led to a chain of events that were unavoidable. You know the tradition, Jink's is a lifetime role. Endor, my youngest brother, was in line to take over, as per our tradition. But he was only just out of his arse sling! Believe me, it was a shock to be grabbed and taken far, far away from Cordelia—'

Lunging at him she shouted 'Corella! You little s—'

'—easy, easy!' Ped grabbed swinging arms before she could register a true, solid strike.

'You deal with him, Ped. I'm done!' Her face was full of anger and hatred toward Ebby, which was only punctured by the tongue sticking out before she turned to storm away.

Ped nodded to her and then to Ebby and the two in tow. 'Ebby, she understands. But, why? Why no word back? We have plenty of peddlers and carriages going up that way, and the first stop is always here. Makes no sense! Never did. We haven't seen nor heard from you, not directly, for years. You know Corella, and how she must have felt. And why wind her mother up even more?'

'Dunno, maybe just trying to sever that cord.' Jink looked at his feet, one was swinging in the dust, the other still shaking from nearly joining the elders' spirits beneath the trees. 'Know it was bad. Just didn't know what to write. "Hey Corella, sorry, can't ever see you again, well I can but it has to be here! Away from all you love!" Was better for me to just let it be!'

'Maybe. But was that your choice, or one that presented itself to help make it the *desired* choice? And it shouldn't have been yours to make either …' Ped eyed him, a flare of anger came forth, but was suppressed with a wipe of his mouth with the back of a thick hand.

'Ped, I get it, though we really should be on our way. I might skip through Caliopa and make our way to Remoria. Do you think the High Elder would give permission to take these two through the *tunnelway*?'

'Not a chance, laddy. I reckon though, he may give some assistance by way of getting them through the forest road. He may have had forward word of your arrival, but you were not due for a few another day or two.' He then chuckled as he looked at his wife as she slammed the door shut. 'Lucky you did arrive today, and early too. She was setting aside time this evening to sharpen a few butcher knives.' Ped chuckled some more, a little too jovially for Ebby's liking.

Semoni rubbed his hand along the wall that rimmed the expansive well. It must have been at least ten body lengths in diameter. He then looked into the chasm below dauntingly. A draft hit him hard, but he didn't back off, instead he inhaled the air rushing past him. A pecbor's sensitivity to sight, smell and sound was not lost during his time away from Pecboria; he could almost taste the crystal-clear waters filtering through the surface, the musky aroma of the mushroom covered walls that must decorate the caverns, the salty sweat of the eberacru working furiously to open up the network leagues beyond the below – deep within the tunnels.

They were waiting on an outcome of the decision to allow them to travel deep below, or to carry on above ground – beneath the Famnagira's massive canopies. They had initially been rejected. However, with Ebby's standing within this glade, they were offered a chance of appeal.

Semoni was brought back to his senses, then knocked immediately back out of them as a wailing shriek echoed up from the bottom of the cavernous void. Panicked, he looked to Missy.

She was the first to react. Looking over the well wall, she saw a floating figure spiralling up towards them. She didn't baulk until the figure turned its head half a circle and locked its gaze at her as it continued to ascend the blackness, hovering smoothly above the twisting stairs.

'Shit!' she cursed as she crouched to hide behind the wall, dragging Semoni with her. 'What is that?!'

'What is it? What did it look like?'

'Pale … floating … old … dead, definitely dead, though holds a strangely familiar face …'

'You must have good eyes to see that far down the well,

Missy,' he said with a quiver in his voice.

Missy shook her head 'No! it was right ther—'

Feeling some sort of a presence, they turned their heads, and looked atop the wall behind them.

Both screamed as they scattered away from the figure looking at them, a toothless crooked smile adding to the terror. Its face was missing bits of skin, its nose sunken slightly, and it was draped in tattered nightclothes. It looked as though it had just dug itself out from the ground.

Suddenly, the recognition dawned on Semoni as he whispered questioningly. 'Morla …?'

'*Yes,* Sem … I see it too!' Missy said, if a little absently.

The figure they assumed to be the revered Morla – the Onberseeler from eons past, one of the six large marble busts that skirted the main entrance to the City of Columns and in the main hall – was now looking at them. At least the general outline was there, and there was no mistaking the pointed ear, the one that remained.

She spoke to them, very clearly, softly as though whispering which would have been impossible to hear from the distance they had scampered back to. 'You do well to recognise me in this state. Good, that will speed up our discussion. And my apologies for my dramatic entrance. Soon as I heard you were here, I made my way as fast as I could.' There was no wavering in her voice, the articulation and pitch was perfect for a being that had been dead for thousands of years. Another figure rose from out of the well and clambered over the wall.

Ebeno Jink – Ebby's, so-called, deceased father sat on the well wall beside the ghostly apparition of Morla, confirmed by the fact that Ebeno passed through her ghostly form. The face that Ebby would one day portray, in another fifty or so years, looked at them. Apprehension had at first stopped Miss Nomellia from approaching as soon as she had seen him; she didn't hesitate once the act of walking through the apparition of Morla had occurred. She raced to him and jumped into his arms. It hadn't registered to her though that he had not been of this material world either. She banged her knees on the wall and only just stopped herself from flying headfirst down the well.

The warm and familiar chuckle that followed irritated her slightly – not that it was uncalled for, but for that he was not there to catch her.

The chuckle died down before he spoke softly to her. 'Dearest Missy, fear not. I am still of this world, which I'm sure you knew already, that you believed it so. We do not have long, this rendezvous has been years in the making, the playing pieces of *Fehlter* have been set into their positions, ready to counter the *Fell*. The Fell to come will be swift and without mercy, though the pieces atop the playing board will not be carved from stone nor cut from leather.

'No. For now we are all players of Fehlter. The darkness has played its hand, albeit sooner than we had predicted, and hoped, but we had also anticipated, and applied the required contingencies, be that it should. This is where you come in.'

Morla then turned to Missy and asked, 'Do you believe that *I'm* dead, that I have passed on?'

Missy's emotions were still being coerced through the unseen waves of the forest, so she didn't hesitate to act on the question. 'You are dead. Dead for … ages!' She then turned to Ebeno. 'But you …' She let a small smile creep through. 'Would have deceived us all. Where the shit are you hiding?! And … why?!'

'Oh, Ebby hasn't told you?' It was Morla that spoke, her voice now almost angelic. 'Well he should have. Maybe not before you left the City. He should have *cleared* up a few things before you got here though. At the very least.' Ebby again looked abashed, he'd nowhere to hide from the constant scorn.

Semoni had mustered the courage to join them; he had

also recognised Ebeno but had not felt the urge to run after him to attempt an embrace. 'Maybe next time you should appear first Master, Ebeno? Just a thought …'

Morla hissed a slight barb, 'There won't be a next time!' losing all angelic chords, now replaced with sharp bite.

'Easy Morla, they know not what they have been involved in. None of the youngers, nor any of the Novices do. Be easy …'

'Oh get over yourself. Big! Teddy! Bear! Jink! I will, once they all get here.'

'Where? Where are we to *get* to?' asked Semoni, all fear gone.

'The pass,' Ebeno replied quickly, 'as a start, you must venture beyond though, to where *they* reside, deep in the Ellemenda Peaks.'

'Who? Or what … is there?' asked Missy

Morla was the one to answer. 'A visitor has approached the main glade, only few know from where they hale. The creature is here as massive, but it does not know why, nor do the dwellers of the main glade, but we do. The creature belongs to the magerana genus, an ampemera; the same species that helped the Eberactu venture and settle in this beautiful forest many, many eons ago, even longer than before we settled here.

'But we know why it, or rather she, is here. The world as we know is about to get a whole lot darker. The spawn of darkness, those whose will is to consume without question, as is their nature, have prematurely made a move.

The messenger, the ampemera, will wander for a while longer, but not forever. You must venture on, you must be there to record the message when the most prominent star in the sky, the Star of Eternity, is at the apex of its transit. That is when it will burn its brightest. The star's burst of light will be used as conduit from another world to send its dying message via the creature who will then speak. You must copy exactly and without pause on the sacred scroll you will find deep within these caverns.'

Missy frantically stumbled out questions. 'But how are you here? How is Eberon here? Wait ... what are we doing here? We cannot travel the caverns without—'

Eberon calmed her before she became even more disorientated – the swaying waves of the pulsating magic had not subsided, only Missy had timed her emotions in rhythm with it. Now they were being thrown out of sync by the unreality unfolding itself around her. 'Calm child, all is in order. You will meet me soon, down deep below. But for now, listen to us. And listen well. On your journey below and beyond—'

All her joking aside, she now had firm confirmation from him. 'What? You, you're ... actually alive? I knew it! I knew it!'

She was about to dive forward again but checked herself, still feeling the throb about her knees. Tears began to glisten. Not from the physical pain she felt but from a relief the affirmation had brought, and what those words meant.

They were interrupted by Ebby and another eberactu, taller for his race, wearing a dark bushy-topped turban known as the Elder's Pikbin which was woven from the halber tree's leaves, hidden deep within the sacred grove, many centuries ago. He held a cylindrical, hard-leather tube which was adorned with an ancient symbol and text scrawled all across its surface.

The elder spoke loudly so all could hear, including the folk who had begun to empty their homes to form a ring around the perimeter of the oval. 'Here ... I hold one of the ancient Scrolls of Vilenzia ...'

Missy gasped and Semoni's eyes widened in shock.

The elder continued on, his deep, resounding voice capturing all in attendance. 'Though the text on the scroll contained within is beyond our comprehension, it must be forward by those marked with the sign …' He walked, flanked by Ebby Jink who now wore a wider grin than he had ever had before – which was a feat in itself – toward the two of them. 'Take this, child,' he said to Missy. 'You must use this to seek out the sacred, tainted scroll – the one marked by the gods. This here will help guide you. Whatever you discover, you must then deliver to *She* who has been marked. But before you do, you must seek out Eberon below …'

Missy looked perplexed as she replied, interrupting the elder. 'But he is here—' She turned to look at the well where Morla and Eberon had been seated, but there was no one left sat there, their presence dissipated, replaced only by air. '*Was* here.'

'Aye, they were here to advise of the path to be taken, I'm sure their powers of illusion have since run dry, my lady. Ebby here, he has delivered you seamlessly, that you are accompanied by this other young fellow too … well that is fortunate.' He winked at Semoni. 'For the path has been set in motion, multiple paths actually, all dependent on when the seventh would occur, and it has, or so is our best assumption.'

Semoni spoke, eyeing the scroll's capsule, 'That's one of the … the ancient, yes mythical scrolls!'

It was Ebby who responded, cutting off the elder before he started to speak. 'Let me, Elder Jacindo.'

The elder nodded; he knew Ebby had a vested interest in the whole charade that had taken place over many years. Just as Eberon had before him, the cycle of Jinks through the city tavern had become a running ritual, filled with humour within the elder eberactu community for centuries – behind the humour was a hope that the prophecies would never be fulfilled, and it was all just folklore. But they knew it for what it was, for the frequent visitation of those not of this world had kept them in check, and also diligent in their continuation of the charade. There had been many occurrences over the ages of the tavern's resident Jink being overcome by members of the Column. The target was never the barkeep, but the feisty girl being hauled away, the last to see the theatrical play conclude with the closing of the main doors – the curtains to the whole saga being drawn. One of those selected from years of searching for the right candidate throughout Vilenzia and beyond.

Before Ebby could speak, he was whacked hard on the head – if he were any normal human, it would have only been a whack across the midriff. He took it well, as he'd expected some reaction from one of his travel companions. The blow did nothing to diminish the smile plastered across his face though. With a small rub across the nose as the other hand adjusted his chin he spoke, 'Deserved. I will take that, though I'm surprised you didn't swing again, Missy.'

'I will save the next one for your bastard father, Ebby!' She smiled too once she had let the frustration out; she would indeed slap the older Jink around his well-known thick mutton chops.

'Bastard, father, you say …' Jink rubbed his chin some more. He had not thought too far that the same fate had become his grandfather. 'Fair enough, but I'm sure by now you know we are not here on a field trip? There is a lot we must discuss. And, lucky for us, we have a long way to go …'

Ebby looked at Semoni who was still transfixed on the scroll, wide eyes following it about wherever it swung. 'Yes, Semoni. Well it is one of only the few that have been recovered so far. Or so I'm told.'

'I thought they were all securely contained within the upper floor of the library at the City?' Semoni looked perplexed, but still in awe.

Elder Jacindo jumped in. 'Only vague copies of what we have found. Very vague, but masterfully transcribed to disguise their true falsehood, as the story goes.' The old eberactu smiled – knowingly.

He lifted the scroll high into the air, which was followed by a rumbling murmur about the milling crowd now encompassing the town's centre – they knew the time to worry was nigh; they were all well versed in the prophecies and the oncoming threat that must be dealt with. They would no doubt be ready: thus the operations over the past few generations creating such a defensive barricade to the forest entrance and the network below. The network below also held a few secondary safety measure – just in case …

Shaking her head, still feeling the effects of the forest, she murmured, 'I still don't understand why. Why me? The pawn in this whole episode, I'm not even ready to ascend to the next level above apprentice. What the piss is going on?!'

Ebby drew close and held an arm around her waist.. He then motioned Semoni over, placed the other around his waist. 'All will be revealed soon. We must venture below to where we need to go … and quickly.' He held them both a little tighter, looked up at each, and nodded with half closed eyes, which seemed to draw a sigh from each as he gazed at them in turn.

# Expose of Darkness

Mesfa looked out, far beyond the balcony to the barren, macabre landscape that was offered. It made her feel a little disorientated, whether due to the void of life or the horizon shifting away much nearer than she was used to. She had been feeling a sickness, overwhelmed by a sense of something she had never felt before, whether it be real or due to her hypochondriac nature she was unsure, but something wasn't right.

The only light offered this side of Kinora was the reflection of sunlight from Seltero hovering in the distance; it wasn't much, but was enough to carry across the surface. Her eyes had always been keen in the darkness, at least for the majority of her life – ever since she was locked away as a stray child in the cellar of a modest vineyard, a vineyard frequented by the Syltenerians located to the south-west of Vilenzia, the *Witches Crook,* on the outskirts of the town Felgorse.

The corona of Inarrel locked its gaze on her, much akin to the eye of a scepteran – an animal much larger than a tiger and much more ferocious which dwelled in the southern ranges of The Divide and very rarely needed to venture any further; their eyes had a glowing hue about the iris. As a creature of the magical divide, its abilities had been enhanced throughout the ages. The oval shaped pupil was shaped for a wider vision when hunting. Similar to the shape of the planet now plunged into darkness gazing back at her now.

The unease had hit her suddenly, she did not know what was happening to her; maybe the fact that Arigal had, what seemed to her, been selected to elevate to the next rung of darkness. Mesfa knew that only one could elevate to such a rung, it was the way … a necessity – she had always been drilled with this notion. But it could not be that, for the slight setback on the balcony had been but a hiccup of petulance from her. She had always been the one to come out, usually way in front of Arigal, through all their studies and trials in and out of the field.

Beginning to wonder about the future set her retching over the cold bone-laden balustrade. She came up for air, wiped away the spittle, then proceeded to make her way inside. Holding her petite frame against the arched opening she pondered, *What future? What comes after this, even if I do get to see after this ... what then? This planet is as barren as my adoptive whore. Is this what becomes of my home world if we are to triumph over those who would try to stop us?!*

She blinked, but the second she opened her eyes the iris of the darkened planet pulsated outward from pupil, and she was drawn to its magnetic pull. Moving away from the archway, back out toward the edge of the smaller balcony – the one she had found for some sort of solace – she reached out with an outstretched hand and also her mind to whatever was calling to her.

Behind, Arigal crept to where she had stood in the archway. Watching her sister move gracefully to the edge of the balcony, she looked entranced by something, but she couldn't see what. *This planet does stir the emotion, I wonder what she is doing. Did she take the soul fire from that little cretin and is now in a euphoric trance? We agreed to take that life together!*

Mesfa spun around, hearing the slightest scrape of nails on stone as Arigal skirted her way quickly toward her. She reached up as Arigal's hand was about to connect with her skull, grabbing the bony, yet still powerful wrist, and spun the arm around, bringing Arigal to her knees. 'So, you finally found some courage to challenge me once again!'

'No! We agreed we would share in any soul fire! We would consume until we had to make the decision to consume each other whichever that *other* would be!'

'Stupid girl. Always so quick to feel the victim. Is that why you were so smug up there on that ledge? Thinking you had bested me?'

'No … no, sister.'

'Then why? Why follow on with the charade to that bitch that you are more worthy than me?'

Arigal roared, 'Because I am!' She spun Mesfa's arm back around as she raised herself up, and doubled the effort. She reduced Mesfa to her knees, and she stood proudly above her. Mesfa's shocked face was a delight to see for Arigal. 'All this time, you actually believed you were better than me? Ha! ' Arigal bellowed, which brought a hurtful gaze from Mesfa. 'The vanity you secrete is nothing short of disdainful to all who have ever loved you. Now you will be forced to submit to my will, and I will be looking to add your pitiful soul to the collection *we* have consumed and double the power I possess.'

Mesfa's arm was twisted but not enough that she couldn't escape. She looked at Arigal but was knocked back to looking at the stone pavers below by a slight narrowing of eyes and a slight twitch of her head which screamed, *Sister, please do as I say, we are being watched.* She bowed her head in a submissive motion. *What is happening sister?* her pleading eyes asked.

Arigal thought the subtle communication hadn't been observed, so she kept up with the charade and whacked Mesfa around the back of the head with a swift knee – it had looked like the head, and a stern blow, but she actually caught the top of both shoulders and had released a lot of the energy prior to impact. Mesfa still fell forward as though the scepteran had swung one of its massive, clawed paws and connected – without complaint.

Mesfa rested on one of five beds arranged in the same

orientation as the five-pointed star shaped room, away from the onyx sculpted figurine standing tall in the centre of the room. A surreal thing, it looked in the same direction toward any, no matter where they moved throughout the room. She finally felt safe enough to speak low, almost only a breath. 'You saw, and felt it too.' Mesfa pointed at Arigal, more in hope. 'It was calling to me, Arigal, you must have been influenced too?'

'So that's why you were dancing around like a lady tramp looking for some cheap coin to come your way?'

Mesfa saw a smile appear at the last and creased her face, before launching a soft, pawing attack upon her sister. 'So, what was it?'

'What, Mesfa?' She looked at her dumbly. 'Probably just the life of that world being radiated by the conjunction, so much emotion would be throwing itself around down there. I had come to tell you that we are ready to return. I have been instr—'

Mesfa interjected. 'You . . ? *You* have been instru—'

'Yes! Listen to me, and quickly!'

Mesfa sighed and threw her head back into the rolled-up cloth she used as a pillow. 'Go on ...'

Arigal detailed the story of the *Roaming Knight* who had stolen *certain* – without any further elaboration – artifacts from the head mages of the Sylteneria and had hidden them away millennia ago. She went on to detail the story told to her earlier, before she had come to the balcony: the *heroes of* Inarrel are being guided by those not of Inarrel, and probably not of this realm, to seek out these artifacts to end the forever eclipse of darkness and the intended eventual consumption of all soul life on the planet.

'But why don't *they* who dwell here, and those beyond this planetary system, go down there themselves and smash them to pieces and be done with them?'

A voice came from somewhere, as an echo throughout

the domed room, similar to that of the cavern back in the Depths of Enteria, though even more direct. 'I *am* of another realm, that which cannot be touched, nor broken, by mortal flesh, nor by the pawns of my choosing. Who, in turn, would choose those not unlike you!'

Mesfa and Arigal looked around the room, then also out into the corridor adjoining, seeing nothing – unsurprisingly. Still, the voice carried on. 'My precious flames! I feel your doubt, your fear, I too feel the pull of that repulsive planet. Do not be concerned with those trying to sway you from your path. I'm your mother, your only salvation, and … I will be obeyed!

'My pawns, at the very least, they know their role. The being you have been assigned to, *my* pawn, is only a few rungs above you in the distinctive hierarchy, but there are thousands like you and she is but many a rung below the upper echelon of those I select to ride in the immortal carriage of the Sylteneria.'

It became clear that they were being spoken to by The *Ultimate* – The Lady! But, as both bowed to the well-worn carpets below, they looked to each other with fear in their eyes. They had been caught with dissimilation within their minds, and not by the being they had earlier assumed to be The Lady, but by *She* … her very self! And also, no doubt, those in train who would be testing every sway of emotion, every sway in their consciousness, those who would draw a final conclusion. Mesfa realised that the sickness she had been feeling was not from her indiscretion, but from the continuous poking of all of her senses by those from *that* other realm. *You fuckers! I hope you heard or felt that too! Whoever … or whatever you may be!* The thought of an unwelcomed prying set her off.

Arigal looked sidelong at Mesfa, and whispered – not that it would conceal much during the exchange – 'I know what happens next, what is expected of us! It ain't pretty, though it never is, hey?'

The voice returned, giving affirmation of prying. 'Be about it then, and be quick. The more you achieve during this alignment the higher will be your esteem! I will unleash the third realm upon them! Be there when that begins! And ready. For those fools will use all resources at their disposal to stop us, not knowing this wave of disruption would be but only a tester. A teaser of what they would believe was to come. Thus exposing, and thus highlighting, a swath of all their supposed heroes we're to focus on neutralising between now and then. An eventual swarm will then occur during the *forever night,* one that will not ever lapse, during the eclipse of those planets, a few years from now. An eclipse to null all. Now go!' A laugh echoed throughout the place, sliding away, leaving nothing but the panting of the two newly ascended acolytes.

The short span of silence between was broken by the all too familiar sound of heels hitting stone that paced up the corridor towards them.

# A Sound From Within

The docks bustled away, fervently, for it was now a long way past midday, and the expected darkness had already taken hold of the city of Sinboran. It hadn't darkened the residents' spirits by any means though. Rather, the jostle had increased in line with the ambience, which was now resounding throughout the streets and the busy docks, elevated ten-fold since the day broke into early night.

The number of patrons gathered throughout the scattered taverns had overflowed onto the streets – the taverns had accounted for such revelry though and had erected barricades that stretched a fair width beyond where their usual custom would be permitted. Thus, with only one way in and one way out, ensuring they snared as many punters into their bottlenecked net as possible, increasing their chances of a considerable margin.

Those same gates – more so the exit rather than the entrance – were manned, every one, by the muscular *engorians*, wider, and much taller than the average man by at least a third. Their greenish skin and no-nonsense demeanour was perfect to quell any brawl that would frequently break out. They had been known to throw the rowdiest of patrons, those causing the most trouble, over the high barrier and to the cobbles beyond the makeshift fence.

The bubble of each tavern would undoubtedly have overlapped if it weren't for the high chain fencing dividing them with the landlords more than likely splitting the cost for the dividing fence to save a few grets.

The festivities had now been in full swing for a while. And, as the trio entered the music hall, all such resemblance of harmonious singledom dissipated into an eruption of chaotic adulation.

For the punters inside knew whom entered: the three most talented beings to ever grace Sinboran. Many had brought flowers, knitted effigies, or some other soft item to throw from the tiered terraces – furnished with wooden modular tables where the copious amount of food and drink during the Festival would be dropped.

The trio made their way up to the higher second platform of the second tier – the one reserved for probably the second-best view, taken so every year by the count's guests.

Marcos collected more than a couple of the ladies' intimate, soft apparel that were thrown their way, bringing the crowd to bouts of humour as he swung them around and then flicked each one of them at Velosko as if an archer. As ever, Velosko was able to avoid every cotton threaded arrow with a bend or swerve and still keep a straight face until they reached their table.

Their table offered a direct line of sight, with no obstruction, to the entirety of the stage below, more so that the count was offered a full view to assess each and every performer, even those less accustomed to the spotlight, to be ogled by the thousand permitted patrons: to assess not only their ability, but also their attitude for a modest offer from his own administrators' coffers.

Once they were at their station, Velosko pulled out a few random pairs he had casually secreted away, to the slight disgust of Amaria, and dropped them on Marcos's dinner plate once he felt it apt. Then he turned and bowed with a flourish which was lapped up by the baying mob – the standard response whenever they were in attendance.

Though they would not be playing their much-rehearsed piece until the later session, they would sometimes jump on stage and help out the nervous or struggling acts, and the crowd knew it, and that is what kept the music hall full for the three days of performances, hoping for the guaranteed extra *appearance* from the few performances scheduled of those exceptional muses who were now in Sinboran.

Second to that was the impromptu aid one or two of them would offer to those who belied the soul for want of engagement – mainly … Marcos.

As they took their seats, the next scheduled performer was due to grace the grand stage after the slight disruption their entrance had caused. Velosko stood back up and raised his arms to the raucous crowd, shushing them to silence; he could hear the fluttering heartbeat of the next performer, the nervousness caught in her breaths, and the clasping crunch of her violin grasped with sweating fingers. Immediately the crowd fell silent as the girl and her violin entered onto the stage, splitting the high hanging curtains as she appeared.

Velosko's act of quieting the crowd had set the already nervous girl's nerves racing even faster; the sudden quiet had hit her more than the blinding lights shining from the balconies of the upper tiers.

Velosko heard the quickening of the heart and the gripping of the violin – it felt as though she would snap its scroll. She missed a small, cushioned chair – laid out as a prop on stage – and bumped into it, making her stumble a short way as she continued on her way to the front of the stage, seating herself on the ornate stool she was to perform from.

The girl rested the violin atop the cushion of a decorative armchair beside where she sat, and straightened herself out, trying to settle her nerves. The ice was shattered once again by a punter's loud heckle "Get on with it, will ya!" which brought jeers and a only couple cheers from the crowd. Velosko stood and raised both his arms, hands outstretched; a whoosh from the crowd replaced the noise. Velosko was to aid the young musician; the signal to the crowd had been seen many times before though never this early on the first day!

Marcos looked up at Velosko. 'What are you doing, man? Can we at least have a few more drinks before we get into it?'

'I'm feeling so alive, Marcos,' Velosko smiled toward him – the vigorous exercise had heightened his passion somewhat. 'I reminisce of my first performance in front of *real* people. She's as nervous in this hall as I was in the grubby *Apple and Partridge* back in Heloniko, and that was only for the five regulars who would remain seated there, even if the place was on fire!'

'Yeah, I can see that – ah stuff it, I'm coming down with you!' Marcos stood and stretched his arms too, then cracking a few joints as his hands clasped together. He shouted to his carrier who was now stood near the backstage door, peeping through to view the spectacle, 'Cello!' he said, followed by a roar from the crowd.

Blinded by the amplified lantern lights – some enhancement through magical means – Anna-Mary couldn't see what was happening until she heard a shout; she knew the voice well, the angelic accent of Marcos. *Blood and mud, Marcos! Shit, I must appear so stupid up here if he is coming to help me out! This early in the day too! Shit …*

As they made their way up onto the stage, the face of Marcos came into Anna-Mary's view. *Oh! Wow! Isn't he just … divine!* She had no idea Velosko was flowing up the steps too, not far behind.

She stood, quickly.

It all became too much for her as he came into her view from behind the blinding lights. She was blacking out, she could feel the blood rushing away from her face before she lurched, uncontrollably forward and began to fall face first.

The landing was not the crashing mangle to the hard timbers she expected; instead, it was as if she was landing atop a large, fluffed-up pillow. *Lucky! I must have landed in the chair. Oh de*— The last image offered was that of Marcos's face coming in close as Velosko held her gently …

Velosko – sensing the blood rushing from her head – dived forward to catch her before she hit the deck. Holding her head in his hands as she succumbed to the panic, he spoke, 'Marcos, hold both her feet in the air a little, one in each arm and jiggle them up and down, should get her blood flowing quicker back into her head!'

As she came back around, fully out of the mini slumber, she opened her eyelids a little to see Marcos between her legs. *What a wonderful dream I'm having.*

'I think she's waking, Vel,' he said as he continued to jiggle her feet with the crook of his armpits.

'Huh … what? Who?' She quickly sat up and blushed. 'Oh, I'm sorry. What happened?'

A soft, though direct, voice came from behind Marcos. 'Marcos, what *are* you doing. Get off her!' Amaria clamped her hands on her hips as she looked sternly at him.

'But … Vel asked me to grab—'

'I don't give a flock what Vel said … *I* said get off her!' She then swung the steely gaze to Velosko. 'And you … we are here for no more than a moment and you're up here!' She tapped her foot as she went on. 'Little one, are you alright?' she eventually asked the daze youngster.

'Yes … I am now,' she said as she smiled in the direction of Marcos.

Amaria nodded. 'Well … will you be alright to perform on your own? I want these two fools back up at that table.' And pointed at where they had sat themselves moments earlier. 'And quickly!'

Anna-Mary nodded. 'Yes, I will be, I should be alright. This is my first time here, I usually perform for the small groups who dare listen to my noise down at the common, though mostly I'm surrounded by nothing more than its beautiful greenery and its colourful, flighty residents. It was your father who recommended me to perform, and he put his name as sponsor. And he's the only the reason I'm able to perform here today.'

'Reason enough. Very well … you must be a talented musician then for such a high recommendation.' The frustration had now left and was replaced with her usual warm glow. Curiosity set in too as she looked at the pretty face. 'I very much look forward to hearing you play. Come on, louts! Let's get settled before— Sorry, flower, forgive me … but your name?'

'Anna-Mary,' she replied, smiling sheepishly, still in awe of the trio.

'What a lovely name, it's a perfect match to accompany that the blossom of a smile.'

'Thank you, I will be alright. Helps I can't see anyone though …'

'It certainly does.' She responded, nodding toward Velosko. 'And, if you ever feel overawed, find no shame in finishing your composition early, believe me, the majority here won't even blink an eyelid. And the minority *I* will deal with …' she replied, full of reassurance, as she clenched a fist. The motherly smile still offered sincerity. 'Good luck, petal!' she offered, genuinely, as she turned away. The three quickly exited the stage, disappearing into an artificial darkness, leaving the girl alone.

As the three left the stage, a few boos rang around the auditorium before Amaria shouted up at the galleries, 'Calm down you bunch of hooligans! Has this coveted music hall now become nothing more than a zoo? There will be plenty of time for these two' – she looked disdainfully at the pair – 'to play! Now … let us enjoy the music of this young performer, who has the much coveted, and the only, recommendation given by his lordship, Count Atinna! Now … shut your faces!' Laughter and cackles followed her rebuke as they made their way back to their table.

*

Anna-Mary breathed in deeply as she waited for the "hush" to be shouted by the resident compere. It was slow in coming, forcing Amaria to stand and turn to face the galleries, she glared from one side to the other, quieting the rowdy crowd. Her gaze swept the room once more, seeking any to challenge – none came.

The compere eventually waddled over and found his way to the front of the stage to introduce, with a flourish, and a swagger, 'The singer, and her violin …' Marcos muttered something to Velosko that resembled bemusement at the strange combination, before the compere finished, 'Anna-Mary of House Gleve.'

Amaria inhaled sharply. 'She hadn't mentioned her surname …' Turning to Velosko, who had heard the words as she took in the breath, she cut him off before he would ask. 'Oh, you wouldn't know the story,'

'What story?' Marcos's interest had now been piqued as he suspected further intrigue. 'Gleve? Why so closed, Amaria?'

Ignoring Vel's twitch of a head to signal his interest in the matter too – *He will find out soon enough* – she turned, comically, to Marcos. 'Well, Marcos. My … my, how many times have you been here?'

'Well I—'

'Rhetorical, Marcos. Come to think of it—'

'Ohhh. I see …' Marcos blushed, now making the connection. 'Annie Gleve? No … it … it cannot be!' He suddenly remembered a woman he had connected with in *every* sense the first time he had performed with Velosko and Amaria in Sinboran. She was also a performer, but not of the kind to grace the so-called sophisticated masses here in the hall. She was a performer of a different kind – a traveller with a troupe that settle in Sinboran, an amazing acrobat, singer, dancer, and her favourite act – which had caught the full attention of Marcos – was dousing a halberd blazing with flame orally, at the massive, multi-coloured marquee of the Gleve Family Circus that was always on full show at the edge of the city.

Amaria looked at Marcos through squinted eyes; she knew the girl was not his and was ready to burst with pent-up laughter at his expense before the girl on stage touched the first string with her bow.

Her attention was instantly frozen, then thawed by the sound making its way from the stage. No, the blissful sound of a perfect chord being struck. What followed was completely unexpected by all but for the man that squeezed Amaria's shoulder. Turning she looked up at her father who had just made it to the hall in time to be seated with the three. Her only response, the only one she could muster was, 'Wow!'

An uplifting crescendo of high, flitting notes were followed by a winding descent of long and short ranges, only to perk back up, then back down again. Up and down, every switch in play brought the audience forward and then dropped them back into their seat again, the swing of her bow, drifting them one way and then the next. That she was able to sing – and with such gusto and poise – with the violin nestled beneath her chin was both uncomfortable to watch and absolutely magical to behold.

Her story, versed in song, went on for no more than a few minutes; the words being sung by the multi-talented soprano were lost on many in the hall – the song was sung in a mythical language that was supposedly from the realm beyond dreams, that of *Parilit*. They were not lost on Amaria, nor the three men, nearest and dearest to her.

The moment Anna-Mary stopped playing, the room stood silent for what felt like an age. No one dared breathe and be the one responsible for puncturing the bubble of absolute bliss. It was only once they had come back to their senses that the room erupted in raucous applause and loud whelps of delight.

Amaria was the first to stand, which cause a ripple through the hall as chairs were scraped by those eager to show their appreciation. She found it hard to applaud and at the same time wipe away the flow of emotion rushing out, so she let the tears flow, carried atop the applause.

Marcos and Velosko too were overcome with joy and all the benefits that brought. The sight of them hugging each other, patting each other's back was a graceful moment to savour for Amaria.

Her father was looking at her – a knowing, wide smile splitting his face – waiting for her to check her emotion and turn back to him.

When she did, she squeezed the wiry old man with a big hug: one tighter than any she had given him since she was a small child. Too old to swing her around this time, he spoke instead. 'Come and meet my new star pupil. I swear the world will know the name of Anna-Mary and the Sinboran College of Musical Arts by the time she is done touring with us!'

'What? You mean she is to come with us? No! Get out of here!' She let go of him and pushed him, a little harder than she had meant to, as he hobbled back a few steps. 'Get out of here! Seriously! She is amazing, Father!'

'Yes, she agreed. But she agreed pending one condition I put to her.'

'And what was that?' she looked at him cautiously.

'That you had to be impressed enough to want to tutor her.'

'Absolutely! As if she needs it though! Who could not …

she is an amazing talent! I would lo—'

Count Atinna butted in with a nod to Velosko and Marcos. 'Not just you, but those too brutes also have to agree! However … I see they are just as stunned as you. As was I when I heard a voice resounding around the common. I was equally enamoured by the fact she had a ukelele strumming away – never mind a violin – whilst singing her merry tune. I honestly assumed some other were playing the instrument, until I inspected – stealthily.'

Amaria replied, 'Gods! I would hate to be following that!'

By now Anna-Mary was making her way to the back of the stage where another sheepish youth was stood in the crook of the two curtains. The boy in his late teens made his way out, lugging a large case, obviously for the oboe. Anna-Mary high fived him on her way past which he made all the effort to connect, but in doing so he dropped his case and stumbled over the top of it.

Upon seeing this, Marcos spoke, 'Leave this one with me! I will help give this kid a show that will be remembered for generations. I am so full of emotion, Vel, after that … unexpected performance. I think I need to have a quick release! And this lot will be the beneficiaries! Vamo!'

Wiping the remaining tears away, Amaria spoke, still under the influence of emotion. 'Granted!' The word came as so too did a large bubble extruding from her nose, this set her off in a fit of laughter which produced a stream of much more, but she didn't care, she was happy, and sad at the same time; a sadness she wished would never come – one day inevitable – as she looked deep into her father's warm, loving eyes.

Velosko approached, checking his embrace to reflect that of a friend whilst under the oblivious gaze of her father.

She whispered in his ears which caused him to step back a little. 'My father has asked if she study with us. But—'

Her father offered additional weight to the argument. 'She can be an awesome talent …' He nodded to Velosko. 'She can be the catalyst for my— for the *City's* college to flourish from our *project.*'

'Seems like you have agreed already to … *our project?'* Not a sarcastic response, he understood her tenacious mentality – completely – and the need for her to fulfil a long-ago, lost dream.

'I have. On the condition put forward by my father, that you would agree,'

'But she is so young.'

'So much potential, Vel! She is brilliant! Though her voice needs some work to achieve that air of perfection, and her follow through with the instrument could be better, if ever so slightly. But were we not, are we not, imperfect? When we first ventured to Jacobs, or the far northern city of Gungenadon deep in the mined mountain range of *The Murakolorians?* Vel, she may have no family here. Let us entertain ourselves developing this young bud. Let us give her a life beyond Sinboran; a life as of our own that we are so fortunate to be blessed with. Let us help her flourish, help her to bloom beyond even our level, Vel! Your talents took you from hobbling the cobbles in your father's estate, if I recall correctly, to the lofty heights of being adored by the most powerful and influential rulers all across Inarrel. Can we do the same for her, that little flower … the one we so often see sprouting through, between the cobbles, looking for the light?'

'Ah, Amaria, let me think of the reasons not to first. I know what you're up to. I know the Academia is competing for the upper echelon of clientele – the monarchy sort – but I believe this place has much more soul than that of Heloniko. That's why I love coming here, to see what your father has built. The artists who come through for these three days, the majority are produced under the tutelage of those who spend every second of their existence teaching music, sharing their passion, to those who do not have the coin to gain entrance at Heloniko, nor the opportunity to be enrolled on merit. As they at Heloniko are too far up themselves to even come here to listen, as they themselves have been brought through the "entitled" way of life and how life *should* work. And they love it, they do it for the joy of music, not for accolades, not for praise, not for monetary advancements. They are happy to teach their religion of music, sharing their soul. And that is a beautiful thing I would like to see continue.

'I promised you that this tour would be the last. I was hoping to go out and retire in style! Let me think on it. She may be the spark that enables that, and also the spark your father is looking for in his vision for the—*his* college.' He nodded to Atinna, who was stood a way back; he had somehow moved himself away from the two of them but had no doubt heard every word.

Atinna closed the distance and reached out a hand. Though Velosko could not see it, Atinna knew it would be clasped with vigour. 'Thank you, Vel. I am proud of the Academia we have; the people who are part of the Academia family are world class in every discipline, but without the financial support from the wealthy of the world, we may not see out the next decade. I have pumped no small amount of the wealth my family grew into creating this shared dream, I just need the dream to evolve into sustainability.' Atinna raised an eyebrow, one that Velosko could never anticipate.

Though he felt the man's dilemma anyway through the straining of his throat. 'I understand, Atinna, no matter what happens, you should be proud of what you have achieved here. We'll speak with a few of the potential benefactors on our next travels. You know … most of them despise the thought of musicians from over the Emerald Ocean coming over here to entertain them with their manufactured strutting and forever repeating compositions. They enjoy the raw emotion and vitality that your students bring to their court. Leave it with me. Though, initially, what are your thoughts on this? If we hold ourselves as judges for a talent contest in each of the five regions we will travel to, we will perform, for the week, once a day! For nothing, no fees, nothing! But … the winner is given a scholarship, and boarding here—'

'That would cost me … this city, thousands. No! Much much more grets!'

'How much in lost revenue would that leave us? We offer a gratuitous performance!'

'Very well then, so you perform, you offer your takings as compensation to provide such offer?'

'Atinna, the offer of generosity is much more appealing than the charge for a further recompense!' Velosko, held the count's shoulder, more for reassurance. 'And yes, maybe it does cost more … initially. Yes, indeed it would. Let me finish though, for the forementioned gratuity that *we* would offer, *if* there was to be a transfer across the Emerald Ocean, to Heloniko, of any pupils from that region or duchy, then there would be a donation of, say, thirty percent of the fees that would be paid to Heloniko during the tuition, into the coffers here, paid for by the treasury of that region in exchange for our services previously offered. I will explain the reasoning and, hopefully, they will see the reasoning. Short term loss for exponential gain. *And,* as an incentive, to agreeing to mark that in their local laws, as edict, everyone from that region who does want to study the arts here would receive,' Velosko made a slight cough, 'free board …'

Atinna staggered back two steps before he spoke. 'Well … I would have to … hmm, let me speak with the treasury and run a few numbers.' The count paled and was ready to pass out himself.

Amaria looked at her father with the same look and poise she held minutes earlier when scolding the two forever men in her everyday life – fists pressing tight on hips. 'Shame! Father. Just raise your fees to cover the expense! I'm sure that's all you care about these days: the coin!'

'Darling—'

'Don't call me that! You only call me "darling" when you know that you're—'

Atinna grumbled, 'Fine! Fine … I'm sure the arithmetic will sort itself out … in the end. It would be good if you could secure some actual funding from these benefactors too, maybe … Vel?'

'I'm sure *our* new protégé could swing a few *funds* our, sorry, *your* way.' He turned to meet Amaria's advance. Too slow to react—

She grabbed Velosko and squeezed him so tight he lost all wind before she slapped her lips against his. She could feel the heat rising off his cheeks before her father looked away, eyes back to the stage where Marcos was tuning his cello.

Trying hard to keep his gaze averted from his daughter mauling away at him, he spoke absently. 'Well … so … should be … a wonderful set today. Here's hoping.' Speaking absentmindedly, he continued. 'Say, we have had some unconfirmed reports of some trouble at Denmore, down the coast, though seems to be a bit farfetched to even consider thinking about.' He rubbed his chin and returned a nod back to Marcos. 'Some huge monster or another …' He began humming the tune Anna-Mary had played moments earlier, and excused himself, returning to his table at the bottom of the third tier, a small platform of its own, cantilevered above the tiers beneath, thus having the most exclusive vantage of the show below.

He dropped heavily and sighed with relief, as Marcos shouted aloud from the middle of the stage.

Outstretching both his arms, bow in one hand, cello grasped in the other, he shouted, 'Let's get this Festival going!' The young man sat in awe, next to his idol, too dumbstruck to even move before Marcos shouted at him, 'Play! Play, boy! With all you have and more my friend!'

Every street that wound its way – in many a direction – away from the hall had been bustling away for a while, as always during the Festival. The hordes of punters now revelling in their offered, then designated areas, had increased well into the afternoon. A minority had indulged far too soon, much earlier, and the majority of those were now being, or had been, ejected into what remained of the public domain of the street, from which they had entered.

It didn't matter in the end where they stood, those in the streets were the first to feel the unease.

A wave of vomiting rippled through the residents of the southern port town of Sinboran. The wave emanated from the port district and seemed to affect everyone who was stood outside of their home, place of business, or semi-enclosed in their section of revelry.

\*

Coming up through the hatch, and out onto the deck, the captain of the *Ethereal Dancer* – the vessel that had voyaged from Dalmetonia as carriage for the three musicians – Jentis observed what he had thought he heard, as though they had all been out on rough high seas for days. His crew, those that had remained on board, were now on their knees emptying every content of their innards across the deck they had been furiously scrubbing to clear away the scourge of the long journey.

He made his way to starboard to see that those on the jetty were also struggling to stand from whatever had become them. It wasn't until he looked toward the bow of the ship that he discovered the source of what was happening.

'Holy sh—! What the fuck is that?!'

Bobbing up and down in the middle of the bay – partially hidden behind a wide expanse of the sea wall – was a blob of green mass, sprouting hundreds or more arms, eyes, and mouths. The little light available reflected off its eyes and teeth, the ones bared. He observed a pulse of darkness continually replicating itself, cascading upwards about its body, becoming darker and darker from every pass until the creature made a leap out of the water and sent another wave of darkness toward the city, accentuated by the large ripple it formed as the wave swept across the bay.

Jentis calmed himself. Immediately observing the crescendo of darkness pulsating up through the creature's body out in the bay, he knew then he had to remove himself from above deck as soon as the creature leapt into the air, to fall backwards down the shaft, even if he knew the landing at the bottom of the hatch would take more than the full weight of his body.

Bouncing down the steps, he managed to keep his vision skyward, watching, as a black wave moved swiftly across the shaft's opening above from where he had fallen – jumped. The wave made a slight swooshing sound as remnants of it crept through, but not enough to penetrate further than the rim.

He readied himself, and accepted with no doubt to score a few broken bones when his body would eventually settle on the landing, *a small price to pay* he told himself. Rather that than the puff of vileness emitted above.

As a traveller of the Third Pillar, and well regarded within the precinct, he had been well versed in all the elements of darkness, including the dark creatures and those swayed by the delight of the forever night – one of which was now making waves, nasty waves across Sinboran. Assigned to travel to Dalmetonia decades earlier, he was to report back intelligence of any potential uprisings of darkness sprouting under the influence of the boon of the Syltenerians. He had done so on many occasions, which led to a return to the foreign state with the required resource and ammunition to snuff out, or plug, any trickling spring of potential darkness.

One such time led him to follow in the wake of the musical trio – he had latched on with the proviso his muscle would be handy in the rowdier suburbs where revellers dwelled in their most rebellious of ways, under whatever influence. The reason he had taken such course was the way their music had seemed to create a barrier – a shield of reflection – against a couple of the Syltenerian mages he had been marking for a while outside what he presumed was their hideout in Heloniko.

He had tailed the dark duo to a cove and that's where he had discovered them happily playing away down on the sand for a few of the local children. The two targets had turned and hissed soon as they came into range of the gleeful music. It was barely audible to him, though was enough to stop the pair.

He wondered if their hideout was beyond the cove and that the reason for their repulsion to the place was because it threw the music with its optimal conics for acoustics and reverberated the sound being played, amplifying the senses of the two mages.

Instead, they had turned and saw him standing there. Recognising who he was, they decided to make their way back toward the music, only to be repelled once again, thus ensuring a fight which had ended with them both with a twisted neck.

He now sported a burned through shirt, the plated orichalcum he was wearing across his chest now fully on show from the few feeble blasts of stinging fire. He had felt his face, quickly, just to make sure the defence to his chest was enough.

Reporting back to the Third Pillar, he was swiftly advised to return and investigate the phenomenon – one that had never been observed by any in the Third, if any of the Columns.

\*

After a while, he eventually revealed his true intentions to the trio, but not for months after his return to Heloniko. They were obviously nonplussed by the revelation and had asked why. He had then revealed himself as a member of The Shadow of the Path and offered the explanation that he needed them to go with him back down to the cove and then beyond where they had sung for the children. And before the city watch could discover the origin of *who* applied the *twist* to the necks of the two men months earlier.

Amaria gasped before he had chance to reveal who, or what, the pair actually were, and how their music had somehow caused them a great deal of pain. He had reiterated the urgent need to venture back to that cove, to flush out the remainder of the cult from Heloniko by invading their dwelling, deep in the rocks at the end of the cove. He also revealed an absolute need to test out their *magic* for a second time, to abolish any lingering doubt that *potentially* there may have been other forces at play, however unlikely ... very unlikely, indeed.

\*

Back to the shit he found himself in. He came to a rest at an awkward angle in front of the bottom step. He had since lost sight beyond the hatch above and was now nursing a few injuries, though he was still able to stand and make his way down another flight of steps and then into Velosko's main bunk which made him feel slightly better.

The well adorned bunk was split in two halves by a grand

bed, its sheets still ruffled, and it looked mightily inviting, very much so for how he was feeling. The bed was not to be his final destination for a quick snooze, even though he very much felt like making it so.

No.

Behind the bed lay a large ornate brown chest – as long as he was high and about as wide as his thick upper arm.

He pulled sharply to break a non-descript chain from around his neck, pierced through another such non-descript item – a weighty, smoothed, black pebble, roughly the size of his palm. He hovered it close to a golden plaque in the centre of the chest.

'A light beyond the darkness,' he whispered, and the pebble suddenly held a hue of light before it then spread outward, skipping through the air and toward the plate. Upon contact, the chest swung open with a dramatic swing, revealing what that lay within.

Dropping the pebble, he swiftly grabbed the crooked, twisted spear with the hand that wasn't broken as badly and raced to clamber back up the steps, hoping the wave of evil had passed – no time to think of the alternative.

He jumped onto the deck, raised the spear high into the air, and uttered three words quickly to animate the weapon.

The blade at one end of the spear suddenly seemed to reflect more of the little light offered much brighter than it could have possibly been received. Of the light it reflected, it helped to create a bubble around Jentis, one that would protect him and, the further it expanded, those in said proximity until it reached its limit of expansion.

The chaos had subsided a little throughout the streets. Many had sought shelter indoors, including the main hall.

The trio had finished playing their impromptu piece only minutes earlier, and were still taking in the standing ovation and rapturous applause offered by those in attendance when that acclaim was abruptly cut off as the large doors to the public entrance flew open.

A crowding of townsfolk rushed in, shouting all kinds of madness.

The majority of the hall's new inhabitants looked worse, much worse, than the street urchins that dwelled within the shanties, their clothing freshly stained and starting to carry some stench, hands and knees spoiled from retching while they crouched, or had rolled around on the floor in pain, soaking in their or their mates' convulsions.

They had rushed backstage, knowing something foul was afoot, and knowing they needed to get word to Jentis. Urgently.

Waiting in a large storeroom, the entourage of helpers had been in full voice and all sort of theatrical antics before they were spotted, then interrupted in their frolics by Marcos who carried his cello and Amaria's violin. 'Quickly! The lot of you, this way.' They made their way over. 'Take these! Quick, we have to get to the ship.'

Velosko stopped them as they were about to head out of the back of the hall through a set of doors that led out to the streets adjacent the markets. 'Wait … wait! Whatever happened before I think is about to strike again. I feel *something* nearing!'

A rumble of the building and the shaking of the doors kept them still as they braced themselves for whatever dark magic was about to take hold of them.

Velosko thought he had sensed something off during their final song of their first performance, but he put it down to nothing more than the raucous tapping and clapping coming from the rafters.

Nothing came as they hunkered together. Amaria was holding tight to Velosko. 'What is that? What is happening? We can't go out there, Vel. We all appear to be safe …

inside, in here …'

'But, for how long, my dear?' Velosko replied. 'We need to touch base with Jentis, for he will no doubt by now hold the spear …'

'He will surely be on his way here … he will be. Surely.' She looked blankly at Velosko. 'He has the means to travel safely, deftly to us, he will know that we do not have the same means to get to him.' She saw Marcos look at her with a knowing smile, one which was immediately met by a frown. 'No! We are not going out there! We are not going to risk whatever has become of these people by singing and playing through the crowds of people clearly not themselves. So, we sit tight here. We go back and help whoever we can back in the main hall. We can play there and entertain those seeking shelter from whatever is happening. It's the least we can do.' She looked to Vel and touched his arm gently – more for her own security but to also advise that is what she wished, for her parents still remained within the great hall.

'Shit, me! That bastard thing be bigger than I assumed!' Jentis pondered.

The creature that bobbed earlier in the cove was now moving closer to the port, closing on Sinboran. It now stood twice as tall from when he had first spied it out in the bay; the leap upward must have distorted its girth, stretched it as it leapt. 'I don't think this spear will be enough to subdue it, I must find Velosko. It's time to see if they still hold that magical chord of repulsion or whatever it may be within them!'

He raced down the gangplank, spear still held high.

The townsfolk and foreign crewmen hit by the second wave were now moaning, rolling about in agony. They had given up on standing, content to be lying on the ground, out of harm's way … they assumed.

He knew his movement wouldn't escape the attention of the bebockle – the creature he had determined it to be from his education within the City – and would surely receive a barrage of projectile bile from many of the small mouths snapping all about its body. The spear's magic should hold off any direct attack, though it was not the direct ones that he was concerned about but the ones that missed, hitting the helpless souls scattered about him as collateral as he held aloft the shield of light.

As sure and as quick as the thought had come to him, so too did the barrage of putrid, acidic bile. It hissed as it touched the bubble the spear had created, and then again as it hit the thick wooden planks of the jetty. The planks held up far worse than the protective shield as the bile sizzled through, corroding them, dropping whoever, or whatever, was on them into the dark water below – fodder for the monster as it approached.

He made steady speed toward the town. He had to go on and hope for the best for the people who lay about him as he ran, though he felt the reality was pretty much doom. Luckily for him, the hall was not too far inside the city wall, for he was already growing weary from the spell he had asked the spear to perform and the opportunistic, swift pace he kept.

*

Looking down from the highest point atop the cliffs – also the last point and the highest that split the bay to the sea beyond – the creature's mind controller stood with her arms outstretched, watching the simplistic but effective attack from a safe distance so as to not become victim herself. Up this high, she would be safe from the outshooting ripple of ill, dark intent emanating from all around the creature she was controlling.

*This is almost too easy*, she thought as she forced the

creature to spout the second wave of darkness, much more powerful and longer lasting than first.

The creature's sensitive hearing captured the sound of despair reflected back from the town, and transmitted it to her, high up on the *Cliffs of Despair*. She revelled in the misery they felt, she always did.

The first stage of the assault was complete. Those who mingled on the streets had now been subdued. Now on to the second phase, the physical attack. She assumed there would be no resistance from any who had stood on the wall, those that manned the big cannons or equally sizeable ballista. She pushed the bebockle forward through movement of her arms, toward the town. *For such a large creature, you're quite easy to move around, big fella.*

A bebockle was a common nuisance on the high seas, even on the best of days or nights, and especially during the eclipse of the planets. The general assumption throughout Vilenzia was that a pair – male and female – of bebockles inhabited each of the large seas and the large lakes that eventually fed those seas. Very rarely – due to their size – did they venture into shallower waters such as this one, unless goaded. A creature that had the mental capacity of a worm contained within such a large mass was an ideal candidate for any with even the slightest ability to carry out such a mind connection or coercion.

*What is that?! It looks like* … She spied a bright light, reflecting, growing brighter, coming from a ship toward the end of the pier. *Hmmm, surely not! The chances! Chance of that?*

'Well … to be sure, I must get a closer look, see for myself, too much of an opportunity.' She began to use all of the creature's defences to attack the figure running between, and over, the peasants that lay prone on the jetty. Firing its bile from multiple orifices, the lucky ones would be devoured wholly, giving it more strength, height and girth as it made its way toward the city.

She could see through the bebockle's eyes keenly – whichever of them she chose – though the staff the man carried was not allowing anything through beyond where he ran.

'It is!' she shouted triumphantly. 'It's the *Spear of Starlight!* We *will take back that which was once ours!* She then pushed the creature forward, faster now, realising what was on offer: an ancient prize she had just rediscovered. *The chances?* she thought once again.

*

Jentis raced through the large gates, now unmanned – they would be too small for the creature to walk through, but he judged by the size of its now observable legs that it would just be able to step over the walls.

There were bodies everywhere, some whimpered, some writhed around; a few lay with glazed, frozen eyes – the pain, too much to take, had ended them. He launched himself into a faster run now he could see the hall, the doors had been closed, not admitting any of the throng that amassed at the entrance, the majority slumped around its threshold.

Instead of heading toward the hall's main door, he decided to make his way to the rear via a wide backstreet where market stalls would have been set if not for the Festival.

He hoped.

As he made it halfway down the alleyway, the one that lead to the back of the hall, he was thrown in the air backward to land on his arse as soon as the sound of the voice that rung and echoed through the street emanated from within the hall. Knowing the spear was a creation of dark souls, he remitted the infused magic and went on. The mortar-fire of bile had since ceased, and instead a rumbling could be heard and felt as the creature made its way closer to the city walls. He made a quick sign of Fah, praying for the souls that lay between him and the bay.

He tried to push the back door to the theatre open, forgetting his broken arm, he flinched, before he decided to kick down the wooden doors. He made his way inside, after first rubbing his knee. *Lucky I didn't attempt throw my knee into the damned thing!*

The plan was to destroy the city, then a couple more towns, without getting her hands dirty – just as she had at Denmore – then she would destroy the bebockle *and* consume its soul fire – that included all the citizens it had consumed itself – then she would have nearly enough to ascend, more than enough to do away with the mindless creature.

She estimated a few more, less sizeable towns, would be enough to have such power for those above to take notice.

\*

But now there was another player involved, another piece to the whole event, one that would halt her from moving her bountiful gains up to the next town on the coast. Whilst the odds were in her favour – as shown with the essence of darkness spreading far and wide across the landscape, enabling her to call on any of the dark creatures that would heed her call, snapped away from their usual dalliances in whatever habitat they called home – she still had cause for the slightest ounce of pessimism.

The bebockle was now making its way toward the farthest point of the jetty, the water now only lapping beneath four chubby knees. Suddenly a large opening appeared in the middle of what should have been its chest, revealing a mouth full of razor-sharp teeth. The chompers lunged forward, snapping away at the jetty and whatever lay atop: timber, rope, bone, sinew.

It didn't matter, all was consumed until there was nothing left to stand on.

It then stepped, with a little difficulty, onto the hard dockyard, and waited there for its next command.

*Hold!* she communicated, emphasised with two flat, outfaced palms. She was contemplating going down to follow the creature into the city and retrieve the spear herself before her mind was made up for her.

Coming down the street beyond the wall, she could see three figures advancing at a slow pace toward the main gate, and the bebockle, not perturbed by its presence.

No spear in sight, she waited a moment before all manner of shit broke loose as she lost connection to the creature, but not before she felt a piercing slice through her head, as though she had been hit between the eyes by an arrow.

*No spear still? What was that?!* She came back to her senses quickly and tried to reconnect, but was quickly buffed with the same intense pain in her head. The same pain as when she had disconnected from the sea creature a moment earlier.

Not game enough yet to try again, she hopped down onto the lookout platform below and proceeded, at pace, down the miniscule path that had been cut into the cliff face, and raced back to Sinboran's docks.

She wondered while she ran if the creature would turn and depart, or if the taste of blood dripping out of its maws would be enough to spur it on. Before she could make contact again, all she could do was watch … and hope for the latter.

*

Velosko led Amaria and Marcos out and through the market street, the dance of his vocals and their instrumental weaponry at the ready, fully trusting in their innate ability to sense danger before it reared its head.

Jentis had explained the problem with the overlap of

their ensemble and that of the spear not being able to function at the same time, not within such close proximity of the user at least.

'Just as Jentis said, we have to keep it occupied enough to stop its stampede, but not enough to send it back into the bay to regain focus.' He stumbled for the first time in a long time, losing his footing, the alcohol consumed in the past few hours still having an effect on his usually keen senses; the urgency and anxiety of the situation also added an extra sense of confusion.

He was happy to sing, to soothe, and calm the anxiety of others, but this was something that they had not done for many years, not since the time when they were caught between Jacobs Well and Angier, travelling through a forest road and were forced to sing, and play for their lives to escape multiple flocks of crazed pigeons.

The problem was that the music they played had to be in total sync, and from deep within the soul. Not just any sort of soulful music, but one of happiness and utmost joy, which was hard to muster by oneself, never mind a shaking trio. And especially in such a situation as they found themselves in.

But he had faith, a faith in something more; he held even more of the same in his long-time friends. He knew they would be as anxious as he, maybe Marcos not as much, but Amaria … most certainly.

The thought of her anxiety brought a memory of her scent after he had been desecrated during the initiation – a scent that trumped all other at that time, one he chose to scent and one he would never forget, a memory which gave him strength, bounds of joy, but also gave him a firm reminder of shame, one he hoped never touched her mind. The eternally revolving memory set his mind racing even more than it should, for he knew he was more capable than most men who held the sense of sight.

He touched her face again, with both hands. Whenever his senses had been heightened through panic or necessity, he never failed to hold her face in his hands to get a clearer image in his mind of the one he would die a thousand times over for, more if offered. He was acutely aware of his senses, but one thing he had longed for was to see Amaria in all her glowing light, and marvel at the face he had so often stroked to feel, and replicate in his mind, his assumption of the perfect sculpture, the porcelain frame before him, she who had loved him for what seemed his whole life.

Now they had to rely on that faith and love for one another. One thing that added weight to his anxiety was the thought of Marcos's consumption during the day, but then he checked the thought as he *hoped* Marcos had plenty more than himself, for they had many nights out together where the love and faith had been exponentially increased for every drink consumed.

*We will be ready,* he finally surmised.

They had decided to abandon the hall after going back onto the main stage and seeing the despair from every corner, from every pair of eyes that gazed upon them. Then the rumbling came.

Amaria's father, Count Atinna, had shouted at them to go. 'Get out of here!' So they obliged, Marcos the first to turn and head back, eager it seemed to offer to fight back – as was his nature.

A signal from Jentis to halt the ensemble, and allow him to get in close enough to strike at the creature, would be a critical moment for the advancing trio.

Untested, they knew not how long their influence on the dark creature, or the general aura of their influence on the immediate surroundings, would linger. They hoped it would be a straight switch-off of energy to allow Jentis the time and space to jump in and jab with his spear.

A fallible plan, but a plan all the same.

Jentis had also suggested there was a distinct possibility that an agent of the Sylteneria was in the midst of the chaos. Confident enough to say there would be at least one, if not more, for bebockle do not encroach unless provoked – and no one would be out in the waters near the city during the Festival, not alone for the revelry, such no one had ventured out on the seas because it would be darkness for three days – the worst time to depart, or be out on the high seas, unless the journey was a long one, for a full day and night of stars was a useful tool to utilise.

A signal was to be given once he had found the creature's heart. With the bebockle's squidgy interior being so cavernous, this could range from any point from the largest expanse of flesh to the skinniest. So hopefully he would be able to locate it with haste.

The upside though, with no bones to pierce – save those at the centre of its chubby legs, and only the snapping smaller mouths to avoid – the spear should find the critical target with ease once located.

Jentis waited as he observed the creature stood on the edge of the dock of the bay. It was now just meandering around, outside the city walls, as if it didn't know what it was doing, as if waiting for some instruction, direction.

That's when he knew for sure.

He began to look about the place, trying to see if any other figure was amongst them, looking for any movement amongst the walls, docks … anywhere.

Then he spied the movement of a shadow and braced, until it revealed itself as just a crow, drifting away across the bay, flying away from the now advancing trio, taking a gamble as to what was out there.

As he peered over the stone parapet that crossed over the main gate, he saw Velosko *finally* appear out into the main street. He could see Velosko's unease as he shivered, trying to hold a confidence and grace that belied the situation he was throwing himself, and his two closest friends, into.

*Be strong, Vel. We got this!*

Marcos followed Velosko, who walked slowly ahead, singing a well-known cheerful song – one so addictive that the folk he would often sing to would hum or sing the tune themselves for days, if not longer – at the top of his voice. He still wore his thick silver framed, blacked out spectacles to hide vacant eyes. *Probably doesn't want the fiend to feel so bad when we skewer it.* 'Hehe,' he let out a small chuckle which did not do anything to falter the stroke of his bow, if anything it brought elevation of spirit which flowed through his body to bounce away at the strings of his cello with added vigour.

Amaria took her sidelong gaze away from Velosko to switch focus to Marcos. She wondered what the chuckle was for … it didn't matter, she knew humour aided their cause, the repetition and crescendo of humour was one thing that they had found throughout their travels to be absolute. It was overwhelming, often spreading like wildfire through all admitted patron.

She continued to slide her bow across the violin's strings, with much more gusto than moments before. The glorious sight of Marcos chuckling in such a serious and precarious situation only added to her unbridled stoicism, which, in turn, only strengthened her resolve, turning any anxiety into absolute power: a soulful emanation … something she saw as she looked about the air between them. Visible in a physical form – something she had never been able to see before.

But now she could see vividly all of what they created, bouncing along with the tune through the air: soul, laughter, love, faith. She could see it dancing around them, then spreading further and further the more they played.

She wondered what would be seen if they played with such poise in any musical hall when all the lights had been dimmed; it was more than visual, it was something that could be felt, touched. She knew it was there.

*Next time I will seek to play in darkness, to really dazzle those in attendance.*

But now, she had to focus fully on the joyfulness of Velosko, of Marcos, the joys of her life. She thought of Anna-Mary and all the emotion she had brought to the hall with her personally, to Vel and Marcos. She played for them: for life, their life, and for the joy life brought.

Velosko sang for the same – she knew – which brought a fresh touch of moisture about her eyes, close to breaching the quivering bottom lid, knowing she was at the forefront of his mind – as always.

Onwards, she graced her strings knowing theirs and the people of the city's lives depended on it … it did.

*

They made headway only by slowly wading through the still writhing bodies in the street – the creature was visible above the city wall up ahead. The massive wooden gate hadn't been closed so they also had a clear view of its shuffling feet. It seemed as though the creature had turned around and was now facing back toward the bay when, suddenly, multiple eyes opened all about its back and latched onto them, their movement drawing attention to its sensitive hearing. As it turned back around, they could now see the front of the creature, and no sooner had it turned than it opened its massive mouth and flicked out a snaked tongue toward them. It slashed away at the street behind the main gate.

Velosko heard the slapping on the cobbles. Assessing the situation, he decided to carry on without a flinch. *Louder!* He thought as if to make communication, though as he was singing he could not speak nor break the rhythm being carried forward. So, to communicate with Amaria and Marcos, he raised both hands as a signal and sang as loud as he could. He had known of the bebockle and how sailors would bang loud bells, drums, even scream at the top of their voices to try and drive them away, and he wondered why it was here, in the city, on such a day!

It didn't take much for him to put Jentis's words to what was happening now; they were under attack from a darkness … *the Darkness* Jentis had always spoke of.

He increased the volume to his maximum. Through his own keen hearing, he heard the growl and shudder of the creature now within the range of their aura, once described by Jentis, as *'A magical sound, that would make the gods themselves weep!'* He went on, driving closer. Jentis had given clear instruction for them to halt their charge at a certain point, to give him enough room and space to drive the spear home. Velosko, however, had a different view of the situation and at how naïve Jentis could be, and had been.

Any creature of the dark would dwell in a cave or wherever, waiting for its potential master to appear and for an alliance leading to destruction: some were subtle, some not so.

He did not feel the pain, nor the whimpering of the bebockle to replicate such endeavour of evil to be such a dark creature; he felt the pain of the creature which had an abundant air of confusion about it. He went on, past the agreed boundary, not ceasing the music.

Jentis stood atop the wall now and looked down, lividly, at the three muses. His marker ignored, he leapt toward the street below, bouncing swiftly off a makeshift roof which barley took the brunt of his two feet, screaming for them to cease. His voice was overwhelmed by Velosko's. As he made his way toward the trio, he looked back to the large creature, now withering in size from its massive bulk moments ago as the onslaught of music took its hold.

It looked to be in two minds as to what to do. *Must be still under some dark influence to react as such*. To flee or stay? What would be its best outcome it seemed to think as it shuffled its feet forward, then back to the bay before it made a decision. It made a lurch toward the broken pier it had consumed on its destructive path into the city and outward into the bay it raced – at a speed that belied its anatomy.

Velosko moved on forward still. He wanted the bebockle out, far away from Sinboran's potential response of retribution, for it had not been the creature's notion, nor nature, to attack the city, or any other city. The city's folk, most only now coming to their feet, would want to embark on some journey of retaliation for such a fatal menace.

He eventually stopped and dropped his hands once he could not feel the pain of the bebockle anymore.

The music stopped too.

Then another confusion was heard all about the dock district – and no doubt beyond – up to the music hall.

Panting, the three rested on the ground, sweating and struggling to breathe. Expecting the worst to be over, Velosko spoke, 'There is something else out there, near here maybe.' He lurched forward and retched. Not much came out. Spitting out whatever he could, he spoke again. 'I sense a darkness here. Jentis, I know you meant well, but that creature was scared, scared of whatever was in its head.'

'So you surmised, Vel … and a correct deduction at that, maybe.' Jentis helped him up. 'Whoever is here, and believe me, they are here somewhere, they will want this thing no doubt.' He looked fully up and down the spear twice before nodding at it. 'A necessary exposure. Now, we must be ready for whatever *its* contingency plan will be. No doubt it's already in motion!'

She had seen the movement taking place down below as she raced quickly along the barely visible pathways cut into the rocks, and eventually onto the docks as the fallible creature – *and all that soul fire!* – was now making its way back out to the sea and beyond the cliffs. She paid it no more mind, that cause was now lost, as whatever had driven it out would do so again if needed, and she needed what they had, it was worth far more than the few hundred souls consumed … much more so.

She stopped as she saw the man with the spear helping an older looking handsome man with unusually dark, tinted glasses, especially random for this time of the year. *Ah …* she twigged. *The famed Velosko! I'm sure you wouldn't remember me, nor would your wife, that little bitch Amaria. But he will! Well then… I'm coming!*

*

Marcos's sweat ran freely as he hefted his prized possession; it was heavy and awkward to play when carried – the cello crafted for the old king of Debronta, crafted by the Master of Arts at the City of Columns, an expensive and intricate instrument, constructed over many years, using only the finest of materials. It was aptly named Holto's Bane and the bow, Lenjora's Blade. It was priceless, beyond compare. He held it tight to his body as he stood while watching Vel rise up off the ground with the help of Jentis.

They had made it a hundred paces past where they were to halt their adlib composition, but they had carried on with all the sinew in them, to the outer wall and beyond as Velosko had increased all vigour and volume. He settled Holto's Bane on the edge of the pier that had been demolished, point to the hard cobbles below.

As he turned to speak to Amaria, he saw something beyond her shoulder. A slashing reflected over her head, two blades swinging from a woman making fast tracks toward them. She was a mirage. There fully then invisible, save the two blades. When visible a distinct muzzle and equally distinct angry eyes presented themselves.

Alerting Jentis, Marcos spoke, 'My gods! She is stunning, look at that poise, the control of those daggers, the determination in those pretty blue eyes,'

'How the hell can you see the colour of her eyes, Marcos?' Velosko asked. 'How far away is she?'

'Far enough away not for any of us to see,' Jentis spoke. 'Marcos, you obviously recognise that maniac. Who is she, and how in the whatever hell is she known to you?'

'Huh?'

'Man! How can you know her eyes from this far away?' Jentis shouted, walking the small steps to Marcos to shake it out of him.

'She is, she … well I thin—No, I know her to be someone *we* have met before, but it cannot be … she is one of the daughters of the Master Smith at Silverdale!'

'Great! I hope she isn't here with some sort of vengeful ambitions from a past tryst.' Jentis's eyes rolled slightly.

'No, no, that is the much talked about Slayer and her spinning daggers, the Blades of Chaos,' retorted Marcos.

'Doesn't matter.' He quickly huddled the three together. 'This is the plan …' He asked them to follow his command with at least a small amount of the conviction they had displayed minutes earlier.

Spread at arms' length, they waited, at the ready. The onrushing woman was now closing the gap between them with frightening speed, a screech now audible to all, not just Velosko. Marcos shot an uneasy look at Jentis – the distance now within blade throwing range – but still a hand was raised, holding them. It wasn't until the woman released one of the blades that he dropped his arm – the signal. With haste, the first brush of a string produced a wave of a harmonic beat that reflected the dagger back, as the barrier from the blast of sound emanated outward.

The rebound of the dagger had struck the Slayer on the upper part of her thigh – not with the blade end but the butt. The initial impact shook her; the second impact, that of the wave of sound following through, shocked her as she tried with all her power to advance.

Coming to the conclusion she was being baited, she released the full extent of held power that was helping her stay on her feet. Moving slightly to her left, another shockwave hit, throwing her over the ropes of the dock to disappear into harbour's murky waters.

Jentis halted them. With spear raised, he raced to the spot where the woman had disappeared over the dock. Skidding to a halt before he too found himself in the drink, he used the staff to reflect whatever light could be garnered.

Nothing. There was no sight of her.

*How long can you hold your breath in that filth?* he thought as he waited. Impatiently, he held the spear over the rope, to get as much light into the water as possible.

A mistake …

Clinging precariously and with much difficulty to the dock wall – digging her toes and fingers into the flaking mortar and broken brick lining the revetment wall – she waited. She had hoped the staff would be used to illuminate the murky water now lapping up and wetting her feet. She just had to bide her time.

Failing that, she would spring up into the man holding the spear before he could react.

The music had made her cautious, so she had to be quick. In the end the man was indeed … impatient.

Seeing the spear and the blade, all possible light extinguished, it made her black heart skip a beat. One of the daggers wedged under her arm pit was quickly released.

With a large arcing motion she grabbed it and sliced at the hand holding the shaft. Unable to release herself and get enough momentum, she agonisingly watched the staff disappear below before she could release her weight to follow after.

As she dropped to the black abyss below she didn't miss the three stumpy fingers floating on its surface, nor the cry of pain that was snuffed out as she hit the water in search of the spear.

*

Clambering up onto the rocks at the far side of the bay, she clung tightly to the spear – as a new mother would their babe. Now away from harm, she shouted ecstatically, 'Mine! Haha! Mine! Once more.' She looked at the piss weak quartet still flitting around on the dock, frantically trying to make sight of her; she had called for aid with some energy stored for such a moment, and, with a stroke of luck, a pair of *synoguile* – shark like creatures with long snouts, layered twice with razor-sharp teeth – had been feasting on what the bebockle had missed on its way through.

Luckily, there been two, maybe more, nearby. With their speed in the water, she had entrusted the spear with one and clung to the other's long neck as they raced away from any further problems those up-themselves musicians could cause.

She would have to make a move soon. The mission to consume the life soul of any more seemed irrelevant since the bebockle had moved back out into the deep. And as to what she now held in possession, those searching for her had more power than they realised. And she would not forget any of the faces that had held beheld charge. *Especially the handsome, devilish, and rapturous lover ... Marcos!*

*

Jentis rushed frantically about the dock, pacing from one side to the other. He did not stop until Velosko placed an arm on his shoulder. 'Friend, please! I can hear the blood pumping out from your hand, never mind the spatter on the floor. Stop ... and apply some aid.'

'Vel, I cannot, my stupidity and impatience has cost us dearly. Many lives— no, not just lives ... *souls* will be lost with that weapon back in the hands of darkness! I must act now, otherwise I—'

'Jentis, there will be another day, man, but not if you do not stem that wound. Jentis, please ... I understand the urgency, but I will not see you buried for such a small wound.' Bringing his arm up to wrap around Jentis as though brother, he knew words would bring no sense, so he quickly whipped his hand down to strike atop Jentis's spine. This drew a face full of anger toward Velosko as Jentis offered a slowly fading and burning glare.

But neither the sound of rage, nor anger, would escape Jentis's lips as it had moments earlier.

Amaria shook her head ...

Marcos could only sigh.

Velosko could only smile.

# Echo of Silence

A ripple of light in the darkness could be observed atop the residence, a building akin to a non-descript logger's home, deep in a dark, dense woodland. That is … if any were there to observe, which would have been nigh on impossible. The night wolves would have sensed – with their enhanced detection of any scent – and pounced to take care of any who had ventured this far into the woods, beyond the outskirts of Menton Green. The night wolves were not present during any other time of the year in this vicinity, or any other location within close proximity to even the sparsest populated areas.

A few of the local children would sometimes venture into the woods, mostly as a dare … but … sometimes, they would be drawn in by the magnetism of darkness calling to the void to shroud their gullible souls.

The bully. The one who would amputate small animals, involuntary, for sport … the one who crushed helpless insects as they made their way by. Any who contained such tinder, ready to be lit by the darkness – the call would be the spark for much more evil deeds.

It was well known that evil lurked there during the long dark night in the woods. This, in turn, still made the town folk sceptical of breaching the periphery of the woods during the time period either side of the three days of night. Thus strong advice was given to the children to stay well away, but that was misunderstood by them as folk tales, thus exploited on the most innocent through peer pressure from the belligerent souls whom themselves would not dare chance such a foolish adventure. Unless they truly held evil in their heart and soul.

In this instance, however, there was one who had observed

the ripple, the distortion of reality about the place. He stood from his crouched position, hidden behind one of the felled tree stumps.

He was not hiding, he was just unsure of any materialistic collateral discharge by way of the visages entering this realm, or from quite possible, far beyond as the ripples increased then suddenly stopped. It didn't matter, he was sure he was in the right place. He had read many tome in the town library about such ripples, texts issued as a resource by the City of Columns.

A lifetime of being beaten down physically, and more often than that, mentally. A lifetime of being told he was useless … that he should be left in the dirt to rot … *A nobody gets nowhere but the dirt …*

It had all hardened his heart such that penetration of any more harm was now frivolous, past the point where now he was immune to the pain from such words, or beatings.

Exposure to the flame of emotional and physical abuse had set the beacon off, and he felt it shoot outward like an exploding cannon full of flamework. The beacon had been spotted during the previous Festival – most recruits to the Syltenerian cause had been enrolled during the three days of the Festival, it seemed to elevate a level of passion to do evil which was easy to sense from those trained to detect such evil … plus any depraved deeds while they were at it.

Bareleno stood up, awe filling his mind as the ripple subsided.

He hopped over the felled trunk toward the residence. Having walked unhindered through the forest past hungry eyes and the snarl of the dark shadows that drifted in and out between the tree trunks and undergrowth of the dense woods, he felt no fear as he approached.

They had made him uneasy early on as he ventured through the woodland, though he had quickly stemmed the chaos and anxiety in his mind to a feeling of total calmness, as would have been expected by those whom he assumed were even now watching – into himself.

He was met at the edge of the residence by two acolytes, more than likely the same two who had spoken to him about his troubles and bruises the year earlier. They had known there was something off about him by the way they seemed to connect instantly on a level of relative empathy, rather than sympathy; something he was so accustomed to from strangers, and those from beyond his outer circle of not many.

He was taking a chance he had mentally agreed with himself – *its either here or the gutter*. The acolytes had assured him they could, and would, quench his thirst by alleviating and avenging all the pain he had suffered in his most innocent years.

By offering himself to a team who would make all of those abusers obsolete, in the physical sense, they had offered him the chance to see their ultimate demise through consumption of their souls, however little they may contain.

The acolytes had communicated to him that he was to make the journey, on his own, to this point, without any elaboration of what he would face on his way.

However, they sternly advised, and without remorse, that should he turn back once he began the journey, the darkness would pounce … and without hesitation once sensing the weakness of his fallible and unworthy notions.

He had no fear, not anymore. Only a determination to see this through, whatever the outcome may be.

Moving closer, up the small steps that led up to the timber deck of the lodge, the two acolytes who had befriended him in the town didn't remove their hoods, but he had now no doubt, a feeling inside told him, it was they.

'Welcome,' they said in tandem, bowing slightly. 'Welcome to eternity. A *very* special and much revered, and much unexpected, guest awaits inside.'

'On we go then!' he replied, if too confidently.

*No fear …*

One of the acolytes cast a spell, followed by a wave of a hand over the middle of the door, revealing hidden markings upon the wooden casing which now glowed a bright purple – the shape of three triangles crossed over each other at different angles, the signet of *Malok*. Another word from the acolyte set the glyph spinning, accelerating until it became an image of a circle. Then he pushed a hand to the centre of the circle. Instantly, the whole door disappeared, and in its place was the slight shimmer of a threshold.

They made their way through, inside.

As they crossed the threshold, the door replaced itself with a crackle, to that which stood moments before.

They walked up to a low height wall.

In front of the wall was a wooden bench adorned with flowers, candles and some other macabre looking objects.

'Take one item, Bareleno. And one alone,' the other acolyte said in a slow rasping sound. Obviously the boy.

The girl, then, must have been the one to disappear through an internal door, and into the darkness beyond, leaving them alone. But he did not feel as though they were the only ones present in the room.

'Which?'

'Ah, maybe you should take the most sadistic item to please our Mother …' the acolyte answered, a little too passively. All friendliness he had shown the year earlier had now been displaced with an air of animosity, or scorn – he cared for neither.

Hovering his hand over a bloodied stump that looked like a forearm, but without the skin, hand, or elbow, he paused.

The acolyte removed the hood dramatically, to reveal it was indeed the boy from the market, however his face was now much paler and fleshy in a few blotches.

Smiling at Bareleno, he offered again. 'Go on, choose one, be quick.' The acolyte winced slightly as his lips moved, opening up cracks of unhealed sores.

Bareleno confirmed his suspicion of another in the room. An innate sense he seemed to possess itching at the back of his neck.

He picked up the tallest candle, the one with the brightest flame, and turned sharply, not too fast to extinguish the flame, but enough to catch the hidden figure off guard. A fleeting shadow swept across the wall. From the size of the initial frozen shadow stuck to the wall, it had been stood just over an arm's length behind his back.

A rasping sound came from the corner hidden in shadow. 'Smart boy. Unlike you, Tomlin.' The acolyte bowed deeply toward the corner the voice came from. 'Lead the way, my boy, lead on. I will follow and observe—'

'Who … who are you? And how are you doing that?'

Tomlin jumped in. 'None of your concern, maggot. Follow me, and do as you are told next time.'

'Now, now, child … do not let such enmity and anger cloud your responsibilities. He saw through your attempt at trickery. Deal with it. And deal with it quickly!'

'But I was testing him, Mighty—'

'Shush . . Quiet! Now!' the woman shouted. A box of produce was thrown from the opposite corner of the room to hit the acolyte, shattering into pieces, to reveal it was not produce from the farmyard at all, but bones: hands and feet – some too small to be beyond an early age.

Bareleno paid no mind to the two in the room, nor the scattering bones of children. Instead, he followed the first who had left the same room – the girl.

Now out of view as he passed the threshold, he was still,

however, within earshot of the room and heard one more volley of abuse aimed at the hapless Tomlin. Once again he paid no mind, he was determined to see where this journey would end. *Vengeance and a new beginning? Maybe! Or the sweet embrace of nothingness,* if he failed.

The latter thought had come far too often for such a fledgling now in his late teens.

Seeing Bareleno appear through doorway, through a portal of blackness, she smiled devilishly at him. 'So … you finally found the balls to follow through here.' She looked seductively down at him. 'How'd you know which way to go?'

Bareleno was bumped into by Tomlin who rushed in to catch up, post reception of the brunt of rage of whoever was following them.

'Ah, brother … I see you are still second best at everything you do …'

'Shut it, Keller!' Tomlin had just regained his poise before Keller raised her hands, clasped them together, and then shook them.

A blue hue tried to escape from between her closed hands … and all fell silent.

She walked slowly, but purposely and with a slight sway, toward Bareleno. 'I … I can see the fire in your soul, raging! A fire that is burning so so bright with the urge to avenge all who have wronged you.' She raised a palm to rest on his shoulder. 'I see your pain … though I cannot feel it … and you cannot see it, but you do feel it if obliquely. I can help you, if you would let me … let us.'

She let her hand fall down off his shoulder, and brushed past a now silent Tomlin who held no more motion then that of a block of ice. 'This one here fails to seek help. He won't let go of the anger, he fails to embrace the bigger calling, and it won't be long before our Lady discards him.'

She brushed the same hand through his hair as he remained motionless and smiled at Bareleno. 'I could hold this spell for much longer, if I wanted to …' She smiled seductively at him again. 'How long would you last, I wonder?' She bit her lower lip as she slowly walked back to where he stood; he was unaffected by the spell but the gaze she offered froze him to stone.

'I … I … I, erm,' he struggled to get any response out before she grabbed him by the crotch with the still glowing hand.

She immediately jumped back and laughed loudly before moving in close again to cup him. 'Ah, I was expecting much more than what I saw. I cannot feel the warmth of any memories down there. Haha!' She looked up at him playfully, without malice, only seduction and curiosity in her eyes. 'You have never been with a girl before, have you? Just you and that naughty, naughty wrist of yours …' She twisted hers a little.

A slight groan escaped his lips and his cheeks flared bright. 'What is this?! Another test?' He grabbed her wrist and pulled it away before they were interrupted by the shadowy figure lurking once more somewhere about the room.

'Such innocence will not get you very far here, young man. You need to embrace the soul fire you so seemingly possess. You need to feel that rage, but also find a way to release it. Now … back to where you were.' She finished the last with a giggle that tapered away.

Keller once again grabbed him in the middle of his crotch. 'Aha, so … there is something down there, it wasn't there a moment ago. Do not worry,' she nodded to the still Tomlin, 'he cannot see us. His mind and body has been frozen to a point in time.' She moved her body in closer to him, still holding on. She was now touching his chest with hers. 'Should I do the same with you, as you are, right now

…?' she pondered.

Bareleno tried hard not to look and stare down beyond her chin, down at what he knew was heaving upward as she bobbed slightly against him as she spoke.

Another laugh, one from each female in the room. He opened his mouth to speak, to offer objection once more, but the potential of protest was doused with moist lips, closing around his.

*This feels wrong, what am I doing here …. She is pretty, but surely, she is not all there in that petite head of her's? Oh shit, what is she doing now?* His eyes were closed as she released her lips from his. Before he opened them, he felt a tug at his slack and dusty breaches … then the fresh, cold air hit … followed by a rolling warmth that soothed any more thought of protesting.

The world fell to bliss. No legacy of pain, no sound, no noise: only echoes of silent waves pulsating through his envigored soul. He embraced it with a passion – a vigorous and rapturous passion.

He was absolute.

He was free.

Mesfa watched on from the opposite side of the threshold to the next room. The portal about the door offered a one-way view – *lucky*, she thought as an arousal spiked her body. She was alone in that room also. *Lucky!*

She was sure the boy's soul jolted away from its mortal cage, only to suddenly leap back in the moment the young acolyte fell to her knees.

She finished herself quickly then waited. Standing at the doorway she realised the boy had more passion in him than she first thought – the comments of inexperience the young acolyte made only aroused her again.

Stepping over the threshold to reveal herself, the boy

looked up, directly at her, but did not relinquish the rhythmic thrust he had found to enjoy. Though his face did twist with a little distortion which brought her humour *I'd best not show any reaction to put the boy off. I want it … now!*

Her thoughts were interrupted by a silent message from she who she had travelled with earlier from Kinora. *If you want him … why are you waiting? Standing in the shadows! You are above these acolytes, as a given right by her Lady … finish him!*

*It's not him I'm interested in, let him have his way then I will have mine with her,* she responded, trying not to quiver her knees too much.

*Hmmm, very well then! Uhmm … you never cease to surprise. But. Before you do …*

Out of nowhere, the woman who had greeted her on Kinora, the one who had belittled and beguiled, now dropped her mirage of shadow and appeared before the four of them. She dropped her long shimmering dress to her waist, and then to the floor as she approached Mesfa.

\*

The impromptu show of passion was too much for Bareleno, who now thrust harder a few times before he groaned loudly, gazing at the two beautiful beings who had appeared suddenly before him.

He dropped to cling to the girl he was holding as they both panted and sweated. He tried to kiss the nape of her neck, but she nonchalantly bumped him off as soon as his lips touched her skin.

She stood and made her way, uninvited, to the two women at the far side of the room.

He didn't care for the slight received as he rolled over to lie with his back on the cold floor. Looking sheepishly at the prone Tomlin just behind, he was sure he saw a tear glisten on the cheek. *No matter.* He was not ashamed; he was now rather amused by the whole episode. *If this is my life from here on … I'm fucking in!*

The thought was accentuated by the echo of another passion reverberating around the room.

Seeing Tomlin's other cheek glisten, he smiled; the first genuine smile he was willing to accept after so many years.

He winked at Tomlin. For the humour was, for once, not at his expense.

# Change of Plan

They had been traversing the marshes of the Odigan Territory for most of the day, the quickest way to The Divide … if you could levitate – for Jasquirea, that was the case. However, lugging along the brute Bendim was cumbersome at best.

'Ah! You should have gutted me while you had the chance, little man. Pulling my sorry arse through these shit heaps has slowed you no end!' He laughed some more.

'Quiet down, stool.'

Jasquirea pulled up on his end of the makeshift stretcher that Bendim was strapped to, letting the man's big head drop below the surface of the murky water of the marsh as a reminder of who was in control.

Spluttering, Bendim shouted as he came back above the surface. 'You bastard, I'll rip out both your eyeballs for that, and shit int' 'oles left behind!'

Jasquirea whispered, sharply, 'Quiet … I hear something …'

This only brought further loud remarks, and some obnoxious song from Bendim, who was taking no little delight in the reversal of discomfort.

Not being able to hear, he dropped the stretcher completely, submerging it and Bendim below the waterline once more.

He focused, and heard someone, or something, dragging their legs through the reeds and waters of the marsh not too far away. Clearer now, once the commotion of splashing below had subsided, the sound drifted to him through the air. Not one … no, but at least four pairs of legs were waddling towards them.

He risked a cautionary glance over the reeds – barely swaying in the slightest of breeze – hoping to capture some movement, little aided by the scant light offered from the red planet

There were, indeed, four pairs of legs … though where he'd erred – forcing a wide smile to split his little face – was that the four pairs were driving one massive body forward!

He was spotted as soon as he flinched at the sight of the massive form of the arachnid, its body blotting out all available light with matted fur, from its legs to its head.

Green balls of light flickered as they moved around, searching for prey. They all had instantly locked onto him before he had chance to drop behind the reed line.

Pulling Bendim up above the mirky waterline, he made no noise. He saw the fear in the man's eyes, reflections of his own. 'Quiet, an *archnadess* approaches. Be still, make no noise, and most certainly … do not move.'

'Ha, no chance there!' Bendim looked humorously at his body strapped to the makeshift stretcher.

'Quiet, I said!'

Before Bendim could offer a smart reply, a massive haired head appeared over the top of Jasquirea, followed by four raised, segmented, arms.

Seeing the oaf's face stretch and contort with despair, Jasquirea let go of the stretcher once more, releasing all influence of the magical bond of levitation applied.

He leapt forward, leaping over where he had dropped the big man. Before he could turn, the splatter of marsh water washed over his head from the impact of the strike from the archnadess.

Bendim bobbed up above the surface, the beast had just missed with its massive pincers where he was submerged, but the wash had flipped him over. He had enough time to take a deep breath before he found himself face down. *At least he can't see me,* he thought.

He was wrong, one of the *archnadess's* claws mauled at the

stretcher, eventually finding sure purchase, locking a sharp pincer between the back of the stretcher and the straps that encaged Bendim.

It lifted its leg high in the air, leaving Bendim to look out high into the abyss of darkness, before another, even more terrifying, abyss approached by way of two large, sharp fangs closing in on him.

Bendim used all his strength to push his whole body forward to try and escape the stretcher; he hadn't needed to, the creature – obviously hungry from lack of prey in these parts – was too eager as it brought its sharp teeth down, grazing just enough of the taut strapping to split them and drop him from a fair height. Any relief of escape from the stretcher was swiftly cut short as he hit the water below.

Once again he was trapped; the high fall had given his body enough momentum to spear into the marsh bed, leaving him plugged in the mud up to the waist. He struggled, but thought better of moving about. So he just waited there. *Better to die in the water than the slow painful death of being decomposed inside the massive stomach of … that fucking thing!*

Not for the first time in so long he was he wrong, for this was not a male of the species, but female, and with a large sack in tow – the *archnadess* was well known by all who dwelled in the area surrounding the marshes. The offspring brooding in its sack would consume all others in the sack, until only one remained. Only then would the mother allow the sack to be split open, and the one remaining offspring allowed to feed on flesh and bone of anything other than its own kin.

He felt a rush of water wash over him and saw a shadow as he opened his eyes, much smaller than the creature that just tried to skewer and consume him but much larger than Jasquirea.

*Where is that little bastard? Probably left me for dead the little shite!* Then he saw the shadow return, and saw what seemed to be thousands of tiny eyes shine with a green hue. With a rush, it raced toward him. Even in the gloom of the marshes he was seeing its movement as clear as if observed in daylight. The pain struck him harder than anything he had ever felt before, causing a manic echo of pain to resound through his entire body.

It wasn't long after the initial impact that he eventually realised he was now unstuck from the mud, from the stretcher, from the creature, and finally … from Jasquirea.

The source of the pain pulsating through him became evident once he had reached a fair distance from the commotion. Perching himself atop a long ago fallen tree trunk, he looked at where his arm should have been – the realisation hit him as he had tried to elevate himself with both hands to mount the fallen log, instead hitting his chin as he flailed an absent limb to find an impossible purchase.

He pulled on one of the now broken straps which was still looped around his shoulder and used it as a makeshift gauze, stemming the blood flowing freely from just below the elbow. The creature's babe had obviously sensed the movement of his arm as he raised it to shield himself from the onrushing attack. Then, following the initial impact, the dragging and subsequential pull of his arm had been enough to dislodge him from the mud he had been encased in.

*No mind, such a small price to pay for my freedom. Will just kick back and enjoy the show before I kick on home … Wherever that may be now.*

Bendim raised his only hand to his brow, searching through the darkness for any sight of the little man.

*

No sooner had Bendim's thoughts set in then they diminished after finding no sign. The surprise of Jasquirea jumping up onto the log to sit beside him made him stumble backward. 'So … do you want to keep your other arm or are you going to bolt again? I will give you one chance … one chance only to redeem yourself and not give me the ultimatum of dragging your arse all the way to Ectora, where you will live an eternity of sorrow. What will it be? I need to know, before that thing realises where we are …' Jasquirea nodded down the slope to the marsh below. 'Oh, and before you decide, I believe this is yours …'

Jasquirea threw a torn and mangled stump – still discernible as a forearm and chubby hand – toward Bendim, who, in turn, attempted to catch it with the phantom hand flying toward him. Before he realised, it was flew past him to the floor behind the log.

'I can heal it, well … so much so it may once again be used, with some limited functionality, but it will still look like—'

'Do it so I may one day have the chance to strangle your sorry arse with both hands! You little prick!'

'Do me, and yourself, a favour and be quiet. You do realise I saved your worthless life back there.'

'Not from where I was rooted … seems to me I saved my own skin through good fortune and misplaced judgement on *its* part!' He waved an elbow into the air, blood still dripping out of the makeshift gauze.

'No. Not back there in that bog. I offered to take you with me, teach you something that may be of use: some respect at the very least. For I do believe you are worth saving.'

'Horseshit, they left you with me because that fucker Somendel took the *Bite of Deign,* and you needed to take back something rather than nothing to prove you are not only a failure, but also a scourge to the clan you represent.'

'No, I slit that worthless piece of organic mass's throat like I would yours if I saw you to be of no use.' All façade of grace the man seemed to forever hold was now gone.

Bendim gulped. 'Well, that would achieve nothing, hey! Much less, in fact. You wouldn't get to know what I know then…'

'Exactly! So, shall I attach that limb back to the already festering elbow you're waving around?'

Bendim nodded toward where the hand had disappeared behind the log, and waved the bloodied stump at him before he disappeared.

Bendim fell backwards in a rush, and did not take long to show his prize – the once attached appendage – to Jasquirea.

'Bring it, quickly. Those mini beasts in this marsh would no doubt be already infesting the limb …'

The thought made the big man lurch forward to empty his stomach at the thought, before he presented the appendage to Jasquirea, wiping the remnants of drool away from his mouth after he handed it over.

'Before I do this, you need to swear fealty to me, and me alone! I assure you, it will be a harmless offering. One that would only benefit us both! Believe me …'

'But I cannot. I swore oath to the Lady, or more so to her minion that follows her!'

'But for me to attach that now stinking thing back to your arm, and not slit your throat, thus leaving you here as food for the creatures of this marsh, I need your word. And not just your word, but unbridled commitment. I am sure your oath was just a convenience of noise flapped from your mouth to those representing the Darkness, or am I mistaken?'

Bendim nodded, if too eagerly.

'What I require is utter submission to my way, to the way of the light, and much more so, to the way of the ancient race I am of, and represent.'

Jasquirea looked at the man, only to find thought of any commitment from him troubling. In the end, he thought that was a trait he could use to his advantage. 'What say, you …?'

'Well, suppose it's a better option than being spider or grub feed. Will give it a go, but I ain't promising anything other than what we have already discussed.'

'I need as much information as you possess, though not necessarily your recollection of those followers of the Sylteneria before I met you and that sorry band. I'll need it all!'

'Whatever it takes, then,' he said shaking the dirtied hand in front of him. As he did, an elongated crawler made its way out through the wrist and he shook it harder, trying to drop the centipede to the floor but failing. 'Fuck! Yes, whatever you want! Just sort this out!'

The green dagger he had used on Somendel, the Syltenerian Cleric, was pulled out once again. Being barely conscious at the time, the big man had not seen fully the events that transpired with his former Pecborian master, but he had certainly heard the men talking in the tavern afterwards.

He now saw the blade firsthand. 'Say, what did you actually do to that bastard Somendel? Heard he spat up his soul or summat!'

'Not quite … well, yes, part of it. He is being used by the light now and does not know it, but he will find out … in the end. I cannot divulge any more for now. Say, you're looking a fair bit paler now. So fear not this dagger, Bendim. Fear the past, *your* past, and embrace it.'

They made their way out of the marshes and onto a grassy hill that overlooked the marsh at a safe distance. The arachnid and its offspring had disappeared. They were safe, for the archnadess wouldn't cross the marsh's outskirts. It wouldn't leave its marked territory. It also seemed immune to any dark influences so far as Jasquirea could tell.

*Could it be used for purpose of good?* Jasquirea thought, then shook his head. *No that is not our way* – the idea of good was that free will to do good was always the option, the only option available to those who followed the light, though the sway of free will through communication of information could be just as effective. As was now the case.

He then looked to Bendim, recognising the contradiction to this thought.

Bendim had now lost the pale complexion but wore a familiar blank stare, a state brought about by the dagger's influence.

'What …? What did you do to me? I feel … weird!'

'Like you don't know who you are? Like you have jumped headfirst into a lake filled to the brim with feathers?'

'Yeah, but …'

'But you remember everything?'

Bendim nodded. 'Mostly.' He rubbed his head and shook it slightly. 'So this is how you get what you want out of my head?'

'Kind of … you just need to arrange those thoughts floating about inside your head into some sort of chronological order, as that is critical to what I need.'

'Chrono—what?'

'Order of events, longer ago to nearer now, Bendim. You need to start from the beginning. We have a long journey. So, I'm all ears.'

'You're not wrong there,' Bendim quipped, displaying a wry grin.

Jasquirea cut the smile off the man with his next words. 'I was going to wait a while before I took your arm … but time is short, and we need to be elsewhere. I can feel it all about the air!'

Bendim stopped, though remained relaxed. 'You knew … knew we would be ambushed by that thing?'

'Yeah,' Jasquirea chuckled now, 'I thought one of those

cognisant of my kind would put on a good show!'

Slowly he spoke, all inhibition to rip the ectoritor's head off … gone. 'You bastard, you set me up!'

'And how does that make you feel, big man?'

'Well, you've known me for long enough to know the answer to that stupid question …' They walked a few steps more before he spoke again. 'However, I do not feel in the slightest agitated by such a shitty revelation; it makes complete sense to me, to scare the shit out of me, chop my arm off in the process, then have me submit myself to get it stitched back on. ' He looked over the forearm where the limb had been reattached. 'And not a bad job at that, wish I was compos mentis – or whatever that means – to see the magic happen. But, man! There could have been an easier, less dramatic way, surely?'

'You sure did pass out quickly. The blood loss had left you weak, the pain of the incision, though, topped you off. Believe me there was no magic at play, and it wouldn't have been a pretty sight for you, even for such a big man.'

'And why is that?'

'Well … that little fella before, the one that crawled out of your loose hand … well, he made a run for it, up into the exposed flesh of your stub. I had to squash it up around your shoulder before it could do any real damage.' The small man chuckled again.

Bendim fell to his knees and felt around the shoulder. After feeling a firm lump underneath his skin he was immediately on all fours once again … retching.

# Apportionment

'"The night is upon us" she conclusively said to me,' Grehn said.

'Who said?' asked King Benjamin. 'And what in the seven realms of darkness possessed you to leave the castle grounds on such a night?'

Grehn shifted slightly in her seat from the admonishment. Peron was sure she wore a slight smirk – the crinkle about her eyes added weight to his assumption – at her father's remark of 'possessed'.

'Father, there are things happening here that you don't understand!'

'Aye. That would be right! Your grandmother thinks she knows all. Did she tell you about this …?' He showed her the scorched mark underneath the ornate vambrace.

'Yes. Yes she did! And that is something you should have told me long ago, Father.' She rose out of her seat and stood in front of him, hands on hips. 'I always wondered how you knew, when I was little, when I would disappear and you could find me anywhere I hid with crazy haste.' She settled back into her seat, wrinkling her nose, irritated.

'Had good reason, my love,' he lifted both hands up and rubbed them over his tired face.

'Yes, Mother Ursen said as much.' She mimicked her father. 'But now it seems as though we should let it all out, put it all on the table ' She went on to detail the events that had transpired after breaching the castle wall.

Morla had been waiting for them. She stood atop the steps Peron had stumbled on his first day in the city – stood was probably not the word, 'hovered' was more apt.

The brave town folk who had remained at the periphery of the square crouched low, some peered from behind more solid structures and others through shutters in the rooms overlooking the square – there were not many. The wagons – housing those from the Medica – remained where they had the day before; the sisters, it seemed, were not too perturbed by the apparition of one of the founders of their city floating in close proximity to them.

She had appeared from nowhere late in the morning, and disappeared within a blink, only to return a few minutes later, appearing to solidify before gently smudging back to ethereal form.

It wasn't until the mixed band, escorting two glowing figures, entered the square that the apparition took any notice of her surroundings, as though a switch had been tripped to startle the ancient woman.

Peron, Mother Ursen, and Grehn led Holtonos and Lenjora as they approached.

Now in the square, the glow had faded around the two not of Inarrel – they made their way directly to where Morla was stood, now looking directly at the merry band.

Ignoring the three in front, Morla spoke to the two just a short way behind. 'Ancient ones, welcome. It is good to see you again.' She then turned her attention to Mother Ursen. 'Now, child …' Mother Ursen shot her a disgruntled look. 'You took your time coming back here—'

'Look at the state of you! And what the hell is wrong with you?! Possessing the young girl! You could quite as easily have come to us sooner! But no! No … you persist in this hole of a building!' She now jabbed a pointed finger toward Morla and carried on. 'Please tell me, I would like to hear it … why are you even here?'

Morla let out a laugh, an extended laugh that eventually died down after a long while.

She took a deep breath and spoke. 'You of all people know the ways of the world. The spirit realm, the realm of sadness, those of joy, laughter … despair. I have been able to navigate all to make my way back here, to this time, to this place. It seems to be borne from this "hole" that the affluence of those who would dwell within for leisure have some communicado with all those realms; it's as though they dwell there for a short, short, while, dependent on how and what they feel. They touch, but do not know. They feel that realm for but a moment before the realm of … well, this world drags them back, right back to their place of things …' Looking at Holtonos she spoke. 'Well, old man, how do you do it? How do you link them all, or are you only but a pawn in a much bigger game?'

'Not here, Morla.' A sternness about his face shut her down. 'Now the prophecies have been realised, let's get to diffusing the realm of darkness and all its false offerings. So … why are you here?'

'I am a servant for good, you should know that Holtonos. However, to that end, I have travelled far and experienced much. Much more than even you could realise.' She looked pained all of a sudden and dropped her solidity to almost a shadow. 'Come, please. We have much to discuss. The others have been alerted and are on their way to—sorry! Come inside, quickly, all of you.

'What does she mean "others"? What others?' Ben eagerly jumped in.

'I'm getting to that you big uff. Just sit there and listen. It is very important that you listen, for there are operations afoot that you must coordinate, based on the advice about to be given. But first listen, and listen well.' Grehn smiled at the last as he settled back down.

Mother Ursen shook her head a little at Ben and his interruption.

Ben looked at the two immortal figures, who intently looked back at him also. 'So, where's that old bag of sand Everos? He would've lightened the mood a little.' He let out a short, sharp and hesitant laugh, before he realised all in the room – all those who had heard the words spoken at the Grousing Potter – were deathly pale at what was about to be unveiled to the uninformed.

Once through the infamous doors of the Grouse, the figure resembling Morla became more solid. 'The feelings of folk linger in the atmosphere; this truly is a wonderous place. They emanate a certain … thing. I don't know how to describe it: the aura brings life, transverses realms so it's such—'

'Get to it, Morla. I'm still not happy with the whole episode atop the Arches.'

'You were taking your time!' Morla interjected. 'And still took your bloody time, old woman!'

'Ha! Old woman? Look at you, you degraded crone!'

'Let's get to it shall we?' Morla's voice was now stern, verging on rageful. 'An apocalypse, of sorts, is upon us. We need to enact the strategies assembled through countless generations. And swiftly!'

*

King Ben interrupted the telling once again with the start of a question but was quickly shot down once more by all in the room with a chorus of quickly shaken heads. 'Go on,' he eventually managed to get out.

'As I was saying …' Grehn went on, trying to hide the smile cast at her father's now downward stare.

'The world as we know it, is now at its darkest. The sky burns with darkness. From all the observations, throughout the centuries, that subtle tinge should have lasted for no more than mere minutes, but it still holds! So that tells us that the darkness is holding the orbit of Kinora in check, between the blue planet and the blazing star we all swing around.

'So, the darkness seeks to play its hand … prematurely. Whether by way of impatience or arrogance, or even some other subtle play, who should care? But us … we must! So, we must be wary. No doubt the dark-orientated creatures of this world are about to rise, or have already risen, from their relative sanctum from the light. With this in mind, the City needs to enact the first of the six edicts through their network all over the world, and not just here in Vilenzia. So! Mother Ursen, can you begin the enaction of the First with the help of those outside? As I mentioned, it must be swift for their early intrusion shows much, trying to catch us slightly underprepared, but not wholly unprepared.' She winked at Grehn, though the eyelid struggled to rise back to fully open.

'You, child, have been marked by the light. Stories of the dark and the light have always played part in all kinds of tales, stories, folklore, as they must. Though now we are faced with a darkness to rival all those stories you may have heard and many more that you may not – knowing your lineage, the latter. In light of this, we have to strike back. We have to play our hands, one at a time before … snap!' Morla emphasised with a quick slap of her hands – the whole of the Grouse reverberated with the echo of the clap, the sound further enhancing the intended shock, thus gaining the required attention.

'You see, the first edict is an alert sent throughout the network that the darkness has begun its play. Generally, throughout the ages, and let me be clear, this is not the first time Inarrel has felt the brunt of an attack from the darkness, and it won't be the last. The First will be followed almost immediately by the Second and Third edicts. The Second is to respond with force and in kind to any immediate threats to local communities against whatever threat is upon them. The Third is to evacuate any known hot spots ripe for invasion, to prearranged venues or locations in the local vicinity, hoping that any time gained from this before an attack is enough not to enact the Second. For once the First is in motion, the Second and Third are available to be enacted.'

'So what's the Fourth or Fifth? Or even the Sixth?' asked Grehn.

'Those cannot be discussed without knowing we have full encapsulation, away from any prying from those *women* out there!' Morla pointed toward the square where the carriages resided. 'Don't trust all in that troupe!'

'My ladies are all vetted, Morla! They are the epitome of subservience within the City and, in fact, of all Inarrel.'

'Yes, well, so are the dark lords and all their underlings of darkness. They have no other way. Also, I take it that the recommended "mind intrusion" inductions never took flight for the newly initiated?'

'Not a chance, not now, not ever! All candidates are interviewed and selected humanely, with only the—'

'Could save yourselves some time,' shot back Morla.

'No! Not ever happening!'

Holtonos finally spoke, 'Ladies! We have an issue here. A big one!'

'Damn right we do,' Morla pointed a finger at him. 'What have you been doing up there? The folk down here worship you demigods not realising they worship a bunch of bludgers! And in saying that, where is the ultimate bludger himself? Everos!'

Lenjora answered. 'Hold that tongue of yours, wise one. Do you remember your abstention? You had had enough of this world, and the role you had been given. The light, the dark … it all got too much for you and the others. That you were the first branch, the branch of light that the mortals now descend from, you gave up your duty to uphold the values of light.'

'That … is … piss, and you know it, Lenjora! I feel your mind has betrayed you quite sufficiently enough that you forget what you and I spoke of … before the betrayal.' Morla looked pained once more before going on. 'I gave my life and soul to this cause while you lot sat up there hoping for the best with well wishes and kisses to send on to whoever pissing takes them from the cattle of well-wishers – the subservient down here. To that end and to nip this one in the bud, let me finish. We all have a role to play in the next few phases. Whether that be in the next few days, weeks, months, years, or even another millennia: we cannot show our full hand until the eventual finale occurs in the course of history. There will come that time when you, and all of us, have to disappear for the next cycle to take place, the contraction of all matter. Thus, the creation from the resulting explosion – a monumental breath in, then out for another countless millennia, so don't become too comfortable. It will happen one day. Blink and you'll be replaced by yourself but not as you know it. It could be a billion, billion, billion moons from now. But, eventually all of that that makes you … *you* will one day reintegrate itself after that implosion of life into itself as *you*, here and now, but so rearranged you would never know! It could be the next explosion after all, but eternity is a fickle thing, it could throw you a doozy and rearrange your being one billionth different as you are now presented but the chances of that are as slim as me being as beautiful as the rose we must now nurture, Grehn.' Grehn blushed the same hue as such flower mentioned. 'So, we must be well prepared for that finale, pass the knowledge forward through time. Saying that, though, it does look ominously obvious that that time is drawing near.'

It was Holtonos's turn to speak. 'Yes, we are also but mortal beings. The breadth of our lives are not so short as your own, it would seem.' He chuckled, before looking at Grehn. 'Grehn, those dreams you harbour?'

'Mine … and mine alone! I hold them dear. For they are all I have.'

Ben was visibly shaken at the revelation, but he understood her reasoning.

Holtonos looked at her, genuine remorse in his eyes which softened Grehn's armour somewhat. 'I see, and also understand your need for privacy.' He offered her his hand. 'Would you walk with me, Grehn, instead? Away from friends and family? I will only ask three questions, and only divulge the answer given for each to Lenjora once I process the meaning of each. You see, there could be vital, unfound information contained within, critical intelligence, hidden knowledge in a sense that we need to tap into to break the wards set about your being, an avenue untouched by physical barriers. What I mean is this' – he whispered – 'the realms of emotion extend beyond the physical, like strings being strung, they vibrate across the cosmos on so many levels, like conduits, all connected to the One source, the beginning of all. Even the slightest connection from an early age could have damaging effects on the outcome of what is to eventually take place, not only on this planet, but on many others also! The balance may be on the side of darkness, and we may not find that we have been left cold sided until, well, when we would eventually find out.' Again he chuckled, but the gravity of what he was saying weighed on his eyes.

He asked Grehn again, 'Please, child, come with me. Give me what you may, and in return I will imbue a special skill upon you, adding to a repertoire of skills you, no doubt, already possess!' He said the last loud enough for Mother Ursen to take note. 'For though we are not immortal, we do have the tools to build artistry in how we see fit!' He bowed his head and spoke a few mumbled and indistinguishable words before holding out his hand. It glowed with a blue hue, and in his palm was an outlined shape of a triangle, all three sides of equal length – the signet of Jora. He mumbled three more words, before holding out his other hand. This time his whole palm was aglow as a bright green light shone from deep inside his hand.

As he clapped both hands together, he shouted, 'Balter!'

All in the room, all but Holtonos and one other, were thrown backward, away from unseen, gushing shockwave of energy that had shot forth from his glowing palms.

The candles in the room, though, were not the slightest moved from their constant flickering.

In what felt like real time – but watching the others fall to the ground all was happening in a mere fraction of time – Holtonos walked over to Grehn and held the awestruck girl's hand, then nodded.

Grehn, caught in awe and dismay, asked innocently with her eyes if the spell cast was to be that she would learn. A nod of the head from Holtonos affirmed the unspoken question.

Grehn held out her hand, oblivious to the wild ranting of Lenjora …

*

'Every time! Every time I hear it, it still gets me. One day I will learn to buff that spell of his … the old git!' Lenjora grumbled, offering a questioning smile to Holtonos.

Morla agreed. 'He showed me that trick eons ago, but he never could show me how to avoid it. Ha!'

It was now Peron's turn to speak. 'So … where have they gone? What's next!' he asked, with no little concern in his voice nor upon his face as he worried, obviously for Grehn.

Mother Ursen, still blanched by the few days of drama, jumped in. 'Do not worry, young man, if that is the spell of

"Bal An'g Fer" they are probably only seconds away from returning. Judging by the sign of Jora on his sorry old palm, I'm guessing they are already on their way back!' She began to push him back away from where the two had disappeared. 'Don't want to be standing there when they come back young man, unless you want to be conjoined with Grehn should your bodies eventually merge.' Peron blushed uncontrollably and rushed to the corner of the room quickly, which brought a swiping gaze from Mother Ursen. 'Or that of Holtonos!' she corrected, blushing herself.

Morla smiled – with what was left of her mouth. She had sensed within an instant that Peron found Grehn attractive, by the way he glanced away from her as she would look toward him. Who wouldn't? Add in the title of princess and heir to the oldest region in Vilenzia, and now the prophesised saviour of mankind … *Pffft mankind, such a spog* – no, of all that lived and breathed, both mobile and that which was rooted to the earth, she would be a magnet to anyone. Would he be the one to carry that admiration forward, past all the pleasure and pain to come? For the prophecy of the saviour was to unite all in a backlash to the coming storm! By any means necessary. Could, in fact, the young girl caged inside the fortress her whole life find the courage – if what was to be believed – in the next few days, weeks and, maybe many more beyond, to repel and expel the darkness.

*Possibly, she is of good kin,* she thought, looking conspicuously over at the girl's grandmother.

Though she was not of Mother Ursen's blood, she could sense much of the same determination. *So it seems the intended lineage is not hereditary. Also, if the darkness had found its way through her dreams, so too would have the light!* She plead, and hoped that was the case …

Morla spoke to Peron with a reaction she herself could not check, for it was immediate, a spout of impulse. 'You must protect her!' She was aghast at the impromptu verbal outburst. 'By protect I mean you must guide her! I feel your heart, though your mind is not pure—'

'But I am an honcura—'

'Shush, Peron! I was paying you a compliment. We don't have much time. You are to aid, help nurture and educate the saviour, if that is what she will be! Even though she may not be, we cannot take the chance. Your heart is pure. Use it wisely, and if the urge from *both of* your impure minds evolves itself into something more, then so be it. But if you are for the cause, that of your oaths to the City and then those further beyond – that of The Shadow of the Path – you will swear the penultimate oath to me … save only one other.'

*

Morla winked at him, the ancient, decrepit eyelid still half closed; Peron was sure it would soon eel away.

*Penul*—Peron suddenly realised what she had said, and understandably paled. For he longed to grace the creaking timber of the world-famous Grouse; he could just as longingly sink beneath the timber boards below, and then beyond, to the other side of the world.

However, now he was here, and with some important people. He did remember those oaths sworn in the City, and those sworn in the secret covenant as initiate to The Shadow of the Path; though he paled at the thought, he was ready to abide  by those oaths, no matter where and with who they would end up.

Standing tall, he looked at Mother Ursen who only shrugged her shoulders. Then to Lenjora, who also shrugged her shoulders – she also offered a cheeky smile which eventually, after a few moments, bared teeth with malicious intent, accompanied by a raised eyebrow.

Standing an inch less taller than seconds earlier, he eventually nodded. 'Go on …' He accepted his eventual and ultimate fate.

Morla began, 'The almighty Lenjora bear witness and say aye.'

'Aye!'

'The ever graceful, healer to many, and mother to all, Mother Ursen, bear witness to the words, and say aye.'

'Aye, but hurry. We run out of time!'

'Noted …' She turned to Peron before she spoke. 'Now, Peron, do not take this oath lightly, it is a forever assignment, one to protect her, and a sworn fealty she may never hear of. I ask you firstly: are you pure of heart – by that I mean, are you a servant of the light and only the light? Do you have only a pure response to evil and its seductive entrapment? Bow your head and speak truly for each answer given.'

'I am pure and true!' Peron spoke resolutely as he bowed to look at the feet of the woman floating just in front of him.

'You are now,' she continued, 'but could you be swayed in the future? Answer this honestly Peron! I will give you a few seconds.'

'Darkness is all around us,' he began, though we cannot see it, our bodies give off shadows even in the brightest light. Some creatures only see that because they are looking for the darkness in all they see. I see light in the opposite, I see it wherever there is the darkest of shadows, for light must also exist there to cast such!'

Morla looked to Lenjora, from the corner of her eye, for affirmation. Lenjora closed her eyes and gave a slight nod.

She then looked to Mother Ursen who tapped her knee twice quicky with her right hand. To offer affirmation – if unconventionally.

'Quicker,' Mother Ursen spoke, with urgency.

Morla ignored the interruption and focused intently on Peron. 'Secondly, you are a man. Did you know we only recruit females, eunuchs, or creatures that do not abide to such sexuality to that of keepers of the realms? Though you may see this as irrelevant, ascension is out of the question for you, but it may apply to Grehn to ascend beyond what she has been marked as. How does that make you feel?'

'It is of no concern to me ... However, if Grehn is to ascend, as per the stories read and issued through my earlier tuition, then it would have been an honour to share the same breath with such a woman!' He blushed at his own words.

'*Have* been an honour? Such modesty. Though it be the truth.'

Head still bowed, he almost dared a glance to Lenjora, but she warned him away with a sharp mental snap – *No! Stop!* – before he could react to his own urge to see if affirmation was offered to support his answers.

Luckily Morla sought affirmation from Mother Ursen first. A nod toward Peron with the 'aye'. A nod and the 'aye' from Lenjora followed before the third question was asked.

Peron still had his eyes down when he asked, 'Thought they would be back by now?'

The answer came from Lenjora, who dropped her palm into his eyesight, blocking off the sight of Morla's crumpled brown sandals. The blue glowing triangle was the answer he needed.

'Now. The third and final question. Ready yourself young man. For it will be the most difficult.'

Peron nodded his head.

'Who sent you here?'

The question took him aback. It was an easy answer, the easiest of the three. He had waited for this assignment for years, but now the obvious answer escaped him completely.

He couldn't recall who had given him the order to attend Anatoma, the offered mage from the City to Jacobs Well, and then to travel beyond, up the coast. He sought the answer, but could not recall. With his mind's eye, he sensed Lenjora shake her head. 'I … I am unsure who? But it was … Damn, for the life of me cannot recall who issued the missive.'

'Who else knows?!' shouted Morla.

'Well … all that were there … all who were supposed to be there. I think … I can't remember now, it's like a dark cloud descending on their faces when I try to remember who—'

'Focus on their clothes, Peron. What were they wearing?' Mother Ursen jumped in.

Ignoring her, he scrambled for a response. 'Surely the same person would have given me this assignment, the Onberseeler – the head of The Shadow? Even the Tembor would have been present to give at least two votes required for such a menial assignment.' Peron looked perplexed. He then took Mother Ursen's advice and tried to remember what the assembled had been wearing, but that again failed to materialise in his mind.

'All I remember is that others were sent out into the world, to research and provide assistance to those who had discovered any strange occurrence.' Peron still looked down. 'Others were also summoned to attend the Third. The urgency was what was the most unsettling.'

Morla looked at Lenjora who was smiling at Peron. 'He speaks true.' Lenjora nodded back to Morla once she'd averted her gaze to the young man. 'What heralds from his confusion, Morla?'

'The old boot has been successful in cloaking his identity,' Morla looked pleased. 'Do you remember where the others were sent to?'

'Yes.'

'Where to, may I ask?'

'To the … ummm, to the—'

'No worries, Peron. Again it seems he was successful,'

'Who?'

'No mind, better you do not know yet, there are still those who could use such intelligence for their own gains.'

Lenjora then released the spell of Fresia and a sudden rush of air filled the tavern.

Holtonos let go of Grehn's hand, and now she was relieved to be left alone. They had instantly disappeared from the Grouse, and were standing roughly fifty paces from a large door cast in a frame which extended half that distance vertically. The suddenness of the move had jolted her senses, causing her to stumble a little and feel a little nauseous.

She turned around to see in every other direction what was there, but she could only see the doorway in front and rolling hills of green everywhere else.

'Where are we?'

Holtonos looked at her, measured an answer, one he thought would be appropriate. 'Think not of where, or when. Also, where can be subjective. And what would that matter? We could be anywhere. So, in saying that where would you like to be, Grehn? Where have your dreams taken you?'

'I have seen this doorway before …'

It was now Holtonos's turn to look around in every direction, for her answer had spooked him.

All he could see now, other than the door, was smouldering fields, blackened from grass that had recently been aflame. Placing a hand on Grehn's shoulder – reassurance but also to steady himself – he spoke. 'Child, this is the realm of dreams, a realm of my own. You see for every living thing there exists a realm, too, of their own. A sanctuary … of sorts. We can invite others into this realm and also create a landscape from nothing more than want. But … there is also an element of this realm that reacts to emotion, be it love, fear, anxiety, it all becomes relevant. To master this realm is to be at absolute peace within and with yourself.'

'So, why suddenly all the smoke?'

'Fear, my child! You see you should not have been able to see this door. This door exists only in this realm, my realm, and one other place.' Still holding her shoulder, he went on. 'There exists another door, one identical to this. For we can only ever see the face of the door that we see now.' He stepped a few steps in front of her. 'Come, walk with me. I will show you.'

They walked a constant arc, keeping the same distance away from the threshold of the massive door. No matter how far they walked along the arc, the doorway remained as was – the full face of the heavy door standing before them.

'I fear the doorway you saw was the same, however from the other side.'

'Why is that such of a fear to you? And what is behind the doorway?'

'I don't know, though I imagine there is something on the other side. However, I have never been able to open it. One day maybe I will. Once I muster the spirit to try.'

'What? You haven't tried?'

'No, child! For I fear what could, or would, be on the other side …'

'Explain further. You are not making any sense of it.' Grehn still felt the unease of him holding her hand and holding her shoulders. She wanted out of his dream already.

'The fear I hold is that *I* am on the other side of that doorway!' Holtonos now stood straight, facing Grehn. 'For if I am on the other side that would mean there is a version of myself that is the opposite to what I am. If that is the case

I fear that he would step through into this realm, and then who knows … the fear I hold is that I would unleash a terrible being upon our world, upon even our universe! We have enough problems to worry about already.'

'That is a very fickle and presumptive answer, Holtonos.' Grehn laughed a little which took Holtonos by surprise. 'Are you not a god? Could you not just shut the door quickly if your fear turned out to be correct?' She continued to laugh as she walked toward the doorway. 'If you are not that brave to open the door by now, how will you ever be?'

She was now at the doorway.

Holtonos was astounded at the thought that she would open the door, but before he could move, the fear of what she was about to do took hold of him, and he was strangled to the ground by thick vines coming from the same. 'Grehn, stop!' he managed to shout before his throat was strangled, rendering him silent.

She pushed the large door open with the faintest touch. It swung open as if barged by a herd of wild bovine.

What she saw horrified her.

Stirring back at her – as though a mirror had been planted in the opening – was … an image of herself. However, the girl reflected had an evil, twisted face, and arms adorned with talons dripping with blood.

She screamed, revolted at the sight.

Grehn pulled the door closed before the being on the other side could react. Turning to Holtonos, she cried, 'This is my dream, you bastard!' The vines tightened around him but she did not care. 'You dare to lecture me on fear, of where or what we are?!' Holtonos gasped for air. Every breath released brought less for the next breath. 'Show me! Show me your realm! Show me!'

Holtonos hesitantly held up a hand. A red light shot outward like a ripple in the ocean. Everything became hazed, then shimmered into a new landscape.

Now it was Grehn's turn to gasp.

They now stood upon a rock, jutting high out of the ocean raging beneath them – there was just enough room for the two of them to stand on it.

She looked at Holtonos with a pity she had withheld so far. *So much, so much for the man to contain. His doorway is out of reach.* The same doorway they had observed moments earlier floated but twenty paces beyond the rock. *Probably a good thing he has been so reluctant to open the damn thing! He is probably right, the creature on the other side would pale even my evil reflective being. Well, at least I know I'm the good one!*

'This, Grehn … is where I was going to bring you. But I let you lead; I apologise for such guile.' Holtonos looked about, arms outstretched as to take it all in. 'You see the raging ocean below? That is reflection of a constant fear I hold for all souls. I think of it even when I am awake, the emotions that run through me, shadows of the raw love, the raw beautiful energy I strive to provide for all of you!' He waved his arms up and down as if in time with the rushing, rhythmic sound of wave hitting the rocks. The sea calmed. 'You see, I serve The Greater. My sanity – be it flawed and incoherent at times – is sound for the most part. You know, maybe the doorway is only a doorway, a portal to the higher echelon of this life and the next. Maybe. But it could also be a reflection of what we could become, if strayed from the light … maybe. Maybe one day I will take that chance, as only as a last resort.'

'Does the doorway appear in everyone's dreams?'

'No, that is what shocked me so, that it appeared to you … I thought that I was initiating the mirage of the doorway, but when you said you had seen it before it stumped me. Then it was real.' He waved a dismissive hand. 'I am able, and competent, at calming all the voices I hear and even able to control the flow of emotion running through, thus calming the rage below, but that rage below is a constant reminder of what I am trying to achieve.'

'And that is?'

'The greater good! One day this world, the universe and all the good beings within it, will be able to live out their existence in peace, unafraid, with a sense of neutrality that swayed beyond the neutral bar and toward kindness. Who knows what a world without evil would be like? I observed your soul turn a little to the dark when you opened that door. You cannot become that which *they* want you to become!

'I fear though… I may say that quite often, though fear is a good thing, a good trait to have, for without fear there would be no check to what we are doing. We would surely end ourselves in a heartbeat! It is what stops us poking an arm into the fire, or jumping off the tallest cliff,' he emphasised by leaning dramatically over the rock on which they stood. 'My newfound fear, thank you for giving me that, may I add, is that you are being shadowed to veer off the intended path, through a manipulation with the slightest of nudges.'

'By whom?'

'That, I do not know, but I presume there have been subtle attempts to break your stride.' Holtonos twitched his moustache as if both cheeks itched. 'Now, I will give you a test. But before I do, you must acknowledge that there is more to this world – which I'm sure you are now well aware of – and you may *or* may not be its saviour. And … currently, Peron is being quizzed as to his true nature, and intentions as we speak. He was sent here by Master Johltor, Onberseeler of the Third, from the City to meet Anatoma. Unbeknown to him, however, he was sent here to see your elevation through the ranks at the City and then, hopefully beyond. A play was made weeks ago to secure you, hence the arrival of Mother Ursen was indeed no accident.

'Morla however, was, and still is, a massive bump in the

road, one that we knew was there, we just didn't know when. How she is doing it, we have no idea. I'm of the opinion she is of substance, somewhere, but what we are seeing is a projection of the play she had set up, thus, there may be many such remnants of her currently playing out her merry tune throughout Vilenzia, to many other players in this game of good versus evil.'

'Can you not feel her presence then?'

'No, we are limited, for why? I know not' Holtonos chuckled.

'Oh.' Grehn twitched her own imaginary moustache. 'Well, with such power then why do you not act with vengeance to all that is wrong with the world, *your* world? Can you not just snap your finger and rid the world of such evil?'

'No, it is not right to presume all that does is!' Holtonos made a cross with a finger which changed the landscape below to a beautiful golden orchard. 'Look now, you see all that rage below? Gone in an instant, replaced with a majestic orchard full of life, teeming with colour. Now watch!'

He twitched his finger again and the smallest of sparks crackled before it dropped and disappeared beneath the canopy of golden leaves below. 'You see … the world as we know it is filled with such occurrences of … mishaps, that which has the potential to cause such violent harm and damage. We assume there was a cause … Now watch.'

Suddenly, a pillar of smoke made its way up, through the canopy below.

'You see? That wildfire does not know right from wrong; it burns anyway, unaware of its destructive capabilities.'

Grehn nodded slightly, knowing that the spark was indeed not evil and not striving to take over the world. An obvious observation.

'Now … what if I were to tell you that those doing evil's bidding are the same as that fire down there. Tinder, per se?

They'd be unaware they are causing such pain and suffering, and it is only second nature to them.' He looked at Grehn who was now growing weary over the lecture of right versus wrong. But he went on, and Grehn listened – she was not bereft of manners, if patience. 'The sun is a source of light, one we found to be almost perfect, but it is also a source to inflict such pain by causing the fire to begin in the first instance. So what do we do?'

'We use water to extinguish the flame.'

'Why not the sun?' he asked her.

'Because all would fail, I would imagine ...'

'True, and that would be a monumental feat that may require the use of every single drop of resource in this realm.'

'And, why water? Why not magic?' she asked, matter-of-factly.

'We could, but that would be an immense amount of magic. Why not wind?'

'Wind would fan the flame.' She sighed. 'This is all a bit tedious now. I do get it.'

'Do you? Do you understand yet that evil is not necessarily evil? Even though it does evil it may not be at all evil?'

'Yes, you explained that already. Tell me why we are really here, Holtonos.'

'Here? Did I not say before that that is irrelevant? When is the appropriate word!'

'Okay then, when are we?'

'We are now, or at least at the best of my ability. Time has slowed all around us allowing us to step in and out of these realms without much notice. But I can hear the calling of Lenjora; she too has slowed time during the questioning of Peron. We must leave soon. But, before we depart, your question as to why: well, turn around and see for yourself.'

Grehn instantly turned and saw that which her dreams

had been showing her all throughout her life, each and every one of them melding into one another.

'Back to your question for a moment. We are somewhat powerless on Inarrel. We never used to be though. The more life generated and multiplied here, so too did our abilities diminish. Maybe a balancing act, who knows? Though we are still able to counter dark souls, not necessarily those of this world with dark hearts, the belief is we created so we can heal, thus generating more to send forth, onto wherever – from the oceans that sway up on Seltero!'

Grehn wriggled her cheeks, not fully believing it. Though she thought of a set of scales in Anatoma's chamber – always level, even if one plate seemed to carry more bulk.

'Grehn, you entered my realm from the very beginning. I have been striving to calm your waters this whole time. However, the rage you saw before was that of your own, this is still your dream, one that I have access to! There must be more at play here than you or I realise …'

Grehn nodded, she understood the why of the intrusion. She shuddered to think of the alternate intrusion, from those seeking to bait her, those baying for her to become their fire – or those who lurked on the other side of the door now staring at her, the image of her evil twin's plaque now forever etched upon every door she would open from here on.

Holtonos went on, sounding pained once more. 'Time! In the end … time is all we have … It ends just as suddenly as it begins. Time is a funny word, for it does not account for all within. We only ever think of time when it's about to run out. Your time will come and go, as will that of all. But time can be many things other than such, it ticks on forever forward; that is correct, once that tick ends though time does not, it begins once again. So … with that in mind, where do you think we are?'

'In my head?'

'Come on, Grehn, your much smarter than that. When are we?'

'The end?'

'Precisely, and where are we?'

'We are at the edge of reality, that which time does not—cannot replicate?'

'Again, well done, so what is next?'

'We extinguish the flame before it spreads?'

'Not quite, but yes that will come soon enough.' He pointed at her, at the chain hanging loose around her neck. 'Pass it to me.'

She hesitated, but eventually bowed and brought the chain over her head, sensing it was the right thing to do. The chalk she had yet to present to Mother Ursen was still contained within the locket.

She handed it to Holtonos.

He unlocked the case with a wave of his hand. 'This is your realm, remember  Why is it that you are what you are, seeing that we are in a dream? Even all immaterial items, such as this, and the clothes we wear?'

'I don't know the answer to that …' she dared not take a stab at what she thought.

'Is it because we have traversed the realm of reality to be here?'

'Ah! Here! This is not real. I get it now!'

'Here, take this. Sign a glyph that would take use back to the Grouse, back to your grandmother and Peron. But … before you do, I want you to extinguish the fire raging below using only this elegantly crafted item.'

She took the locket from Holtonos's hand, and opened it to take the chalk. She drew a shape in the air, that of an hour glass. She blotted the bottom section, as though full of sand, and left empty the upper chamber. She smiled at Holtonos as the flames below disappeared. He returned the smile – that of a proud teacher who had only just found out his pupil was destined for great things. She had not missed his subtle hint – before he knew what she intended to do, he nodded.

Grehn drew an arcing arrow, from top to bottom and mouthed words that flowed together. *'Unparte-nexa.'*

The time glass flipped on its central axis. And a rush of air threw them both back, back through the landscapes where they had stood in her realm, finally back to the familiar faces of those back in the Grouse.

Dazed, she saw a faint glow diminish in Lenjora's hand, then noticed an astounded look, and an exposed relief upon Peron's face. *Looks like he has been to all the hells and back!*

She looked over the long timber bar, to a large ornate mirror that traversed the entire wall behind, up to the floor above. All she could see was the reflection of demons where all others stood. *Hmm, so that's the way it is now.* She blinked, hard. *Better.* The reflections were now those of heroes, embellished by a glowing golden hue, one she thought resembled glory – the saviours of mankind, of all kind, on this world and beyond.

The most striking reflection was Morla, who resembled a woman in her middle years, bearing a shield and broad sword strapped to her back, face painted with some primitive colouring – stoicism personified.

She understood now, more than ever; all made sense in her world. The years of constriction and confinement justified. Absolutely. She let out a sigh, before hugging all in attendance, one by one – Peron a little harder than the rest, for while she had been in transition back to the real world, her world, every word he spoke echoed through the space surrounded her, settling her.

She was eventually granted leave to return home by Morla. And a smile from Lenjora once she released the spell.

'And that was that!' Grehn announce triumphantly. 'Father! I understand my role! And also understand what you have been hiding me from all this time!'

'That's grand, petal, but you are not to—'

Holtonos grumbled, Lenjora coughed, and Mother Ursen stood hands on hips – all looking at the big gruff man.

'Well, whatever you need to do. You will have myself—'

'My life is yours Grehn, my blade, my soul! As it has always been.' Kneeling down, King Ben's brother, Kimo had entered the room silently, he had obviously been eavesdropping on the whole interchange.

Grehn looked at her uncle; she knew there would be no worth regarding his word as bravado.

Entering from another door, Grehn's mother rushed to embrace her only child – tightly – with much energy, save squeezing the life out of her.

'Sweet Holt—errm … sweet Mother! Is there any privacy in these walls!'

King Benjamin rubbed his chin roughly. 'So, what transpired upon your return to the Grouse? It can't have just ended at that? You have my full attention, for I will need to know how to help, where I can.'

'Well, no, we talked.'

'About what, Grehn? Mother Ursen, care to elaborate on what was talked about?'

'I'm afraid not, Ben. That should be something best left unsaid for the time being,' Mother Ursen said abruptly. 'There are too many ears in this place. As you well know, Benjamin.' She walked closer to him, made a slight gesture with her right hand and spoke softly. 'Echo of my voice, be near.' Moving even closer to Ben, she held both hands to shield her voice as she held them between her lips and his ear. 'The time is nigh for your annual speech to the masses of Jacobs Well. I ask you to walk with myself … and Grehn immediately afterwards, or as soon as possible, for there will be much to discuss away from those creeping beyond these walls.'

King Benjamin Jacob Aurelia looked at all; all those that nodded had been in the Grouse earlier. He spoke, knowing no further details could be derived from them, 'Where would you propose?'

Still at his ear, Mother Ursen whispered again, 'The Catacombs of Silence, at *the Efflame*; for that is where it will all begin ...'

# Flame

The guests had been invited back to the castle grounds following the disruption to proceedings the day earlier, when Grehn went missing. Which had meant the castle locked down and all festivities – including the king's annual speech – had been cancelled or postponed.

Due to other commitments, two of the permitted attendees from the previous evening had not been able to attend – they were from one of the taverns and were most likely already missing out on the most lucrative time of year – so they had offered their places to their two girls: two members of the Artisans Guild in the city and quite well connected – two young female artists who had dressed elaborately for the occasion and were goggling and giggling uncontrollably.

Grehn did not miss the two walking by – in a somewhat swaying route – from where she stood behind a stone wall, welcoming the guests back through. Though the majority of them had returned, she was sure many wore a reluctant smile and were afraid to offer any slight to the accommodation and respect shown by the royal family for inviting them back to their home – she smiled inwardly, a longing to feel joyful bliss. *My time is coming.* Looking over the top of the two young girls, she saw her father perched atop the wall of the well – the symbolic centrepiece to the town, and that from which the recollection of stories came to guide his monologue. He did not miss the two either and smiled, before he noticed her looking in his direction. He returned a pained smile with his eyes dropping before hopping down and making his way towards her.

The journey across the courtyard was taking much longer than he had anticipated, being accosted at every step was not helping. Instead – when he had the chance – he waved

Grehn toward where he stood, then pointed.

He made his way back to where he had stood, following the flow of traffic entering the square from the main gate.

Grehn fared no better, she too was struggling to get through the dense throng of guests. She was just at the precipice, about to break free, when the two new additions to the list threw themselves in front of her, squealing and carrying on obnoxiously – intoxicated.

She embraced the two of them and led them forward to the foot of the well wall where she spoke to them. 'Stay here! And be good or my uncle Kimo will switch you both back across the Arches if you so much as raise the slightest commotion!' She winked at Kimo standing not too far away, he in turn banged the pommel of his sword against his breast plate which brought a yelp and a gulp from the duo. He smiled an evil grin back at her. 'Stay right here …and be good. Understand, my ladies?'

'Uh huh, of course, of course, Princess!'

'None of that … Grehn will do. Before I jump up next to my father, your names?'

One of them was dumbstruck for a moment – either that or incapable of putting two words together due to the grog, which was exposing its neck out of her night purse, still missing its stopper. The reply came from the other. Even if slightly incoherent, Grehn understood. 'Me, am Pomora and this be here me mate Clarissa,' quickly followed by a hiccup, which brought laughter to all three.

Grehn screamed at them, loudly, and in the vibe of a *night crawler*, which brought a shriek of terror to the duo and a boom of laughter from her father and uncle who had been trained on the exchange – for Grehn was seldom in company of girls her own age.

Grabbing both of them by the shoulders did not help her cause in calming them for the night crawler was now on the attack. She quickly drew a glyph in the air with her chalk in the shape of a wave and pushed her palm through it toward the pair who immediately calmed and came to their senses once the wave of magic had washed over them.

Grehn looked at the chalk. All the studying, all the painstaking hours of confinement had now begun to bear fruit – she was amazed – for she had practiced the strokes of each potential spell hundreds … no, thousands of times.

She quickly followed up with, 'Sorry, I was always told a sudden fright was the best cure for hiccups!'

It was Clarissa who was the first to laugh, followed by Pomora then the booming laughter of Kimo and Ben. Grehn just stood for a moment, placed her chalk back in the locket and joined in with over-the-top laughter to just fit in with the moment, bringing a higher, sustained laughter from all in the attendance.

Amused by the theatrics, Grehn fell to a full and meaningful laughter that burst out in spasms – portraying the light and joy of her soul.

Pomora felt her legs begin to dampen, the copious amount of liquor consumed, aided by the laughter, was now seeping through. She quickly scrambled onto the wide wall of the well, crouched on her haunches, and let a warm flow trickle down the well, bringing bemusement and the whole chapter of laughter to a grinding halt – beginning with Grehn. Ben and Clarissa still enjoyed the episode unfolding. Grehn joined her on the wall, shielding the view from those congregated below with her loose cardigan.

Grehn turned to her father and whispered so as to not be overheard, 'What's got you so amused? How much longer should we be standing here? I am eager to discuss with you that which was foretold by the apparition of Morla before she—erm … tell you that later. Here comes Mother.' She winked at him and hopped down off the wall to embrace the graceful flowing form of Jahnna.

Pomora pulled up her leggings quickly, now finished.

Ben helped her down before his brother approached and hovered over the two young starlings. He spoke abruptly, not liking what he had been witness to. 'You two need to come with me … Now!' He turned on a pivot and began to walk toward the corner of the courtyard – the most distant point to where the annual decree would take place, and the furthest point in the courtyard from the well.

The two girls looked at each other, then both pirouetted a full two turns before falling into each other as they walked to follow, chests held high mimicking Kimo. Kimo glanced over his shoulder before locking his gaze back at the corner he was leading the two to; a smile almost touched his lips before he saw Sentok making a beeline for him, carrying some sort of makeshift box with a few tubes sticking up out of it. *Not now, Sentok!*

'Hey, Kimo, you wanted me to keep these away from the folk right? Where's the best spot?' Sentok put the box down and rubbed his bald head, removing the beads of sweat as his hand slid across the glistening scalp. The box was heavier than it looked, full of a dense mixture of explosives – the night's entertainment, the sky flames.

Kimo responded with a dramatic wave of his hands. 'Certainly not there, Sentok. Put them in exactly the same locations we agreed for yesterday's show. Say, where are those larger ones you were carrying around earlier?'

'His Majesty told me to put them somewhere else. He was very adamant, and was Anatoma at the time too.' Sentok instantly sprouted more beads of moisture upon his scalp, and now also his forehead, which he quickly dabbed away with the big palm of his hand, leaving a sliver of lamplight to reflect off his scalp. 'He told me to not utter a word to anyone as to where I put them …' He gave himself away as he looked nervously over Kimo's shoulder toward the well. 'They maybe not be in there, Master.'

Kimo shook his head slightly. *Why is Ben getting involved in such menial tasks, wonder what the man be up to?* 'Well, Sentok you—Hey! Girls, leave those alone!'

Sentok and Kimo quickly stole away the tubes the girls held, pretending to duel, banging them against each other's, giggling away unaware of the potential catastrophic consequences such an idiotic action could cause, not only to themselves but those in their not so immediate vicinity.

This brought another dramatic rebuke from Kimo, dragging them both away as he held tight an arm of each, to be deposited in the corner and told that under no condition were they to leave until he came to remove them. The ensuing reaction of the girls was as expected, both in tears, hugging each other as they crouched lower and lower.

Pomora looked up at Kimo, but was set back down with a shake of his head and a hard point of his finger to stay put. 'Sorry girls, this is not a time for silliness, there be flamework happening shortly. It's for your own good health I leave you both here. Understand?' Rhetorical. They needn't have nodded their acceptance.

'Sentok! Walk with me and talk about the night's light show. I want every detail. *All* of it! And I don't give a shit about what *he* said. I can be much, much more brutal than my brother!'

Sentok gulped then nodded, understanding the level of the threat – he had seen it firsthand. 'Well … there be seven large tubes – huge – strapped inside that well there. Them be the big ones. All the colours that always brightens the sky on the third and final day of the Festival, Kimo.'

'What? Inside the well? But the well roof will be blown to pieces.'

'Aye, that's his plan, don't know why … there be some charges on the roof and that to drop it down the well before them big ones go off!'

Kimo rubbed his chin. 'Very well. When are they likely to go off?'

'Once the annual edict has been given.' Sentok looked at King Benjamin, the glance was immediately returned with a shake of the head and a smile to show he knew what had just transpired in the short transaction between the two large men. 'They be big ones, sir. Bigger than ever! They will light the sky for forever around to view. King Ben had them placed to his liking with the advice given from Anatoma: apparently, from the bird's view, and a show to that evil planet up there, the arrangement is of – well – a signal, or glyph, or the same, I don't quite know.'

'Is that so?' Kimo again rubbed his chin – this time much slower and less agitated. 'Well then, let's not dawdle, let's finish up. Hey girls, girls …' They looked up at Kimo, now doe-eyed, trying to avoid any more rebuke. 'You wouldn't mind taking a seat here? Stay here … Yes, stay here.' He then leaned in close to the pair, eyeing them both quickly. 'If you know what is good for you, you will remain here and cause no trouble. No trouble at … all … do you understand me?!' As he finished, the flash of lightning spread across his eyes, transmitting more than words ever could to the docile pair.

'Eeeek!' came the joint response from both.

'Sure! For sure!' Pomora followed Clarissa.

'And, before I leave you two,' he pointed to Clarissa's waist, 'hand it over …'

'Eeeek!' Clarissa handed Kimo a small, glazed hip flask that was tied around her inner thigh.

'Thank you, sweetheart.' He grabbed it and took a long swig before passing it to the hulking form behind him. 'Ah … vintage?'

Before Clarissa could muster a response he hushed her gently. Sentok confirmed the year, then followed up after another swig. 'Bodett. Not of their general yield, but one of special harvest.' He eyed the pair before asking, 'How is it you have in your possession such a rare Bodett?' He gestured to Kimo to come closer.

Clarissa looked to Pomora, who had now turned white as snow. 'A gift?' she eeked out.

Sentok whispered to Kimo. 'This is a very expensive drop, Kimo ...'

'Aye, it does emit such characteristics ... the value you would attach to such a "rarity"?'

One of the girls began to speak but was shot down by Kimo's gaze.

'Hush, child, the question was rhetorical,' Sentok interjected.

'Retoclocle?'

'Nay mind, child.' He grabbed Kimo by the shoulder and turned him away from earshot of the two youngsters. 'Listen to me well, Kimo. Only the Grouse has such stock and not much of it at that. This stuff is not, I repeat not, for purchase. It's cellared for royalty, and royalty alone ...'

'Thought I recognised it'

'Uh hum. Kimo, this stuff— and beg my pardon – it's not even offered to anyone else, other than ... you know, royalty.'

Kimo looked at Sentok from the corner of his eye. 'I am royalty, eh? Sort of.' He chuckled before putting an arm around Sentok's shoulder. 'Do you know what resides down that well there? Well, not directly at the bottom of the shaft, but down one of the many tunnels that burrow under the castle and down into the rock?'

'I have heard stories,'

'I am telling you now, Sentok, the real truth!' He turned his head around to look at the two before returning a side glance at Sentok. 'I have an avid nose for such, and I have been fortunate enough to sample ample offerings from that estate ... on many occasion. You know for a fact Ben won't touch the stuff. And believe me – but do not repeat this, for your life is not necessarily worth extinguishing for such lack of confidentiality – Ben has ten bottles of every vintage from every estate in Vilenzia stored down that very shaft!'

'So … Now, what are you getting at?' Kimo slowly turned Sentok around – arm on his shoulder still – and approached the two girls.

Sentok spoke, a little too loudly. 'They be thieves! For sure, sire, and that is me being the slightest bit modest!'

Clarissa squeaked once more before jumping up and lunging at the big, bald man. 'Thieves?! Thieves! You balding twat! You wouldn't know a thief even if they stole your goopy looking eyes!' Luckily for Sentok, she wobbled as she lunged.

Kimo stopped the charge with a big palm to her face, holding off the swinging arms with his other. 'Stop, child! Stop this madness! You drunken fool!'

Clarissa slumped to the floor and began to sob.

Pomora came to her and hugged her tight before looking up at Kimo. 'It was my fault! Sir, it is my err … I was the one who decided to open the bottle and store it in the flask. My father's donation, to bring it with us, as a gift to the king and queen, for he was unable to attend due to some *events* happening at his … err … *establishment*, so we happened to attend in his stead.'

'Tell me, child … who is your father?' Tell me it isn't Sir Derimor!' Kimo eyed her, knowing already the answer – she was the mirror image of her mother, Parabella.

'It is, sir … ' her eyes dropped to the floor.

Kimo barked a sound that almost resembled laughter, something he rarely ever did – at least not in the public domain. 'Child, why didn't you just say so!' Kimo shook his head after wiping away the tiniest amount of moisture from his eye. 'You will,' he continued to laugh, 'if I know Lord Derimor, be in a lot of trouble, young lady …'

Kimo grabbed the glass flask and threw it as high as he could manage toward the high wall. It shattered upon impact and dropped shards of glass into the flowerbed below. The wine smeared across the wall in all directions and dribbled down to the flowerbed, looking like someone's head had been smashed against the wall.

He then said, 'Well, His Majesty, the king, thanks you for your offering and he will be sure to pass on his thanks personally once the Grouse is rid of its—hmm … issues.'

The two girls squeaked and hugged each other before both each grabbed Kimo's legs and kissed his knees in unison, uttering thanks and praise to the almighty!

Nudging each away – with not just a subtle kick – he spoke. 'Now, you will behave yourselves or I can just as easily have Sentok here take whatever shards he finds and drops them with a note to your dear father! Understood?' Both nodded before he continued, 'Now that is sorted, Sentok, show these two chooks to where they can observe, out of trouble, on that there wall above the flowerbed. And if any trouble becomes them, come fetch me to draft that note … understood?'

'Come on girls,' Sentok began, 'sorry for mistakin' you both for cretins, though I am sure I wasn't too far wrong looking at the state of ya!' He chuckled as he walked toward the flowerbed – the one with a few tubes sticking up and out from the bedding soil. *Best fix that up'n put 'em somewhere else, don't want to be barred from the Grouse for an eternity!*

Ben was not amiss in letting his terse gaze drift from himself to the two girls and the tall, bald man – he had not misheard the disgruntled laughter from his brother; he was genuinely interested in the exchange. With a nod, he motioned Kimo to approach.

As Kimo got close, Ben spoke. 'What has gotten you so riled into a frenzy?'

'Apologies, sir—'

'Ben, always been Ben, Kimo.'

'If you say so, sire … those two miscreants there are the offspring of Essen Derimor and his other half, the Lady Parabella.'

'You should get out more, Kimo …' King Ben pointed to them both. 'You think I would have let them behind these walls, acting like a pair of *monkenerets*, if they were of any other ilk?' Ben looked at Kimo, smiling. 'You should really get out more, big man!'

'Aye, I should maybe frequent the places of ill worship more often … aye!' He shook his head. 'Only realised it was them when they gave me an indication of where their pa was from, it clocked from the one time I met the owners of the Grouse in the square, oh … maybe fifteen, sixteen years ago?'

'You know that it was exactly seventeen years ago. You do numbers and memories as though ingrained into your palm!' Ben rubbed his chin, not unlike Kimo moments earlier. 'Never seen you so stuck for words in all our lives, even to this day.'

'Oh, come on Ben, 'twas nothing more than a kiss of my cheek, and you know … that was all!'

'Haha, Kimo! You're blushing … we know exactly where she kissed you!' Ben extended his lips a bit further out, emphasising not just a usual pout.

It was met with the full fist of Kimo. Though checked, it still knocked Ben back to the well wall.

A rattling wheeze crept out of Ben's mouth, not unlike the laughter earlier, just more restricted – from the air knocked out of his lungs with the impact of hitting the base of the wall of the well.

'Oof, hoo-hoo, oh, Kimo, it always touches a nerve!' He still chuckled away as he began to pick himself up. The arm of Kimo assisted more than just the elevation of his body back to the upright stout position he always held.

'Sorry, Ben, you know more than all why I just thumped

one on you. Now … play your part of the act, a role to ease the now silent and stricken crowd.'

Ben jumped majestically in the air and pirouetted before striking Kimo on the top of the head, a glancing blow, no harm done. Kimo fell backwards laughing dramatically as though this was just a playful fight between the two most powerful men in Jacobs Well. They both stood up after a few tumbles and rolls around on the dusty stone pavers and hugged each other, more dramatically than the tumbles, which brought an ease and calm about those assembled.

Ben whispered to Kimo, 'She was yours that night, no doubt.' Ben looked at Kimo again, this time more reluctance to meet his eyes – for fear of whatever he would see. 'Say that wine you just plastered on that wall over yonder, didn't happen to be of an exceptional vintage did it?'

'No, Ben,' Kimo winked, 'you also need write a note of thanks as though it was such, and not to mention my decoration of the castle wall …'

'Oh … very well. So, it was a gift of such elegance I so assumed … hehe, no matter, the pompous prick! I will personally write thanks to his lordship. You know though …'

'What?'

'Never liked that woman of his.'

'Yeah, you mention it every time I mention anything to do with her.'

'Seriously, if you knew Derimor now, from when he was that swashbuckling youth all those years ago, you would see she has aged him a great deal.' Ben held Kimo on the shoulder. 'Kimo, it was always the greatest prize for her. I was taken—not that that has anything to do with it, I assume, so next best was the heir to the most famous tavern in all of Vilenzia, or the next in line for the throne, being … yourself.'

'Bollocks, Ben, we know what transpired over those few

weeks that I courted her.' Kimo pushed Ben's hands off his shoulder and turned away, a dejected slump on his face freely visible to all who lingered in that direction of his exposure.

'Sorry Kimo, come on, let's forget that little shite Derimor and that crone he now calls spouse.' Ben's reference to spouse was a slight on Derimor as he always referred to her when she wasn't around as his benefactor. Though in the early days of their marriage – his prize – it was always his beloved.

Kimo chuckled. *He isn't wrong! She would have kept me from my duty, and I would have given her that inner proximity of disposing of Ben discreetly and becoming queen consort.*

Kimo had never married; he had dedicated the entirety of his time and effort to something else. Something he felt was much more important than himself: the protection of the royal family and all within the walls who shared his commitment to absolute obligation. That isn't to say he had never fallen prey to many a woman during his tenure in the castle, and before the abdication of his mother which denied him ventures most appropriate in the valley of sin – The Valley of Fortitude, a port town founded not long after Jacobs Well now full of layabouts, tinkers, and heavy drinkers and the rest of those seedy professions that followed such scourge. It was only a couple days hours ride to the south of the castle, via Naranba. He had given his all to support Ben and the difficult task of raising such a potential prized asset. *No! Such a precious thing.* That was his all, in the fight against the darkness. The odd tryst was usually from being couped up in the castle, when Ben was on one of his touring duties out in the county or beyond the border, to across Vilenzia or further afield. Usually with one or two dignitaries travelling in the troupe while he would hold court – a few ladies he would write to, for such an occasion, and would align such crossover with flawless precision to ensure a private, vigorous, meeting.

The rest of the evening went on without any further hiccup to the proceedings before Ben spoke to all in attendance in length about how the time for unity was more critical than ever before and how – when the time was needed – a unified response to any threat, be that physical or political – the latter spoken to ease the crowd of any impending threat, for what was spoken during this edict would be spread among the general population, and the cascade of information was usually embellished through each passing phase of transmission – they needed to be as one when the time came.

He spoke also of how proud he was to serve the city and the surrounding region throughout, and even beyond Jacobs Well's provincial borders. A small part of the edict was dedicated to his wife and how she too was a stoic negotiator – not only on all political matters but also on what he was to wear when attending formal dinners, including his attire for the evening. This brought a ruffle of laughter from the gathered crowd.

The edict concluded with a lengthy description of how his daughter, Grehn, would one day be elevated to ruler of Jacobs Well: a first for Jacobs Well but not uncommon throughout Inarrel. Along with identifying all her heavenly qualities and how she was the very essence of both her mother and father – elaboration on her stubbornness was identified as being borne of his ilk – this drew another murmur of laughter from those in attendance. That likeness, and the inheritance of her mother's gracefulness and rectitude to her people, those she viewed as only one removed from her own family.

There were near slips of tongue of the upcoming trials, and most certain tribulations that were to follow. He was not yet sure what these entailed as this was to be discussed with Grehn and his wife's foster mother, Mother Ursen.

All in all it was a cheery reception, not as warm as previous years' as there was an air of palatable apprehension around the courtyard, rumours had been circulating concerning the day's events down in the main square adjacent to the Grouse and it seemed as though a revelation was coming, but it never did arise from Ben's lips.

The courteous applause was the correct approach from the generous, though slightly bored, folk.

A few hollers from the two girls thrown into the mix didn't go unnoticed by Kimo and was stomped down with a stern gaze in their direction – obviously they had concealed more drink than they had divulged.

The anticipation of this year's flamework was now beginning to build. It could be felt from the vocal buzz of excitement as the line preceding the conclusion of the edict from Ben had stirred them up to at least be a little more excited.

They had all watched Sentok walk between them, carrying large cylindrical items, some bigger than the big man himself – gratitude for their invite to grace his home was now beginning to turn to a genuine excitement. The tubes being carried by Sentok were only for show, the real ones had been hidden already, and were not half the size of the counterfeits he lumbered around with.

Kimo stood with a straight back and a curious eye viewing the fluidity of head nods between the two: Ben and Sentok were up to something. The fact that he knew truly little of their plans other than the flamework in the well had him on edge; he was nervous and a little perturbed about what was to transpire in the coming moments. Not because he feared any harm to himself, the guests, or the royal family, well … he just liked to know what was going on. He always knew what was going on, and he would have stern words with them both later.

\*

As was custom, the royals would make their way around the group and make introductions, even though they were one of the most famous couples in all Vilenzia. The introductions were reciprocated, both party engaging with meaningful conversation about their day-to-day lives. Grehn this year, however, was hanging back near the main gate with her grandmother – she was usually front and centre of the conversations as it was her *annual* chance to engage "officially" with the folk from over the Arches. This year she waited impatiently for the edict, chat, and pompous flamework to hurry up and be started so it could as soon finish. Then would be the time for Mother Ursen to advise her father on the next phase of proceedings from within the castle walls, and what was now expected to transpire beyond even that – he would have to release the hold he had on his only daughter, one he had cherished and protected so dearly for so long.

She was itching to get on with the tasks at hand, and looked at Holtonos who was also engaging with the general folk – they were none the wiser as to who, or what he was. He instantly looked back toward her; a pained smile made its way across the ageless face of the god-like being.

'Quickly,' he whispered, but the whisper carried far further than the distance expected.

'Quickl—'

'Yes, Grehn. I also heard.' Mother Ursen rubbed both her arms to pat down the creases on her puffy sleeves – a habit of hers when under any uncomfortable or unwarranted duress.

Grehn didn't miss the tick; she leaned in and tried to wrap an elegant arm around her.

Sensing the coming contact, Mother Ursen jumped

forward. 'Child, you startled me. Come on, let's get your father moving with this whole spectacle. We need to be down in the cavernous doldrums by morning, and the way this is going, it looks we will be here the whole Festival, stalling! That's what he's doing … Come on, Grehn, follow me, we are heading down there now via your mother, and we will ultimately let your father know to get this show done and over.'

'No, Grandy—'

'Don't call me that child. Grandmother is simply fine – even if it makes me feel the slightest bit … weathered.' She nodded as a prompt for Grehn to continue.

'Sorr—'

'No need, go on, continue.'

'I actually thought it was quite relevant for the edict to be a little longer than usual. These folk don't know about, or at least don't understand, the true scale of what is about to transpire upon our world of Inarrel. Subliminally he may be preparing their minds as to not panic in a way—'

'Not panic? Grehn, deary, I can guarantee half this lot will not be in any fit state to be able to panic; they will be frozen to the spot with fear. So, I say again, he is wasting our time.'

Grehn was about to speak before Sentok made his way to them to usher them away from the corner where they were standing.

'No need Sentok, we were heading away anyway. Say, when are this evening's proceedings coming to a close?'

Sentok rubbed his hands together, smiled, then carried on making his way past them, now they were out of the way.

Both looked back at him as he turned to look back the way he came. 'Soon … very soon!' He went on to fiddle around with the large box shaped items pointing skyward not too far from where they had been standing. 'Special one this year, lots of surprises involved. Your father has been involved. Very hands on he has been this year. Talking about out with the old and in with the new, muttering it over and over quite jovially.'

As he finished his set up, he lit and touched a fuse cane to a long piece of string. The string began to glow brightly, before subsiding to a mellow orange, the string being consumed by the heat was but a trickle. 'There. Last one … should be raging all about the sky soon enough.' He held a horizontal palm to his brow, looking about the courtyard.

'Well enjoy your theatrical dick slinging along with the rest of these pawns. Come, Grehn, let's get out of here before this oaf does some irreparable damage to our ears or, most likely, some other bodily harm.' She eyed his big frame up and down. 'Wouldn't trust you to set my plate.'

'Grandmother!' Grehn's eyes narrowed in disgust at the rudeness being offered to one of the mainstays of the castle, and his operations, including, but not limited to, this very courtyard. 'Apologies Sentok,' she offered genuinely, 'we really must be off. Have a wonderful time. I'm sure the townsfolk here and those no doubt gathered on the Arches and beyond, back down into the old town, will enjoy every shower of flame you have selected and prepared!'

'Hmmph,' Mother Ursen grumbled at the niceties.

She was about to grumble again before King Benjamin bellowed, 'People here gathered. My people, people … no! My apologies, *The* people of this great and wonderful city that I am so blessed and privileged to serve and devote my life to, to all of you, I declare I am but your servant! Now, seeing my master craftsman has initiated the inevitable countdown, I ask you to sit. All of you sit on the cushions being provided,' A column of servants entered from the two outermost doors. They brought out two things each – a large red cushion emblazoned with gold rope to stitch up the tightly packed goose down within and a transparent tankard crafted from crystalline deposits found beneath the deep dark funnels of the well, filled with a golden liquid that bubbled with a large, frothy head – not the usual draught, but a special reserve fermented in the deepest groves of the Famnagira.

'The drink this year has been most graciously crafted and donated for this very occasion, by the eberactu of *the Middle Grove*. All they asked for in return was … quite simply, and I still cannot grasp the generosity, but … have faith in one and each other.'

'Your father is buttering them up as fast as the lillindrica flower shows its seed.' Mother Ursen rolled her eyes, still agitated at the delay in getting out of the castle and out of harm's way – out of the immediate danger zone, there would be many more to come, but right now this was the hotspot, this was the moment for any evil deviant to make their strike. The darkness of the Sylteneria was obviously well aware of her proximity from all its years of trying to infiltrate not only the castle's walls but those of her mind too. They had known for many years where she was but had always found the indestructible wall of Kimo and Anatoma – if not Ben or her Mother. Even Sentok had been there, when he wasn't trouncing the countryside, to review and interrogate every gift offered, or the decorative flora to weed out any potential hazardous substance.

But now, with the darkness at its peak, it was the opportune moment to make a move. Especially for those animals stirred by the tune of the unrhythmic call of darkness, no doubt being swayed, to move in tandem now at the pinnacle of the eclipse. 'Grehn, let's not hang about and leave things to chance, come … Now!'

They raced between the servants as Molo lumbered along with their luggage behind. Rather than linger around the courtyard and discuss the inevitable goodbyes, they directed their path to Ben. By the time they had reached him and the well, the theatrical introduction to the flamework was concluding. As they approached Ben, he finished his speech and thrust his arms in the air in time with the boom of the first rocket to spiral skyward, colour and heat emanating from the flamework adjacent the main gate – the shortest fuse, the one they had just loitered near.

*Smart,* thought Mother Ursen. *Maybe not such the big uff I thought him to be.* Before she had any more time to consider such revelry, a constant onslaught of colour lit up the sky, like a multitude of multicoloured storms raging above. She grabbed Ben by his collar. 'Ben, what the hell?' With serious eyes she looked deep into Ben's: looking at each eye in turn to see if he had indeed gone insane. 'Your daughter is in danger if she lingers here. Now can we get to where we need to get to?'

King Ben only winked at Mother Ursen, giving her a wide smile showing all his teeth. And he only spoke one word. It was enough for him to calm at least the anger in her, if not the urgency – *'Efflame!'*

She understood instantly: it was the way of the city, the Efflame was the eternal flame that burned forever beneath the well. No matter how many times an attempt had been made to extinguish it, it always remained alight, glowing with its bright, purple flame. The well was not one dug for the water far below, but was, supposedly, bored by something not of this world, deep into the rock by a force greater than anything imaginable, for the walls were as smooth as porcelain, the diameter from any point was to the exact same measurement at any point around the circumference, to an infinitely miniscule tolerance – one that had yet to be distinguished. It was too perfect; it was the whole precipice that the city had been built upon, the well had always been there, the tiny flame of the Efflame had also been there from the very beginning.

Mother Ursen stepped back, aghast at what Ben had said, of what he had said out loud and in such a public forum –

though not in earshot of any of the town people currently present. The flame – Efflame – at the bottom of the well was believed, within the royal family, to be a parcel of hope sent from the gods, one of a handful of such mysterious and unexplained discoveries found throughout Inarrel. Efflame the same word Morla had used to add credence to such a critical venture out beyond the walls, one not yet divulged to any other than the party that ventured to the Grouse.

*Smart boy,* she gazed at him, shocked at her own sudden calm. *I always thought you were capable, and, I am terribly sorry for … what I perceived was the right thing to do … all those years ago.*

Ben abruptly cut off her thoughts. 'Lead on, then,' Ben now moved as urgently as Mother Ursen had commanded moments earlier. 'Say, do you not want to stay for the finale of this whole flame show? One that I have collaborated so tirelessly on with my man Sentok? To showcase the talents of the best flame worker in Vilenzia?'

'You know damn well we don't!'

He chuckled. 'Of course. Well, then … lead on.'

As they made their way to a heavily guarded doorway, the one barred with a massive log between two thick iron supports, an eruption of flamework shot skyward from the well – an arc segmented around the circumference as each individual colour lit the sky.

Grehn laughed, as did Ben – one segment had failed to ignite, the rainbow was missing one colour: yellow. She looked to where the two girls now sat, Pomora's face as white as snow, Clarissa faring no better – even though she was the soberest of the pair.

'Shit … Pommy! Your weak bladder has stuffed up the flame show …'

They laughed in tandem as the old rotten roof structure of the well blew itself back up in the air and obliterated into millions of splinters, falling harmlessly to the courtyard floor.

Sentok quickly realised and rushed through the smoke that was hovering around the well, pulling out his fuse stick from his belt as he did and clambered over the side of the wall, disappearing through the smoky mist and into the gloom of darkness inside the well.

He reappeared, scurrying over and away from the wall with haste, bringing more giggles of glee from the pair, aimed at one their earlier tormentors.

Not long after he cleared the wall, the blast of the final flametube shot skyward, creating a vibrant colour of yellow smoke as it rocketed to the sky above, before it exploded …

Upon reaching its intended terminal height in the sky, the massive plume of yellow light spread outwards as though a large mushroom's cap.

Grehn looked up and gasped, as did all those in attendance who bore witness.

For within the flowing cascade of light, a sign bore through the plume, a shape – that of a snake's head, black as onyx, spreading outwards and growing larger the further the flamework spread.

'Father, it is as Morla foretold earlier. We must make a move quickly. Come'

'And make it quick,' Mother Ursen interjected. 'We should have been on our way, way before long ago!'

'Yes … yes, let's be on our way.' He looked toward Kimo who was making a sign of his own as he hovered a thumb in front of his face.

'Kimo!' he finally attracted the man's attention. 'Follow me. It is time to enact what I presume Morla also told you about.' Looking at Grehn and his mother-in-law, then back to Kimo. 'The Signal of Aphorin. It's time!'

# Assimilation

Down deep, deeper than that of the deepest known cavern in Vilenzia, a chasm of darkness as large as the most locally populated point of interest upon the surface, in the town of Tellbrush lingered a dozen robed figures.

The pocket of inaccessible space they now inhabited was constantly submerged just past the ankles with a crystal-clear water from the River Arneld, filtered through the crumbled rock and then on again through the fractured layers of sand and limestone.

There *should* have been thirteen figures assembled upon randomly chosen daises, all of those that had reached the same rank of he who was not present … Somendel.

All looked at each other – though to know how they knew he was the one missing was impossible to determine for they all wore hoods over their heads and only a slither of an opening for their pecborian eyes to peep through.

A high-pitched drawl escaped the lips of he who was most likely to make some noise for he who was not present.

'He dares mock us, once again. And that of our own glory by not appearing as he should. Surely this must be the final time …' A chuckle escaped the figure stood in the middle of the chasm, stood atop the central dais before they spoke again. 'No matter, he was always at the edge of despair. That despair his own right from his involvement away from here, to the higher powers that be the Syltenarians. May he rest in whatever realm that would welcome such shite!'

There was a murmur of agreement from the majority of the others assembled.

He spoke again, 'Is there one of our kind ready to take up the mantle? His mantle? And to follow in our ways?'

Three of the dozen raised an arm, then moments later, a

second arm to copy the first.

One spoke, a female with a low, slushed voice. 'I may have an asset, though he is not yet accomplished enough. Given time and the finalisation of his training he may be of our equal, wise Hoblelt.'

'Thank you, Mekara, I know of whom you speak,' said the taller pecbor. 'However, we can only ascend one *fully* of our own, and as you are all well aware, the ascension needs to happen within days, provided that self-serving scrote has met his overdue, and timely demise. Are there any others that would fill the role?' The man looked around, peeking through the slit beneath the hood.

Another of the three spoke, but not before the remainder dropped both arms and retreated, back to their daises. 'There may be one, and …' the pecbor seemed aged, for he wheezed for a breath, 'she is more than capable …' he wheezed again, 'last reports were … she was causing some trouble down the coastline towns … using the alignment for her own plunder.'

'Hmmm, we have been there before Ghenka. She is a hard one to tame. And she too has her own priorities that do not reflect or align with those of this gathering. Nor is she a full breed.' He moved his eyes across the remainder of the group. 'So, if no one has any further advancements on the aforementioned …' He waited for an answer. 'No …? Well, then, let us hope that Somendel is on his way, for we cannot locate the *Shard of Drecordian's Hammer* without that spot filled. '

The Shard was a large, mythical item to those other than those of this circle – without a full thirteen using their abilities it was impossible to create the required twenty-six fissures within this cavern to locate the item. The very reason they met here, for over the past millennia, was to prepare themselves for this very alignment; for there may not be another for centuries

'So now … I suppose we at least use what we can assemble to narrow the location enough to search through whatever terrain we find ourselves in. But until then, I suggest we wait for Somendel. As much I despise the thing!'

One of the others, who had yet to speak, walked forward, piercing eyes glowed in the dim space, light thrown off by the few candles that burned around the large, globular space. He pulled his hood back. 'She can be persuaded. She covets the possibility of having in her possession all of the artifacts of the *Mythical Beings* from way, far, away, or at least the battle items.'

'But the hammer is not a battle item, Merga! It's a forging tool, a building tool, at least part of one. It is what will build our kind the most extravagant city to rival even those in which those do-gooders reside on the other side of the divide.'

'Yes, Hoblelt, it is believed to be a tool of shaping the terrain. Though, she is vain, precious about her reputation with those within this circular's view's underneath, and even beyond the umbrella of Sylteneria. Think, what would she desire more than a palace of her own? Heck, she may even be ambitious enough to take over that blue rock in the sky once the darkness of the Sylteneria has extinguished all the weakness down here. They won't be silent up there, their precious creation on Inarrel will be extinguished and they will need to act, and they will be squashed also when all of the tribal sects, similar to ours, combine and finally see off the weak …'

'So, we double cross the double crosser …? She would see it coming a mile away. What would we offer her as bait? For surely, she is not stupid enough to believe we would just hand it to her on a platter … She would bash all our knobbly heads like the kids do at the summer fair, though the prize attained would be far greater than a knitted animal …'

'What does she desire more than that of which we

desire?' Merga clasped two hands together and shook them with vigour. 'She desires the ascendance, the reason she has been so reluctant to join our sect is that she believes in gaining favour of her Lady, whereas we believe in the ascendance of as many pecbor once the formalised fate of the weak has concluded; the hive be pecbors, the queen, the pecborian race.'

'But she is only quarter pecbor, Merga, so she cannot be allowed to be part of what we will become ...'

'And what is the true value to us, this *Shard*?'

'To forge a city beyond rival.'

'Why? Once those shites in the City of Column's light has been extinguished, once the great cities spread throughout the state of Vilenzia have been cleansed of all shite they preach, we being the most favourable race to her Lady, we could establish our population throughout! We each could reside in a palace or castle in one of the many great cities. Let her have the *Shard,* on condition bound by an oath of blood. Then she has the *Shard,* but it would be unable to be used on this continent: from Vilenzia down to the Southern Highlands. And ... she would only have it once we have built, and enhanced, the pecborian empire.'

'An open-ended timeline which she would not agree too, nor would I. Actually, nor would any other here. Though you bring an argument which could bring favour to the cause, albeit ... farfetched. What say those gathered here?'

The smallest of the assembled now moved forward to stand beside Merga; she too dropped her hood to reveal an old lady's face. 'We need this to happen, Hoblelt. Give her the damn piece of hammer, for she is less likely to bash our nodes than that shit Somendel!' She then elbowed Merga away a little before waving her hands to create a ball of light which, in turn, expanded, though it faded the bigger it grew. 'The last known sighting of "The Slayer".' It showed her last actions, before she disappeared into a mirky darkness leaving only a ripple.

'So …' Hoblelt began, 'she holds the Spear of Starlight, as referred to by the weak!' he walked toward the old form of Abrenca. 'How true do these images hold?'

Crinkling her eyes and shaking her nodes, she snapped back, contempt in her voice at the question of her ability to call upon such images that *had* happened, 'True as your small cock, you imbecile!'

A chuckle came from just about all in the room upon hearing the oldest chastise the youngest but most powerful there. The only one other than Hoblelt that didn't make a sound was Anhale. The silence from the man was not lost on Abrenca. She turned to look at him and whispered an apology – for Anhale was tricked at an early age by Somendel, as his apprentice, to remove half his manhood, so as to focus on being as focused as his master to follow the path of glory forever in the Lady's eyes.

Hoblelt spoke with slight humour, 'Careful, aged one, let's not reflect on the fact: if you would have accepted the cock you would not have been here, a choice not of your own choosing, for none were forthcoming to touch you, it needn't have been rumoured …' He went on. 'Can you cast the same to spot that imbecile Somendel?'

'Oh, get on with it you little bastard, you know very well that he cloaks himself, whenever he is up to shit,' she shot back.

'How many of the mythical objects does she now possess?'

'Just the one, for the others have yet to be revealed. Though we expect those to present themselves soon enough, once the Union of Jenine enacts their *precious* edicts.'

'Incorrect, Abrenca. Do you understand my urgency or is that lost in that little grey head of yours?!' He shook his, longer than was necessary to make the point. 'The revelation of all these items has already been granted to those on the surface to make a move and collect such. Again, they are irrelevant as we are only chasing the Shard which is not mentioned on their fickle list!'

'So, we are hiding here 'til all the fighting has taken place?' Abrenca said.

'Correct, well … unless we make the vote, one to persuade "The Slayer", or if Somendel appears with his sorry arse in this cavern. Then … yes! We are staying here until at least the end of the Festival when most of the weak would have been extinguished and we can be on our merry way in search for the Shard unimpeded.'

'But, if we convince her to come and aid us in our search, we could mobilise immediately?'

'Again, yes, we would be able to pinpoint the Shard within a stone's throw. And with that, now the time is nigh to actually cast that vote …' Hoblelt turned the full circle, to look at all within the void.

Eventually, everyone moved back to their daises, even Hoblelt. Though he spoke the loudest and most frequent he was far from the most senior; that role fell to Merga.

'All assembled here, we have a vote to cast. All those in favour of the motion put by Hoblelt to pursue the elusive Slayer, raise your left hand for the aye.'

Four immediately raised a hand, followed by two who hesitated slightly before raising theirs slowly. This was always the case, there would be those who would, for no other reason other than the political, try to apply mediation to ensure the correct decision would be reached. This would entail a faction of four members that would break away, multiple times – through a multitude of combinations – to discuss the option, or other options, available which would invariably end up with the motion passing in the aye majority.

What they were forgetting was that there was a possibility

Somendel was still walking his arse around Inarrel – which could dispel any notion in chasing down the Slayer and the requirements of such an outing: a point made by those in the nay section of the sect.

But time was of the essence, there needed to be a plan to locate the Shard. The reason this was of such importance to the sect was that the shard was known to those who followed the light as trivial – a piece broken off an irrelevant hammer. But to the sect who had studied the recovery of the item, those who had discovered the texts, they had skewed it away from being a battle item and more a benign *thing* to lessen the focus. That focus by either the light or the dark was to be trained on the other items scattered throughout Inarrel – most notably, the majority had been deposited around the more densely populated Vilenzia. What had been derived from such intense involvement in the Shard had been that it was not a shard at all, but the actual hammer of Drecordian itself, one of the most complete items dropped – whether purposely or not by the higher beings – and buried around Vilenzia.

There was also another problem facing them, to fulfil their long-held ambitions: the population of Pecbor. They had to be convinced to turn from their mundane ways, which the majority surely would, as they held high contempt to those not of their own kind. For they believed they were viewed as monsters throughout the remainder of Inarrel, as though they were of a lesser kind, even though their sensitivities in every sense would actually ascend them above any other average being that held residence on Inarrel.

But there were also those – the minority – that held the loudest voice in the communities and believed in changing their outward hatred and to showcase their abilities in trying to integrate on a larger scale with the world outside, beyond their definitive boundary. A boundary defined by the solid, high standing and impeccably crafted stone wall that skirted the perimeter around the whole of Pecboria, acting as a way of keeping them all in, rather than as a defence to any attack – one which had never transpired during their tenure upon Inarrel.

When all combination of quadruples had been extinguished, a new vote was cast.

The outcome: again, a stalemate. But this time, rather than left arms raised for the aye, the other six had raised their right arms stipulating another option was to be considered – one that must have been put forward by one of the members, which was rare.

For millennia, a split vote had always resulted in the aye whereas the last vote was always neutral if it was a six to seven split.

It was the oldest of the group, Abrenca, who represented the alternative to speak. 'Those who have voted with their right, they will not stray from their decision as is their given choice. Though the right has put forward a motion that would suit all, and actually involves and supports the first motion, for all its merits are sensible if not feasible. So, as we are all aware of such through our discussions, I request a revote to invoke the alternative.'

The most senior, he with most sway, Merga, agreed to put forward another motion to the floor. 'A vote to split our *esteemed* members into two: one to—' he slapped his head with disbelief to what he was actually saying '— Piss me! To locate that bastard, Somendel. The other group to try gallantly, if not perversely, to persuade the Slayer to come to *our* aid, to help us retrieve the hammer. For fuck's sake, if it comes to it, I will let them fight it out to the death! In this cavern if both are located and … *he* be not dead! Though my preference is for him to … well, have his head removed, if not already!'

Before the vote was cast, Hoblelt spoke. 'What about the

hammer?'

Merga answered, 'Believe me, Hoblelt, it would be much quicker to have the location pinpointed than trouncing around the hills, or depths, of sod knows where for days, or even weeks, months, on end. We need to have all twenty-six fissures extrapolated and triangulated, so we can be digesting all of the information presented to us.'

'Very well then … let's get on with it!'

The results, the first round of votes, yielded a unanimous decision for the aye. All in favour.

The first time ever.

# Interlude

'Father …'

'Yes, child?'

The boy wriggled ever so slightly in his bed, the slightest of mobility he was able to muster.

'I have been having strange dreams of late.'

'Yes, and? They're of?'

'No … well … I have been having these dreams … of … well … the stories you have been telling me. I am having the same dreams as those in the stories.'

'Oh,' the man chuckled, 'then I suppose you *are* listening to me then.' He chuckled a little louder.

'No, Father! Your stories … they are that of *my* dreams.'

The man bristled, suddenly serious. He stood from where he sat at the edge of the bed, and proceeded to walk over to the large window.

The temperature outside was cold and he could feel it cut through the glass pane. For snow had dropped heavy over the past two days and had only just ceased. The criss-crossed wooden frame had a frost creeping around each of its glazed corners, refracting the little light the low sun threw through. Though it was now a little brighter than when the earlier dark blankets rolled through the sky. The rainbowed refraction was subtly noticeable on the dark timber that lay the bedroom floor.

He held a hand up to rest his palm on one of the panes of glass, then gently applied pressure. The ice-cold touch settled him, if slightly. As he looked into the distance, he saw the lights of the town, nestled far away, at the bottom of the hill, beyond the wall cut through with a tunnelled passageway, glisten a silent orange and gold.

Pulling his hand away when the cold grew too much, he looked at the slightly shaking palm, now moist: a different, more agnostic glitter flickered across his palm. The source – the familiar candlelight and burning hearth, flickering inside the boy's room.

He looked again out the window, down at a steeper angle, toward a few stacked crates he had packed before the snow blew in – they were destined for the same town. He had meant to take them, but his wife had not come back in time from the city over the river beyond the town he gazed upon. So that meant there was no one to hold fort but Chester the mule. *She must have been caught short by the storm. Oh well. The snow should keep it fresh,* he chuckled again.

'Son?' he asked without looking back to the boy, no doubt eyes trained on him.

'Yes, Father!'

Silently, he grimaced upon seeing the boy's forever big green eyes come to light in the reflection offered by the glass. By now, sixteen winters had passed since one of the Higher had come knocking.

'Tell me … what will happen to Somendel? Not that which we have read before – for we know he just disappears and is never returned – but, in your latest of dreams?'

The question seemed to knock the boy back a touch, his eyes dropped and lost their sparkle, though for only an instant, before he raised them again to look in his direction.

'… I don't know yet, you haven't read that part of the scroll yet, you always seem to skip such a passage … amongst many other!' The boy smiled at him, bringing more angst to his already heavy heart.

'Boy …?'

'Yes, Papa?'

'Tell me of it, you're old enough now to … entertain my curiosity.'

He saw the boy's eyes drop again. 'Only … only in my dreams, hey? Father.'

'Aye, child. Hmmph.' He rested both palms on the

window now, more so to block out the reflection paining him. 'Well?'

'He ... ermm ... has his nodes ripped off!' the boy said, matter of fact, which surprised the man.

'Hmmm,' the man wrinkled his lips. 'Sounds ever so violent. Say, by whom?'

The boy looked downcast again, not keen to say any more.

When both hands had numbed completely from the cold, he walked back over to where the boy lay on top of the quilt. He removed the thick cover and wrapped both hands around the boy's left calf.

The boy yelped, before he looked at his father.

With tears in the boy's eyes, the man returned the smile; he too holding at bay a few tears.

'By whom?' the man asked again, gently.

'A shadow. There is one figure I cannot see, but it speaks to me.' Still tears falling, he asked, 'How long to go?'

'I'm unsure, child. Your mother has been to the city to bring back a healer. *The* healer. One who is said to perform miracles on the children who are cripp— err, children who be like yourself ...'

'I felt the shock of your cold hands, Pappa! It felt dreadfully sharp, but so amazing. I don't feel anything else though.'

'Give it time, you will be up and about in no time ...'

The boy looked out of the window with a distant look in his eye, toward the clouds parting slightly. 'I suppose I will, in time. Though, in the end, time is all we have left, huh?'

The man agreed with a nod, and a sigh.

*

In the distant city, beyond the town and over the river, the man's wife walked through narrow cobbled streets. The snow had been pushed to the centre, to allow free passage on either side for the residents to tread freely. She was heading to meet The Jester, or The Healer, the man rumoured to be able to heal the sick and, most notably, the crippled, mostly children.

Luckily, the snow had delayed his departure from the city. Rumour was – she had found after asking around – that he was settled in a non-descript tavern near the city centre, creating a stir with some crazy stories. So, she wound her way there carrying a sack full of gold coin – most of their saved coin – and a few other precious items, including most of her jewellery, to sweeten the deal if he was found not to be initially forthcoming.

The Jester was sat upon an overly large, cushioned chair, rested upon the upper balcony of the tavern, looking out down on the square below; it was more of a circle but that didn't bother him, he enjoyed things that were not what they were supposed to be.

Something eventually piqued his senses, making his nose itch and his ears burn – an odd ability to sense when he was in need, only rarely, though, did his nose itch.

Intrigued, he scanned the periphery of the courtyard, quickly noting a woman pacing briskly in his direction, not changing the line to accommodate those making their way across her path, nor the piled snow as she ambled up and over the highest portion. *Hmmm, determined. They usually are before they become overcome with despair.*

She locked her eyes, hard, onto his, before they dropped quickly to see where she was going, checking for any other mounds of mush to traverse.

*Best get downstairs and set up near the hearth. Another one! Though she must feel like ice herself, that stare alone …* He shuddered at the promised, imminent intrusion – one he was much accustomed to.

'Barman, another *warm* one,' he said as he made his way to the floor below.

'Of what?' the barkeep questioned.

The Jester looked incredulously at the barman.

.'Horse piss, though that would no doubt taste much … much … better! Man, what the—Geremi! Cider! Now! Please … No … actually, make it two.'

The barman grinned, another prodding of the man, trying to find that pompous bite of his!

Pushing the large door open, she was surprised at the lack of resistance from it as a draft of cool air rushed in from behind her, bringing a sullen grumble out of the majority of the punters sat warmly inside.

She walked up to the man lounging, legs crossed on the big green leather sofa beside a roaring, open fire. 'You that Jester fellow?'

'I am that Jester fellow. What brings you into my presence and need?'

'I think you have an idea?'

'No. No I don't. Despite what you have heard I am not a psychic, nor do I possess the ability to see into the future.'

'Are they not the same thing?'

He rubbed his chin. 'Maybe they are. Here, this one is for you.' He passed her the wooden mug, frothing with a warm cider and motioned for her to take the space adjacent.

'Thank you.'

'Now, sit, and tell me … what troubles your heart?'

'My son—' was all she managed to get out.

'Ahh, now I see your need for urgency. Did you know I was to leave town yesterday?'

'Yes, and it should have been with me.' She gulped down half the contents of the mug. A warmth spread through her body. She let out a satisfied sigh. 'Thank you. Again.'

'Do you believe in fate my dear?' He looked at her intently, looking for something before she could respond, then smoothed his facial expression, showing her a friendly smile. 'Your name, my dear?'

'No I don't, fate is what we make, not what is, if that makes any sense,'

'No, it doesn't, but I like the simplicity of the answer.'

'Gretta. Gretta's my name.'

'Well, Gretta, I'm Jesse.'

'Why the question about fate?'

He smiled and took a long gulp himself. 'Because, or so it seems, fate has gotten in the way here, or maybe it was always meant to be.' He looked out of the window, nudging his head to take note of the cold snap that had drifted through days earlier so suddenly. 'Or, maybe, there's a reason for you meeting me here this day, at this exact time. Maybe.'

'Maybe. I mean, whatever, I just need you to come with me. Here I have—' She began to place the small sack of coin on the table, but he reached over and placed a hand on it, pushed it back to her, back toward her waist.

'Lady Gretta, whatever you may have heard about me, it be mostly false, I do not take coin for talking to strangers in need. I find enough coin from … elsewhere.'

She looked deep into his eyes, looking for something more. 'Can we talk somewhere privately?' She took her gaze away to scope the surroundings and the many ears pointed at them in the lounge.

The barman came over quickly to jump in, thus confirming Gretta's assumption people were, indeed, eavesdropping. 'Yes, my lady. Here, come with me. This way.'

Jesse smiled. *Smart, I wonder what such caution could entail.*

The barman led them around the hearth to where two chairs sat in front of the fire, directly opposite to where they had been sat before but a smaller space giving them at least a little more privacy. The privacy she sought.

'He's special.' she said as soon as they sat down.

'I'm sure he is, just like any other mother would say.'

'No, he is special. Though, he isn't my son, but adopted, I would say gifted to us, in a way ...'

'How so?

'Come with me when this snow clears,' she asked, pleading in her eyes.

'So ... what's wrong with him?'

'We don't know. He is bedridden throughout the day, but at night, when he dreams, his body becomes full of life, fully functional. It's as though his dreams bring him to motion in a physical sense. He disappears throughout the night, gods know how, and to the same location! But when he is in the house during the day, it's as though he is just ...' She held both hands around her mug then drank the rest of the contents.

Wiping her mouth, she smiled – a sliding smile – before continuing. 'He is as nimble as they come.' Then a small, croaked laugh escaped her lips.

'So why? Why do you require my help?'

Gretta drifted her hands about a little before answering, looking for some sort of focus. 'Because he is a cripple while he is awake. And then he is what could only be perceived as an acrobat while he sleeps.'

'Oh, so he is, that is ... odd. Does he have the draconic scales, or the slightest whiff of the aforementioned scent?'

'No ... No!'

'Hmm, so he is sentient?'

'What? What kind of question is that? Of course! What a thing to say!'

'I see.' Jesse smirked.

'What? Why is that funny to you?'

'It is. Quietly, the functionality of the thing—'

'My son!'

'Ah, my apologies. Yes, your son, he sounds oddly like the old man spoke about in the old tales. Alone, residing in the isolated tower on the mythical isle of Cantera. Do you know why he—'

'Yes … I know the tales – he was locked in there, behind a magical barrier for his and every others' safety, for he was a madman whilst he slept.'

Gretta pulled her knees up to her chin and wrapped her arms around her shins – a subliminal action to make herself as small and compact as possible, to avoid any barrage of hate that may come her way.

'My husband,' she spoke through her knees, 'he mentioned the boy has begun to feel. Only the slightest of feeling, and only in his left leg.'

'Miss, I feel as though you jest. For the man in the tower would not feel a thing until his dying day. The day he knew he was dying he was able to move about as freely as if in the night. Do you know why?'

'That part I have never heard, maybe because it is only a tale and nothing more.'

'I will enlighten you as to why.' He leant in closer to Gretta, which only made her fold even smaller into herself. 'There is nothing wrong with your boy's body. It is his mind that is causing immobility. The stillness and nothingness of his muscles and other associated senses, though, there will be a reason, a cause from something that I cannot, and am unable to assimilate a reasonable assumption from what you have told me thus far. There must be more to his story.' He leaned back, ready to measure any bodily response of Gretta. When she still held tight, he assumed she was hiding more and was afraid to let it out.

'Tell me something unrelated to your boy. Tell me about your husband. What is his trade? What does he do to keep warm your household. Can he also make enough coin to set off—' He looked at the sack. 'Unless …? Please tell me you were not offering me your life's work for my services?'

She held herself even tighter than before, burying her

eyes into her knees to avoid any chastening eyes.

He moved off his chair and kneeled before the woman. 'My dear, Gretta. For what has my reputation preceded me?'

He stood and pulled her arms up with him, bringing her out of the clamping grip she held to her body.

Now kneeling upon the chair, her head rose up to his chin, she lunged both arms around the man's slender, wiry frame, holding him as tight as she had her own legs moments ago. All the years of anguish and despair at the boy's condition had suddenly let itself free. She sobbed – though tears would never be enough – quietly into his shoulder.

'He *is* special,' she whispered. 'You must accompany me back to my *humble* abode.'

'With all haste, my lady. And I will pray to the gods to aid us with a favourable tail wind and a clear sky until then!' he said back to her, offering hope, no matter how hollow he felt.

*More than you could ever have known,* she thought before squeezing tighter, for she felt an ease and calmness that the man abounded with and it seemed to seep its way through her body and into her soul.

*I have no doubt you will be the boy's saviour, and maybe of all.* She kept that thought to herself.

*

Back at their humble abode, the man stood by the window once again; the sun had begun to make its descent behind the tall hills beyond the rooftops that topped the skyline of the town below, the sky cascading from a deep purple hue down to a brilliant, bright, orange, the low hanging clouds dabbed about the horizon shone a deep red. 'Ah, the gods see us blessed, son. We should have the fairest weather by the morn, if not sooner. Your mother should be heading home with that Jester fellow, hopefully they'll be here on the morrow.' He pulled closed the curtain and went to turn down the blankets on the bed.

The boy struggled the best he could to hold up drooping eyelids, as they now sagged half closed.

'One more chapter before bed?' the man asked taking note of the boy's condition, delaying the inevitable.

'A short one though, Father. Maybe … tell me, do you have anything scribed on the whereabouts and condition of the pecbor Somendel? I would just like to corroborate with the changing visages in my own dreams.'

The boy shuffled in the bed, trying to pull himself up slightly, and succeeded. He then looked at his father who carried a shocked expression.

'Papa! My legs! look! My whole body moved … did you see?!'

The man raced over: amazement, happiness, pure joy on his face at seeing the boy's gleeful reaction and the stare that reflected that of his own.

He hopped onto the bed and hugged the boy who tried to do the same before realising his arms wouldn't move much from their resting position, thus draining a small portion of the happiness out of his face.

'Small steps, my boy. Small steps …' He let the boy go, sat back a bit, and patted the boy's legs. 'Now, shall I find what you were after me to read?'

'Yes!' Small, half open eyes looked at the man pleasingly.

'Well then, as we are skipping ahead, give me a minute to locate the chapter or verse you're after.'

The man walked over to the wooded shelves and pulled the small ladder away from the books he had sequestered up high in the corner of the room – though the boy could not move, he still could not leave to chance the boy finding some way to gain access to the most secretive writings, those issued years after he had gained the scrolls from the goddess-like woman who had once again, issued via a higher source during a fleeting second visit. She said she had come to deliver the word of the unknown: written, this time, on pages of thick parchment and bound between leather covers.

Those volumes were only to be read after a pertinent signal – for they would not open fully, not even enough to glance a peek, until that signal granted permission.

The man had asked what, her, or their, plan was about. Her response was that of a riddle which, he would, in time, make sense of. He would know the sign when it came.

'My plan? I do not have my own plan … I do as told, or more so guided. For he has a plan, though none of us know what that is or what the end would look like or appear to be,' she had said 'I see a pain about your eyes. Why?'

'Us?'

'Yes … is that what pains you?' She looked questioningly at the man. When no response was forthcoming she went on. 'There are four of us right at this moment, delivering exactly the same message and material to those just as devout as yourself.'

'Where are these other men, Your Holiness?' he had asked.

'Bah,' she cackled, '"Holiness", no need for that. And did I say men alone carry your burden? Anyway, they exist, but not as you would know it.'

'How so?'

'That I cannot divulge, nor can I elaborate any further. What I can give you, though, is assurance.'

'The boy?'

'Yes … the boy. He should become a powerful man one day, one of great power and not a little potential; to sway a war that has been waging since the beginning of time, and forever beyond before.'

'I know I have asked this question before, but why us?

Why Gretta and me? For it is surely a burden and not so much a blessing.'

'You see the boy as a burden?'

'Yes … well, no … though he cannot move, and he isn't ours, really …'

'I see. As I mentioned once before, long ago, this was not my plan. Maybe ask your beloved wife how she feels. If she is in agreement with your abhorrent disregard tof the boy, agreeing he is nothing more than a burden, then we will remove him immediately and allocate him to a more suitable family. To be developed appropriately, and nurture his soul to the level we would expect.'

'Wait! We do love the boy … unconditionally, we have always wanted a child and we both were ever so grateful when you answered our prayer to deliver us a son—'

'Then why?'

'Ahh … it's just—'

'Do not concern yourself with what others have for you need to understand you are not only nurturing your son, but believe that the boy you so adore is potentially of a forever legend. As cliché as that may sound, you need to understand that.'

He shook his head as he thought of *that* conversation and how embarrassed it had made him feel. He made his way back to the bed after he had retrieved the boy's requested scroll, aptly titled "Somendel's Despair", the scroll itself still contained within a cylindrical, leather-bound case brought from the square holes atop the bookcase's shelves, just below where the rest of the scrolls were deposited.

*Lucky I indexed them all!* he thought to himself, relieved at the little time it took to find before he noticed the boy's eyelids dropping even further.

'This one here,' he spoke loudly, trying to snap the boy out of slumber, 'is not too far along the timeline we have been following, and as instructed by—as we were … hmmm it's only a couple scrolls beyond where we—'

He needn't have bothered elaborating, for the boy's eyes were now fully closed, lips slightly parted, and his head lolled to one side on the stuffed pillow. A certainty given how late it was before he would succumb.

His legs however, flickered ever so lightly; too slowly at first to notice, but the longer he lingered the more they fidgeted, until a rhythmic vigour shook his whole body to eventually move to the unheard rhythm of … something.

He pulled over his leather chaise and began to read anyway, muttering to himself in time with what the boy was whispering in his slumber – as though the boy was, himself, contained within the writing of the scroll as they recited almost in tandem.

… almost.

As the man read, he watched with amazement as the text distorted and reshaped itself. He had always thought the parchment he read from was not of this world, and he also wondered if the text he read to the boy during his earlier years would be the same as he read back now. Even now, he was sure he felt the scrolls he reread over that period, up to that point, had changed ever so slightly, subtle enough to not show any wholesale change – the generality of the literature had always remained the same. Now he wondered, as he heard his fostered son – the boy he would undoubtedly give his life for, his soul even more so – whisper in time with the text he read.

# Iteration of ... "A Dream"

'Papa?' the boy opened with his usual initial line of enquiry, if barley awake.

A distant and far away voice echoed through his mind, *No child, this is not so.*

He opened his eyes fully as he rose to sit up in the bed. It was always the same: a greying haze, a curtain of nothing but a blurry canvas confronted him. Though this time he was sure the grey was a little clearer than before, a little less confusion about it as it shuffled its pixelated mass about itself.

As the response to his question was aired, a faint ripple emanated from within the fabric of the same.

He was unaware of such until a second response came, from the exact direction where his father would have sat.

'What do you remember of me?'

The voice sounded not too dissimilar to his father's, but it was ever so slightly drawled out to be truly his.

The boy blinked to discern the question before responding, 'You ask the same question you used to ask. Why again do you ask such?'

A ripple again that was followed by a hearty chuckle. Much more similar to his father's now.

Nothing but silence ensued for a short while before another question to counter the question from the boy. 'Why do you *think* I ask?'

'I am getting stronger. I promised myself I would one day walk, even push past that impossible dream to even run. But here ... in my dreams, I feel a connection to a world not of my own ... well, not of the one I am used to.' He moved up onto his knees and shuffled to the end of the bed, and reached out an arm to touch the grey.

'You ask because I think you are afraid.' A finger of his

approached the greyness, growing colder as the approach became closer. 'I think you are afraid I will be able to escape this dream. You should know, *this* dream is not the only dream that recurs. Usually, when I fall back to slumber in *this* dream, I awake in another: teaming full of life, full of intrigue and wonder.'

'Is that so?'

A face appeared in the now flowing ripple. A face that was identical to his father's – though there was no colour, the contours were unmistakable.

The boy gasped as he opened up his palm and caressed the features protruding from the blanket of grey. 'Father?'

'Not quite … though kind of. But not of the kind you would think of. I am *He*. He who knows. Is all, well should know all … I appear in this realm from a place far beyond here. Far beyond even imagination could take you, I suppose.'

'But why? Why are you here?'

'To keep tabs, I guess.'

'Why then are you wearing the face of my father?'

'Why not?' The ripple continued as the face disappeared, back to a flat canvas. 'Would you prefer this one?' A new face appeared in the same area – a rounded, petite head, distinguished with the two nodes and a short nose.

The boy straightened up and, with shock, shot back toward the head of the bed.

'So … you recognise this face, hey?' The face receded and reappeared as a more friendly image – that of his mother. 'Do not worry child, only a mirage. Tell me, though, how do you recognise the features of Somendel? I do believe that is the villain you are familiar with … from *my* scribe?'

'Yours?' The boy eased a little, and approached, cautiously, once more. 'Father believes the scrolls to be magical, infused with the ink of the gods …'

'And you …?'

'I have never actually read from them. So, I wouldn't know.'

'But … your tone indicates there is more?'

'I dream of that world, the one my father reads about. Those writings come alive within me as I dream away, as though I am witnessing first-hand the scenes unfolding before me from behind hidden eyes. I'm unsure if he knows, but there are subtle changes to the story every so often. I seem to dream ahead of the writing the more we … *he* reads.'

'How many cycles of those scrolls have you been through with your father to notice such?'

'Those ones … a few, but they are the most sporadic by way of consistency … of storyline.'

'Is that so. How so?' The being switched its face again, this time to the long, strong, angular features of Gurengal.

'In the previous cycle, as you put it, Gurengal doesn't make it out of the fight with Somendel. He is overwhelmed by three scottles. However this time there were only two. And Somendel's "new" companion has some interest in taking Somendel back to his home country. But Gurengal kept hold of him instead. Why?'

'I have no idea … So, would you say that the world of Inarrel is a safer place in the latest cycle?'

'Potentially … The atmosphere amongst the general folk seems more of cautious optimism, as though they are only slightly worried about this year's Festival.'

'Hmm, you speak of as if you are there. And how would you know how they felt, feel?'

'The background chatter. The words spoken are of a lessened worry and how they are much more open to celebrating without fear of—'

'What? Impossible! You can hear them? Chattering away? Hmm, that should be—'

'Like I said, I *am* there.'

'Very well, let me ponder some of my time on this. Now, were you not to be somewhere else by now?' The boy nodded eagerly. 'I will return soon, to let you know my thesis of this observation. For those bystanders should surely not be in the scrolls I have scribed … multiples of times I may add.

The grey mirage dissipated, almost to a nothingness. Then that nothingness began to spin on a central axis, faster and faster, creating a whirling pattern that stretched further and further apart, to bring in additional colours one by one. It spun so fast the whirls were now blurred before eventually forming an almost discernible picture. Faster it spun until that picture became full of motion.

As always, the boy was enveloped from all sides as the vista encapsulated his whole vison with images of its own.

The boy stood up, not now on his bed, but on a small rock no bigger than half his height that jutted out of a mossy, grassy blanket A green blanket that rolled on until it met a wall of thin greying trunks shooting out of the ground. These trunks bore no leaves, only skinny outshoots of limbs high above the ground.

He turned his head, to look to his left. Two men were moving across the emerald blanket – the wind rolling low across the ground swayed the small expanse of green like large shoals of *pingorts* being hunted by their senior kind, *pingartas* – one of the men laboured, while the other seemed to move as though gliding, he was unsure. But he was sure they made their way to an opening to breach the treeline, where maybe healthy trees had once stood. Again, he was unsure as his eyes failed in focusing for more than a moment.

He made no immediate move himself for his eyes were still adjusting, trying to time in with the cycle of the sphere's spinning pixilation – he knew to let the adjustment settle before he would allow his legs to make their move.

Then, the imagery vibrated, rippled, not too dissimilar to the moments earlier with the grey. Again, he let his ears adjust, to align his receptors to that of this new environment; one which played out by way of different sensory rules – those he had now been attuned to through time spent.

He listened, hearing the voices a little more clearly. The voice of the *ancient* and the brutish, constant dribble of Bendim. Then he realised why he was here.

A murmuring came from outside the realm he found himself in; though discernible, his current sensory perceptions were still slightly askew, so it was hard to understand. The tone, though, was unmistakable – his father's.

He was reading to himself more so than him as he was asleep, it seemed, before it abruptly stopped, only to be followed by a mumbled curse. The boy smiled to himself. He understood what had happened. The scroll the man was reading had become obsolete, the text disappearing, waiting to be forged anew. This had never happened before, he would usually be met with a wracking pain through his entire body by now, as if running through a brick wall.

He wondered, *The past has been written, but ... but the future too has been written, and is now being rewritten. Changes are afoot, knowledge of the past shapes the future, the final outcome; that final chapter will now be up for grabs – for both sides. Hmmm, both sides,* he again wondered, *there is another player in all of this. not yet revealed, and unlikely to reveal itself until the right moment.* He was sure of it. He had begun to sense a presence, hidden, much like his own. A presence of something, it was influencing certain outcomes through minor manipulation, he was again sure. For he knew the outcome of most of the text within the previous version of the scrolls; the outcomes this far had diverted off, carried on a new tangent, to a whole raft of changes.

They were fundamentally different, branching off in multiple directions to multiple offshoots of eventual outcomes. He wondered once more, *At the end of this cycle, I don't think there will be anyone to record such.*

He heard the murmur, or more the rumble, of his father's voice once more. *At least the writing has continued, to some degree, maybe … hopefully I will be wrong.* He listened as the two realms diverged then contorted only to swing back to rhythmic alignment. Followed by his senses.

The man waited a few moments before he began to read again. The boy had moved suddenly, and he had watched the boy sit up and crawl to the edge of the bed then backwards as though petrified, then stop, as if curious of something.

Though the boy spoke, he could not understand what he was saying. He did recognise occasional patterns of speech to discern that it was not at all gibberish – some unknown language … perhaps  One he was not aware of.

At one point, the boy looked directly at him, eyes glazed, up close, real close, before he smiled. This was a first – Or was it merely a coincidence? – and the man couldn't shake the image of the boy's blank gaze enough to think anything that could resemble sense.

The man read while the boy fidgeted about on the bed. Right up to the point where the boy suddenly leapt off the bed within an instant, onto his feet, before he bounded out through the window – the man had left it open, slightly ajar, before the eventual, nightly incident – and onto the snow heap, piled below the timber ledge.

The man dropped the scroll onto the end of the bed, placed a small weight to mark where he had read to, and made his way to the window just in time to see the boy disappear over a small knoll that rose up slightly between the house and the woodland.

The man remembered the very first occurrence, and every subsequent time thereafter.

\*

The first time had shocked, alarmed, scared the wits out of he and his wife. Once, with his age only past seven winters, the boy was subdued and brought back to the house: the second and third, and a couple of times after there also. But eventually they followed until the boy stopped running. To stand as still as the dark in the night.

Though they both panted from the exertion of keeping up with the seven-year-old, the boy seemed not the slightest bereft of breath.

He had stopped in the woodland where a small obelisk had once stood – all that remained, though, was the plinth upon which it once stood. A plaque remained, bolted to the plinth, and most of the words had since been worn away over time. All that remained was a symbol, punched deep into the brass plate, that of three crescents inside an encapsulating, larger circle.

Rooted to the spot, he stopped. He did not flinch – no matter any change in his surroundings – until the sun near touched the horizon. Then he would bound his way, unaware of their presence, back to the house and back into the bed he had leapt from the night before, clambering up the façade of the house beneath his bedroom window.

The woman had learnt to deal with the frequent washing required over time. Usually, only the feet would remain soiled upon re-entry, so she lay a cover over that section of the mattress with old cloth to alleviate such a chore.

The tempered glass, though, was an absolute blessing – taking out hours required picking up shards of glass in his room and at the foot of his window in the dirt below.

Tonight … the man decided to follow the boy once

more. Change was afoot; there was something different about every step from the usual cycle he would navigate throughout the night. He was intrigued, and more than a little worried for the boy's wellbeing.

As he made his way from the window to depart the boy's room and enter into his own bed chamber to change into a more rugged attire, his attention was drawn to the scroll now lying on the bed. The text had started to burn into the scroll, flaming a bright red before disintegrating the ancient fabric – a new text, to be forever etched into the ancient scroll.

The man gasped, then hurried quicker to his room at the end of the hall. A change was, undoubtedly now at hand. Was this the crux the goddess had talked about. He made a sign, hoping not, *No, yet …*

*She said she would return before … before he was ready.* He was stopped mid-thought as a black mist hovered at the threshold of his bed chamber.

The shape of the mist resembled a hulking figure, though he was uncertain as it had no legs or arms as such, but it was immediately clear that it was sentient as it sensed his approach. It then communicated, clearly … and concisely.

'What have you done to advance the child's capabilities? What do you believe you have done for the boy other than read that dribble to him every night? You are weak, mortal, even scared, and not the slightest bit pathetic!'

The man trembled, believing the figure was of ill intent.

It went on. 'Let me take the boy. I, and those who know how to enhance the abilities of the *weapons,* will get him ready for whatever the Higher has in store for him.'

Another voice startled him from behind, a shrill, echoing voice – it carried a weight that dropped the man to his knees; it was one he knew well and would never forget.

'Dagda! It is not his time! Begone, we cannot rush this one like the others!'

The black mist arranged itself to now show, at least, a humanoid form. It barked a laugh of contempt before replying, 'You jest, you have no idea. Now … now, is even too late. The others feel it too. There is something at play here that we are not privy too. We have all been excluded from the realm of—'

'Enough, Dagda! Leave those details to ourselves, and ourselves alone, these mortals need not know—'

Again, Dagda barked a laugh. 'Mortals! Do you forget so easily? You old crone,'

The woman raised herself on tiptoes in front of the man as he solidified into something more tangible. A man that could only be described as beautiful in every physical way: long, flowing, voluptuous hair. A wide, stubbled, angular jaw, olive-toned skin that glistened – like an array of stars – under the lamplight. 'You and I were once, such. We devoted our *mortal* lives to finding a way to better the places we would find ourselves.' The woman grimaced, pained. 'You move too quickly, Dagda.' She sighed.

Even the sigh of the goddess-like being sounded as if nature had burst into song. 'There is still time …'

'Huh!' Dagda grumbled. 'What is it we are let known, so, so often by the elders? About time?'

'Time, in the end … time is all we—'

'—have.' finished the old man, finishing the familiar words. Words he had heard spoken by his boy many times.

*My boy!*

The woman looked at the man questioningly, surprise held in her eyes.

'Quiet!' They both spoke in tandem.

'No! No! I will not be quiet!' The man threw his hands up in the air before dropping them again to slap his thighs. 'You come here without warning, without any concern for the boy's safety other than … than some big all ending plan you and your lot have set in motion.' He pointed at both of them in turn before going on with the rant. 'And ... then you tell me ... he is one of many? And how many *others*, exactly, are we talking about? And what happens—no! Let's hear what happened to those *others*!'

He stopped the gesticulation and the pointing to face the two with equal measure. He then dropped his gaze to the wooden floorboards creaking under his feet.

It was Dagda who spoke first, a low rumble, a resonating tone. 'The boy is not like *those* others. There are trails of an influence, even our masters cannot detect its source.' Dagda looked at his counterpart and nodded his head. She returned the nod before he continued on.

'We believe he hangs in a balance, between two forces, maybe even a third. Could even be a fourth. We're unsure what is happening. But it has the whole Union of the Jen— '

The woman spoke before he could continue. 'Uhumm ... he is special, he has been groomed, through hidden shadows, for much greatness, a greatness that will flow to all of they who follow the light, the good. But you will have to let him go, eventually. Set him free from the shackles of the scrolls he most dearly ponders about every day, each and every evening. He is not yet ready, but soon he will be. I know you sense it too ... can't you?'

The man sighed. He was still inspecting the ever-widening cracks in the hard timber below. *I must get to that someday.* 'I suppo—'

Dagda interjected before the man could speak further. 'He is as ready as he will ever be! Come on! let us see for ourselves, for the scion of *Elimbah* is calling, can you not hear it? It is a wail of a madness, of chaos! Of despair!

'We must move swiftly and decisively. We must enact the saviour's remit before all this ... this and all that we have known fades into a crumbling madness we would never be party to!'

All were silent for a short while before a sigh from the middle of the three broke the unspoken strain.

The man trained his eyes on the boy's bedding lying crumpled behind the woman. Heavy eyes sunk to a realisation that what they both had spoken of was truth. What weighed heavier was the words spoken by Dagda, for those words reigned truest.

A change *was* afoot, one he could sense. Though the boy had not spoken of such, he sensed the change upon his nightly routine, the jumbling change of the text within the scrolls; even the unnatural changes here, on his own plain, had him on a never-ending sense of a dubious keel, always ready to reveal its ugly self.

All three were looking in the same direction, viewing the bed the boy would lie in for the majority of the day, through every waking hour.

The woman shook her head slowly. The weight of expectation and responsibility seemed now weighted heavy tenfold upon her shoulders. She was in a fell situation, she had nurtured him so much through dreams and an intertwined, semi-reality of interaction – or refractions of the same. She knew also, there was a pull away, something she had never felt from the *earlier* candidates.

Her voice had always played a part in his dreams, acting as subtle commentary, or narrative, highlighting all that should have been the most poignant moments – amplifying any critical words, even third party talk from a peasant, if he ever became distracted. Those distractions had become more prevalent the past few years to a point of complete insurrection of thought, or reception to her voice.

*A good sign,* she hoped.

Both Dagda and the woman noticed the unfurled scroll, held down with a bird's head shaped paperweight – a miniature falcon, shining with a golden haze. It was not lost on either, the scroll's impudence of solidness changing face then being set. Forever! The same way as every other such occurrence before a new revelation.

Both immediately ran to observe, but dared not touch one of the sacred scrolls – for such a thing would bring an immediate exile of all realms the scrolls speak, of what they present. A banishment none, nor anyone could afford: Vilenzia was critical. So they both held back, even as the words shifted and then burned through the vellum beneath their eyes.

'It's been happening since a short while ago, but lately the whole text beyond where we have been reading shifts and changes. I have sensed subtle changes since the first time I read them, but now prevalence has taken the place of subtleness. I had hoped the boy wouldn't recognise the change, but *I* knew something was amiss ...'

The two not of that world looked at each other, slight concern reflected.

'This is a good thing, I surmise. Correct?' the man asked, sheepishly.

A long-drawn-out silence ensued before both shook their heads.

Together they mouthed, '*He be whom shapes beyond the current! He is who will be for all, he will be all, and more!*'

*

The boy stood still. Still dreaming, still stood on the same rock he had before the two men, still a fair distance away, made their way to the thick woodland.

A loud screech came thundering through, shaking the bare trees at the precipice, and he himself.

Still not adjusted fully to the environment, he fell to his backside. Then, feeling the moisture of the moss seep through to his imagined breaches, he jumped back up, a little higher than he had anticipated, thus falling forward and onto his chest as his body moved quickly through the air. Moisture now seeped through his light vest – and he shuddered from the cold touch that grabbed both nipples.

Bendim smiled as he was dragged over the moist, mossy mounds, toward one of the last checkpoints before The Great Divide – home to the Ellemenda Peaks and all manner of mythical creature – the last such point before they were to venture into an expansive country he knew all too well. There would be many beasts who would not hesitate to take his head once they scented the remnants of blood crusted about his clothing, if not the lingering stench of his previous employer.

This was his only meaningful hope for escape, hoping his captor was viewed with the same regard – for keeping alive one who had aided and abetted the man who had taken so much from their magical, mountainous world.

He was hoping for any opportunity no matter how slim. He began to wonder, though, would he take it. The confuddlement of such a decision that should have been obviously taken, should a chance of freedom present itself, scared him more than the sounds coming from deep in The Divide. He eventually decided against it.

*

The boy held his tongue, just as he always had throughout the playful motion of the dreams, scared he may alert whoever was in the vicinity to his ethereal presence.

The boy knew his, and ultimately their location through an experience of the multiple iterations supplicated by the scrolls – he had been here before, in a dream a long time ago and many times again. Again, thrown into the same place where he currently stood – perception always a little clearer. Though the prey, this time, was of seemingly low importance. *Shouldn't I be witnessing Somendel's head being chewed off again soon? Like last night?* But it was far from such as Bendim was now in tow.

The border of broken ash trees that separated the mainland from the country of the mythical beings only a few miles yonder meant that soon a death awaited; it always happened just beyond that mystical divide – though not entirely the same way, nor by the same hand, or talon – of what lay beyond.

Then something that had never happened before occurred.

Jasquirea stopped just prior to entering The Divide. He looked directly at the boy, squinting as if to see something, sniffing quickly as if to smell anything in the air. He held the same pose and posture for a short while. Eventually he shook his head and turned back toward the thicket through the trees. Another quick glance back, to catch someone or something off guard, preceded their disappearance into the coppice.

Another loud screech, different than before, followed by a similar rumble echoed throughout the forest and plain where he lay. This time he held his ground before walking gingerly, following the trail the two had left behind.

Before Jasquirea crossed into The Divide, a voice from above, as though from the heavens, stilled him for but a moment. He smiled.

*Read on Papa ...*

*

'This makes no sense. None at all!' said the man as he read.

Dagda blankly gazed out of the open window.

'We must go to him now. We have to tell him who he is, where he came from, and what needs to be done!' the woman said quickly.

'So ... now you agree with me,' smiled Dagda. A cynical smile that split portly, supple lips. 'Now do you see?'

She shuddered, but nodded affirmation.

The man read on, not believing what he was witnessing, nor speaking. The text was etching itself through the vellum as he spoke. That was not the most extraordinary development, for the words now contained an additional character, one not conceivable to be in such a scroll.

The man grimaced. *Hang on, Getty. Hang on mate, we're coming to get you* … 'Hang on son.' He mumbled as he stood tall.

'Let's go!'

They found him stood in the same spot as they had so many years ago, absolutely still, like a statue. The aura around him had grown brighter every time. Now it was bursting out tiny tendrils all about the slender silhouette of his body.

Many years ago, the man had been curious as to why he had always stood in the exact same location. They had soon discovered that – after a few scrapes away of the dirt – a plinth was buried beneath the ground; its diameter was no more than an arm span and its depth unknown as they gave up digging after a few feet before filling the hole back in.

He began to make his way to his son before Dagda held him back with an outstretched arm. 'Hold on. Give him a few moments more. You see those tendrils?'

'Uh huh,' the man saw the unnatural aura, like worms plucking out of the earth, searching for air.

'Well, they're not normal. This is a new development we are witnessing, even for us two.'

The man looked at the woman, who nodded.

'What do we do then?' the man asked.

Before Dagda or the woman could answer, the boy's body began to dissipate, then reappear in its full form.

This prompted the man to move again.

'Getty!' he shouted. He was held back again, this time with two arms – one from each of his otherworldly companions.

He did not mistake the concern in the woman's eyes as she looked to Dagda, who had now lost the pretence of a stout, foolhardy joker, he now held some serious concern across his face too.

Another ripple of nothingness rose through the boy.

This time, the promptness of the woman was impeccable as she leapt the full twenty lengths to tackle him away from the pull of the plinth.

Both skidded across the snow, bringing up fallen wet leaves from beneath which stuck to their clothes, until they came to an abrupt stop not far from the central obelisk in the middle of the clearing.

The boy opened his eyes briefly as he raised himself up off the cold woodland floor before he flopped back down, closing his eyes once more.

The woman brushed the snow and foliage from the boy, then herself, and picked up his teenage weight as if but a twig to carry him as gracefully as would an ice skater carrying a flag upon a froze lake during the Wintertide Show.

The man rushed to take the boy but as the weight was shifted onto him, he almost fell forward, so the woman took the weight of Getty back onto her chest

The man slumped to his knees, the wet woodland floor not deterring such a pose, feeling the weight on his shoulders exponentially increase. It was too much for him to comprehend, such a burden. One he had carried for so many years – for so many winters.

He held the same sacrificial pose until the boy began to stir. The woman shushed him, and the boy, with a whisper – it was all that was needed to calm them as a welcome, enclosing darkness appeared, surrounding his vision.

*

'What happened back there?' the man whispered to Dagda

as he looked desperately at the slumped boy in the graceful woman's arms as they made their way from the clearing. He himself was still a little groggy but full of a relief from the lifted hidden weight.

She walked beside him. 'He was slipping out of this realm and into that which the scrolls show us. He has set the path from all time before, and that cannot be rewritten. I am sure if you go and pick up that scroll you dropped in the snow, the etchings would have ceased upon *my* contact with the boy.' She went on after a small pause. 'You see, the boy is of neither world, he was spawned in another timeline, under a very different sky. Plucked from obscurity and thrust into a real world from a long way away, much … much further away than our imagination could ever take us.

'All I know is that I was tasked with assigning a family for the boy. One that would care for him deeply. Believe me, I had no idea that the boy would be called upon so soon, nor so desperately. My heartfelt apologies I offer you and your wife … truly,' she bowed slowly.

The man shook his head, even slower. 'He is such a blessing. He really is. I don't want to lose him … he has brought so much happiness and, no doubt, as much sorrow to us from our inability to help him. We always thought that was a temporary flux, but as the years went on … and on, we had finally given up on hoping and started to begin loving him as he was, as he should have been. And for that I will forever hang my head with shame.'

The man rolled up his sleeves as he chuckled, also while he wept. 'Look at these arms, look how big they are … hehe. They have carried this boy everywhere; I only wish they were a hundred times as large, so I could take him to the stars above where he so belongs.'

The woman gazed wistfully at the man, obvious emotion brewing from deep within. But she contained it well before she spoke in the same tone as the whispered voice earlier.

'He will one day own the stars, for us, for everyone. All that he will see. All that he will be … it will be because of you and his mother. No doubt … it's doubtless your love and commitment to the boy has spurred on a flurry of confusion throughout all the other realms. Other times, and beyond … surely.' She looked at the boy who was now sleeping peacefully.

Looking again at the man, directly into his eyes, she said, 'All I can now ask of you … all *that* I can ask, is that you see this through, you must give him as much time, guidance and tuition as you have done before, only tenfold. That … and to believe in him.

'The gentleman your wife has gone to procure for your son's condition, he knows much. Listen to whatever he has to say … though he can be a menacing fool at times, he means well. He always has, and—'

'Do as he directs you to do, for sure he will only have the boy's best interest at heart …' Dagda finished as he approached.

Dagda came to the man's side, helping him stand as he placed big hands under his armpits and eased him to a stance. He patted the man's shoulder, dabbing away the tears so they would not soak into the man's coat.

'Easy there. We will help take him back to the house and, once there, leave instructions to follow until we can decipher what is happening here. It is much more than we are party to it seems. The winds of change are striking upon us once again. I fear though, more than hope … this time could be the last …' He said the last as he looked, with some concern, at the forever etched scroll.

# Darkness Descends

'Father?'

Nothing. A long silence ensued before a loud bang was heard downstairs.

'Father? Papa?'

Nothing. Once again.

Getty lay in his bed, shivering. A slight numbing sensation was accompanied by a shaking throughout his body; a feeling he had never felt before.

Another feeling, above his left hip, ripping through to his lower back – a grinding, niggling and sharp feeling.

He was feeling uncomfortable, though he felt very little pain.

'Yes? Getty!' The man mumbled as he clattered through the wooden door, holding a tray that held his breakfast.

'I feel strange,' the boy nodded toward the hip causing the discomfort. 'Pain, I assume?'

'Ah … yes.' The man placed the tray on the floor and pulled off his flat cap to wring out the moisture collected from the rain falling outside as he waited at the front gate, gazing down the long straight road that disappeared under the archway into blackness. He had been waiting there for hours – waiting to see the silhouette he knew so well.

He continued, 'I was trying to … erm, you know, change your bedding.'

The boy blushed.

'I, err … pulled them a little too hard and you came with 'em and caught your side on the bed frame there …'

'Oh … sorry, Papa!'

'No, no. Hush my child. My fault, really.'

'But the sensation of pain is good, eh?'

'Aye, 'tis!' The man smiled and rubbed a hand through the boy's hair. 'Tell t' truth,' the man moved over to the window, eyes trained on the black archway that led underneath the town's artificial waterway which supplied fresh water from the peaks not far north of the woodland, 'your ma should be back soon. With that fellow I told you about. You know the one who can apparently help the crip—um, the …'

'Papa, it's alright,' the boy laughed, then looked down to gaze at prone body. 'Look at me!' he laughed again.

The man joined in with his chuckle. 'Aye, very well.' He moved back a step, then two, but no more, keeping a line of sight on the archway and back to the bed. 'You have such a spirit, you never seem to upset about your … erm, well … all of it, all the things you should be doing. All we do is read, bathe you, dress you then maybe feed you – dependant on your behaviour.' The man chuckled, as did the boy.

'Maybe I like that you do all that. Heavens! Could be I'm just a lazy uff! Just like Bend—'

'Don't say that name!' the man interjected, a little too quickly, before looking back toward the half-circle of darkness punching through the distant wall at the end of the road, down at the bottom of the hill. 'Sorry, child. Just bear with me.'

\*

The man walked back into the alcove to where the scrolls were placed, above the books below.

One was aglow.

He began to reach for it but then jerked his hand away as a searing heat emanated from the now brightly lit scroll.

*Hmm, what could that be? Another? Heck! Who knows what's going on? They were once tattered, battered things but have become sound over time. A change is surely afoot!*

'Papa?'

'Yes, child! I'm coming. I'm coming back.'

The boy noticed him rub his hand as if to mentally relieve

some pain.

'I think we leave this next chapter 'til tomorrow at least, laddy.' He ruffled the boy's longish hair again, then proceeded to fold a few sheets on top of a large chest beside the bookcase. 'Your mama should be back soon enough. Should be getting ready for her arrival and preparing the spare room by the kitchen in anticipation of our important guest. You know, I reckon he will be able to work something into you. You seem much stronger than I have ever—'

He was broken off by a slight gasping sound from the boy. He turned to see the boy had drifted off back to sleep.

He glanced back at the narrow, tall bookcase in the alcove. The scroll had begun to burn a brighter red, so much so that he could feel the heat from where he now stood.

He whispered, almost inaudibly, 'Easy, child. Let's get you walking first. Plenty of time thereafter before you get your chance to run …'

*

Mesfa joined Arigal who had been on her own. She sat on a warped wooden bench cut from a fallen tree trunk, overlooking the lake on the outskirts of the small town of Menton Green. Mesfa sat beside Arigal, both watched on in silence for a while – they were both watching the boy, now full of verve, splashing about with another figure with long hair, a slim waist and a large chest.

'You trust him?' Mesfa asked.

'No. But then, I don't even trust you,' she answered, laughing.

'He is young, full of pain. That much I can sense. He made his own way. He was not afraid of anything that was following him. Nor was he afraid of any of us or … or her!' She pointed deftly at the woman bobbing in the lake, dark eyes shedding no reflection of the candlelight from those placed around the edge of the lake by forever-faithful acolytes. 'And that is what I'm afraid of. He has endured much for such an early age.'

'From what you tell me, his first seventeen have been quite … trivial.'

She put an arm around Arigal but was flitted away with a sharp switch of a hand.

'She is watching, though it would appear she is in full revelry … who knows with those dark eyes. We need to reserve such affection for when we—'

The woman in the lake snapped them a direct look.

'See …' Arigal whispered.

They watched on as the whole enigmatic scene took place. Underneath the rippling surface there was probably more at play. They were now fully aware that her eyes were not just on the boy, but they were always on all. Ears too, so it would seem.

*

Arigal walked over to stand in the water, moving in no farther than where the water lapped just above her ankles. The small, smooth pebbles shifted under her weight and soothed her aching soles.

The ripples had since subsided and now only the boy, floating on his back, remained, keeping himself afloat with short twists of his wrists and subtle kicks of his ankles. Their superior had long-since departed, carrying a non-distinct smile.

She turned to speak to Mesfa, though held herself with a shrug. For she too had since departed, to follow the woman back through the woodland trail, to where she had suddenly, and unexpectantly, appeared bringing a long rebuke and punishment for such disobedience – one she was still paying for, with her body, so it seemed.

She trained her eyes on the boy relaxing in the dark water

staring at the dark sky above, he was oblivious to her gaze. He looked ready to sleep, floating upon the surface.

He raised a hand, without looking at her, and waved for her to come in and join him.

She gestured with her fist and obstinately shouted, 'Fuck off, scumbag!'

Bareleno laughed, before he replied in kind, 'Fuck you too then! Hey?' He raised his head and angled it slightly to get sight of her. He laughed again, louder now and then dropped his body beneath the surface.

He resurfaced not far from the spot where Arigal had stood moments earlier, only to see her also disappear through the woodland trail.

'Ah, she is a stickleback bitch,' he grumbled. 'Oh well, back in I go!'

He leapt bakwards, arms at full reach behind his head, into the water, unaware of the boy stirring at him from the far side of the lake.

Floating on his back, he thought he caught a glimmer of something move beyond the far bank of the lake. He flipped to his front and looked in the direction toward the sudden flicker of movement.

Nothing.

He flipped over again. Then flipped back just as quick to look back in the same direction.

Nothing.

Feeling a little uneasy, he swam back to where the three had departed, keeping close to the candlelight as if now suddenly afraid of the dark.

The boy watched on from behind the wide mess of twisted, spindly trunks, fully aware that the swimmer had noticed something – no, not something, someone. That someone being him!

He pondered a short while before moving on to follow.

He had never seen beyond this point. His father always skipped over the next few sequences of events. Over the few – or many – chapters he was now viewing.

He was curious as to why.

So, he went on, and followed.


Arigal waited outside of the large dwelling the trail had led back to. She held out her palms to look at the fluorescent purple streaks that had appeared on her palms and wrists only the day earlier. She had noticed the same on the odd high mistress, but hers had many more, violet coloured, and they shot right up to her elbow until they disappeared into that hideously fashioned, tight fitted garment she always wore. Even in the lake earlier she wore a similar outfit, only losing her leggings as they drifted off with the lap of the small waves produced by a brisk, if inconstant, flicking breeze.

'Maybe gloves are not such a bad idea. Maybe Mesfa had it right.' She spoke a little too loudly.

Bareleno heard her. 'Well, I think, though I have little familiarity for such a thing, that your hands are … quite … well, they're much, much, softer than that woman's, your mistress.' He grinned at her.

That annoyed her. That crooked smile. She shot him a dark look and raised her hands, muttering to summon a spell of some sort to squish the fool. 'She is not my—'

'Easy … easy.' He raised both hands too. 'A compliment, Arigal.' He still had his hands raised as he approached slowly and stopped at the railings at the end of the porch. 'You that far past all reproach for a compliment?'

She giggled inside as she replied, 'Say, maybe that I am. Then maybe I should just swipe your head off for such a reproachful comment to one of a higher station.'

She studied the boy, his palms not raised quite high enough to hide the stone-cold beauty deep in his blue eyes.

She found herself fighting away the butterflies that had suddenly begun to flutter in her stomach – and also somewhat lower – every time he came near her. Mesfa had had her way with him. *Damn that girl I love so deeply!* Or was it the other way around?

He had tempted her out at one point, later in the day, to the outskirts of the woods, only to be interrupted by her superior before anything more than touching had transpired. The woman then demanded penance from him for sneaking away from her chambers. A penance it seemed carried over to this morning's escapades.

A muffled crying out could be heard from the window not too far from where they both stood. *That crone is such a whore. Does she ever do anyth*—

The boy interrupted her train of thought with a raised eyebrow and a slight quirk of a smile then a nod back in the direction to where they had vanished the day before – a small clearing hidden within a dense expanse of trunk.

The butterflies intensified as he dropped his hands only to raise one to encourage her to grasp it, and follow. *Stupid girl, you are the lady incarnate! But then … look—no, listen to that bitch inside!*

She grabbed his hand – strong, nothing soft about it. Years on the streets would do that. She let herself be led.

The grasses close to the building brushed against her knees, adding to the tingling sensation now thriving all through her body. That tingle of anticipation, and some sort of release from the frustrations over the past few days set her off. *I will be better than my dear sister! I will be better than that fucking effigy of our Lady! I will encapsulate not only his body, but his soul to do with as I please. I will—*

She was cut off again mid-thought as he turned half a head to see her fully. A smile not befitting a street urchin weakened her knees, causing her to stumble slightly. He held her hand tighter, saving her the embarrassment of floundering around on her back in the knee-high grass.

*Shit, what am I becoming?! Some farmyard wench! So it would seem. So it does seem.*

She smiled back at him and instantly, in that moment, she felt a darkness fall away from all around her aura. She felt as though she would no longer be able to commit her all to her sister, for this boy had stirred something inside her, something that brought back chronic memories, something she hadn't felt for what seemed many an age. *Semona … that was my name, once. And I was … umm! Though … those eyes. Ummn!*

He pulled her faster once they breached the perimeter around the grove of the residence.

She overtook the boy, Bareleno, and pulled with all haste, all the while unbuttoning the front of her close-knit dress.

He grappled to let go of her hand and raced ahead, regaining the advantage of position in front of her. He then steadied himself for the wrapping impact.

She leapt high into him … hard – legs wide, ready to snare her prey, hoping to knock him down and land atop to devour.

He caught her weight fully and twisted his body to drop hers softly to crush the brush below, both not caring now for their intended destination a short way ahead.

She dragged him down, fast, from his knelt position, grabbing his loose hanging shirt front close into her heaving body – the exertion from the mini tug of war they played almost leaving her breathless. She kissed him deeply, while pulling at the buttons keeping his slacks high up over his waist.

His clothes were dry, though they should still be damp from the lake as he hadn't dried them with a dry cloth, not one she had seen. She forgot herself once again as he nibbled at her neck.

Eventually she gave up with the buttons that wouldn't

give and began to pull instead downwards about the cloth that held his thighs from the air, trying to find purchase in that task while now attached to his lips as their teeth clanged together a few times, bringing an excited giggle from each until it was muffled by the resumed locking of lips.

In turn, he had already succeeded in his attempt to free the dress from around her waist and that which drooped between. He let her fumble around a while before pulling her hands where his pants circled his waist, and shuffled his hips to help her free him – free him of the only defence to nature's kindest and most important element … air.

Now fully exposed to the boy hovering his weight above her, she waited, expectantly, without releasing arms now held tight around his neck. Though now their lips had ceased contact, hers hung devilishly close to his ear, which she couldn't help but take a soft nibble.

She felt the inevitable coming before it happened, before it transpired. She whispered softly into his ear, 'I … I am *Semona*.'

The slow slide forward of his hips punctured her very being. It fractured her entire make-believe world. There was no pain as the butterflies made their way to flutter chaotically all throughout her body.

Lost in a world of chaos. Lying on the damp grass, watching the pulse of darkness, interrupted with tinges of crimson that danced all about through the miniscule but ample punctures in the dense canopy.

He whispered a reply, 'I know! And … I have wandered this world, and many more to bring you home!'

Darkness.

Nothing.

*What* …

She lay in the crumpled undergrowth. There was the sound of heavy breathing from both. Though she had heard perfectly clear, she had let the boy continue on. Her mind was now racing with non-comprehension and a spattered relief.

She subtlety reached down, to feel the instep of her tanned, leather ankle boot. She fumbled for a moment then grasped at a small dagger tucked inside a small ankle pouch.

'Easy,' he said, and reached down to gently place his hand upon hers. 'Easy, Semona …'

'I am her no longer! Thule!' She pulled swiftly on the hilt, but his hard hand stayed the weapon where it was sheathed.

She knew those eyes, that smile, the way he moved. Her mind was constringent to processing the fact that had just presented itself. *Those eyes!* That it was he who had dealt her the final blow into being who she had now become. *Why now? Why after all these years? Why* … she whimpered

The boy brought himself up slightly, up off her body, his hand still holding Arigal's near the ankle.

Now she saw fully. The face of the boy had eroded into the man she knew many, many years ago – her teacher of magical arts: Thule. He had tutored her from being a benign if silly little fledgling from a broken crop of bad people. Her, and her sister, Mesfa.

She left the dagger where it was to grab him by the shirt again and kissed him deeply once more. Deeper this time.

'You must leave, Thule, now! If Mesfa finds out it is you, then we are both dead! No, we will be worse than dead! Our souls will be taken and absorbed into their ongoing ascension of the Higher Power. We … No! You must get gone, now! I will not stand by and see all I have attained stripped from me for one stupid folly with a perverted old man like yourself!'

'Ha!' he laughed, joyfully. 'I may now appear older, but I was once that vigorous lover you would run to when that so called family of yours would give you a bruise or two!' He released their connection with a short move backward to now hold his upper body weight on his knees – rather than her chest.

She felt the release of pressure between her legs as he slipped out, which brought with it its own wonderful sensation.

After a moment of digesting the sight of the man before her, she looked between his legs and giggled. She held a hand over her mouth to smother the laughter and rolled away, onto her stomach. Still laughing, she raised her hips, still exposed beneath her dress, to a treacherously inviting height.

As her laughter grew louder, he asked. 'Semona—'

'I told you! Not my name! Anymore!' She was looking away from him at the wooded mess ahead of them.

'Ok then Ariga—'

'Do not call me by that name either!' she shouted, more inpatient than angry.

He watched her roll over then saw her inviting smile as she turned her head back to him. He then looked to where she had been looking – non placid once more. Then at what she was presenting him. He let a small grumble escape before he grabbed her by the waist …

Finished.

Exceedingly intense and much longer lasting than the first iteration of the long-lost passion. He kissed the nape of her once bare neck, a soft, virginal space of skin which now bore a large, inked symbol – that of the swallow. An unnaturally bright blue bird, hidden behind the smoulder-black mane – the symbol of peace. *Not much befitting.*

He shuddered again. This time not from ecstasy, but from the paradox that was the girl panting heavily beneath him.

The second shudder of his hips brought another giggle from Arigal.

She still shuddered from the first, the second brought a little more of those butterflies to shoot away from her midriff.

Then pain.

The first: a sharp flick of darkness – from the sky to the grass that now suddenly brushed her cheek.

A physical pain came next.

A third: the sight of Thule's distorted face fall close to her own, to look at her, confused – out of mind, out of sense as the blood poured to close those questioning eyes.

The fourth: the sound of the wretched woman's non consistent drawl.

'*I am … I am. Semona,*' she whispered to herself before all pain, and the world in front of her became a wall of nothingness. But in that nothingness, right before the total blackout, she saw a glimmer of something … a body maybe, a shape that moved from behind one of the massive, twisted trunks beyond her reach – too bright for her to make out what it was, and she was too short of consciousness to comprehend anything more … before Semona succumbed to darkness once again.

*

'Papa!' the boy cried out.

He sweated profusely all over his body. But that was not the reason for the boy's startled cry, nor was it that the dream had affected him in a way as never before. For he found himself stood tall, stood on the bed he had been so accustomed to only lie in for more than a decade.

The man rushed in through the door only to see the boy slump from the rigid standing position, down onto the bed. A heavy fall, about to be even harder as he bounced off the side of the bed.

The man was quick, much quicker than he let on, so quick that he made it to the bedside in a flash to cradle his fall and deposit the boy smoothly back atop the padded quilt.

He blushed as the man looked at the boy's pants, but the man paid no mind to the boy's erection.

'How the bloody hell did you get up there …?' he asked, with a slight chuckle.

'Don't know, Papa!' He shifted slightly, much more movement than the hours that had passed since the boy fell to slumber.

'I just woke up, and then … woah! There I was.'

The man touched the soul of the boy's foot. *Warm still. And not muddy, nor scratched.*

'Anything else, child? Did you see anything unusual? Feel anything unusual?'

'No, Papa. Just woke up here.'

'Well then, I suppose that shows then that you erm, well … 'tis not your body that's the problem but …'

He trailed off as he saw movement – a speck, then a second speck – appear through the darkness of the arched tunnel, down the at the bottom of the hill.

They became larger, quicker than he had anticipated, but there was no mistaking that bobbing, swaying mane of Gretta and the funny run she bore.

He soon deduced, from their speed and frantic arm waving, that they approached at some pace.

They were being chased.

Suddenly, black shapes followed through the opening and spread all about the road, hard on the heels of his wife and her unknown companion.

Five shapes in total, dark as dark could be, all possessing webbed, bat like wings and hunched legs which hovered constantly, ready to pounce upon their prey.

The man raced from the bed to the window and slammed the window shut, then pulled on a draw cord to release a secondary layer that dropped from the pelmet above – this one made a rattling metal-on-metal sound as it came down.

Next, he raced past the bed and disappeared out the room without saying a word.

The same rattle occurred a further seven times – equalling the number of windows scattered about the house.

The boy shifted a little, feeling more than a little helpless. He was unaware what his father saw, though the fear wrapped all over his face as he raced past indicated something severe was about to transpire. So, he listened, as he always did … though ever more so intently.

*

The man held the door open with one hand in readiness for the two to enter. The other held a cord, ready to drop and block the entrance.

He could see the frantic look on her face as she neared. It was tired, she was grinding her teeth which shining through staunch lips, determined to reach home, full of absolute, resolute will – one that would see her home. He knew, or at least wished, it to be true.

The other's face, not nearly as disturbed, frightened him. And that he thought he saw a wry smile on the man's face frightened him even more. The male figure held Gretta's arm tightly just above her elbow. An instant pang of jealousy touched his mind – that he was unable to provide aid of his own – but was soon extinguished by the fact that the man had obviously coerced and coaxed her on through what must have been a terrible flight through the long-barrel of darkness – that of the tunnel and what, patently, must had ensued prior to its entrance.

More movement beyond, behind the two, further behind the pack of darkness chasing them; the whole mouth of the tunnel seemed to grow larger and larger until it consumed all available viewable space about the walls.

The tunnel continued to spew out the same black animal-like creature, overwhelming the man's sense of sight; he feared for the life of his beloved.

He acted in desperation as he left the post – left the last bastion that safeguarded half of his world – to race forward and add what little, if any, aid he could offer.

He pulled the chain-linked chord before he left, paying no mind to the clatter of metal.

*Be safe my boy!*

He raced quickly to close the gap between as the dark shapes began to consume all but a few paces behind them, hard on their heels, almost within a distance their flapping wings could swipe and find a true purchase. He wasn't close enough, not yet, to offer anything that he meant to.

Resignation crept into his mind and it began to fester but it was soon purged, snapped back by a deep, ingrained, and innate resilience. He found that extra step – another level of himself he very rarely could find – and roared a shout to match the hurried, suicidal steps.

One of the creatures made an attempt at tripping the pair. It made a sharp swipe of its translucent webbed arm toward the ankles of Gretta but failed in finding its target. Instead, it overbalanced and tumbled sideways, knocking over the identical creature to its right. That space though was soon filled by two others.

He succumbed, finally, to the inevitability of the whole situation; a realisation he had known throughout the short episode. And now the cloud of rage had dissipated to only despair; he accepted he was too late to even get close to her.

Then, once he saw the fallen creature's substitute fill the void left and it closed on her, raising its wing for a close swipe, he knew she would succumb to a blow, be it her legs, chest or head: it would be all that was needed.

He was too late …

She must have sensed his panic. For rather than showing a fear that should have been cast all over her face, she only smiled, directly at him. A smile he hadn't seen for many years. She whispered something too. Was it *Getty?*. He couldn't be sure – his mind was ablaze with every emotion which made it difficult to comprehend anything but the inevitable about to transpire.

She moved her lips for what he thought would be one last time, but a shouting broke in. *Not hers!*

Senses aware, he heard loud and clear, 'Get down! Now!'

Without pause, he dropped flat, and the momentum rolled him forward multiple times. The final roll ended with him on his back, looking toward the light-grey clouds above. The clouds disappeared from his vision, replaced with multiple arcs of burning light that shot past, temporarily taking their place.

He could feel the heat of each scorching arc as they flew by, not far above his head. He dared not raise his head, but he did turn it enough to see the other two had also dropped down low.

Beyond the pair, the black creatures were being scythed into pieces from the relentless barrage from behind him. He turned his head over carefully to see from where the barrage had originated.

Standing near the doorway which he had left unattended, two mirages of light stood, arms outstretched and legs wide apart. It was no doubt those that had dropped in from the heavens earlier, and the very same two that had immediately disappeared without a goodbye once they helped Getty back to his bed. The same who left *another bastard reading, this time a tome,* to only be opened once the boy turned his next year over.

The blades of light shot through without pause upon impact, as though the animals – or whatever they could be – were made of nothing more than rolling smoke. The only noise when the arcs made contact was a hiss, a sound like that of water hitting the cookpot at a high temperature.

A gurgled mess was the only sound the animals made;

there were no footsteps, no vocalisation of pain, no thud as they hit the ground.

Eventually, the darkness that had descended upon the pair had either been destroyed or retreated back into the temporary haven of the tunnel.

That wasn't enough for Dagda. He leapt the full expansive distance over to the dark archway and continued to let loose on those trying to flee, lighting up the darkness, turning the tunnel into a flashing beacon of bright light.

The man finally heard them make a natural, vocal sound, a howling wail that echoed throughout the landscape; a howling that scattered all living animals to the air or through the closest brush.

Emitting from the tunnel entrance, rising into the air, was an acrid cloud of yellow steam. He was sure the foul creatures' very essence was now dissipating into the cold atmosphere.

The goddess-like woman helped the three to their feet, nodding to the man and his wife. Then she nodded to the stranger, winked at him, then embraced him with a squeeze that rendered him mute.

'Ma'am,' he let out once she had released some of the pressure. 'I see Dagda still has that extra bounce in his gait.'

She nodded and looked at Dagda now walking his way back to where the four stood, hair swaying from side to side ceremoniously. She softly spoke, 'More than you could ever imagine, Jesse. More than you could ever know ...'

# A Solution. A Remedy

The boy listened intently for any sound of movement – no matter how insignificant. He had heard lots of noise coming from the direction of the shuttered window of his bedroom. No voices, though, no screams. *That's good, I suppose.* And no shouts – until that of his mother.

The sound of her voice left him cold and uneasy. Where it should, instead, have brought a warmth, it wracked him with an icy, frosty sensation throughout his body.

Sparks of light flittered through the slightest of gaps around the frame of the shutter soon after he heard his mother, fleetingly lighting up the dim room now that the candles had burned themselves away.

A howling wail rent his body to a shiver; it sounded inhuman, which brought its own little comfort for it sounded nothing like his mother or father. The howl also sounded nothing animal like either. He shuffled slightly, more than he had ever before, but not enough to make more than the slightest movement to where he wanted to go.

So, he just lay still, as always … and waited.

He trained an eye on the shutters, without taking the corner of the other away from where his father had departed so suddenly, remaining alert for any movement near the door that led out onto the landing.

He dared not drift away either, even though he was aching to sleep. This was not a dream, this was real, this is where he was, though he generated a ripple of excitement at the thought of something a little like the events in his ever so vivid dreams …

*But this is real! Whatever is happening, whatever is out there, could rip me apart. That … and my papa and mama!'* He shrunk a little lower down into himself and the bed he was so accustomed to.

A little while passed …

Muffled voices eventually broke the eerie silence. He detected at least three: his mother, his father, and another he thought he had heard before, the sound of a woman's voice he recognised. However he could not attach a face nor a name to it – he had very few visitors, so he found that strange. Though the fact that he could distinguish his parents from the few muffled voices enabled his spirits to perk up a little.

The downstairs shutter was being raised with seemingly a little difficulty, before the front door banged against the wall as it was swung open.

Fast pattering steps could be heard, firstly across the tiled floor between the front door and the main stairs, and then on the timber treads of the steps – he counted five, which meant the ascender had missed at least two treads for every leap.

He need not have guessed who would bound in, just like so many times before, though this time much more fervently.

Tears welled in her eyes when she didn't miss the slightest shuffle of the boy's hips as he readied for the onslaught of affection she was about to dish out. As she was about to smother him, he twitched, which only gave her more cause to squeeze a little harder.

Moments earlier she had seen the end, *her end*, and had even embraced it. In that seemingly fleeting final moment, she recounted every single moment and memory of his existence, and nothing before. She knew she now had a duty to ensure the boy would walk, would run, though his waking mind denied him the ability. She would see him fulfil his full potential, be it with those celestial *things* that seemed to rear their heads at the most inopportune of times. She would see him love, laugh, sing … would pull him away from that *bastard* vellum his father read to him constantly, the fallacy of fiction – so she had ascribed it – from the constant dribble the man would talk, about how this and that had changed in whichever scroll. She had wanted to burn them all, burn them all and roast pine fruit in the company of the boy, over the ashes of the bullshit being fed to assimilate his mind and into their way of things.

He took the brunt of the embrace around the chest, an area he had had very little, if any, sensation in before – it hurt.

He smiled. Widely.

'Oooof!' he eventually cried out. 'Mama, easy …' He tried to raise his arms to pull the embrace even closer but they only reached high enough to hover low above the mattress.

It was enough for his mother to notice; she grabbed both hands in hers and squeezed them tightly, which again brought a small welp of pain, one that was welcomed joyously by both as she let out a little laugh at the sight of *her* boy for the first time sensing her touch.

Feeling the squeeze made the boy smile wider too. 'Mama, I feel, I feel you!'

'I know, my child! A blessing it sure is …' She looked skyward, mentally throwing a curse through time and beyond space. A thought silenced by four other bodies entering the bedroom of the apparent saviour.

She rolled her eyes – just enough for the four not to notice anything askance – and released the boy from her grip as she began to move away.

Grateful for their assistance she surely was, and now she had the time to offer gratitude to the pair, one of whom she had met before, the other obviously of the same ilk. She bowed.

'Higher Ones, welcome to our home, I offer my thanks and praise to you bo—'

'Say no more,' the celestial woman intercepted before titles could be offered and accepted. 'That you have offered so much of your life, devoted to ensuring the continuality of what we are striving to achieve … I *thank* you, Gretta.'

The boy blushed, upon seeing the woman's face. Fear was replaced with an unconscious, lustful feeling. He recognised her face immediately. Though obviously much more aged, she was still as beautiful as he remembered her.

He whispered, slowly and low enough none could hear, 'Arig—'

The woman interrupted with a stern gaze in his direction. Dagda had also heard and turned towards her. Her eyes stayed as her head flicked from side to side to silence him before returning the gaze back to Gretta. 'Now, Gretta, I introduce one of the other Higher—'

Before she could finish, Dagda moved forward to kneel before Gretta and held her hand tightly as he bowed. 'My name's Dagda! And may I offer you my full protection from here on?'

She shook his hand away, placed her own on her hips and replied, 'No. No you may not. I would be better off never seeing you or your like anywhere near here ever again!'

Dagda stood up. 'Ma'am, the boy needs protecting … especially in these trying times. We can be his protection. As you saw outside, we are quite a force.'

'Hush, before I wallop you!' She now stared at the boy who looked like he was having a bad dream. 'All of you, out there, with me, now! Downstairs with the lot of you. We can discuss the boy's *treatment* downstairs.'

With that, all but one left to leave the boy to his own thoughts and conclusions as to what the hell had just happened outside, who the mysterious figures who had walked in behind his mother were, and what the hell *she* was doing here!

The stranger that remained – obviously at the behest of his mother – was no doubt the one she had sought to find on her arduous travel through the town and over to the city.

*Wonder why he's looking at me like that?* the boy wondered.

The stranger smiled as if reading his thoughts.

'Boy, do you know who I am?'

'No, not really. My mother did speak of you before she left. She said she had been waiting for a long, long, while since hearing of you, but she had never had the courage to travel beyond the mountains.'

'Smart lady. Though there are those that do travel that course. You know, couriers, peddlers, merchants … they all could have delivered a message to me anywhere I may have been.'

'Maybe she had her reasons.'

'Of course she did. Maybe. Can you elaborate on your assumption as to why she would refrain from doing such?'

'Maybe she didn't want anyone to know about me?'

'Smart lad!' He smiled again, wider than before, and nodded.

This brought an air of warmth to the man, relaxing him a little before the strange man spoke again.

'Why would you assume she would not want anyone, but *I* know, to know who *you* are? No … let me simplify that. Why would she not want anyone else to know about you?'

'Ugghhh, you sound just like him. Too much tongue without actually saying much, if anything at all.'

'Who?' the stranger asked sharply.

The boy took his time to measure the response, not missing the directness in the man's tone. 'Oh, I don't know his name. But I see him quite often, you should know.'

'Nay mind, then. Now … tell me about you. What is it you believe to be your *supposed* ailment? And how do we fix it?'

'Isn't that why you were sought, for you to figure that

out? To help with that?'

'No, your ailment is your own. It has nothing to do with me. I am not a healer, as such. But I can help *you* help yourself. And, from what your mother told me, it looks like a slight miracle has occurred since her departure. Am I right? Or did my eyes deceive me?'

The boy looked at the stranger before asking him a question, one that he already knew the answer to. He asked anyway. 'Who are you?'

'If you do not know the answer to that by now then you are far from help. Well? Who do you think I am?'

The boy made another disgruntled noise, not too dissimilar to the one moments earlier. This brought another smile from the stranger.

'Alright then. Enough of the to and fro, hey? I am not who you think you think I am. I have never met you nor have you ever met me, in this realm, the next, the prior, the after, nor the similar, though I know you know of others who could be me. For the record, I have never met them nor their kind … save a few, to be true. And so here we are … back to a question, *the* question … who am I?'

'A long surmise for such a simple question. Only to end up back at what I had originally asked.'

'Apologies for boring you. I was just settling my thoughts out loud as I lose myself somewhere sometimes. For I *know* of those who *you* would assume I am or *could* know of. I have heard stories and also read a few passages in my time upon this world, and before you jump in with cries of contradiction, I have only ever ventured my long, skinny legs upon this world.'

'You talk … way too much!' the boy chuckled.

The stranger chuckled too, adding weight to the boy's softening impressions of the man. 'My name is, as I'm sure your mother told you, *was* The Jester. However my real name *is* Jesse … Jesse Hasconito of the Hasconite Tribe.

You ever heard of them?'

'No … not ever. Jesse, was it?'

'Yes, you jest.' They both chuckled again. 'Oh, I'm sure you would have heard of my tribe if you—'

'Jesse, of the Has … cot … whatever, I have never left this house!' The boy looked at him, now showing a slight anger. 'Well, maybe I have, but never have I been pushed as far as the tunnel at the bottom of the road.'

'Yes, of course, your mother mentioned such. Sheesh, those *deathslayers* certainly did me a fright!'

'Huh?'

'Ah. Again, forgive my ignorance. You have no idea, do you, hey? Well … to put it bluntly, me and your mother almost lost our lives a stone's throw from this very residence.

'Your mother asked that I be open and honest with you from the very moment I accepted the request to accompany her back here to see you. So, I will be. And I will try to be as becoming as possible. However, if I could permit your input into *certain* matters then I will not be so frank. So—'

'Deathslayers? Whatever could they—'

'So, you missed all my words beyond deathslayers?'

'It would seem so. I'm sorry, do go on …'

'Well, as I was saying—hey!' Jesse clicked his fingers to draw his attention away from the shuttered window.

'Have they all gone?' he asked hesitantly.

Jesse walked over to the window and pushed the shutters hard, back into the pelmet above, and swung open the window to reveal a deep grey vista, scattered with miniscule sun rays poking through the offered punctures all about the rolling blanket of cloud cover.

'Some escaped, but from what they would have witnessed out there, I would safely assume they will think hard for a long, long time before mounting such an assault again. If, more importantly, they could hold such a thought!'

Jesse closed the window once more to block out the draft that brought a cold air into the room. A scent of burnt oil hung on said draft which made  his nostrils twitch.

'But, you should know, from what I have heard about them, they will come back. You do understand that? Oh … I assume you don't, from that look on your now wretched face. Oh, come on child! What are you doing? Look at you, you are wriggling like a plumber bird's prey. Gods, you're such a wretch, look at you! You maggot. Get up! Stop being such a ninny! Stop being such a floppy cock. Sort yourself out, will you?!'

They boy's body was reacting to the hurtful spiel projected at him. He knew it was meant to be motivational, which made the spasms of laughter all the more enjoyable, for it had been more than he had ever moved before.

He laughed uncontrollably, like a young child in the throes of madness brought on by attrition of sense. He had never heard such profanity before, in the real, *his*, world at least, and it made him feel … joyous, rapturous to the bone.

The man kept on with vile spiel, the viler the content the more the boy's body reacted, up until a point where the boy was literally bouncing up and down in the bed, helped by the spasms of laughter rippling through his wrought body.

The man smiled then laughed too at the sight.

He continued the comical barrage of insults until the boy could physically take no more. The boy's body seemed as though it were about to break.

Jesse stopped, to pant profusely, out of breath.

The boy panted heavily too. He could feel the pain from stretched muscles and cartilage, a stronger pain than he had ever felt before. But he didn't mind; his body had moved far further than the miniscule amount he was used to.

Jesse was satisfied. It was his way of assessing the reaction of those afflicted by immobility. Almost all of his patients showed no sign of what could only be described as a bodily emotion – only a vocal anger, humour or pain. What he had just witnessed would ensure that he earned his penance fairly.

*This boy, I reckon, can be saved! Not only that, but this boy is also more than I could have ever imagined! He could be the one to save us all from the forever destruction that all the seers have foretold of. He is, potentially, the one I have been searching for, for so, so long!*

He spoke to the boy, in a matter of fact tone. 'So, now do you accept your body as it is, as it should be? Do you accept your body is fully able to be taught that which you had always thought was not possible?'

The boy replied in matter-of-fact manner, 'I have never doubted my body. I know *something* may be askew, for I seem to always wake up with Papa or Mama washing me with the softest of sponges, the merest tickle of sensation wherever they apply such. And considering I am crippled from the neck down, I should not feel anything, so therefore I must have done some serious damage for them to spend so much time tending to my wounds. So, as you would say, I doubt my own filiation and things of that nature.'

As Jesse drew closer, the boy suddenly threw his hands towards him at such a speed it took both by surprise.

Jesse smiled as he held the boy's hands. 'Well, if you are unlike any of my other patients, this shouldn't take long at all, hehe.' He rubbed the boy's hair, a friendly gesture. 'Tell me, boy, why do you doubt your mother and father?'

'I never said I did!' The boy looked confused. 'You misheard me, Jesse. I would never doubt them or their love for me. But … are they mine? You know, like … erm. I don't know, I just feel different to them somehow.'

Jesse pulled over the chair his father had used for sitting on over the many years and heaped into it, an audible sigh followed.

'Tellin' you now, boy, feels good to rest my arse and

weary bones. That walk damn near killed me!'

Getty giggled at the joke, before asking, 'So what do we do next?'

'Well, that is entirely up to you and how fast you want to improve your body's responses.'

'So, what are you going to do?'

'Right now?'

'Yes. Right now. What are you going to do?'

'I am just going to sit here and talk to you for a while.' Jesse shuffled to make himself more comfortable, moving into the divots left by the man's arse cheeks, and then crossed his legs.

Silence ensued for a short while. Getty looked at Jesse, waiting for some sort of response, but Jesse just shrugged his shoulders and held his hands out as if prompting Getty to speak.

'You're just going to sit there?'

'Yes. Well, if you fall out of that bed at least I'm in the perfect spot to catch you before you could damage anything.'

'Very well then. What did you and my mother discuss on your way here?'

'Ah! That I cannot tell you.'

'But you said she told you to be—'

Jesse theatrically stood up, out of the chair, swung a finger around in the air, then sat back down in a heap.

*Weird,* thought Getty.

'Do you know those two people who followed your mother into the room?'

'No … I don't think so.'

'You do or you don't?'

'I don't know!' he shouted. And, as he did, his legs kicked up in the air.

Jesse smiled again. 'Very good. It seems anger may be the

key to get you up and about.'

The boy tried again to move his legs but was thwarted by the lack of response.

'Ugh, I could feel a sharp pain on my hip for a second then, when my legs shot up, but now it's just a niggling sensation once more.'

'Let me take a look.'

The man peeled back the cover and bandage to examine the wound, a fresh wound amongst numerous other scars that had been cleaned and tended to. It looked to be no more than a day old.

'Looks like you have been on quite an adventure, Getty! We will get you right as rain, just as soon as we can. That be, 'til your body permits itself to be guided by that not-so-simple mind, stuck inside that hefty sized donkin of a shell of yours.'

Getty laughed. 'Donkin head, never heard such a saying. Not ever. It sounds so—'

'Ah! Then I have much to educate you on. About the lands to the south, past the southern ridge of this massive caldera. About the golden sands that stretch forever beyond the highest ridge at the northern sector of the caldera. About my homeland, and that of many others, that seem to pop up high out of the ocean far beyond the ridge, those that gets smashed by waves of a size no man has ever been able to reach. Not too far east of here, the same waves, if you listen closely enough, you can hear from the western rise of the caldera's highest peak.' Jesse closed his eyes and held up a finger for silence to demonstrate any evidence of the fallible statement. He breathed in and held it for a moment then sighed a satisfied sigh, obviously hearing such a thing in his crazy mind.

Jesse opened his eyes and motioned, with a nod, for him to replicate, as he pulled both hands up to his lungs and took a deep breath once more.

Getty followed suit, holding his breath. He could indeed hear the sound beyond the eastern ridge, or was it ingrained as a thought offered by Jesse? He didn't care, it sounded surreal!

Both exhaled in tandem; the same satisfaction shone upon their faces.

'How did that make you feel, Getty?' Jesse asked.

'Good … it felt really good. Not just because I heard what it sounds like when you put up a cup to your ear—'

'What? Why would you put a cup to your ear, Getty?'

'Not my idea. Papa said that we don't have many shells around here so to replicate what he had read about the large conical shells found on the beaches, he assumed the same experience would result from a cup. I don't know … don't think he did either.' The boy laughed. 'Has some funny ideas, does he. He means well though, tries so much stuff to cheer me up like that, but I'm just happy for him to read to me, takes me to places far beyond my bed and the confines of this house and its immediate surrounds. So, it's good to daydream of faraway places that are of my own world for a time, if be it from a cup!' He laughed again, joined by Jesse.

'Tell me something. I'm a bit curious. How do they get you down the stairs? And why the bloody shite would they perch you up here instead of downstairs?'

Getty laughed a little. He was beginning to warm to the strange man; he was genuine and spoke genuinely, when he wanted. Which he liked. 'They have a type of contraption, a mobile chair with wheels, that gets me about upstairs and downstairs. They just pull off the wheels and put on some other square ones to make it easier going downstairs as they don't have to drag my "donkin" head back up the stairs.' The boy laughed, now at ease in the stranger's company. 'Why do you believe my mama and papa harbour me so?'

The question caught Jesse off guard, for he stumbled for an answer. He knew the reason, just as he had known the man and woman who had come to his and Gretta's aid.

He composed himself, to measure a response. 'That, Getty … is for you to find out. No, not find out; you must experience much more before the … ah truth can be revealed, for the truth is much more than a … *any* single answer.' He again rubbed the boy's head. 'Do you understand what I'm saying?'

'Do I have a magnet stuck to my head?' he said before he answered the question as Jesse finished ruffling his hair. 'No, not really. Not yet … but I'm sure in time I will. So, what are that lot doing downstairs?'

The stranger smiled. 'What would you guess, Getty?'

'Trying to listen in on us?'

'One hundred percent correct. They're listening as hard as they can.'

'Oh,' the boy blushed. 'Would they have heard my earlier consideration regarding my lineage, or more so whatever the opposite would be?'

'Not a word,' Jesse pulled out a conical shell from one of his satchels, the size just bigger than his palm. It glowed with a slight amber hue. 'Not a single word.' Jesse smiled as he hefted it up and down in front of him.

He patted the shell and the boy smiled once more. Though his body had no response, Jesse was sure the boy lay before him, the one that had been sent two – not one, but two – of the highest within the Union of the Jenine had a special calling for him.

Jesse uttered an unspoken prayer, one to keep the boy safe through the trials and tribulations he was soon to follow. Ones of many he was sure the boy would undertake. He just had to find the key to unlock the boy's mind. He was sure it – his mind – was holding back, afraid, even if subliminally, of what was to come, what was expected of it. Was it afraid? Did it know? Did it want to just lie there forever knowing what was in store for it? He felt that was the case. From all he had seen and heard about the boy, it seemed as though his mind was holding the body back, as if offering the body its own manifested afflictions.

*They say the heart isn't separated from the head ... until it actually is. Well, that would seem the case here!* he thought. *But who could blame it?!*

He looked at the boy, contentedly.

'We will get you ready for what is to come. You feel it, don't you? A pull, a presence, an ache in your heart, a reluctance in ... in your mind to accept what must be from all assumptions you have made over the years. That you are an element of light it would seem, and I think you know it. Not exactly what, but the purpose of you being sheltered here.'

'Jesse ...'

'Yes, child?'

'I'm scared. I have always been scared. Not for me, but for my mama and papa.'

'Why so, young one?'

'Well ... they have always been so hesitant to do anything with me outside these walls. When taking me outside they are always looking to the heavens as if waiting for me to be spited and cast down by some unimaginable spurt of anger or evil!'

'So? Is it such a bad thing that they care for you just as any parent would? Why would you assume you're any different?'

'That's just it, Jesse. I ... do ... feel different. I think they are waiting for that strike from above to wipe me out, or at least take me away, so there is an added hesitancy in the way they approach everything. I think I know why papa is so adamant I listen to all the scrolls taken from that there nook. At first, I enjoyed the scrolls, most definitely those set around Inarrel.

'I loved most the sound of the ancient paper rubbing against itself as papa would unfurl them. I loved seeing the ancient text – the one that I could never understand – and the way he would pass over certain verses, chapters, or completely miss a scroll. Now I know it was to avoid such difficult questions from myself around any sexual rendezvous, a head being sliced apart, some extravagant cursing not too dissimilar to that which you uttered earlier, or some ghostly inclusion. It seems *all* was accounted for in such writings.'

'As it should be,' Jesse grunted affirmation.

'But they changed. The older I became, he was more focused on the writings within the collection of a writer unknown. But I think I know, as well as you do, who the writer may well be?'

'Who, Getty?'

'The unknown? Almighty? I assume he's the one who visits me, as imposter, between a world of reality and a world he has recorded, that I call my dream world, and the in-between which he calls the ... umm, realm of ... oh, I cannot remember. Huh ... strange.' Getty shook his head slightly. 'Though the recording, if that what it is I'm witnessing in my dream, seems to alleviate the unknown the more I am read to, I wouldn't call it education as such, but more of an insight, a vision into all the probabilities playing out until a final one has to be where all is night, and thus the world of Inarrel, and potentially beyond, is in serious peril.'

'You okay?' Jesse asked as the boy took a deep breath. 'Much of what you speak is *probably* a truth, but who would know? I have met young boys and girls not unlike yourself. But they had never come to any conclusion other than they had been a cripple. And they had only ever been here. And ... they had never any recollection of meeting the "Almighty" as you put it. If that is what, or who, it may be.'

Jesse stood, relieving his arse of a comfort it did not

deserve, and his legs sighed to that effect.

He pulled off the remaining coverage of blanket, off the boy's legs, and spoke. 'So, this is where we begin. We are now at the beginning. Forget everything you knew or thought you knew of the scrolls behind that makeshift curtain. I don't give a shit that the scrolls seem to be aglow – changing what is written upon their meek surface—'

'They have become more solid since, less flimsy! The older I have become!'

'Yes, yes. That is because the past, present, future or whatever the fu— whatever is going on and in whatever fu—whatever realm! Is what it may be. Our goal is to get you moving, to enable you to achieve your full potential, and then maybe some answers will reveal themselves. Now, such a curious mind wouldn't mind telling me about that interaction with Arigal moments earlier? For I am sure to not let you leave this room before some sort of explanation for her shushing you before anyone had even uttered a word?'

The boy blushed. Jesse walked over to the scroll, one hastily deposited back into its pigeonhole and plucked it from its temporary perch. The glowing had subsided, but not fully, and it still held some heat.

Jesse opened the scroll fully, holding it high, as it spread a full span from his outstretched left hand to transcend across to his right.

'Oh. Oh, my. Oh she did … Oh, he did what?…. Did your father ever read this one to you?'

'No! Well, some of it … half of it, but then he always skips past heaps and on to the next one.'

'And you know what happened within this chapter? Without it ever being read to you?'

'No, I have no idea! Well, not all of it.' The boy turned his eyes away. 'But it's the only one missing, from a series of events I should never have known. You see my father will embellish over such sensitive, brutal, or morbid details. That one, I assume, contains many such within?'

'Then tell me, and be quick, the sudden appearance of a woman who made you blush your mighty little *donk* off, and the coincidental scroll being, or not being, unfurled fully as you say to be deposited back as quickly. How would you know? You seem to know who Arigal is, or was. But not who she is now known as, The Angel of—'

'Sincerity?'

'Correct. But how do you know that? How?'

'An assumption, the Almighty does offer inklings, even if it doesn't know it …' The boy chuckled once more, followed by a wracking wheeze from his chest.

Jesse asked, 'How about other such … interactions between man and woman?'

'Nah! Nothing. All up in here, filling the gaps as such.'

'Now, and I am assuming quite a fair bit of shit that will no doubt flow my way, we have to get ourselves away from here. And your father – or Papa – is to read no more to you. That will become my role. I have much to teach you, and I will select what is relevant to your progress. Including revelations have been left out, some you will never have heard within a tome that contains much more than these flimsy scrolls.'

'Who are you, Jesse?'

'Let's just say that I am the only one in this world that you would be in need of right now.'

He walked over to the window and looked absently outside. *Hope those bastards are gone!* He pulled the shutter down to where it had been earlier when the creatures had made their ascent up the hill.

Making his way back to the large, wooden bed, he spoke, 'Getty, I will ask you another question shortly, but I do not want you to answer it just yet. Mull it over in your head until I ask you it again, okay? Spend a few minutes each day pondering your response. A response I say, as there will be no correct answer—'

'Why ask it then?'

'Because I will do. And you will do as I say so long as you are in my care.'

'What did you and Mama agree to?'

'That I would assess you and make a call on whether you are able to be helped. Secondly, you have to be of those I seek out in this world. And thirdly, you must agree to it!'

'Papa will be devastated!'

'He would, if he was staying. However, I only said that your father was to stop reading to you. He embellishes too much, your mother hates it! She hates all of these writings, and understandably so.'

'Huh?'

'They are both coming with us. Well, they will travel with us, but we will be alone most of the time once we have reached any of our many intended destinations.

'Get some sleep, Getty. We have much to discuss tomorrow. I will also have to catch up with my old friends, see what they have been up to, at the very least, on their otherworldly travels.'

'The question?'

'Ah, yes! My question, for your response,' Jesse jumped onto the chair with much gusto, settling in again with a twist to find the grooves. 'The question … ready?'

The boy nodded slowly.

'The sky above us, and beyond, is infinite, is it not?'

He began to muster a response, but was shushed quickly by Jesse as he held his palm over his mouth.

*

'What were those things?!' asked Gretta.

It was Arigal who answered. 'They're the souls of those encapsulated into an eternal service to the darkness. Forever to be told they would be released once they had carried out the required biddings. Which never can happen, as you have just seen.'

'So what happens to them then when they get whipped away?'

'They just die. Eternally. They will never rise again. Anywhere! Ever again!'

'Oh, so they're dead, dead?'

'Yes, they are dead in all and every possible form.'

'Oh, that sounds horrible.'

'Yes, it truly is. Now, what is taking that crazy man so long up there?' Arigal asked rhetorically, clearly agitated.

'I have been trying to listen—'

'As have I,' the boy's father jumped in. 'Can't hear the darndest thing,' he finished whilst dropping the cup from his ear.

These had been the first words he had spoken since they had returned to the house.

He then asked, 'Is it really him? Will he help us or not, Gretta? Seems a bit of a strange fellow to me.'

'I believe he will. He seemed a bit unsure to begin with but the more he listened, the more he seemed to be drawn in. I may have acted a little … theatrically.'

'He will help you, the boy, or gods help him!' Dagda spoke.

Small chatter continued for a while. Introductions carried on. Even small snacks were offered – none were rejected. Eventually, a slow creaking of a door being opened drew their attention toward the top of the fine, ornate staircase.

Jesse backed away slowly as he closed the boy's door. He stood atop the staircase with a finger to his lips to quiet the small gathering that milled around not far beyond the bottom step.

He made his way down the wooden staircase, slowly testing each step for any further creak that may disturb the sleeping boy.

As he made it to the chequered, black and white marble tiles that welcomed the bottom step, they all heard a bang upstairs. The wall above the door shook. Then another bang. Another thud – the same outcome.

Jesse spoke, impressed. 'Boy's got strength. Look at that wall shaking there!'

Not so soon after, on the sixth attempt, the shutter upstairs broke into a mess, landing outside near the front door. All rushed outside, only to see the heels of the boy disappear through the trees and into the woods.

'Shit, Gretta!' Jesse said, surprise in his voice. 'You were not exaggerating. He really can move and, *boy*, can he move!' He smiled and casually walked into the kitchen to follow the scent of the pastries, hoping they had indeed left a few behind for him.

He was in luck.

# Ethereal

Gurengal jumped up from his bed, startled, narrowly missing the low hanging wooden beam with his forehead. His quick reflex stopped his nose a hair's width from hitting the thick timber holding up the pitched roof he slept under.

He sat back down on the bed and rubbed the back of his head briskly. *Real?* he thought. *So vivid.*

He'd been tracking a small animal in a dream, of a kind he had never seen, though it resembled a rabbit. *So it must taste good,* he had thought. The trail he was following led him to a large opening that split a high, vertical rock face.

The fox now stopped, knowing it was being followed. *But was it not moments ago a ...?* It turned to look at the hunter, held his gaze for a few moments, then bowed its head, low. Its front legs arched backward to the ground. It then turned and bounded through the crevasse that had appeared as if from nowhere.

Gurengal followed. Though now he did not step anymore but drifted above the grassed terrain below. He looked down to observe the blades of greenery that brushed past his tanned leather boots.

*A dream,* he said to himself. As soon as the notion escaped his mind, he dropped with a soft thud to now find purchase on the soft ground with the souls of his feet. *Better.*

He made his way slowly toward the opening in the rock that had recently presented itself where the rabbit-fox had departed. No sign of it. *Why was I chasing it anyway?*

'You were not. It was leading you. Leading you here to me.' A voice, akin to that of an old frail woman, broken in parts, but its intent was clear, meant for him. 'I summoned you. I have a request for your service. For you seem to have piqued an interest from beyond. I speak with you here as my energy dwindles so. So much I must reserve what little is left for the waking world, for one final message, before I depart this realm, and many others, for good.'

Gurengal spoke. 'Morla … I presume?'

'You know history, or at least the Edict of Time, Gurengal.'

'I know what I need to know. Now, why are you here? You would seem nothing more than just a figment of my own imagination, I presume. Though I feel a presence, *your* presence. A strong one, even though you claim the opposite.'

'That may be so here, but I assure you, I'm virtually done for. There is something at hand that has been steadily brewing up close to the rim for more than an age. And I need you to have a hand in the future of Inarrel, and all it contains.'

Gurengal stepped forward, moving deeper into the darkness.

'Stop! For would you crush me, you big oaf!'

He immediately halted the advance into the bleak nothingness, and looked down to where the voice had startled him.

Curiously, he raised an eyebrow. 'You were being serious. But honestly, surely you could have presented as someone to stand much taller than my knee.'

Stood a short way from where Gurengal had stopped stood the old woman. As Gurengal had said, she was no taller than his knee, changed from the rabbit and fox he had seen earlier. The ratio of arm and leg to body was well within the normal proportion, though, which made the image seem odder than it should.

'Does that bother you, big man?'

'No. Not at all. Here, let me sit. Get down to at least see eye-to-eye. I'm interested in what you have come to me for …' He crouched down to sit on his backside and crossed his legs. As he did, so too did Morla, mirroring his movement.

Gurengal raised both eyebrows and shrugged his shoulders as he looked down at her once again. 'Ah, well … Morla, I think I know why you're here. And as I have told those who have come to me before you, I am not this hero you all seem to think I may be, or could become.'

Morla laughed. 'Those cretins I once knew have sought you out already? You of all people. Do not get ahead of yourself. Though you have a good heart, you are not the hero here. No, the songs played over time will not be sung to honour you or your passing, nor will any tome or scroll be etched for you in history as anything worthy of even the smallest respect of mention. No.'

'Good! That's how I want it. Just want to live out my life here and with enough coin to see me by. And then … maybe … one day, a family '

'Bah! Such vanity.' Morla stood back up and pointed a finger. 'That can be arranged. But know this, the king's daughter is in the crosshairs of this darkness. Necessity puts it so, for she is the one marked.'

'Oh. I see. King Benjamin's girl?' Gurengal nodded his head, showing genuine concern. However he was reinforming himself of that knowledge attained from one of the Syltenerian scum – information given by the man under some considerable duress.

'Yes, the very same.' Morla eyed him cautiously as to how he knew instantly who she was referring to, saving her the punch. 'She needs all the help she can get.'

'And how am I to help?'

'Really? We are going to go through this?' She sat back down. 'A man of your—'

'Yes, yeah, I know where it is.'

'As do I. But as I have told you, I am not long for this world. You must use it to find one of the keys.'

'What? It's just an old scroll. One that I was paid quite

handsomely to locate, retrieve, and hide away 'til a day not unlike today, hey?'

'Again, really?' She shook her head. 'You know damn well what it is. It is one of the Scrolls of—'

'—Vilenzia? Yes, yes I know. Tell a truth, thought it would have been a bit bigger, heavier, glowing or something like that.'

'Do you remember where you hid it?'

'Yes. And I'm sure you would remind me even if I didn't.'

'No … No, I have no idea. Now, this is urgent, we believe the darkness is using this whole assault as a ruse, a false pretence to make us believe they are assembling their move. You must retrieve the scroll immediately and do as it says!'

'Ruse to what exactly?'

'To gain access to the hidden artifacts. The ones the scrolls will eventually lead you to. The ultimate defence: only the one marked can enact. You must use the scroll, find the key, then the associated artifact. And then you must join up with the assembled group with it. Time is critical. Lucky for you, the rendezvous point is close by. I do believe *Salino's Pewter* is also.'

'Salino's what? Compensation for such a task? And why would we give in to their ruse then? Let's just sit tight!'

'Complete this task, you must! We have our reasons. Lead the king's daughter through all adversity—'

'There's more?'

'Do this and you will die a happy man. And so too, when you do succumb, you will leave a well-to-do family behind …'

'Rendezvous point?'

'Quinnbo Vale.' She held up her hands as if apologising.

'Oh … '

'Oh, indeed.' She dropped her hands.

Gurengal pulled out the thin, cylindrical tube from under his makeshift bed.

*Hmmm, wonder what shit I'm getting myself into now!* The thought held tight as he struggled to unscrew the cap, as if his mind was forcing him to stop.

Before he could slide out the contents of the tube, the shackled body sat in the corner of the loft started to stir. It shuffled slightly and moved its head up from a slumped pose.

Still holding the tube, Gurengal walked over to the pastel, greyed form that melded itself into the plastered wall that held the weight of its back.

'You are going to tell me what is going on, more than I have drawn out already, or I will rip those fucking nodes off your head with my own teeth.'

The pecbor just smiled in its own way, cheeks held up high. Not so much of a mouthy smile but Gurengal knew his words and demeanour amused the being.

Gurengal only grumbled and turned away, knowing he would be wasting his time even if he did bite the fucker's enlarged nodes off – the very thought of it made him shudder and want to gag.

*Would taste like shite anyway.*

Somendel raised his eyes to look at Gurengal. 'I see you hold something there.'

He turned back. 'You are correct. Do you know what is contained within?'

'No idea. Should I?'

'No … No, you definitely should not.'

The pecbor's eyes dropped back to the floorboards. 'You may as well just finish me off for I will not be welcomed back. Not after the humiliation of being defeated by such … commoners.'

'Hmmph. You think me and my men be mere

commoners? More fool you, I say. And too, more fool anyone, or anything, that assumes along those same lines.'

Gurengal crouched down, looking deep into both of the grey man's eyes, hovering at the same level. 'Worm, I have no need for you. Where you will end up eventually, that is a place I would fear. They will extract all of those dirty little secrets you hold inside, from within that corrupted mind of yours, and I wager they will make you pay for every shitty thing you have done, no matter how slight. Over and over the ancient ones, or those at the city, or whoever, will punish you. You may break and tell them all you know, and I hope you do; for all you know will be used against those you once called friends.'

'Bah! Friends! And that is the most I have heard you say without taking a breath since I met you. You feeling, okay big man? Friends!' A cackling wheeze escaped Somendel. 'We have no friends; friends are for the weak. We only have opportunities. The easiest way to ascend relies on our ability to refrain from the very thought of *friends*.'

'Well. You will find none here, nor where you'll end up.'

Somendel raised his eyes once more. This time they shone with realisation; something must have clicked as Gurengal had been speaking.

'You … you're not heading to the city!'

Gurengal slowly shook his head.

'Hah!' The grey man brimmed with devilish delight. 'You delay? I wonder why? Ahh, I see now.' A smile that was not returned gave him a clue as he took his gaze away from Gurengal and focused them on the tatty tube he held.

Without saying another word, the pecbor leant the full length of its back on the crumbled plaster wall and closed his eyes to conclude the latest interaction between the two. Clearly to agitate Gurengal.

Gurengal was wise to the bait. He turned around and walked back towards the bed. He took a look behind him at the pecbor, its eyes still closed, enjoyment still hovering about its face.

He shuddered.

*I guess I could just swipe its head off!* He smiled, before thinking again how much the man was worth in the right hands.

He took out, and unfurled, one of the ancient scrolls. It seemed much heavier than the last time he had held it.

*I wonder how Morla would react if she ever knew where I kept such a treasure,* he wondered as he kicked the large travel sack back under the bed.

*Well, well,* Gurengal smiled with satisfaction as he scanned the illustrative instructions, *seems as though I have already eliminated the threat. Now I just need to find a way to get in there and hope it be the only one that resides up there!*

*

Velosko stood beneath a marble archway, the one that lead back to their assigned chambers. He listened sporadically as Marcos and Jentis argued over something. Intermittently, when the wind dropped, he could somewhat piece together what they were saying.

*Probably in disagreement over what that old woman, the wraith called Morla, asked us to do last night. Huh, last night, if it can be called that this time of year.*

She had appeared not long after the scuffle on the pier, once all hell had been calmed. The music, she had said, brought about a light that shone brighter than the sun itself, piercing through this realm and rippling through into the next, and, undoubtedly, beyond even that.

Velosko decided to approach the pair before it came to more than just words. He knew though, heated as it was, the pair were as close as brothers.

They did not miss his approach, nor the form of Amaria who suddenly appeared to stand exactly where Velosko had been stood.

Both turned to accept the approach of the man. They were still in awe – after all this time – at how well he operated in the world of the unseen.

Marcos spoke. 'Apologies, Vel. We were just at odds as to how we follow those instructions the lady thing … err … Morla gave us.' He looked about as if waiting for a curse to be struck upon his soul.

'No need, Marcos. I understand.' He shook his head

Morla had advised them they were to seek out a man by the name of Oberek, who resided in the Hills of Drauch, a few days ride from the city, to the north-west. By *they* she had explained it was to be only Marcos and Velosko.

Amaria and Jentis were required to remain in the city to thwart any counter threat posed by those who would follow up on the onslaught from the night before.

Jentis spoke, fear making his voice tremble. 'We cannot leave you alone out there in those hills, Velo.' Jentis raised both hands, one padded with a great amount of bandage, to chest height and beat them, gesticulating wildly like a wild *babanol* – the wild and ferocious animal that roamed the very same wooded hills. 'I won't! I will not! I must be there! With you, Velo!'

'Easy, Jentis. She spoke true. There is a danger in the air still. Much more to come, I assume. We must go, as she advised. You and Amaria must remain here for the good of these people. The events of yesterday still linger as a shock to all. Having yourself and Amaria remain will give them confidence to strike back this time. I don't believe the bebockle will return, but who knows what she will return with next time …' Velosko, reached out to touch the padded hand of Jentis. 'You need to rest, let that heal also. It will only fester if you are out and about in the moist, swampy playground of muck anyway!'

'I haven't left your—'

'I know. I know, Jentis. And for that I am forever grateful. I assure you we will be back way before long—'

'But it's dark still out there.' Jentis offered whatever he could to dissuade him.

Velosko sighed, a sigh to ease Jentis. 'It is always dark out there for me, my friend.'

'Maybe Jentis has a point, Vel,' Marcos added.

He glanced quickly past Velosko, to where Amaria stood. 'He is much more equipped than I to protect you. Hell, I don't even know why it is you who is going in the first place.'

'We made that quite clear to the old lady, Marcos. She was also quite clear that only I will be able to find whatever we are looking for. Ha! Looking for … And, she also made it quite clear that you were to be there to watch my back … Quite clear, as she swatted your complaints away with a screaming burst of anger that made you cower like a little—'

'Yes, yes, Vel.' Marcos again glanced past Velosko. 'But Jentis is a seasoned fighter, one of the Third Pillar, Vel.'

'No. Marcos, I need you to do this. As was told'

Marcos held himself for a while before all air escaped his lungs with a big sigh – acceptance of an immediate fate. He looked past Velosko again, slightly shaking his head.

Amaria dropped her eyes and drifted away from the scene, from the unlit archway, into the bleak darkness so stealthily that even the *magnificent* Velosko didn't detect she was ever there.

\*

Miss Nomellia was the first to spot the old woman again. This time, she appeared much more solid than up in the glades of Caliopa. *Probably the surreal darkness down here!*

Ebby Jink was the next to spot her. He froze for a second before he looked to Missy, face like freshly painted plaster.

Semoni was the last to spot the hovering form in the

middle of the dark tunnel, though he was the first to speak. 'Missy, Jink, is that her again?'

The ghostly form rushed at him, quickly, rather too dramatically. 'Hush, child,' she spoke in a ghastly tone once more, 'time is short. You took your merry time!'

Missy screwed up her face. 'Well, it was you who told us to wait for them.'

This drew a stare from Morla that would almost have scared the darkness away from the dark.

She then moved over to Miss Nomellia. 'You, child. You must come speak with me … alone, away from prying eyes, and quickly for things have progressed quite so …' She looked at the two others with suspicion in her dark eyes. 'We have not much time. Walk with me a short while.'

Missy shook her head and followed close behind the floating apparition, almost disbelieving the whole episode again, once more.

Though no fear shone in her eyes – as they reflected the minimal, sporadic, candlelight flickering throughout the carved-out tunnel – Semoni was sure she was afraid, not of the sudden appearance of the woman but of what the woman was about to say. As was he …

Ebby Jink spoke to him. 'See here, young lad. Something be afoot here.'

'You don't say, Ebby.'

Travelling further behind, just far enough to keep sight of them, Kost and Shanlar noticed that the small party they had been following since Caliopa had abruptly halted.

They moved quickly to catch up and investigate the sudden stoppage.

By the time they reached Semoni and Ebby, Miss Nomellia had disappeared way ahead, into a darkness tinged with a waft of smoke as the candle lit lanterns had suddenly been extinguished.

Semoni turned as they approached, and spoke, a bit of a falter about his voice. 'Master, she appeared again!'

'And we missed her ... again. How convenient.' Kost shook his head with a few short, sharp sways. 'Ebeno? Was he here again also?'

'No. Just her,' spoke Ebby.

A voice came from deep in the darkness, coming closer as it spoke; a familiar voice. 'I am here. Give me a moment to make my way there ... all of you stay.'

Ebby began to make a move towards the figure now emerging from the smoke.

'Stay there, I said. Dammit, boy, listen!'

There was an unceremoniously long pause, accompanied by a silence that was only punctured by a slow tempo of a clicking on stone as the pre-proprietor of Jink's Rooms made his way to where the four waited.

Ebeno winced with every slow step, as he held his weight on a crooked stick. It clicked on at least twenty stones before he reached them, which took the surprise out of the air – replaced with comedic silence between each click.

'Good to see you, old pal,' Shanlar patted the short, older man on the shoulder.

'Good to see you also, Shanlar,' the old eberactu barkeep tapped Shanlar in the groin with his stick and wheezed out a broken laugh. 'Still can't find it ...'

Shanlar doubled over in pain but was unperturbed by the bait. 'Should have tapped my knee then ... old man.' They all laughed.

*

The laughter and chatter amongst reunited friends was broken by a shout from the darkness.

'Help!'

*Sounds like Missy,* Semoni thought, knew.

Another shout. 'Help! I cannot see ... a fucking thing!'

*Confirmed.*

All but one of the party raced toward the distressed call. The one that remained spent the time to relight the still smoking lanterns.

'She's gone,' whispered Miss Nomellia as the party approached, 'she gave me an insight of what is to come. Gave me an instruction that only I must see to. Then just … vanished!' She shook her head while looking down at her feet. 'I'm not sure I can do this. It is all too much for me to be able to comprehend, let alone fulfil!'

'What did she say?' asked Semoni, impatiently.

It was Eboni who answered, coming from far behind, the clicking a little more erratic as he tried to keep pace. 'She cannot reveal that.' He clicked his stick to the stone a couple more times. The action scattered a few of the vermin that hung around the edges of the darkness, also shooing away any potentially prying ears. 'But, I will tell you this: not far from here is an opening. One that opens into a smaller tunnel, one not of *our* carvings. It was happened upon while we were excavating these *worm* holes. It has been guarded ever since we discovered it.'

'Guarded by whom?' asked Shanlar.

'Not whom, but what … you see, the visitor above, the one eviscerating the grotto, the one from the pass, we believe its partner is the one who is holding fort – and has been for many years.'

'That is such a long time! This whole time?' asked Semoni 'Poor creature.' She finished with a genuine bout of empathy.

Eboni paid no mind to such. 'Young Semoni, who knows why? Why did it take so long to come looking?'

'Errm, because it's stuck down here, in a hole that is in a larger hole maybe?'

'No child, maybe time to them is but a fraction of what we see as such? Maybe? I don't know t' tell truth …'

'Nah,' Semoni found his voice, 'I'm going with the

following: it has been all over the place, all over the world, looking for its mate and it finally got a scent after all these years looking—'

'Maybe,' jumped in Ebby, 'and it's mad.'

'Oh shut up, the lot of you. These creatures live for an exceedingly long time. A long time! Believe me, I have been party to some serious chatter and information over the past few years. The one that has taken up residence down here came as soon as we broke the seal to the entrance to that secondary tunnel.' He again tapped the stones, harder this time, then lowered his voice. 'She appeared through the tunnel behind, so I have been told, screeching now and again.'

'So … What *is* beyond?' asked Semoni.

'Yes, what is beyond the tunnel, past this so-called mythical guardian?' Kost asked, curious.

'That is … unknown. Only Miss Nomellia may pass. And only Missy may know why. Of this I am sure Morla spoke?' He nodded to Missy.

She nodded back. Then spoke after a long pause. 'One thing I can tell you, I need that scroll. I need to present it to pass, then on to where I need to be.'

'And where is this entrance?' Shanlar asked.

Eboni pointed his stick down the dark tunnel. 'Half a decent walk from here.'

'And what are we supposed to do?' Semoni was starting to get agitated at the whole situation. 'Just let her go down that hole on her own? Stuff that! I'm going with her!'

Miss Nomellia looked at Semoni, face pale, replicating the same pasty glow of the ghostly figure of Morla and his not too long ago. 'No you're pissin' not!' Again, she shook her head. 'No, Sem, I must go alone. Morla spoke of much in such a small amount of time. But one thing she made clear, even though *she* was unsure what lay beyond, was that I must venture into that tunnel, and whatever lies beyond, alone, and record the messages when they were presented.' She gulped a large breath of air, swallowing down any tears from the uprising fear, which made her cough a strange sound.

'She gave me one more instruction. You are to continue on. Find the other – its other half that be prancing around the glades above – and make a connection. For ... or so I was told, once I return, *when* I return, the tunnel will be closed! Sealed forever.'

'How is this relevant to its mate? Can't you just bring the creature back with you?' asked Kost.

'There is more. She believes the entrance to—'

Eboni tapped his stick violently a few times to abruptly interrupt her words. 'Child! No more! Those reasons, and such information, are yours alone. We must move quickly. You lot will come with me. There is another glade close by, one only known to the eberactu and no others'—he pointed down the dark tunnel, lanterns yet to be lit—'the outward tunnel, not too far past where we must leave Missy. One where our *maar elde* have deemed it necessary to congregate. For they all foresaw the subtle shade and shadow encapsulate the Famnagira within a seemingly shared dream.

'This glade we will venture to, the one where the *other* mythical creature has taken residence, is also the closest opening out to the above world to where its beloved could potentially be scented from. Hence the need for such an undesirable congregation. I may also point out, it is the birthplace of the eberactu, not to mention the Famnagira herself, so it is believed. Thus written.'

They all looked at each other. Missy smiling at Eboni. Ebby smiling at Eboni. Semoni glum as he gazed at her. Kost and Shanlar looking at each other, shaking their heads in disbelief.

Kost eventually broke the mood. 'Let's be off then. Semoni: pick your chin up and get to what you were sent here to do.' He walked over to Missy and hugged her tight. He whispered, not so quietly – just enough to be heard by her alone – 'Be careful.' Then, without anyone noticing, he slipped her a sharp piece of metal, no bigger than the size of his palm.

She felt the cold from the slip of the metal touch hers. Instantly after she felt the cool blade, she heard another whisper from Kost

'Hold this, and say these three words twice, *"vela en actinia"*, and I will know if you are in need of aid—'

That was all he managed to say as the onrushing remainder of the party came in for their piece of Missy, to offer words of their own – if even inadequate.

First in, to wrestle Missy out of the others' way, was Eboni. Unsurprisingly to all there, not a single click of staff to stone was heard as he made his way swiftly over. He was eventually followed by Ebby.

Semoni, though, held himself back, still glum.

Missy, too, was feeling a little glum. Not at the coming predicament she had been left to bear, but instead for how much she would miss the shy pecborian's slight glances in her direction, the soft, unforced touch around her – be it a swishing *accidental* connecting of a hand, or just a brush from his muscular broad shoulder slightly against hers. *Fucking hell. What am I in for? Why me?!*

She gave all comfort with words of false encouragement before making her way to Semoni where she let her head fall into his chest. The warmth and the power his arms supplied as they were wrapped, protectively around her, she would remember forever, no matter the outcome nor how long that may hold.

As she was released from his solid and meaningful embrace, she felt all that power slip away. So she kissed him … tight, with purpose. A kiss *he* could always remember her by. She knew nothing of love, nothing of the sort. But she knew Semoni. She knew he loved her. *I must return to see where this will lead!* She had had fleeting lovers in the past, all with much more verve and vigour, but ultimately, that had always led to the same finale, away from the one that ultimately mattered.

Semoni was different, he was not the cocky forward type she had always been attracted to – or rather, she attracted. He was different. *Maybe that is all?* she thought. *No! He is a better man than all of those slugs, every . . . single . . . one of them! He is my Semoni.* She pulled away, slowly. Away from the stunned face she had planted her lips onto. *He hides behind himself. He hides behind what he is perceived as to be. No more the boy! Yes, he is more … more than all of those bastards combined. And I will bring out the best in him. He … the boy! No! The best person, the best man, I have ever known!*

She turned away from the group, hiding a tear or two of her own, and many more that flowed freely as she strode away.

Without looking back, she spoke a few words as she held up a hand and pointed toward where she was headed. 'See you all again, really soon! That's my only promise!'

*

Arigal looked to the man she had known from many, many years prior to his sudden *interaction* in her new life.

Shackled to a wall that filled the small space between floor and soffit – no higher than a man could stand – his head was slumped. Above him, where his head rested, twisted against the wall, a barred opening offered little to no light. Only the sound of the creatures that had remained in the woodland beyond the small clearing around their hideout could be heard.

He stirred a little, as if sensing he was being observed.

Arigal held onto the cold steel bars that separated the two. *What did you tell them of us?* She thought. More so, she worried.

The man stirred a little more and twisted his swollen face. Just enough to show an upward movement of cheek. Enough to communicate as best he could. *I know you're there.* He let the smirk drop.

Arigal let go of the bars and turned to walk away.

As she walked away, she left eyes on the man in the makeshift cell and bumped her head into the chest of Bareleno who had just arrived, covertly with bare feet.

He apologised for the unintended collision and held a comforting arm around her. One flicked unceremoniously away.

A small silence hung in the air before he spoke again. 'How did he do that? Make himself … me? That's some talent there! Will I get to learn that one day!'

The man in the dank cell tried to raise a hand, and succeeded. Then he tried to raise a finger, to show he had heard, but fell short of raising it high enough before it slumped to graze the floor.

She backed away from Bareleno and looked at him, intently, for longer than a moment, measuring the cruelness in his soul. She eventually barged past, shaking her head, muttering a violent comment under her breath.

Bareleno looked at the incarcerated man. He felt a small amount of pity. For what, though? He was unsure.

Mesfa shook her head at Arigal. 'What in this world, or any, for the sake of madness, were you thinking?'

'I wasn't!' Arigal held a finger to her lips, which prompted Mesfa to cast a small spell of concealment, one she herself could never quite fulfil.

Mesfa spoke into clasped hands, then opened them up as if throwing a songbird into the air. She then nodded.

'I had no idea it was him!'

'Oh, come on, Arigal! Don't lie to me … you horny, little wench,' she laughed and punched Arigal in the shoulder. 'I knew it was him as soon as I got near him. He stinks. Reeks of the same shit he always used to.'

'Oh, I had an inkling that was because—but I was beginning to think of Bareleno, and he just appeared as he. I thought it strange. There was something about his eyes that were different, but also something remarkably familiar.' She rubbed the back of her head. 'But did you have to … did you have to hit me so hard?'

'Yes, for your own good! Absolutely I did, and I took little, if any, enjoyment in it, before you could say anything stupid, something that you knew the man behind you who was Thu—ewww! No! No … not going there!' She scrunched her eyes with distaste.

Still rubbing her head, Arigal asked sheepishly, 'Does she know?'

'No, she still thinks you thought it was our newfound, other horny, little friend.' She bit her lip which drew a sigh from Arigal. 'But … if he starts talking, you're in deep shit. Which then means I will be in a whole heap of shit, too. So … what are you going to do?'

'Nothing! I cannot! He will not flush me out, of that I'm sure. He said, though, he has been searching for me for a while, in all manner of place—'

'Well then, I will do it for you. I never liked the creep! And where has he been all these years? And why is he only showing his crusted face now?'

'That … is what I need to find out.'

'Not a chance, that isn't happening. Far too risky, we should just snuff him out now.'

'He won't talk, Mesfa. He won't!' Arigal pleaded with her sister.

'That I'm sure of. Sure, that they are his intentions, to remain silent. But, as you know, there are ways of persuasion to make someone talk. Inflicted by those devoted to *our Lady* … as we have done so before. We have had these subtle conversations before, Arigal. You must decide if you are fully committed to what we have worked so hard for. For I *will* only carry you so far—'

'Huh, you? Carrying me? I remember a few years ago when you almost lost your head over the Cliffs of Dagmoraan—'

'But—' Mesfa tried to butt in but was cut off.

'Do you also remember? That snake from The Shadow of the Path? The one who had you wrapped up in all sorts, let you reveal all before he tried to pierce you – with more than his fancy black-as-night blade – through your black heart? Yes … I'm sure you do. And, I'm sure you remember who was there to save your pimpled skin.

'So don't go tellin' me you're carrying me, or have my interest at heart. You are only doing this for yourself. Caring nothing for what happens during the next episode. For fuck's sake Mesfa, were you not listening up there, or ever when they told us: there will only be one of us ascending up to the next rung of that long, dark, and lonely ladder?!'

'Hush, you stupid bitch! I can contain a whisper, but not you shouting your mouth off! Now listen, before I bang your head to sense once more!'

Arigal came in close, close enough for Mesfa to whisper in her ear. 'There is a way forward, for both of us—'

'Ther—' Arigal tried to get a word in.

'But! You must want it. I cannot keep you from perishing any longer. Not with your constant doubt to the cause. Though I know what lies beyond for me, I am one hundred percent committed to … well … not perishing! And half as much not seeing you gone.'

'How? How do we both elevate then?'

'We must sort out that bitch, whatever her name is. Same as the demons, we take what is hers. As ours. We take her power! Survival of the strongest, for a greater power, I have heard it called, but I prefer my own adage: "King Dingaling plays on the swing!" and … I want what she is swinging around on up there! So then, soon, a slot will open up in their eyes, and who better to fill that than I – the one who bested the slutty bitch. And … you can stay on this steady path upward; along the fine line you have been treading for so long …'

Arigal looked vacantly, pondering for a while before responding. 'Very well. But I will not let you slay Thule. I must at least find out why he is here … of all places, after so long. We have to get him out of here!'

'I will not help you, Arigal. Though I will not try stop you either. And I will not help you if you are caught in whatever mess you end yourself up in. I will not hesitate to take his head to keep you safe … understood? Or, if he undermines anything that I have achieved thus far!'

With that done, Mesfa clapped her hands.

The not-so-distant noise of the woodland returned to fill Arigal's ears. Alarmingly so.

Mesfa spun on a heel. Leaving her to ponder what she would do next.

Arigal again pondered. Longer than she needed to. Longer than she felt necessary – but she pondered anyway, weighing up all scenarios presented, just to be sure. She then walked toward the door on the opposite side of the room Mesfa had exited. She was now *fully* sure, and fully committed to her next move. Be what may.

# Flashpoint

King Benjamin winced, stoically, as he ascended the hundreds of steps that followed the spiralling staircase back up to the courtyard. The pain throbbing above his wrist grew stronger and stronger – so much so, that it had started to pain his elbow and parts of his arm higher so. How much more would it affect him before he would succumb? He knew he would not.

*So long as I feel this pain, my darling Grehn, it be such a glorious feeling, for I will know my little girl is still with us!*

Grehn walked through the tunnels deep beneath what had always been her home. Her grandmother, Mother Ursen, walked just in front, holding aloft an artificial orb of blue light to guide the way, and also to deter any animal that fancied a welcome snack. The tunnels were so deep, the channel above seeped through miniscule cracks to drop salty fluid onto the pair; the dripping slowly faded and eventually ceased the further along they ventured.

Twenty paces in front of them, Kimo walked, alert for any hidden danger. He did not walk a straight path, but zigzagged to every crevasse, every pothole, sticking the long blade he held into each and all.

Not too far behind the women followed the large hulking form of Sentok. He had been drafted in to help carry Grehn's minimal belongings – Mother Ursen's would follow through, and out of the city, to a select location beyond the city's walls. Sentok too, looked around at every angle, walking backwards for the majority of the time, nervous, awaiting a hidden onslaught of ill intent.

None came. Be it that any threat was distinguished before it could appear through Kimo's inquisitive blade, or there was just no threat there in the first place. Still, caution was the better option than optimism. They continued on at a slow pace.

Their goal was to reach a thick, well armoured hatch that would open up beyond the main gate of the city. A heavy opening only accessible, or operable, from the inside. The alcove beyond that non-descript door opened up into a large clearing of rolling greenery – not that it would reveal such splendour during such a darkness.

*

Kimo had been instructed by his brother, His Majesty, to firstly seek out Sentok. Then to gather up some immediate supplies and then meet them deep down at the *Efflame*.

Ben had been reluctant to remain behind, but Kimo reassured him that the king must remain in Jacobs Well, for there was change afoot, and the people needed their leader to guide them through whatever was to come their way – no matter for how long that could be. Kimo also gave him absolute confidence that his daughter would be safe, vowing to never leave her side.

Ben knew there was no one more dedicated and well equipped to ensure her safe return. For if she did not return, neither would her uncle; for they would have both been captured or, worse, extinguished – Kimo undoubtedly first.

They were not far away from their destination when a rumble from above sent small rocks and worn timbers to crash down behind them, cutting off their only way back.

Kimo assessed the distance they had travelled thus far, and surmised they had just passed underneath the main gate and were only a short walk away up the steep incline to their intermediate location before their immediate goal of escaping the city. What he had no idea of, though – something that he had always struggled to deal with – was what was causing such commotion high above them.

'We halt at the exit until a calm has ensued.'

There was to be one other who'd make the journey, out beyond with those traversing the hollows below.

He'd been asked to travel above to where they would converge outside of the city and had grumbled at the thought of not celebrating with the many others at the supposed culmination of the Festival … if even it would happen at all. Though he understood the urgency, and such regard to what was upon them, he still felt a little off. And from what he had seen during the few days prior, he was a tad relieved – even if he wouldn't admit it – to be leaving such a pressure cooker of evil, one brewing all about the city. He could feel it, bubbling away beneath the surface.

And he'd been asked by the demigods to look after the girl, protect her, be a reliable, strong ally when all else would seem nothing but absolute peril.

Peron rode the mare hard, one gifted from the royal stable, a fine specimen, from a well blooded stock too, he assumed, for she reacted instantaneously to his every command, even countering any obstacle without, avoiding any need for instruction more often than not.

Looking at all the faces that gazed in his direction as he rode fast over the Masked Arches, and into the main town, then through the cobbled streets, he sensed their seeming, and understandable, fear, no doubt from the evil scene playing about high above the city.

The mustardy tinge of flamework dispersed high and wide from within the castle walls now covered the entire city. To stare hungrily down at them all below with an unknown intent.

Of maleficence, he presumed they assumed as they made signs of all kinds in front of their faces.

There were moments during his flight through the city – a flight indeed, at times he seemed to drift over the hard cobblestones – where he felt shadowy figures would almost reveal themselves, to dance about atop the slated rooves. *I hope Morla, though so decrepit, still has enough spirit left in her to help fight off the inevitable onslaught of darkness.* He sat back into the finely appointed saddle, to hold in a panic that threatened to disperse from his bowels about the mare and the street below.

He saw it late. Though not too late to react.

As he raced toward the main gate, the soldiers stationed there were hastily trying to close it. He wondered why, as the instructions were to keep it open until the messenger with the bright pink helm riding the famous mount *Windfell reached them* – there was only one person in the city wearing a bright pink helm atop such a magnificent beast.

*So why?*

That reason was suddenly offered. As the guards ran away from the portcullis, fast, even more hastily once it had closed fully, slamming down to the floor below, two long, bat-like wings flapped on either side of a bulbous body – a torso easily the size of one of the modest houses he had raced past.

It erupted quickly from behind the main gate and landed heavily on its four feet in the main courtyard between where the mare had reared and where he needed to go through.

The large creature snarled at him and clawed cobbles viciously from the square, flinging them far behind and over the city wall, some damaging the timber of the thick wooden gate, only to rebound away over some distance. Some broke through the large planks to create an opening if any would be brave enough to venture between.

It was a creature he had never seen before, but he had read plenty of text to know that what crouched, ready, before him was a *great languim*. They had not been observed for centuries, at least not in any way to mark parch about – for such observations would have been met with quick digestion by the creature.

He had a quick glance around before he made his next move – one he had not yet pondered. As he did, dark shapes, those he had thought to have seen, relieved the rooves of their miniscule weight.

The black creatures approached from all sides, towards he and his mare. The soldiers running away, now behind him, were immediately swooped upon and devoured with an almost audible glee as the dark creatures hissed and howled.

As they approached, the creature standing in front of them batted its large wings to create a large draft, causing Peron to shield his eyes and his mare to turn, shying away. The motion was intended as a warning, as it sent all the shadowy figures scurrying back to where they had previously perched. It seemed to know its prey and not another thing, no matter what, would become between it and its supposed prize.

*Why? They portray themselves as being docile and quick to act, but, this thing here seems to be waiting … Waiting for something, or someone. And that is worrying me more than the bastard thing itself – or its massive, forked tongue cleaning its long pair of fangs, or its razor tipped talons.*

As soon as the thought had left his mind, he would be greeted with another answer for his thoughts.

The yellow clouds above began to swirl, faster and faster until they formed a spout, descending from the sky, down to where the creature crouched, *waiting.*

The great languim raised its head toward the sky. It then opened its massive jaws and accepted the funnel to enter.

Instantly, upon contact, the entire volume of cloud disappeared into the creature's mouth, clearing the sky above of all foul precipitation.

Peron looked at the daunting creature as it looked dauntingly at him. He was sure it gave him a wink – they eyeholes now full of the same colour as those clouds consumed – and a smile. He had no further time to wonder as the creature's eyes began to burn a brighter yellow in lieu of the soft mauve it originally held – the orbs of black in their centre now contracted to sharp slits, akin to an angry serpent on the hunt.

It was then that Peron knew what was required. He had to make it back to the Grouse. And, hopefully, that blessed, old witch would be able to help, or lend some aid.

There was no need.

A figure fell from the sky. A faded, tattered, red robe acted as a parachute. The billowing robe was punctured by two skinny toothpicks you could call legs – even skinnier than the staff the lump of a figure held as it descended. The plump figure landed directly in front of the creature.

The landing, however, had failed to cover the figure below its neckline, as the robe was caught over its head.

Before Peron, stood a bare bellied plump of a man with skinny bare legs, holding an ever-familiar staff.

The new occupant of the square rotated and adjusted its stance, to turn to him before righting the robe for its intended purpose with waving, stocky arms.

*Everos!*

'Everos, you old bastard!' shouted Peron.

The short, balding old friend of Peron and forever dweller of Seltero spoke with a widening smile, and a warmth filled the air around Peron. 'Good gods, boy! You have given me just cause to leave my home world once more. If it's not bloody *shadow wolves*, or some other delinquent creature, it's a bloody big rat looking bat the size of a large dwelling!'

A new, louder, hiss and howl could be heard behind Peron. Obviously, the figurine of Everos was well known by all the dark figures and was more than likely a high priority target – a much larger prize to be sought and cashed in for whatever rewards were given. He knew of not, nor did he wish to find out.

'Peron,' Everos spoke, if a little too jovially, considering the sandwich of shit they were in, and they were indeed the stuffing of said! 'Good to see you again, boy. Seems we have a bit of trouble on our hands?'

The creature struck out at Everos, trying to devour him from above with a sharp snap and a sudden extension of its stubby neck.

Everos shook his head as he sensed the movement. He raised the wooden staff above his head and held it horizontally. It seemed to extend outward at both ends to instantly fill the entire width of the creature's maw about to swallow him whole.

The creature snapped back quickly to retake its original stance.

It then spoke, just about intelligible enough to be understood – if smoke held the ability to speak, it would sound as such. 'You fool, Everos! You think you can just come here, during the cusp of our reign of Inarrel and further afar! Hahah! Maggot, you do not have the resource to stop us this time!'

'And to whom may I respond?'

'It is I, the Lady,' the creature growled

'Horseshit, it is,' Everos jumped in, 'she'd not dare show her face down here, for she is the absolute epitome of cowardice, the ultimate coward!'

The creature struck again.

The same outcome ensued.

'You're nothing but a pawn. One of many such scattered amongst this cosmos and any other realm she would foul. Now, tell me who you are before I lay waste to this poor creature you would dare take advantage of!'

The creature snarled before it growled loudly.

It then spoke again, 'I know you would do no such thing! And … we know the Union's intentions! For such we have made contingencies for each and every outcome. We will rule Inarrel, your waste of a planet, and all of the known cosmos forever to come!'

'Hmmm,' Everos leant on his staff, 'did you know that we have our own weapon? Yes, we have a weapon to null anything you may throw our way! You, and all you serve to cause disruption, and that is all you do, no more than that. We all may be nothing more than a replica of a previous self from a previous time, but we know how all things end.' He wriggled his body as if imitating a maggot or a worm. 'Your lot squirming back into a self-dug hole of meekness and sadness, then that of nothing but the mud that will end up surrounding you.'

'Ha-hah, well put, old man! You do have balls! Not that I could see them on your way down,' the creature rasped, before it came in closer, close enough to whip the man with its tongue, so close he should be able to feel the warm breath emanating from sunken nostrils. 'But we have our own weapon this time: the ultimate weapon. One that has been brewed within the ranks of one of those so-called Pillars in that detestable city you so covet. So ... do me a favour, and just hide away, like you have done for so much of the many millennia passed by!'

'Impossible! And you know that I know you're lying. For a testing is carried out on every single potential student and, sporadically, during the time in the Union's care after their acceptance.'

'Well, Everos. Watch this space. For the one I speak of be not one of the students. And ... it is too late for you to sway any of the next sequence of events from their intended course. Now, where were we? Ah yes, I was all about ripping your grotesque head off old, sagged shoulders!'

The creature then reared up high in the air, unfurled its tattered wings, and spoke again.

'Shall we begin?'

Though creatures of the dark scared the life out of Everos, he was never once scared of what power he possessed, nor what that power could do to the dark creatures – when warranted. He also understood that some creatures were not of the dark and that their easily influenced docile way of thinking invited such darkness in – this being one of them.

That he hated even more.

For he would not use his power to smite the beast. So he, instead, made an offer to whoever was controlling it.

'Tell you what … get down from there, wherever you are, listen in, and you will no doubt agree to my request. One to swallow me whole! Swallow me whole and let the boy pass beyond. He is nothing on that bounty scale of yours. Let him pass and I will stand here, arms crossed and accept my fate. But you have to agree to only swallow me whole, no teeth, I'm not one to be shredded …'

'Why? And why in one?' the smoky rasp responded; intrigue still detectable.

'So that the beast may feel me pass fully through its tiny arse, ripping it apart once you have fulfilled your use of its shell. In hope you are still present in its pain as well as its thoughts.'

'Muwahah, a joker to the end. Very well.'

Peron was hovering around ten paces behind when Everos turned to Peron and ushered him to come closer.

He did.

Not close enough.

Everos ushered him to come even closer. Much more than the arm's length away he currently sat upon his mount, staring at the delighted beast with shock and no small amount of panic. Everos then jumped up and grabbed Peron's head and dragged him off the mount, whispering in his ear as they fell to the ground and a little beyond. 'Boy, you understand that thing is the puppet. Now, when it lets you pass, whoever is out there – most likely in eyesight of the great languim – will likely follow you and cut you down as soon as you are out of the gate. You need to trust and do exactly what I tell you next … to the letter. Understand?'

Peron nodded with hesitant affirmation as they both lay on the ground.

His face hidden from the beast as they lay on the ground, Everos spoke. 'Good. Now. When that thing there swallows me up, I will cast a spell from inside its guts, understand? And then you must quickly relocate to where it will look to. Run there as fast as you can and distract whoever it may be then—'

'You'll do nothing of the like, Everos!' a familiar voice shouted.

Lenjora appeared from the same street Peron had galloped through on the mighty mare.

'You will do no such thing!'

The shadows on the rooves slinked down onto the street below and began to encroach closer to her. Some formed a barrier between her and the man to whom she was shouting.

She hissed at them all. Spinning a full circle, to show her contempt for such foul creatures.

She then shouted again, this time not to Everos but to someone else. 'You see now, you see now why we do what we do? We need to eliminate these evil puppet masters before they do any more harm.'

Holtonos appeared stoically from the same street. He looked angry, a man on a mission.

He shouted back as he began to raise his arms, 'I have always seen the need to what we do, Lenjora! Now we will scatter these excuses of darkness across the cobbles for the most basic of lifeforms to feed from. That is if they have any substance of a soul left.'

Too late.

Everos turned around to face the great languim, and

shouted. 'Deal. Take it, quickly before I change my mind!'

The creature nodded – although no smile could appear on such a maw, someone, somewhere, was smiling in its own way.

He knew that for sure.

Peron hopped swiftly to remount his mare, just prior to Everos striking his staff into the mare's rump. She reared up so high that Peron was almost touching the cobbled stones with the back of his head before she set off at a great gallop toward the city gate.

'No! Noooo! Everos … stop!' he heard Lenjora cry as the creature flung its tail, scooping up, and then throwing large cobbles to knock down the wooden gate between him and freedom – it's end of the bargain – before opening its maw to envelope fully the awaiting, still prone, Everos.

Peron traversed through the cavernous opening, the only that lead out of the city, as the timber and steel debris rained over and all around the path they navigated.

He had one last look behind, seeing a bright ball of light appear from the staff as the creature swallowed the small man. The ball of light then travelled along the creature's throat and then into its midriff.

He then extended his glance around to espy the creature's master, or tormentor …

Nothing.

It all went dark. It all went as he had hoped, had prayed for. The great languim were written about as hasty eaters, eager to fill their stomach, unlike their lesser kind, the languim which preferred to first immobilise their prey by biting off the head then hide the rest of the carcass for a future, measured, feed.

It was also moist and Everos was quickly encapsulated in a thick mucus. His exposed skin immediately began to burn. *Best be quick, Everos. I suppose, though, I could add to the records of this observation, for I doubt anyone has ever been able to experience such a thing and still would be well enough to ... well, ever see the light of day again, or the night!*

He kept his eyes closed whilst humming a small tune which was just a vibrating thrum rather than any melodic sound – a sound as though he had been submersed in water. He grasped the staff he was holding, now with both hands and hummed a little louder. The end of the staff was now aglow with a bright yellow orb. Though he could not see the light directly itself, the brightness let itself be known all about his hidden vision as it shone through thin, aged, eyelids.

Almost instantaneously, he felt his head being sucked up into the creature's gullet and flipped upside down as the great languim raised its head to aid the next step of consumption. Now his whole body was being squeezed as the throat muscles contorted and contracted, pushing him further toward the stomach. *So far so good. Still have my head, still have my staff. But could have done with strapping my sandals on just a little tighter. Oh well, at least they will be dry when I slip them back on ...*

Lenjora knew instantly what he was up to as soon as the light shone, shaped like a disc from her perspective, visible in the foul creature's mouth. She looked at Holtonos, who was now smiling but also shaking his head, slightly miffed.

She winked at him, he at her simultaneously – a prompt.

Both raised their arms in tandem, chanted in chorus and shot an identical booming ripple of light that accelerated exponentially in every direction, scattering towards the effigies of darkness that cowered, awaiting their imminent doom. Be it in shadow, or on the rooves of houses where they had sought some sort of refuge.

Shrieking echoed throughout the courtyard, hissing as their wispy bodies sizzled into nothingness.

The onslaught seemed not to affect the great languim –
mercifully … it was not that far gone over to the darkness.

Yet!

Peron made his way, at speed, through the large arched
opening. It took many strides to come out from underneath
the hanging stone blocks making up the archway. He
glanced once more, back toward the trail of commotion.
The ripples of light now tracing toward him, he instinctively
ducked.

They rippled through the tunnel, lighting up the stones
on all sides as they passed through.

*There!*

He saw something.

Clinging to the soffit of the archway, just shy of the
opening out to the courtyard, a figure had wedged itself
between two of the larger blocks that formed the arch.

Though he couldn't see the figure's eyes, he need not
have guessed the shading of crimson was indicative of the
Syltenerians. He also knew instantly it was the one mind
linked to the languim. He halted his charge down through
gauntlet of stone and shattered timber.

As he stopped and turned his mount to face back to the
courtyard, he heard a howl. The great languim was in major
discomfort – no doubt somewhat irritated by the old man
and whatever her was up to. Or from the blast of light that
shot forth. Or a combination of the two. It looked at one
point that it wanted to flee, but it shook its head violently as
the figure above him seemed to clench an outstretched hand
into a ball, to pull at the mental reign tighter.

The creature stopped its rattling and focused itself again.
It turned its massive frame a half circle, now looking at
Peron with evil intent. Peron raised the half sword strapped
to the mare – the little available light did not diminish, more,
it grew, the amber glow of the script blazing up both sides

of the blackened blade.

He pointed it toward the now crazed great languim.

The beast laughed. A smoky, surreal, rasp. 'You little man cannot, and will not, stop me. Not even one of the masters of Seltero could stop me!'

Peron smiled. 'Oh, I wouldn't be too concerned about me and my little sword …' As soon the words left his mouth, he cringed a little inside as the creature diverted its gaze from his head to his crotch resting on the mare.

'Oh, Peron, you should know I was to have my way with you once I had levelled this shitty excuse of a city … though, do not worry, I have ways of supplementing the lack of experience and increasing the size of such a problem …'

*Was that all they ever thought about!*

Peron couldn't see behind the hulking form of the great languim, but he knew the two other from Seltero would be angling for an attack. He understood their intent, to not mortally wound the creature, for it was an offspring of their evolution, from their creation. In the limited interaction he had had with the three from above, he knew them to be good, though he always seemed to think that was a weakness on their part.

But who was he to argue?

He understood it was not the creature's nature to come into a city and attack the innocent through unprovoked attack. The limited stories written of the languim were from those who escaped "luckily" with their lives while trying to poach the mighty beasts' dense fur – for even such a small specimen would fetch nothing short of a ransom paid by a king for his first born, it was that rare. But now it stood there, snarling at him, hungry to escape from its prison and make its way back to wherever in The Divide – if indeed it was The Divide – it would call home. So, he understood, just as he always did in such a situation, a second nature.

All he could do was hold faith, waiting for whatever was

to happen, from any of the three before he would raise his short sword and point to the vermin hanging in the small crevasse of the stone ceiling. He was sure his knowledge of the whereabouts of the creature's tormentor was still unknown to them, and it.

The creature suddenly belched and let out a slight grumble. As it opened its massive maws, Peron spied a light, the very same colour as Everos's staff that had been flitting about within the beast's innards. It seemed the other two were reluctant to do anything while Everos was still arsing around inside the languim.

*

Everos, still holding his breath, squirmed his way back up to the languim's gullet. He tickled the beast's uvula – an easy target as it was quite large, so he gave it a good rub. He espied Peron through its now open jaw, the toxic saliva earlier emitted must have been part of the process of consumption, as the sting had now disappeared. Peron was holding his short sword. *Good lad,* he thought. *Now, let's get this to a close. Seems as though you know what I do not … yet.*

Everos hummed another chant; he was unable to open his mouth as there was little air available to breathe anyway. His staff now glowed as bright as the sun and the colour almost too bright to be called any colour other than white. He touched it to the creature's oesophagus. The sting returned instantly as the creature instinctually reacted to the inflammation in its throat.

As soon as the creature opened its jaw to let out a roar of pain, Everos was on the move.

*

Peron, upon seeing the small man rushing – as fast as a man crawling could move, he was at some pace too – out of the creature's mouth, raised his short blade to point at the exact spot where the effigy of darkness was hiding.

The creature did not see, nor could the tormentor, until it was too late. Everos had also missed the intent as he struggled, eyes closed once again, to escape the creatures flapping tongue with all its toxic bile spewing everywhere.

Holtonos, though, had not just been stood idle, stood there for show. For an old man, he had not lost any of his guile, nor instinct.

Blinded by pain, the creature thrashed around. The dark figure did not break its line of communication, though it seemed agitated as it clawed a hand about as if trying to wrest back command, which was its undoing. This always seemed to be their way; they would prefer others to do their dirty work while they hid in the shadows.

Peron felt a shock of pain run through the hand holding the short sword, then that same pain shot up his entire arm, up to the shoulder. He held firm, as he assumed, more than saw – as the brightness burned his eyes – what was happening.

Holtonos, blind to where the Syltenerian was, had trusted the aim of Peron to be true and had thrown a large amount of energy at the arm of Peron, that same energy that had mingled in with the minimal battle magic contained within the scripture etched into the blade.

The amber glow had now changed to a bright blue.

Peron held his grip, tight, though his strength was waning the more he sustained the pain, waiting for whatever would happen next.

He gasped, held his breath to ready himself, for he knew it would become far more painful.

A beam of light, of iridescent blue, shot forth from Peron's short blade, knocking him backward. The stirrups caught his feet which stopped him from falling off the mare and smashing his skull on the stone pavers below.

Holtonos had followed Peron's tracer line to its ultimate

destination. As did Lenjora.

So too did the great languim.

But it was all too late.

The dark, puppeteer fell and grappled for any sort of purchase, but none was to be found as it fell through the air, grasping helplessly at nothing.

With the connection broken, the creature coughed with such force that Everos was flung out, lucky to avoid the two rows of sharp teeth by the measure of a bug's dick.

Eyes returning to normal, it looked a little more than disorientated as it stumbled about the yard.

The dark figure fell, crunching to the large pavers. Though the look on its face suggested it seemed not to feel so much, as if it had landed on feathers.

Its back had been sizzled, smoking as it stared at Peron with a deathly gaze. Peron should have not been the target for the death stare, for now Everos was making his way, staff high in the air, toward where the now revealed woman was plastered to the cobbles.

She spoke, without the previous rasping, smoky drawl forced through the great languim's jaw. It was a soft, budding flower of a voice. 'Fool, you think that you have what it takes to take on the might of the Sylteneria? You are a fool … you too have now been marked.'

She made a quick sign in the air in front of her face with her left hand. A shape in the form of a triangle shot forth and smacked Peron in the head, just as he had regained his composure and posture atop the mare.

He immediately felt fluffy all over his body. The feeling dissipated just as quickly as it had struck.

But that was all it took to know he'd been marked by the evil beings. *Well, finally, they have taken notice!*

He had also been marked by the light. *Awesome, a piece of both, what a fun, eventful weekend I'm having here!*

Though the light required him to see *it* and Grehn

through whatever was to come. *Rather me take the brunt, wrath, sordid little deviants! Better that than Grehn.*

He would be the deflection, the shield, the barrier, whatever it took, to protect her from all, and through what she needed to achieve. He was fulfilling what The Shadow of the Path had been readying for over all those millennia prior. He was the *one* all before him had been trained to be, the guardian of *The Ember* – the spark to ignite the weapons of the light.

She spoke again. 'I will return, as you well know!'

The disconnection from its mental captor had led the great languim into a disoriented meander as it made its way to, again, snap at the snack it had just spewed out, still hungry.

Everos made a quick step forward, toward where the prone broken pawn of the Sylteneria now lay. Staff raised high, he began an arc of a swing. He would aim at her head, for she was beyond salvation.

He was knocked off his feet as a large mass moved over his head. Before he could regain his composure and return to standing, a scream pierced the air, echoing through the narrow opening of stone. Everos dropped the staff and smothered his ears with his hands.

The scream was abruptly cut off and replaced with a loud groan, which, in turn, was replaced by the outpouring of one final gurgle as the great languim devoured the woman, quickly biting its way up her body before raising its neck to swallow the pieces.

Holtonos looked to Lenjora as the creature snapped its way through the gateway, squeezing its bulky body and dragging its large wings through before it leapt high into the air.

It then flew away at such an improbable angle, the unbalanced distribution of its hefty weight versus its languid slowly flapping wings quite remarkable.

'Well, or so it would seem that … ermm …'

'Yes, Holtonos,' replied Lenjora, 'evolution of a long-ago creation, it is all part of a bigger plan. Not mine, not yours, not anyone's really.'

'Yes. But—'

'No buts about it my old friend, our intentions all those years ago. Many, many years ago. Those instructed through instinct, ingrained through many iterations of the replication of life – of how many cycles I am unsure, but I am sure a vast unsurmountable number indeed—'

'Yes, yes, Lenjora. I get it! Evolution is a thing we have no control over. But did you see that?'

'What? What did I see? I saw it rip into that snake of a thing like it was its toy.'

'Exactly! The great languim, as we have observed does not chew its prey! It devours them whole, slowly digesting until its next meal.'

'Ahh,' responded Lenjora. 'I see … It got pissed at the one tormenting it! Brilliant!'

'Lucky I wasn't tormenting it too much, hey …' chuckled Everos.

Lenjora went on, ignoring the jest. 'And did you also observe its resistance at one point to being commanded?'

'Yes. It is a strong creature. Both in spirit and physicality. I see why the folk of this world seek it as a prize, though I do not agree with their execrable reasoning for doing so. I for sure would not like to face one with even the slightest intent of ill.'

'Free will. Isn't that what we begin with? It is also where we leave it: free.' Everos stood a few yards before them.

He had ambled over nursing a knock to both knees. But his hearing was still sharp. *Sharper than ever* Lenjora thought.

'And it is that, Everos.' Holtonos squinted his eyes a little at seeing a stream of blood trickle its way down one of Everos's shins. 'The darkness seems to think it can sway the course of nature with its constant interruption. But in the end, only evil, be it through choice to seek it out, which I very much doubt any creature would choose that path, or those we have given enhanced intelligence to, which will always bring about persuasion from those seeking to enhance their own fictitious standing on the Syltenerian ladder. Fiction supplied from the cascading chain of their commanders. In the end, they all serve as puppets to believe they are the maternal babes of the Lady, the mistress of absolute evil itself. As the same who would, without a shadow of doubt, toss them into a never-ending hole of nothingness, to be never thought of again. But ... that is what is.'

'And what do we do about it?' asked Everos, a touch angry.

'We do what we do ...' Lenjora spoke. 'We do nothing. Isn't that correct, old man?'

Holtonos frowned, for he knew they were angling for a response in line with their expectation. One that would bring humour at his expense.

In the end, he only sighed, left a pause, then responded. 'Our use—no ... I apologise, our only purpose, that attributed at our very inception I must repeat once again, as I have many times, is conveying the life force of the *good* things, the good we have been able to manifest from our very early involvement in the creation of life on this fascinating planet which so many call home. So much that it should be celebrated. So much sustained, and a beautiful contribution to keeping that bitch at bay!' Everos choked, struggled to catch a breath. All from the shock of Holtonos's curse. One that he had never heard the ancient being speak ... ever.

Lenjora, too, sparked her eyes at Everos, gasped and held a hand to her mouth, covering the amusement spreading about her cheeks at such an unfamiliar outburst. He had bitten at their bait, and it made her want to laugh out loud. *The small things,* she thought. *Ah well, at least Everos finally got to join in and enjoy some of the festivities!*

Everos, though, was not so discreet. He had now controlled the urge not to choke on his own saliva. He wheezed and slapped his body with a merry tone.

A clopping echoed through the air and became louder as Peron approached, still holding his short blade, his arm in the air. 'Everos, you're a mad bastard! What the shit were you thinking?!'

'Distraction and protraction my young friend …'

'But could we not have handled it without you being eaten by a *pissing* monster!' Peron retorted.

'No friend, I had to be eaten, swallowed at least. It was the only way, as these two were dawdling behind at such a pace the whole city would have been overrun by the time I was discharged out of its rectum.'

'Eww, Everos, such a charmer you are,' Lenjora admonished with fake disgust, matched with an over-the-top, scrunched face.

'But why?' Peron asked.

'Well, as I said, the distraction was merited.' Everos twiddled his still saliva-laden matted moustache with a stumpy finger – unusually shaped as it twisted at different angles – and an even stumpier thumb. 'I was a prize too good to let go, and the distraction of such left you to explore. Though, now I doubt you had any intention to do such!' The hunched old man, holding his skinny staff – topped with a large, twisted, vinelike head, tapped the cobbles with the metallic base.

The staff instantly became the same size as Peron's blade. Everos tucked it into his robe and straightened his arched back with a loud groan, followed by an audible crack as it found its place. The old man sighed with satisfaction. 'Darn good to have a bit of exercise than trouncing around with not much happening up there.'

Peron also let down the blade he was holding, back into the sheath strapped to the saddle. 'So, has the danger passed?' Before anyone could answer, Peron looked quickly to the dark sky above. 'And … how the f—' He held his tongue, sensing Lenjora's and Holtonos's reaction to another curse would be unwelcome, 'How in the—did you get down here?'

Holtonos backed up Peron's question. 'Yes, old man. How did you manage to drop out of the sky like that? Seltero is on the other side of that forsaken rock there.' He pointed toward Kinora hanging between where they stood and the massive homeworld of the three, the sun unable to shine beyond.

'Well, I got here same as you two. And thanks for waiting for me! Ah, look at that there! Been looking about for them!' He walked over to where he had been consumed and slipped his bony, sinewy feet into the only footwear he possessed. Crinkled, mustardy toenails wriggled as he set his feet fully in underneath the worn leather strapping.

Lenjora bit back. 'What! You were quite happy to remain up there and not get your hands dirty it seemed. Lounging about in that tower you have recently constructed. Just like Jhehbl, you like to keep out of harm's way and spy on things with your new toy.'

'Well, well! Where is the grumpy old bastard?'

'Working on something, he last said,' Holtonos spoke.

A familiar voice came from behind them. 'Actually, I'm right here.' Jhehbl walked gingerly toward the group, followed by the now familiar ethereal form of Morla.

One other trailed behind, keeping a distance from the two ahead.

Peron slipped off the mare quickly and walked at pace to

the first. He grabbed him and squeezed tightly.

'Stars above, Jhehbl! Look at you! You look like you haven't aged a day since I last saw you. Though, to tell the truth, that dark wolf would have discouraged me for more than a few years, maybe even to never return! Not seen you since then …'

Before Jhehbl could register a breath, never mind a response, Peron looked to Morla. A grim smoulder of a smile touched the face of the potato sack returning the gaze.

She spoke, quite clearly for someone dead for more than a millennia. 'Your help will be limited from these three. They must return to where they are most useful – keeping the seas of hope and harmony swirling – for they will be unable to aid you from this point on, that I have observed. The evil you will face from this point on will have substance. By that, I mean no more apparitions, no more of those that crossed from another realm, those now dissipated from this world. At least not for a while. Those you saw, heard, and felt, earlier were nothing more than a mirage. So, I repeat, the creators have no role here any longer, and they know that. There are no more festivities to be had down here, not this year, at least not while that thing on the horizon remains in its haunting locus. Though I do believe it will leave soon, only to return out of kilter in the next few years. So, we must not waste time. No doubt the edicts have been enacted and must be followed through. We must be ready for their onslaught. We must also be ready for their constant disruption before the next, or even second or third alignment from now. For they have teased us into action. They will be ready to pounce on any weakness. I can guarantee reports of such similar disturbances will filter to ears throughout Vilenzia. All will know of the darkness that hangs, ready to blanket and then consume. What we do next is critical!'

Her image flickered slightly. 'They,' she pointed to the

three celestial beings, 'must continue to absorb and send forth, to whoever, or wherever, the good that is left in this world. That there is still so much.

'You see, trying times bring out the best in people. But it also spurs on the evil, given the slightest bit of hope that their challenge will gain traction and ultimately succeed.'

Peron was about to speak, he had been trying to in the whole time she was talking to him. She shushed him with a look that oozed only dread.

She went on. 'Grehn has made it to the exit of the old shaft. There she waits. There is no danger, none present in or around Jacobs Well, so you will have a small window to depart undetected, unseen by all those eyes peering through the slightest of gaps from the shutters facing this square.' She turned to survey the full perimeter. As she settled dead eyes across the arc, shutters were visibly slammed shut, as if to emphasise her point. Hence, the need for Grehn to travel by unconventional means.

Peron turned to where Morla now looked, beyond the main gate, into the rolling grassland beyond – one that would have been shimmering with shifting emerald waves any other time of the year. He saw nothing but swirling dust that hung in the air, remnants of the great languim's less than swift, and far from elegant, departure.

'Boy, I see her light, shining like a beacon straight to join the heavens above. And I no doubt suspect that I am not the only one to view such. Just as I saw your light, albeit a darker shade of blue – the colour of a new rank of sorts, I assume – as you raced through the town.

'My time left here is short. I have two more strings I must tie into this web – to Grehn's web – before I ascend, beyond this world and the next, to wherever? I may never know. Then you are on your own. But do not worry, I believe in you and those I have marked to see through this and another challenge. There will be others, though that is not currently a concern to you.

'But, also know this, Peron. The eberactu behind me will aid you. For he too has been marked by the light. What? You look disturbed, Peron. Did you always believe that only those ascended through the ranks at the city, the one I helped create may I add, could ascend onto the path?' She laughed, before returning to the severity of the situation. 'There are others, a few from the city, but also others who have abilities that will enable you to bring out the best in not only Grehn but the whole group, not excluding yourself.

'Now. Before I depart to the next, a scroll awaits collection. The scroll was deposited in a vault only I and Grehn's father know of. It has text and instruction to locate a weapon, one that I had hoped to never unravel. Though the threat, and the sudden aggressive assault, has given me no other choice. King Benjamin has handed to the man named Dresdor, under strict instruction to only hand to you or Grehn, no other! For he was scared sick of the punishment I offered Ben to procure.'

*Did she just chuckle, or was it a cackled wheeze?*

Morla interrupted his thought. 'The other three scrolls, scrolls containing instructions, will be given to those I have already, and those I will soon appear to. They too must seek the objects related to their designated scroll.

'What? Your questioning look, you expect … *me* to retrieve such items … baha! I would not last a second wading through the trials! You would last much longer than that I could!

'This is my last act on this planet, my soul energy has been slowly burning away over so long. Now the threat is so great, I must use all that remains. Oh, and if you ever bump into the proprietor of the Grouse, please apologise for the mess I left in his cellar!'

*Again, there! Was that humour?*

'For now I must depart, excuse me while I say my

farewell to the good people, the creators of life on this world. My – *our* – creators.'

Morla made her way gracefully, without a bob or misstep, to the four creators.

Peron joined Dresdor. They clasped hands with a loud clap.

The stump of a man spoke, with a mythical gruff sound. 'Peron, my good man. Good to finally catch up to you. That up there party and fire show went down like a lead balloon, aye! Thought to make me way back down to the inn, the Ox, t' collect a few things before I caught up with you. And would you believe it … that there snake of a man was still sittin' in there all dark lookin'. But … would you believe it, Malek? He smiled at me. Smiled at me as though I made him the happiest man in the world. Truth be told, when he told me – backed up by Belrough – that the one responsible for conveying the riddance of the evil in the basement of the Grousing Potter had been to drop off the bounty, I nearly fell over. So here, not only do I have in my possession one of the fantastical scrolls,' he winked as if knowing what was contained within, 'but also a smaller scroll. This one I could unravel, decreeing the bearer unlimited access to the Grouse so long as they can produce the decree and it be legible.'

'And what else? I see a not so small sack now hanging from your waist. Much larger than the one I noticed you hid away a few days ago.

'Ah … yes. Hmmm, yes. It do be coin. Malek took the majority, as was the deal, if you remember.'

Peron shook his head slightly, eyes fixed on the miniature decree, rolled up and tied off with an intricate red ribbon. 'Hmph, figures … We must be on our way, the other party is waiting for us. Seems as though the ride through town was a good distraction as Grehn is out safe. For now.'

They made their way to the ethereal group on the city side of the main gate.

Hugs were given all around. Pep talks and encouragement aplenty. The creators bowed and made their way toward one of the streets that led back through the town, that lead, ultimately, back to the castle.

Everos, though, remained behind.

'Peron. Know that I will be watching … intently. I for one am not bound to the oaths the others took for Grehn. For I never uttered a word.

'There are also ways around "defeating" one of our own creations without actually … killing it, though I would rather not.

'Know this also: If you need me, if you are ever in need of guidance or just a friend to talk to, just give me the *finger* – the one you so often throw my way when you're in a temper, or some ill luck has befallen you, and I will find a way to reach out to you.'

'Thank you, *old friend.*'

Peron hugged the old man tightly, taking in the musty scent of the man's robe, now magically dryer than it should have been.

The very same old man who had found him as a young adolescent, wandering through the glades of Famnagira, fourteen years earlier. That boy had unknowingly been stalked by a *dark evolen* – a bird-like creature the size of a large bull but as nimble as a fox, and flighty as a finch. Everos had also been stalking the dark evolen, observing its traits and behaviours for clues as to its new-found preying nature. For the dark evolen was a creature of The Divide, and creatures of The Divide seldomly ever ventured beyond such. Even the name misconstrued its true nature – for being known as *dark,* a mythical legend from earlier days, drawn up by those who had observed it tearing shreds off the much larger creatures of The Divide that dared venture into its habitat. A habitat that was occupied by its offspring, mothered intensely for the first nine years of their upbringing. The reason for its pursuit of Peron had to be observed, as a matter of urgency, to avoid any chance it had been influenced by those with a *dark* intent. Eventually, it was discovered that the intended prey was not Peron but another. One who had ventured into The Divide, intent on plunder – to pilfer the dark evolen's orichalcum weighted feathers. But had, instead, left with a much loftier prize … a darker than shadow black orb … one of its eggs, one of only three it would yield through its lifetime. Why it chose to stalk the pair, Everos did not fully understand, though surmised that it was going to destroy whoever or whatever was also involved. Upon instinct? To create a safer future for its kind? it was all beyond their comprehension.

An eventual understanding, of sort, formed as Peron and the plunderer crossed paths in the mythical glade. Coincidentally. The unintentional interaction between the two as they collided into each other, as they moved through the overgrown mass of leaves drooping low off a twisted elm, brought an instant assault from the dark evolen. The attack was swift and, luckily for Peron, the initial target was the one holding the soon-to-be offspring. *Was it taken for trading as a future pet, weapon, or raconteur act?* They would never know. As soon as the creature had sliced the egg thief into many pieces, not caring for a quick and dirty meal, it set a gaze on Peron. The egg still lay on the ground. Peron still held the foliage covered branch that had caused the confusion, and pulled it slowly to hide his face, hiding from the inevitable. Awaiting fate, he wet his trousers – seeing the swiftness and severity of violence set his ability to hold such to zero. Luckily he hadn't eaten for a while prior, saving himself and any other from any further stench. Instead of being swatted with its razor-sharp radial-bone hidden deep within its fluffy shadowy plumage, he heard a clicking sound. Not a random clicking, but one that followed a pattern, and not always of the same tone or pace. He bravely peeked a look between the two leaves that shielded his face from the creature, to see an old man holding up the creature's egg with two bony hands that shot out through two overly large sleeves. The old man was on both knees, bowing as he held up the egg to the dark evolen, the creature clicking its beak in return, as if communicating. The old man responded to every communique with a slight twist of his head or a movement of his arms. A two-way conversation was taking place he was confidently sure. The man then began to glow with an amber hue, so too did the egg. The creature pecked once atop the egg, then the man turned it a quart upon its axis and tilted it at a slight angle. He did this three times further, and each time the creature tapped with its hooked beak. On the fourth tap, the egg began to vibrate. Quite noticeably at first, though the longer it shook the harder it was to visualize as the shaking became faster, backwards and forwards, until it was only a blur of blackness that gave the egg a bigger girth. Then the man turned to look where Peron was peeping through the veiny leaves. 'Come out, young fellow. Come here. The creature will not harm you; I explained you were merely in the wrong place at the right time. Come.' He left his place and the slimmest sanctuary, to approach at an immeasurably small pace. When he was little more than an arm's length away, he stopped. The creature bowed, then clicked its beak once more. The old man translated, 'She offers an apology. For scaring the life away from you.' Peron looked stunned at the old man. But that gaze was broken by the shell of the egg beginning to become less of a blur and more solid once more. The old man communicated again, in the clicks and twitches. 'Ah, my apologies too, you magnificent beast. Here, take your child back home, to your home, before it has any chance to escape into this world of humanoids and all that madness that follows, away from whatever would harm it.' At the same time he gestured with his arms, shoulders, and a few head bobs. The black egg was passed into the creature's outstretched palm – which bore a slight resemblance to that of a primate – which appeared slowly through the plumage. He looked at the creature with what seemed joy, a burning pride. The dark evolen tapped the old man on his head with its hooked beak. The man laughed as if sporting a private, silent joke. The dark evolen took the still vibrating egg and deposited it inside a sack, hidden somewhere inside its blood stained, puffy-feathered midriff, and then took flight. Everos, eventually introduced himself, including who he really was, and explained the whole episode. He had then asked, quite blatantly. 'What, for the shit of and all that is shit, are you doing out here young fella? Alone too, I presume, without a doubt!'

Peron smiled as he thought on the long-ago memory, trying to believe his mind had not embellished it through time. It was more likely the opposite.

'How *did* you get down here so quickly, Everos?'

'I took the portal. Same as them. Then a good old friend accepted my call.' He winked at Peron before looking at Dresdor. 'You know of them, I'm sure, wise one.'

'Bahhh,' she cackled, 'wise one! Listen to him, Peron. Haha! Full of sh—'

Everos pulled out his staff once more, extending as it swept the legs from underneath the stumpy eberactu before he could get the full word out. Dresdor hit the floor with a thump, and all contained breath whooshed out his large chest.

Everos stood over him and held out the butt end of the staff.

Dresdor grabbed it, and was then shocked at the strength of the old man as he was hauled from off the cold pavers – still speckled with a darkness scattered about the entire place moments earlier. Dresdor gave a nod to Everos offering his unspoken respect.

'Goodbye, Peron.'

Before Peron could reply, Everos crouched, splitting his skinny knees sideways, and disappeared into the air with an extraordinary leap, almost comically.

A shadow swept in from across the skyline behind the city, over the wall and toward where Everos had ascended – high above the adjacent dwellings. Both disappeared in a blink of an eye, the same direction from which the shadow had originally appeared.

'Best be on our way too, mate.' He nudged the lump of a man with his foot. No response from the startled man. 'Dresdor!'

'Aye … we best,' he finally acknowledged as he shook his head, to shake the reality of what he had just experienced away, from an undoubtedly foggy head full of a lingering hangover.. 'We best, aye!'

'We best, and we must,' replied Peron.

Peron remounted.

The sky above had lost the earlier mustard tinge and now held to its previous hue of a not so evil looking crimson.

The danger, the evil so presented, had seemed to have passed, at least in Jacobs Well.

*Here at least. Here seems safe from danger … I can feel it. Or rather … actually, I can't,* Peron looked about, all around.

Suddenly, he saw a light burst high into the sky, a brilliant and bright light. A beacon. From where Grehn had undoubtedly emerged from the entrance to the tunnel deep beneath.

A magnet. A target.

*A big bloody target!*

He sighed.

'You see that, Dresdor? That light there?' He pointed to the source, pinpointed from the ground and rising up beyond the sporadic clouds, high, directly behind the main gate.

Dresdor shook his head, not seeing anything.

Peron's stomach sank, and his bowels moved once more. He clenched tight to allay any unwarranted discharge.

*This is so … soooo far from over … And—oh no, no … oh no!* Peron's innards strained, audibly. *I am far from feeling comfortable!* Peron squirmed as his bowels bubbled and grumbled again.

'Back to the Ox!' he shouted, sharp and quick. 'With all haste!'

Peron held his stomach with both hands, reins squeezed tight, and leant inward, toward the mare's mane, to relieve the pain. He then managed enough strength to dig his heels into the ribs of the mare before he gasped and groaned painfully as Dresdor stumbled his way behind to follow. 'I … we, must go … go quickly … before … before I shit myself!'

# A Welcome Dawn

The woman who had admonished the pair for the past few days stood before them, arms crossed, tapping an impatient foot, if a little too quickly. *Maybe a tick.*

'Arigal? Do you know this worm?' She twitched her head, almost toward what once was a man now splayed across the cage's iron bars, arms outstretched and tied tight with rusted chains. Head slumped to the side, legs slightly askew from the knee down to the stone floor, naked … fully exposed. As too, was the entire groin region – skin and tackle removed. A clean shot of sinew shone through the redness. The same heated poker had removed his ability to talk with any sense, as the tongue had been charred to now flap painfully, excruciatingly, between bloated and bloodied lips.

She couldn't look again at the man she once knew, so she didn't. 'Yes … once—'

'So, yes. You do.' The woman's head tilted from side to side, as if to crack some strain in her neck.

*So, you do feel, you bitch! Be it only agitation. Still good.*

'And can you tell me why he was … sticking to you? Hey?'

'He was a replica of Bareleno, he tricked me!' Still averting her gaze from the man, she went on. 'He led me to the woods. He was him, flesh and *attitude*!' She pointed to the boy leaning nonchalantly against the wall.

The boy raised both hands before he shook his head.

'Fool! Such a fool …' her hands now resting on her hips. She shook her head. 'Fuck am I to do now?!'

It was Mesfa who answered. 'I believe her—'

'As do I, Mesfa. That is the problem!' She turned to look at the man hanging on the bars. Then slapped him … hard, across the side of his head.

The man grunted. Probably more so that he was still alive than from any further pain being inflicted.

'Still alive then I see …' she crunched a palm into the bloated face once more.

Arigal could feel his gaze upon her. She hesitantly looked at him while the woman's back was to her.

With what seemed a monumental effort, he raised his head, just high enough to wink at her.

She saw no pain in the man's eyes. Just what seemed a pending sense of a relief to follow. *Why now? Why here, and why now?*

He dropped his head once more.

'My Lady—'

'Do not call me that, Mesfa!' The woman turned to Mesfa and dropped her eyelids slowly as if upset as she slowly lifted her head back. 'My name is Heashia …'

Mesfa looked to Arigal with shock. For the woman before them was much more elevated than they had thought her to be. She was at a level of superiority only the highest clerics could trump.

Both knelt and bowed, hastily, before Mesfa stuck another knife through her heart. 'All mighty Heashia, slayer of kings, armies, of gods and more, give Arigal the opportunity to prove herself to you, to all who voyeur this place.' She pulled a blade from her ankle and slid it across the floor toward the woman.

The woman, Heashia, merely lifted a foot with the ball of the heel, ready to trap the blade. She suffocated the clattering noise it made as it skidded its way over to her across the floor. She bent down to lift it up and inspected it intently. An eyebrow twitched, questioningly. 'A fine blade you have here, Mesfa … not of your world, that I'm sure of. How did you acquire such a rarity?'

'It was a gif—'

'No matter! It will suffice.' Turning it over once more,

she looked down the length of the blade, finding no flaw, and pointed it toward Arigal.

Arigal could feel the heaviness of the blade being pointed at her. Though she dared not look, the blade was stabbing at her a thousand times.

'Arigal. A child of darkness, she who best an entire *Legion of Swords* in Dalmetonia. What say you?'

'Give me the blade … Almighty Heashia.'

'Do it! So we can be rid of this foul planet! We will save our strength and recoup much more before the final onslaught of Inarrel. For the defence will be strong, be it a pittance, once we have sufficient resource to follow through to glory once the signal from our Lady is given. We will find and pilfer their precious tools of defiance, defence, even those they deem forbidden, and use them as our own to crush all here and everywhere else!' She turned and walked away, expecting only one outcome.

She grabbed the boy, Bareleno, as she made her way out of the small room and pushed him constantly, violently, in front of her.

*He's on his way out anyway. I'm sure he would wish for his soul fire to be imbued into mine rather than anyone else's. Or did he find another … may he have a family beyond here? And how the fuck did he get here? And where has he been for all of this time? The fucking idiot! There must be more to this, his appearance …*

All answers she needed to know.

All answers that would be revealed once she took the life of the only thing she had ever *genuinely* loved, never mind cared about.

A gurgle – a struggle for one last breath – was followed by a splash upon the stone floor.

Heashia grinned as she clenched a hand, tight, around her groin.

She pushed the boy faster in front with the other.

Velosko stood, arms outstretched, in the same hall he had performed days earlier. Before all chaos had let itself loose upon the Sinboran.

Marcos sat a short way behind, back straight, holding his mighty cello – finely crafted, as was the stool.

Before them sat the ruling family of Sinboran – his wife and her parents, Count Atinna and Countess Maria.

Atinna had asked them both to perform before they left. A song to remember them by, should the worst befall them.

Standing in the shadows, behind the main stage, stood Anna-Mary. She waited impatiently to hear once again the magical duet. She was eager to learn from them, from Amaria, and all they could teach. Also, she was bursting at the seams to hear all about their wonderful lives, of how they had wooed crowds of many thousands.

Marcos struck the first chord: a haunting, long sweep of his bow. It set the tone for the few verses Velosko would narrate with song, though his voice echoed with a melodical haunt.

The second sonnet was no lighter.

The third harboured upon the finest threads of despair.

The last. There were no words to be sung, just a haunting melody of a bow touching the very fibres beyond the physical that were strung, of all that is … or was … or could be, a *sadness*.

Eventually, Marcos's bow – the source of such despair – was released and left to hover over the resonance of string.

All in the room wept.

Save Velosko.


Peron finished washing down and drying the sodden mare, not to mention its sorry saddle. The mare was not too fussed as she munched away on half a pot of left over potato pie –

one that was to be thrown away.

He hesitantly glanced over the houses between where he had arrived and to where he was meant to be. The beam of light, the one Dresdor failed to see, was still making its way toward the heavens. He sucked a breath of air in. *Best get to it*. He was about to jump back into the saddle when the eberactu he had befriended caught his attention – as did the two men who were tailing him. The larger one held two frothing tankards. The small shady looking one held his cloak – now shining clean.

'Ah. Very well, just one, to remember us by, aye Dresdor? As we must really be leaving, like an hour ago …' He took a good gulp, removing all froth. 'Did you find those extra mounts I asked you to find?'

Dresdor wiped his mouth, dripping with froth, then nodded toward the stable yard, the one adjacent to the crafting boutique. 'Aye! Waiting for us over there …'

*

Grehn wondered what was keeping Peron. They had emerged from the destined exit and seen a massive bat like creature flying, albeit lazily, shabbily, above them.

The draft the great languim's wings created pinged their already fragile instinct to run and hide, back toward the tunnel for cover, though it was now sealed, for it was one way out, not in.

She looked toward the gate, to where Peron should have been rushing through, and thought it odd no guards were stationed at the entrance. *Very odd indeed!*

Squinting at the opening, she thought she saw something far beyond. A faint blue shard of light tapering up to the sky, just past the city skyline. She turned to Kimo.

'Kimo, look over there,' she said and pointed over the top of the gate. 'Do you see that light there? That faint column of light?'

Kimo squinted, shrugged his shoulders, then shook his head.

Grehn looked to Sentok, who was close by.

Sentok mimicked Kimo's response as he reached the same conclusion.

'Hmm. Well. It seems to be moving this way.'

They all waited … and waited. Until hooves clipping stone could be heard in the distance. Growing louder.

Eventually, the source appeared. Two men leading a string of horses. The sound of song could now be heard from one of the two. Grehn needed no further hint as to whose booming voice echoed through the portcullis.

Peron and Dresdor joined the party just as the sky had begun to brighten.

The whole sky, from horizon to horizon, shifted as if a tap had been turned off, only to erupt with a brilliant, shimmering light.

They all gasped as a swath of colours began to shoot across the sky to the horizon directly ahead of them.

'What does this mean, Grandma?' asked Grehn.

Looking at the dazzling colours bouncing off the sea of grass and stumpy trees beyond, over the hills even further, she answered in tandem with Peron.

'Time …'

Both looked at each other, before Mother Ursen went on.

'I suspect we have at least another year to be fully prepared. Maybe more, but not many … if any. However, we must discover *all* of those Scrolls of Vilenzia, and attain what they will ultimately lead us to – the items left hidden since before the dawn of ages. They know we seek them also and will be shadowing us until we find them!'

'So no going back home, back up to the castle? Not even

for a short while?'

'No, my child, there is much danger ahead. We must be vigilant. We must leave now, under the cover of stealth so none may know where we are or where we have gone. We need the head start, especially now that all is, thankfully, brightening up again. We must be far away from here before any of the darkness' spies discover our whereabouts. For I'm sure there will be some lingering, hidden in the city, awaiting some sort of bargain to elevate their chance of joining the darkness even as their current station, in the eyes they choose to gratify, belies that of an urchin.'

Grehn looked fervently at her grandmother with a bristled look on her face. 'You know more than you let on. Is there anything else I should know?'

'Yes, there is much, so much more. Of course. But I could have hardly discussed such matters with one of The Shadow of the Path, one resident of the Third, with that Anatoma always listening in.' She waved Grehn's concern away. 'I will reveal much on our journey. As will he,' she pointed to Peron.

Peron looked mortified. His stomach wobbled again, antagonised by the attention.

All but one of the party laughed.

Kimo looked at Peron, with the same look a father would give any boy asking permission to walk their daughter to the closing dance.

Peron did not miss the glare, and his stomach grumbled even louder.

Mother Ursen's instinct knew of the boy's discomfort, and spoke quietly to him. 'I have the remedy for your ailment ...' She tapped her satchel.

'You do?' Peron looked gleeful to be finally rid of his embarrassing ailment.

'Yes, I do ... a healthier diet,' she turned away, not caring for the boy's discomfort any further, for she knew it was all self-inflicted.

# Epilogue

Getty sat upright, sharply. He knew not of where he was nor how long he had been there.

He panicked, if only for a second. For he found himself back in his room once the disorientation subsided. Though the resemblance was ever so slightly askew.

*This feels odd.*

Instinctually, he slung the makeshift blanket from off his legs then twisted fervently to get off the overly large and pleasingly comfortable bed.

He checked himself, a moment before his general instinct would throw him out of a window that wasn't there. Only it was there, just not the same one he remembered in his dreams.

*Lucky,* he thought, as he peered through the impeccably clean glass panes – delicately cast into an intricate iron frame, one that resembled the outlined shape of a crescent – for below was a large drop that settled into nothing but a forever blue hue.

*Hmmm, where am I?* he pondered.

Walking over to the doorway, the one in which his mama and papa would always appear – smiling as though he be the blessed soul of sunshine itself, when the reality was he was such a burden upon theirs – he thought of all those times. The door though, was not the exact same either.

Hesitation crept through his hand to his fingertips as he began to twist the handle.

He opened it anyway, caring no more,

    … and gasped.

We arrive at the end of an introduction to the world of Inarrel. And more notably, in this case, Vilenzia.

Quests have been dispensed. The marker has been set. So too, has the bar.

Evil will not relinquish. It has not backed away, and only seems to grow stronger. For all that I record, there have been a multitude more occurrences of such evil – all extinguished though, as that is my hope, through many a lifetime of planning and the placement of required resource.

Their next onslaught *should* be the last, or so many histories – too many to remember – have led me to believe.

Will it be the outcome I would hope for? One for all time? One to release me from my forever burden of scribe ...

*I, truly hope so ...*

.